LEONARDO'S SHADOW

Or, My Astonishing Life as Leonardo da Vinci's Servant

CHRISTOPHER GREY

SIMON PULSE
NEW YORK LONDON TORONTO SYDNEY

ACKNOWLEDGMENTS

I am indebted to:
The New School, which gave me a second chance.
David N. Meyer, who encouraged me when I faltered.
Jennifer Lyons, agent, who believed in the book.
Caitlyn Dlouhy, editor, who brought out the best in me.
And Katrina, who praised every draft, however terrible.

SIMON PULSE

An imprint of Simon & Schuster Children's Publishing Division · 1230 Avenue of the Americas, New York, NY 10020 · Also available in an Atheneum Books for Young Readers hardcover edition. · Designed by Christopher Grassi · The text of this book was set in Adobe Calson Pro. · Manufactured in the United States of America · First Simon Pulse edition March 2008 · 10 9 8 7 6 5 4 3 2 1 · The Library of Congress has cataloged the hardcover edition as follows: Leonardo's shadow: or, my astonishing life as Leonardo da Vinci's servant / Christopher Grey.—1st ed. · p. cm. · Summary: Fifteen-year-old Giacomo—servant to Leonardo da Vinci—helps his procrastinating master finish painting The Last Supper while also trying to find clues to his parentage and pursue his own career as an artist in late fifteenth-century Milan. · ISBN-13: 978-1-4169-0543-1 (hc) · ISBN-10: 1-4169-0543-X (hc) · 1. Leonardo, da Vinci, 1452–1519—Juvenile fiction. [1. Leonardo, da Vinci, 1452–1519—Fiction. 2. Household employees—Fiction. 3. Artists—Fiction. 4. Painting—Fiction. 5. Identity—Fiction. 6. Milan (Italy)—History—15th century—Fiction. 7. Italy—History—1452–1519—Fiction.] I. Title. · PZ7.G8647Leo 2006 · [Fic]—dc22 · 2005032502 · ISBN-13: 978-1-4169-0544-8 (pbk) · ISBN-10: 1-4169-0544-8 (pbk)

LEONARDO'S SHADOW

MORE THRILLING READS FROM SIMON PULSE

City of Bones
Cassandra Clare

Rash
Pete Hautman

Everlost
Neil Shusterman

Freaks
Annette Curtis Klause

The Dark Is Rising Sequence
Susan Cooper

This book is dedicated to
Eileen and Stephen Grey

. . . and to the memory of Stephen M. Lavell,
writer and friend

I

What do I remember?

"Thief!"

"Grab him!"

"There he goes—!"

"Don't let him escape—!"

I was running right and left, wildly and without thought, threading my way through the stalls of the market in the main square.

Ten paces behind, a great crowd was chasing me, waving sticks and fists, cursing and shouting. Some of them were old, but that didn't stop them. There were women, too. All had sour faces.

They thought I was a thief.

If I was caught I would be strung up by the neck from the nearest doorway and left there to swing, for the dogs to bark at.

So I ran and I ran, skipping in between the market stalls, knocking down barrels of salt fish and baskets of red plums, always keeping a tight hold on my ragbag.

Each time someone new saw me running, they took up the alarm—

"Stop, thief!"

"Somebody take him!"

"The boy must be stopped!"

But I would never let them—even though I felt sick almost to death. I had the fever, I knew that. There was a mist in front of my eyes and I was burning up inside.

But to stop now was to stop forever.

Never! They would never take me while I lived.

I led them around and around, diving under tables and over carts, pulling down barrows and boxes behind me, but still they followed, more and more of them.

The sun was blazing overhead. It was midsummer. The flies were thick in the air, hanging heavily over the meat and fish.

There was a terrible smell. I wanted to vomit.

And then I stumbled—and a great cheer arose from behind me.

"He's fallen!"

"Take him now! Now!"

But I got up almost as quickly, my head spinning, bright lights flashing in front of my eyes. Which way—?

Fifty paces ahead of me was the Cathedral.

The great doors were wide open.

I started for them.

Up the marble steps—one, three, five—leaping over a beggar, fast asleep—

"He's entering the Cathedral!"

"He mustn't—!"

And then I was inside.

Running from the bright white summer light into the dense dark gloom straightway robbed my eyes of their sight. I rubbed them again and again.

The marble under my bare feet was cool. It made me shiver.

High above me in the Cathedral vaulting I could hear birds flapping their wings. The sound filled my head. I clapped my hands over my ears. All my senses were on fire because of the accursed fever.

The windows were made of glass stained blue and green and red. The light streamed through them. I looked at my hands, covered with colored bands. The marble floor was filled with a rainbow light. The colors were swirling before my eyes. I was going to fall—I couldn't stay up—

"There he is!"

No time to rest. No time to think. They were still on my tail.

I took a deep breath and started to run again—

Up the central nave towards the high altar at the far end of the Cathedral.

God will save me!

A priest ran out of the shadows—

"Halt, boy! You cannot—"

No! I pulled myself past him, leaving him to fill his arms with air.

I looked left and right—

The mob was inside the Cathedral, fifty or more of them, fanning out across the vast floor, their cries echoing against the high walls.

"He's over there!"

"We've got him now!"

Then I saw it.

A candle in one of the side chapels gave off a dull yellow light.

A half-open door.

I ran between the benches, falling over one old man praying—no, he was drunk, by God, and let out an awful groan—

Across the aisles and to the door. I pushed it open.

A staircase leading upwards.

Nowhere else to go—

I started to mount it at a run, counting the steps in my mind as I went.

Twenty . . .

Round and round, the stairway wound.

Forty . . .

A small, barred window. I looked out. Below me, roofs and more roofs.

Sixty . . .

The dizziness came over me again. I leaned against the cool white marble wall for a few breaths, until the strange feeling had passed.

The walls surrounding the stairway were so close now that they almost grazed my shoulders as I made my way ever upwards.

Eighty . . .

The only light was a dull gray haze that came from small square holes in the wall.

It was cold.

But I was sweating fit to melt. The fever gripped me in every part. My legs felt lead-heavy. How much longer did I have?

Voices! Almost like whispers, so far below.

At least I had a good start. And they would only be able to climb the stairway in single file. It was too narrow to let them all up at once.

One hundred . . .

My breath was coming so fast I had to slow myself, I was coughing madly.

Up and up the stairway went. Would it never end?

One hundred and twenty . . .

I stopped again to listen. Not a sound. Had they abandoned the chase? Silence, except for my heart, *thump, thump, thump.*

The air grew even colder.

One hundred and forty . . .

And then, when I thought my legs would give way from the effort, I was face-to-face with a small door.

I pushed at it. And again. Rusted hinges. At last it opened—

And for a moment I had to shield my eyes from the dazzle of the afternoon sun.

On each side of the walkway were many carved spires pointing upwards to Heaven.

The wind was blowing a gale up here.

The clouds were so low they were almost grazing the tops of the spires.

Birds were perched on the statues lining the sides. There were nests tucked into the stonework.

I was on the very roof of the Cathedral.

I ran to the edge and looked out between the spires to see what was below.

Roofs, streets, and people small as crumbs.

I looked up. Beyond the city—fields, forests, and, in the far distance, snow-capped mountains.

It was so beautiful.

But I had no time to admire it.

"I see him!"

They had followed me up, and faster than I thought they could—now they were spilling through the little door, one after another.

I ran headlong to the front of the Cathedral.

"He can't escape!"

Nowhere to go now. Nothing in front of me but air. I stuffed my ragbag inside my shirt.

Then I climbed up the marble carvings and stood at the top, holding on to the cross at the highest point.

"Come any closer and I'll jump," I shouted.

They halted, the great crowd of them.

One man, bearded, stepped forward.

"You're a thief. And you've led us a fine dance. Now give back what you stole and we'll hand you over to the Guard."

"String him up!" someone shouted.

"I'm not a thief—I took nothing!" I shouted back.

"Come down, boy, or suffer for it," the man said.

"I'll die before I let you take me," I yelled, and cast a quick glance downward. It made my head spin. Could I jump? Did I have the courage? I hoped I would not feel anything when my head hit the ground. Perhaps it would all be—

"Get him!"

And they ran at me.

I climbed to the very tip, and then, standing as tall as I could—I let go, holding my arms out wide.

They gasped.

"You'll fall, you little fool!"

I smiled. Truly, I did not care.

"I'm not a thief!" I shouted at them.

"Then show us what's in the bag!" one of them bellowed.

I pulled it out from inside my shirt and prepared to undo the knot.

And then—

The great bells started to ring. *Dong! Dong! Dong!*

And at that moment the sun turned its face towards me and my eyes were filled with light—my whole head was bursting with light and sound—I shut my eyes, and for a moment I felt calm and at peace, nothing but the feeling of the air surrounding me—and then I felt myself falling over the side—but I did not try to stop myself or clutch at the stone ledge as I fell—it felt good to be free of the earth and to close my eyes, I did not want to open them again, ever—and I let myself fall over the side of Milan Cathedral, still clutching my ragbag, and as I fell I was so happy that now I would be able to sleep and sleep forever—

II

But I did not sleep forever.

I woke up. In a strange bed. An old woman dressed in black was sitting on a chair next to me, holding a cross and muttering to herself. Her eyes were closed. She was praying. Several times she looked as if she was done, but as soon as I opened my mouth to speak she started up again. Finally, she was silent. She had fallen asleep. That's the only time Caterina is ever silent. And not even then, if you consider how she snores.

"Where am I?" I said.

She opened her eyes.

"Praise the Virgin, awake at last!" She turned round to the door, which was open, and shouted, "Master! The boy is recovered! Heaven be praised, he lives!" Then she turned back to me and smiled. She had only two teeth. I began to laugh, but it turned into a fit of coughing.

"The Master thought he had found you only to lose you," she said, pressing a damp cloth to my head. "It's usually the other way with him—he loses things only to find them again. Like keys. He's such a great thinker he cannot keep the little thoughts in his head—they are always getting crowded out by the bigger ones."

I pushed away her hand and pulled myself up. The light from the window was too strong, it hurt my eyes. I was wearing a nightshirt. Somebody had undressed me, then. *How dare they!*

"Who took my clothes?" I said, trying to shout, though it came out more like a whisper. "Give me back—(*cough!*)—my clothes!"

I had to lie down again; my head felt heavier than a block of marble.

"Won't do you no good," she said, tucking in the sheet. "Burned to ashes. Filthy, they were."

"Where am I?" I said again, trying to draw breath.

"The Master's house. He saved your life, boy."

And then it came back to me: the chase through the market, the ascent to the roof of the Cathedral—

"What happened? I was falling—"

"Now, now," she said. "The Master will tell you everything you need to know."

She continued to wipe my brow with the cloth. It felt good.

"How long have I been here?" I said, at last.

"Long enough."

"And who are you?"

"You may call me Caterina. I am the Master's housekeeper, and have been these eight years past."

She held up my head and raised a cup of broth to my lips. I swallowed. It was scalding hot. I coughed and gasped. Then I took a few more sips and fell back on the pillows, all my strength extinguished.

"You're in the Master's bed, boy. He wants you to have the best bed until you are well, poor lamb. Now sleep."

But before I did, I had the strength to ask: "Who is this master, then?"

She frowned at me. "Why, it's Leonardo da Vinci, boy! Everybody knows him!"

I was in bed seven weeks. Every day Caterina brought me all the news, even when I asked her not to, there was so much of it. The priest who lashed his horse with a whip and was kicked in the head by it, never to rise again. (Caterina pronounced herself satisfied with that result; she hates cruelty to animals.) The new law forbidding ladies to have pearls sewn on their dresses, unless they be the wives of knights, captains, or councillors. Which meant, Caterina said, that a lot of ladies would be lying about their husbands' rank, because pearls were the fashionable thing, and when one lady wears the new fashion in Milan, they all have to.

There were many other stories I slept through, not that Caterina would have minded; for her, the story is in the telling, not the listening. She will lay siege to your ears with a bombardment of words until you wave the flag of surrender, but she has a heart like our Lombardy countryside, full of beauty and goodness for as far as the eye can see. She was so kind to me I had to hide my face from her, or she would have seen me cry. I did not deserve such kindness.

Sometimes, late at night, I would wake and see a tall man standing near the fire; at other times he would be stooping over me. The Master. Once, he touched my hair.

My strength slowly returned to me, but nothing more of my memory. Who was I? Why had I been running from the rabble? Too many questions, my head could not hold them all.

And then, one morning, I opened my eyes to find him sitting next to the bed.

He asked me if I was feeling better.

Yes, I said. A bit.

Then he asked me if I could remember my name.

No. Nothing except being chased and falling from the roof of the Cathedral.

Nothing else?

Nothing.

He nodded, slowly. The fever, he said. It must be the fever.

And then he told me what happened.

He had been working high up on the facade of the Cathedral that day, replacing an old stained-glass window with a new one which he had himself painted. He and three helpers were standing on a wooden platform built for the purpose. They were in the middle of setting the new window into place, when—

"There was a heavy thud as something landed on the canopy above our heads."

"I fell from the roof on top of you?" I said.

"At first we imagined that a piece of marble—a spire, or perhaps a statue—had come off. Our platform shook with the force of your fall—it was not so sturdy, having been built for lightness as much as strength—and we thought it might break up and take us all down."

I could remember nothing of this—nothing!

Then the Master continued: "My helpers were holding on to whatever they could, shouting and praying to God—the platform was swaying, it seemed about to lose its moorings—and then you rolled over the side of the canopy—"

I sat up. "And?"

"As you fell I caught your wrist. With my other hand I gripped the head of a stone gargoyle for support—"

"Yes? Yes?"

"I held on to you as you dangled over the side of the platform, which shuddered and trembled with the strain. I did not let go. And slowly, with help from the others, when they had recovered their wits, we hauled you back up."

"What happened to the mob that was after my blood? Didn't they—"

"They dared do nothing, once it was known that you had been saved by Leonardo da Vinci. I carried you out of the Cathedral without any hindrance."

And the Master told me that I continued to clutch the ragbag and would not let go of it until I had fallen asleep in his house. Then he had undone the knot and looked inside. He found three objects. A silver medallion, on whose face the picture of a bird, its wings outspread, was engraved; a small, plain wooden cross; and a solid, red-jeweled ring.

Now he asked me if I knew where they came from.

I did not.

"You must have stolen them, then," he said, looking away as if ashamed of me. "That is why the crowd was chasing you."

"I did not steal them!" I said hotly. "I've never seen these things before!"

"Then what were they doing in your bag?"

I had no answer to that.

"If you think I'm a thief, I'll go," I said, and I tried to get out of the bed.

He placed a strong hand on my shoulder and held me down.

"I did not say that. But if you are a thief, you will soon be caught. And then what? An appearance before the magistrate and straight to the city jail. Or a hanging."

I did not want either of those things.

"So what will you do with me?" I said.

"I have decided to make you my servant."

Without thinking, I said: "What? Your *servant*?"

"Yes, my servant!" he said. "Is that such an unwelcome prospect, to be the servant of Leonardo da Vinci?"

"I don't want to be a *servant*," I said.

"Perhaps you would rather live as a thief—and die as one, too!"

"Better that than being ordered about all day," I said.

He became angry then and threatened to put me out of the house.

"See how long you last without my help!" he shouted.

I stared back at him, my face red. *Go on, throw me out,* I thought. *I didn't ask to be brought here.*

But I said nothing.

"You had better learn some manners, insolent boy, if you want to keep a roof over your head," he said, and left the room.

After that he did not come to see me for some time, and I had only Caterina for company.

"Well?" she said, one day. "Do you want to be the Master's servant or not?"

What choice did I have?

I told her yes.

Ah, we have had many arguments, the Master and I, since I became his servant, and they always end in the same way. He insults me.

"Good-for-nothing!"

Just because I delivered a letter for him to Messer Dianni instead of Messer Dianno. He has rotten handwriting.

"Glutton!"

Would you call eating fourteen hot cheese buns in one sitting "gluttony"? When Caterina is always at me not to waste food?

"Idler!"

Who is the biggest idler: me, for taking off a sunny afternoon to go fishing in the canal with my friend Renzo—or my master, who has still not finished his most important painting for the Duke after two years, even though a messenger arrives every day asking for news of his progress?

He can call me what he likes (and he does, I can't stop him), but if my master had wanted to put me back on the streets, he would have done so long ago. He hasn't, though, and I deem it unlikely that he ever will. On the contrary, he wants to know where I am at every moment.

Besides, if I was to go, he would have no one to talk to. He is as alone in this world as I am, unless you count a father and brothers he never visits in Florence. I have no family. None that I know of, anyway.

And the Master let me keep the things he found in my ragbag, although I had to plead with him to do so. He even made a box out of dark wood, with a lock and key, for me to store them in. It is not too big, it has no need to be, but it is very fine. He painted my picture on the lid. It looks more like me than my own face, Caterina says.

That box is my dearest possession. I have the only key. It hangs on the leather band around my neck. I never take it off.

As soon as the fever had left me and I was well enough to rise from the Master's bed, the lessons began. "What use are you to me," he said, "if your body grows strong, but your brain remains weak?" He hired a priest, Father Bernardo, as my tutor, who always said "Go with God" at the end of the lesson. Then my master did not pay him for so long that the good priest decided to go with God himself and never came back to the house.

From then on the Master did the teaching, and I could only pray for the return of Father Bernardo, because I was not allowed to rest, even for a moment, and if I fell asleep at the table he would rap my knuckles with a measuring stick. I rose at five, had my breakfast of dried figs or a pear, followed by three hours of grammar and writing; lunch, maybe some broth or dumplings, with an hour off for exercise outdoors, watched over by Caterina, who gave me a good slap if I played the fool; then back inside for three more hours of arithmetic on the abacus and more reading practice. After that I was too tired for anything but a supper of fried cheese on bread, and off to bed. But before I could sleep, I had to recite a poem, a story from the Bible, or one of Ovid's ancient tales. From memory.

I also learned the rudiments of geometry, the fundaments of logic, and the art of argument, known as rhetoric. And having taught me that, how can he complain that I am so contrary?

Within two years I could read anything you like and write anything I liked. Then my master started me on Latin. When I told him that it was too hard, he pressed me even harder, saying that such a great language was not meant for fools, and that he had every hope I did not want to be one.

And he gave me the name of Giacomo.

It's not my real name, but the fever I suffered from took that away from me, along with everything else. I spend a lot of time wondering who I am. Who I really am. The great trees in the Duke's park do not cast longer shadows than those that have fallen across my life.

When my master brought me to his house, he told me I was eight years old, near enough, to judge by my height and breadth. And it is now 1497, and I have been here seven years, so I must be fifteen, or perhaps fourteen, but I refuse to believe I am any younger than that—I have a beard coming, although it is taking longer to arrive than I would like. Caterina says that when it is full grown, I should marry. Marriage is the only path to happiness, she says, even if you have to beat down the thorns as you go, but I think I prefer to walk around them. Besides, my master is not married, never has been, and it looks as if he never will. He doesn't have the time for it.

So this is the story of Leonardo da Vinci and me. No, make that me and Leonardo da Vinci: it is *my* story, after all, even if I owe it all to my master, without whom there would be nothing to tell, because there would be nothing of me, I suppose, except the dust on your shoes.

III

On the last day but one of September we celebrate the Feast of Saint Michael, the mighty angel who drove Satan from Heaven and who guards our city from evil. Some say that he is not doing a very good job anymore and that Milan has become a home for thieves and villains. Others say that Milan has always been a home for thieves and villains, and that Saint Michael can hardly be blamed for it.

It's true that you can get your head knocked in if you take the wrong street on a dark night.

And it's true that if someone cheats you out of your money, your best chance of recovering it is to steal it back from him when he is asleep, because going to court is only for the rich, who can afford to pay off the judges.

And it's true that—but, listen to me, carrying on like a laundrywoman! I might as well complain to the pigeons. I'm a servant. No one listens to a servant, except another servant. And then our masters say that all we do is complain.

But it *is* true that the Duke raises taxes each year, and that the price of eggs is now so high that a good hen is carried through the streets on a velvet cushion. But who dares speak out against Duke Ludovico? He has a spy in every doorway—you can often see their toes sticking out—and if you are overheard, your head will be swiftly parted from your shoulders and rammed on the end of a pike for the crows to peck at your eyes.

Ah, but Milan's not such a bad place. Especially if, like me, you have nowhere else to go.

The Duchy of Milan is one of fourteen states that make up our country. We are usually at war with at least one of them. Then the Duke signs a treaty, and they become our allies. A month later a new state is threatening us, and we are at war again. There are only two certainties: the first is that we trust nobody outside Milan. The second is that nobody outside Milan trusts us.

To our west lie the Duchy of Savoy; the Republic of Genoa; and the smaller, though no less bothersome, Marquisates of Montferrat and Saluzzo. To the east are our old adversaries, the scheming and deceitful Republic of Venice (we say that a Venetian has all the qualities of a dog, except trust and loyalty); the lands belonging to the Marquis of Mantua; and those ruled by Ercole d'Este, Duke of Ferrara (whose daughter, Beatrice, married our Duke).

To the south of us are the Duchy of Modena; the Republics of Lucca, Florence, and Siena; and the territories belonging to the Church. The rest of our country, all the way to the southernmost tip, is ruled by the King of Naples, a man who eats three pounds of olives a day and keeps the stones in a sack made of gold cloth.

So they say; and who am I, not having met the King myself, to argue with them?

And directly north of us, their snowy caps touching the clouds, are the high Alps, beyond which lie the countries of Switzerland and France, where they speak a different language from ours, but no doubt argue with each other just as much as we do.

It's not an easy life, a servant's. You'll see. But that's for later. Right now the great bells of the Cathedral are tolling seven, time for our citizens to down tools and put on their best finery to celebrate the last night of the wine harvest with as much drinking as can be done before their arms fall off.

We have more than a hundred feast days a year, but Saint Michael's is the servants' favorite; after nightfall, the inns and taverns throw open their doors and the city does its best to drink what remains of the old wine, in readiness for the new. If the harvest has been plentiful, many taverns display the only charity they'll ever show, by handing out free cups of wine. Free wine, even the kind that sticks pitchforks in your belly, is of great interest to those of us without a silver coin to light the dim inside of our purses.

I've already had a couple of cups.

I need to put some red in my veins.

I'm off to meet my friends Renzo, Antonio, and Claudio at the Goldoni Fountain, the one with the statue of a cherub that lost a wing and a couple of fingers during a brawl between the Luccis and the Pozzos this May Day past. Terrible enemies, the Luccis and the Pozzos, although nobody knows why.

Tonight I face my big test.

The most important night of my life.

It's not that I'm scared, not at all. Just shaking a bit. You would be, too.

But here I am now at the main square, where a huge crowd is already gathered.

What a sight! What a spectacle! I'll tell you all about it as soon as this giantlike gentleman standing directly in front of me moves to one side—ah, that's better. The great Cathedral, whose facade is filled, nook and cranny, with statues and carvings, seems to have come alive with the light of the torches burning below. All around the square, suckling pigs—dozens of them—are roasting on spits above furnace-hot coals. It's a terrible thing, it is, to see a poor pig's head turning over and over, its mouth still open, as if it was in the middle of asking a polite question: "Excuse me, can you tell me the way to—?"

A gigantic vat, big enough to hold twenty persons at one time, has been erected in the center of the square by the Commissioners of Wine and Leather. The vat is filled and refilled to the brim with grapes from the new harvest. Every citizen is welcome to help tread them down, and there is a line stretching all the way to the statue of old Barnaba Visconti.

Music from drum and trumpet accompanies the treading of the grapes. And it is not soothing music, I can tell you, it is the kind of music they play to keep an army on its feet. Which, I suppose, is the purpose of it.

"Hey, you! Get out of the way! We've got new wine to deliver in this cart!"

That's all the thanks I get for standing here while I set the scene for you.

But I mustn't tarry. It's almost time.

Saint Michael, lend me the strength of your mighty arms! Tonight you send me into battle—

Tonight is the big fight between servants and apprentices.

It's a tradition, among servants and apprentices, at least. The rules are simple: no weapons, no mercy, no excuses. Fight with fist and foot, head and knee, however you can. Knock down one of the enemy, trample on him, do what you will.

And this year I'll be in the middle of it.

If I can keep my courage long enough to reach my friends without turning tail and running back to Caterina's warm and cozy kitchen.

They're not so bad, apprentices, even though we'd happily see them boiled in oil and fed to the grunters. Apprentices learn a trade, a craft, such as carpentry or metalwork, something you can use, while we servants—all *we* learn is how to clean piss pots, wash walls, and say "Yes, Master." There's no one lower than a servant. And that's why tonight we're going to break some heads.

But I've never been in a real fight. A few shoves, a slap, a kick. Nothing like *this*. This is the real thing. I could get hurt. Badly. Or killed. Caterina would not like that, not at all. And, truth be told, I wouldn't either. Someone *was* killed, last year—a servant by the name of Paolo. We knew him well. He had weak legs; he should have stayed at home. He gave his life to warn us of the futility of fighting. It didn't work.

It takes a lot of elbowing and cursing to thrust my way through the crowd and across the square towards the Goldoni Fountain, but once I have turned this corner—

"Giacomo!" That's Renzo, sitting on the rim of the fountain, wearing his customary jerkin with the leather patches. Renzo is the servant of Bernardo Maggio, the carpenter, who does a lot of work for my master.

The cherub in the fountain is spitting a very thin stream of water.

"Where've you been?" says Claudio. "We thought you'd forgotten."

"Or decided to stay at home," Antonio says, giving me an unpleasant smile. He likes to provoke me, that Antonio. He's jealous of my blond hair, that's what it is, he's got hair like a mud-caked wolfhound.

"I'm here, aren't I?" I say. "Every house in Milan has emptied its occupants out onto the street, you can't breathe for the crush. It's like a scene from a painting by—"

"Don't start," Antonio says. He doesn't love art, either.

Renzo takes three strips of red cloth from his belt. He already has a piece tied around his upper arm. He's our leader, sort of.

"Tie these on," he says.

This is it. No going back now. I'm wearing our colors.

"Follow me," he says.

"Where are we going?" Claudio asks.

"The Cathedral field. That's the place this year."

We pass through back streets and alleys, staying clear of the crowds, until—*Saint Catherine, will you look at this!* My heart jumps a few beats and my stomach slops about inside. Every bit of dry skin on me is instantly cloaked in a cold sweat.

There must be two hundred youths here, facing one another like opposing armies, cursing and spitting. The apprentices are wearing green strips to our red, so that we'll know who to hit. Already the taunting has begun:

"Goosenecks!"

"Toadbacks!"

"Ratmanglers!"

"Sheephuggers!"

"Dogfoot maggots!"

"Lilyprick wormstrokers!"

And on and on.

I let fly with a few myself—I love a good insult—but my mouth is dry. I mean, look at the size of some of them—like giants! They're fed well, these apprentices.

The shouting has reached a crescendo. Claudio grabs my arm: "I'm getting out of here, we'll all be killed!" He does not have a figure for fighting, our Claudio, he's round as a roasting pan (and he'll eat whatever is being cooked in it), but I'm not leaving. I want to fight. I want respect. Where else am I going to get it? Not at home.

The signal has been given by someone, somehow—and with a great roar the two lines of green and red are running towards each other—

—and before I can take another breath I'm launching my left fist at someone's face and my right elbow is thrusting at another's head Renzo has someone by the throat a youth has kicked me in the thigh another one has jumped on my back I'm falling I press my thumb into an eye a scream over there

Antonio is holding his head blood coming from his ear I kick upwards and clear a space to rise I'm on my feet a fist in my back I kick behind me jab three fingers into the ribs of a dark youth on my left *watch out Renzo* someone has a stone I grasp the villain's arm and force it down Renzo shouts *thanks* now he has taken the youth's head and God he's twanging it so far back it must break someone right up on me I butt him on the nose trip fall *get up Giacomo* a strong arm has me around the neck and punches my temple and I elbow him in the side—

The sound of a horn, one note repeated again and again—

"It's the Guard! Scatter, apprentices, lose yourselves!"

"Servants, fellows, run like water—!"

Here they come, the City Guard, it didn't take them long to find us—the dogs are here, too, snarl-toothed and froth-mouthed—Renzo is lifting me up from the ground—"Where're the others?"

"Gone!"

"Come on, then, let's get out of here!"

We make for the trees at the edge of the field, and behind us the Guard is already laying hands on some of our fellows, and the battle has been broken up for another year.

Glory. We fought man-to-man, shoulder to shoulder.

And we lived. That's the best part.

Tonight we are heroes.

"You did good, Giacomo."

"So did you, Ren."

He laughs. "What a fight! I took five or more of them down. Your first time, wasn't it?"

I nod. I was too young a year ago.

"Break anything?" he says.

I run my tongue around the inside of my mouth. No holes. No blood on my jerkin, either, thanks be to the Virgin, or Caterina would want to know why.

"We've earned ourselves a cup or two of wine, eh," he says.

We make our way south towards the Ticino Gate and cross the bridge over the Grand Canal, beyond which, snug in the shadow of the city walls, is Jacopo's tavern, called the Seven Knaves.

Now most folk, the first time they enter the tavern, ask Jacopo why there are seven knaves. "Because there are not eight," he says. And that shuts them up. Of course, I never asked him a silly question like that. Truth is, I never saw the sign outside, the first time Renzo took me there. For the lack of a silly question, I got the reputation for being a sensible lad. Jacopo likes me, the wine is cheap and untainted, and the place is usually free of troublemakers.

Tonight the tavern is so full even the mice must have fled for want of room.

Antonio and Claudio are already here.

We squeeze in next to them, and the cups are passed round.

"I'm sorry," Claudio says to me, "I let you all down."

"Don't be stupid," I reply. "If we had died in battle, who would have told our story?" Claudio is a poet, or hopes to be one. We hope so, too. The sooner the better. Because what he writes now, the best you can say about it is that it's not usually longer than a page.

"No, no," Claudio says. "I'm worthless."

We all object to that in loud voices. And after we have finished, he waits a breath, then says: "Nothing but a terrible failure."

Antonio starts laughing. Claudio revels too much in misery, which they say is an indulgence shared by many poets.

"And where were *you*?" Renzo says to Antonio.

"Me? Why, I was in the thick of it, punching and kicking," Antonio says. "And anyone who says different will receive my boot to his head."

Renzo looks at me and smiles. We both saw him running for cover after he had received but a single blow.

"Anyway," Renzo says, "here's to Giacomo, who put up his fists for the servants and showed us what he was made of. Glory to the Duke and Milan!"

We raise our cups. "To Milan!"

And here comes Jacopo himself with a fresh jug of wine. If he's buying drinks, that can only mean he wants us to listen to one of his stories. Jacopo has hatfuls of bad stories.

"Listen up, lads, I've got a new one for you. You'll laugh, I promise!" You see? "Now, then," he says, settling onto the bench, where there is no room for him, but it's his bench, what does he care. "Matteo the peasant was newly arrived in Milan and found himself—"

But then he is called away to stop a brawl, thanks be to Saint Cornelius, who protects against earache, and we are spared. Later, I learn that the fight was between two pickpockets who each caught the other picking his pocket.

We settle down to drink and laugh and forget that tomorrow, sore heads or not, we will be up at dawn to work. That's the servant's life. A few moments of merriment followed by days of drab duty.

In Milan you are what you are.

And I am a servant.

We are all such good friends you would think, were you sitting at the next table, that nobody could ever part us.

Then Renzo says: "I might be fighting on the other side next year."

You what??

He sets down his cup.

"Bernardo Maggio has invited me to become his apprentice."

He picks at a pool of melted candle wax.

Antonio rises from his seat, red-faced, and says, "Talk sense! Where will you find the money to buy an apprenticeship?"

"Maggio does not want money," Renzo replies. "I can pay him back when I am working. And if I learn well enough, he says, I will one day be working for him."

"I don't believe it," Claudio says. "That's five years of hard work, Renzo. You hate hard work, or so you've told us often enough!"

Renzo shrugs. "True, but it's not hard work if you're learning something profitable. A servant's future is decided by his master. A carpenter makes his own, according to his skills and the use he puts them to. What else should I do with my life?"

The rest of us look at one another. Antonio shakes his head, scowls.

"If it was your good fortune, Antonio, I would be shaking your hand," Renzo says.

But Antonio's master, the wool merchant Guglielmo di Palma, would no more apprentice Antonio than give a dying beggar the scraps from his plate. And he's had him whipped more than once, too, even if our friend brought it on himself through laziness and scheming.

"Claudio?" Renzo says, appealing to him.

But all Claudio can say is: "You're leaving us?"

"I've made no decision yet. I'm still thinking on it."

The tavern is so pressed to its sides with shouting and laughter, the beams might crack and the roof collapse. By Heaven, we Milanese know how to celebrate! Yet here the four of us sit with a gray cloud hanging over our heads.

Finally, I swallow enough of my pride to say: "Renzo, we are all grateful to God for your good fortune. We will be sorry to lose you, is all."

I raise my cup. "To Renzo! Milan's next Master Carpenter!"

After a moment, Claudio raises his and repeats the toast. And, finally, Antonio, although he looks the other way while he does it.

"Thanks, lads. But, as I say, I have not given Maggio my answer yet."

"But you must, Renzo. And the answer must be yes," I say.

I am glad for my friend. Even so, I must struggle to conceal my envy. If only my own master showed as much faith in me as Renzo's has in him, I too might achieve the true aim of my life.

I want, I hope—I *must* become an artist.

IV

I have been asking

I have been asking the Master to teach me ever since the first time I saw him at work on a painting of the Madonna for the altar of the Church of San Lorenzo, soon after I came to his house. And each time the answer has been no, with no explanation given. Unless it is that I do not have the coin to pay him.

Because the Master *does* give lessons—to the sons of rich Milanese families. Their parents send them to Leonardo da Vinci (whether to learn about art or get them out of the house, I could not say), and in return Leonardo da Vinci is paid money, which he is always in need of, and gets to hear the court news, which he can never have enough of, though he claims to disdain gossip.

He calls them the cream of Milan's youth. They're certainly thick enough. Well, *look* at them—dressed more for a banquet than a drawing class. One wears a purple cape with a hood in pink silk; another comes in white velvet hose with silver lacework (*white velvet hose with silver lacework!*); the third has a blue brocade cap, an ostrich feather pinned to it with a pearl brooch; and the last one has scented gloves and a codpiece with a lion's head embroidered on it. Their fingers are choked with rings of garnets, emeralds, and sapphires. There's scarcely enough room to hold a stick of charcoal! They strike poses, toss their hair, laugh loudly enough to be heard in the next street, and squawk like parrots if ink gets on their hands.

Whenever they drop something—and they do, often, and on purpose—it is my job to retrieve it. Then they kick my behind. Or pinch it. But I may not leave the room. It is my duty to be in attendance during the Master's lessons, to hand out more paper, a new quill pen, another stick of costly red chalk from the hills of France (wasted on *them*), and, most importantly, to refill the cups with wine. The only reason we keep wine in the house is for the students; my master never touches it. They probably wouldn't come if we didn't.

And when he is called away, even for a moment, they start on me. Their leader, Tommaso Bentivoglio, opens the attack. He is tall, handsome, and a brute. A spiteful, bullying brute. And he can afford to be: his father is Milan's Chief Magistrate. And *he* is a spiteful, bullying brute, too, by all accounts.

"Giacomo," says Tommaso, "come here, will you." Forthwith there is silence. "Must I ask you twice, boy?"

"What do you want, Tommaso?"

Someone sniggers.

"To be your friend."

Yes, you always say that, Tommaso, you hold out your hand, but when I am near enough, you seize me and punch me in the side.

"Then prove it," I say.

"Yes, *prove* it, Tommaso!"

"Show Giacom-in-o just how much you like him!"

More laughter, and the chanting begins: "Giacomo! Giacomoooo! Giacomo! Giacomoooo!"

Then my master comes back into the room, just as Tommaso is advancing towards me with an evil grin.

"Now, gentlemen," he says, "back to your seats, please! I want you all to have finished at least one drawing to show your parents, or they will say I have taken their money falsely."

"Why, Master, never falsely!" says Marcantonio, the youngest son of Count Something-or-other. "My mother says that your lessons are worth ten times what you charge."

"Is that true?" my master says, grateful for the praise. Poor fool.

"Indeed it is," Marcantonio replies, "for it is the only hour in the week when she knows for certain where I am!"

And everyone breaks into laughter, even my master, eventually, who must pretend to be amused for the sake of his business. But behind his smiling eyes I can sense that he is pained by the haughty youth's response. Milan's greatest artist humiliated, and nothing to be done. It makes me mad.

You would think, then, that he would be glad to have at least one student who wants to learn from him more than anything else in the world. Me.

But I am the last person in the world he wants to teach.

I don't let that stop me.

I listen with intent to everything he says and try to remember what the students so easily forget. And when the lesson is done, I hasten to my room to begin my own studies. I long ago resolved to teach myself, if he was not going to. Everything I needed was in the house, after all.

At first I worked on a little panel of fig wood, about two hands square, that I had seen him use for quick sketches, when paper was much dearer than it is now. He left it in the storeroom, so I did not think he would mind if I used it. I cleaned the panel and made it smooth. On it I spread a thin layer of finely ground chicken bones, which Caterina brought back from the market; we burned them in a pot over the kitchen fire, and I mixed the ashes with my spittle. Then I spread it all over the panel and watched for it to be dry. Finally, I took a thick silver needle from Caterina's sewing box, and I started to draw on the surface. When I had filled the panel with my scratchings, I wiped it down and started again. My efforts were childish and unpleasing at first. Sometimes I became angry and shouted at myself. Once, I even threw the panel at the wall. But it was not the panel's fault that I could not draw. I did not do that again. I determined, instead, to practice all the harder.

That was four years ago. Now I use charcoal, red and white chalk, and paper, white or tinted—whatever is left over after the students' lessons. It is my job to clean up, and clean up I do. Everything that is not used by them is used by me. And for a drawing board I use a piece of wood that Renzo took from Bernardo Maggio's workshop. With his master's permission, of course. That's what he told me, anyway.

And I draw.

I draw and I draw and I draw.

First of all, I copy the drawings in the Master's sketchbooks.

You wouldn't *believe* how much drawing my master has done.

Heads. Pages of heads, nothing but heads, heads, heads: young, old, ugly, beautiful, with curly hair, straight, long, and short hair, hair in tresses, hair unbound . . .

Angels. Angels flying, angels pointing, angels sitting on clouds . . .

Flowers. Single flowers, flowers in bunches, fields of flowers . . .

Horses. Dogs. Cats. Lions. Dolphins. *Dragons!*

Saints. Saint Jerome in his study, Saint Sebastian pierced with many arrows, Saint Francis with the birds, Saint Chiara with her bell, Saint Anthony holding a lily . . .

Battles. Pages and pages of battles. Men on horses. Men in armor. Men with pikes, swords, shields, lances. Archers. Foot soldiers. Knights on horseback . . .

Clouds. Rivers. Trees. Lakes. Rocks. Mountains. Seas. Plants. Roots. Stems. Leaves. And buds!

The Master has used up hundreds of sketchbooks; the old ones are kept in stacks in his study. If we ever ran out of wood, they would keep us warm a whole winter!

And one sketchbook has drawings that I look at again and again, of a boy who resembles me so much that at first I thought the Master had been drawing me in secret. But it was dated 1476, when the Master was still a young man in

Florence, so it couldn't have been me. And then I saw at the bottom of one of the pages, in very small script: *Fioravante di Domenico is my most beloved friend.*

I have not forgotten his face.

To do that, I would have to forget my own.

Sometimes I draw far into the night, using the light of the moon through my small window, long after the candle has burned down to a warm pool of wax. If the Master is away, I draw in the kitchen or the front room or the garden. I draw the flames in the fire and the pots on the boil. I draw Caterina's hands, her eyes, her face, even though she tells me not to, it makes her blush, and blushing attracts the Devil. I draw the table and the bench, and whoever comes in to sit on it: Mazzini, the rat catcher, perhaps; or Lucio Vati, the dice player; or Margareta, the housekeeper from next door (all good friends of my Caterina). I fill up every corner of the paper.

And soon—but not yet, I am not good enough yet, not by half—I will show the Master what I am capable of. And then, when he sees that I have taught myself to draw, he will surely teach me to paint.

But drawing comes first. Painting without drawing is like a bird without wings: it will not fly, although, like a chicken, it may make many an ungraceful attempt.

Drawing teaches you to look. It teaches you how to map the shape of an old man's head and a young woman's shoulders, of elm trees and elder flowers, of a baby's chubby arms and laughing smile. It teaches proportion, so that a man's body will correspond in all its parts, as God intended when he made us. It teaches perspective, which creates the illusion of distance, which gives a picture natural depth. And it teaches light and shade, without which a work of art lacks all refinement. Drawing is honest. It is easier to lie to a priest in confession than it is to pretend a bad drawing is good. And I intend to be good. Very good.

I will have to be to win over my master, whose own drawings are incomparably fine. For him to teach me, I must show him just how much I have accomplished without his help, and how much I might achieve with it.

V

To live, even the great Leonardo needs to eat. But when I ask for money for food, the great Leonardo tells me to ask the shopkeepers for credit. So I do. And then they come to *me* for payment, and I go to the Master—and he tells me he has no money. And we all go round and round and round.

Many of them have not been paid for months. And there are rumblings. The name of Leonardo da Vinci is not as welcome as it once was. How long before they cease all dealings with us until we pay what we owe?

Money! We're always short of it, never sure of it. Have been ever since I can remember, and it's not just because Leonardo da Vinci spends so freely on clothes and books and a fine horse and, well, everything else—it's because the Duke never pays him. Here's how it went: My master came to Milan fifteen years ago to work for the Duke. And the Duke gave him plenty of work, too. But then he didn't pay him on time, so the Master fell into debt. And the Duke *still* doesn't pay him on time, or even the full amount agreed, always keeping something back, knowing that my master won't leave Milan without it. The Duke seems to think it is his right, as my master's benefactor, to treat him badly! To stay here longer can only make matters worse, but to go now will mean the end of the Duke's patronage—and no money at all.

So what do we do? Nothing. And the debts pile up.

The Master says that the Duke's purse strings are drawn tighter than the hangman's noose, and he can no longer breathe for them.

And today, while Caterina and I are at the market in the main square, and I am trying to decide which shopkeeper to fool into giving us more food now for a promise of payment later, I overhear two wealthy gentlemen talking about my master. Not just talking, either. *Insulting* him. And loud enough to frighten the birds from the city walls.

"Leonardo lives on partridges and quince jelly," announces the older gentleman, who wears a red cape with a white fur collar, "stores his money in three banks, and has pillows stuffed with goose feathers."

This baldpate is wrong about the partridges: my master is a strict vegetarian, he never touches fowl. All meat is foul to him. And he may have three bank accounts, but there is no money in any of them, that I will swear. As for the pillows, I couldn't tell you; I can only say that *my* pillow is like sleeping on a doorstep.

"The story is that you can never find him when you need him," continues the old fellow, "which seems odd to me. A painter must be *somewhere*—he has to stand in one place to paint!" Then he starts laughing, a sort of bullfrog's croak.

"But that's just it—he doesn't!" says the younger man, toying with his long curled hair (quite the fashion, nowadays). "He still has not finished the Last Supper after two years!"

"Well," the old fool says, "if Leonardo can't do it, I've heard that the Duke will give the commission to another man."

He *what*? Give the Last Supper to another painter? No!

"Giacomo," Caterina says to me, tugging my arm. "We still have our provisions to buy." She can see my face reddening. If there's one thing I will not suffer, it's somebody speaking ill of my master—and if it's two somebodies, that's twice as bad. For them.

I gently remove Caterina's restraining hand and walk up to them. They look at me as if I have just been scraped off the privy wall.

"You know as little about my master as you do about art," I say, "which is nothing, and I counsel you to hold your tongues, or the Duke will have them out and served to his dogs between meals."

That stopped them. But only for a moment. The older one says: "Do you know who I am, boy?"

"Someone who defames my master," I say. "And that makes him, whoever he may be, a damnable villain. And his long-haired son a knave!"

At this the young man draws his rapier—

"You dare . . . ? Father, let me run the urchin through!"

My own hand seeks out the knife I keep hidden under my jerkin. A servant is not allowed to carry arms (at least, no more than the two God gave him), but only a fool walks the streets of Milan without a weapon, even if it is only a slim-bladed dagger.

However, the older man raises his hand to stop his son.

"Who are you to rail thus against your betters?" he says to me.

"I am the servant of Leonardo da Vinci, who has no betters. And who are you, sir, to make mock of Milan's most famous painter?"

A crowd is gathering. Caterina whispers: "Giacomo, we must go before—"

"Make way for the Duke's man!"

A member of the City Guard now forces his way through the assembly, hand on sword hilt. He plants himself between me and the two gentlemen.

"What's going on here, then?" he says.

"Captain," the young man says, "I am Rinaldo Giachetti, and this is my father, Messer Alphonso, the armorer. You know our name."

"No better than you know mine. What's the complaint?"

"This servant has dared to speak against us," the father says, "and we will not suffer it. We want him taken away and flogged!"

"And you," the captain says to me, "what have you got to say in your defense?"

"I was defending my master, not myself. I may be a mere

servant, but I will not have the name of Leonardo da Vinci sullied by these clods!"

"You see, Captain, he still insults—"

"I see, all right," the guardsman says. "You pup's tail, I'll teach you to wag where you're not wanted!"

And so saying, he takes hold of a clump of my jerkin with his fist and prepares to haul me away.

And then Mistress Fortune yawns, opens one eye, and smiles on me, because at that very moment the cry goes up: "Stand aside! There's a horse loose!"

The crowd tenses; heads turn every way. From somewhere we hear the drumroll of hooves on stone—

"Over there!"

"Where?"

A riderless horse thunders out of the shadows, its saddle hanging half off. The owner must have fallen when the strap broke—

"Watch out!"

The horse gallops pell-mell across the square, straight into one old fellow, knocking him down cold—and now a girl child is standing directly in front of it, mewling with fear—where is the mother?

My legs throw me forwards without thinking. I run at the child and gather her up, spinning to my left and shielding her as the horse charges past us and then gallops away down another street. I set down the little creature, still crying, but none the worse for the adventure—her mother is running towards us now—and hasten away.

Someone shouts: "The boy has saved the child!"

"Come, Caterina," I say, "let us make our escape, while the crowd is still distracted."

Before anyone can delay us, we have turned down an alleyway whose walls are slick with dampness and grease. Most of our narrower streets are the same. Everyone dumps their filth anywhere they like. Rotten fruit, animal bones, horse—and human—doings, old cooking grease and tallow, charred wood: it's all here, and it's all horrible.

Long ago, the City Council used to allow pigs to roam the streets, and they would eat a lot of the rubbish. But they also took an interest in rich ladies' ankles, and after a councillor's wife was badly bitten, the pigs were taken off the streets and turned into cutlets. Now it's just the dogs, and they are a lot choosier.

"You'll find your head on the end of a pike one day," Caterina says, pulling her cloak around her. "You should know better than to challenge the word of rich folk."

"I won't have anyone talk about the Master like that," I say.

"Let him defend himself from others' accusations, if he cares to," she replies. "What does it matter to us?"

"A lot, Caterina. We may be his servants, but if the Master falls from grace, we will fall with him."

Just as we are emerging from the other end of the dank passage, the guardsman reappears.

"Now I've got you!" he says, blocking my path.

I could run for it. But what to do about Caterina? I can't abandon her to take the blame that's rightfully mine.

"So you're the servant of Leonardo da Vinci," the guard says.

"That's right," I say. "And you'd better not lay another hand on me, or he will hear about it, and the Duke will—"

"Enough, lad, I'm not here to torment you. On the contrary, the mother of that child wanted me to thank you. It was a brave action you took."

"He's quick to act, is our Giacomo," Caterina says, "except when I tell him to clean the hearth of ashes."

"I don't like the rich any more than you do," the guardsman says. "But I have a job to do and I must be seen to do it. I would have let you go as soon as those two idlers were out of sight."

"Then let us go now," Caterina says. "We have work to do."

"I will, old girl," he says. "But before I do, that gentleman back there said the Duke might give the Last Supper to another painter to finish if Leonardo doesn't—"

"The Duke would never do that!" I say.

"Now, listen to me, will you! Last week I was attendant in the big chamber at the Castle when the Duke told his counselors that he had invited Michelangelo to Milan. Made a big noise about it, he did."

Michelangelo!

A young painter and sculptor whose skill is reputedly greater than any yet seen in the land. The mere mention of the name turns my master's mood to sour milk. Until now, this prodigy has been no more than a long shadow cast from Florence, but what will happen to us if the rest of him arrives here?

"Why do you tell me this?" I say.

"I thought you should warn your master. I don't know much about painting, but I do know that everyone in Milan wants the Last Supper finished—and not by an outsider, either!"

Thank the Virgin that this good fellow does not know that my master is also an outsider, from Florence.

We bid farewell to the guardsman and make our silent way home, passing the Broletto, the council building that houses the offices for many of our craftsmen's guilds and the collectors of various taxes, until we find ourselves on the Sforza Way, which unites the Castle with the Cathedral. Duke Ludovico likes to parade up and down here with a full entourage of courtiers and servants on his way to Mass, and the city always comes to a standstill while his progress blocks all the main streets. There is nothing to do while he passes by, except stare with astonishment at the display of wealth and power, and wish some of it would rub off on you. And cheer, of course, unless you fancy a sword in the guts.

The great road is flanked on both sides by tall poplars, their leaves turning yellow as autumn approaches. Flags and banners in silver and red, green and gold, white and blue hang aflutter from tall poles and high towers along the route, bearing the coats of arms of the Sforzas, Battiglias, Cittadinis, and other important Milanese families.

Now we are at the junction of the Sforza Way and the street that leads to our house. Ahead, some five hundred paces, stands the Castle, its redbrick walls looking out over the city.

Just as we are about to turn off, the high note of a horn sounds sharp and clear, and a troop of horsemen comes cantering towards the Castle. They are not wearing colors or bearing pennants identifying them, which can only mean that they have ridden here in secret—but wait! Borne on two long wooden poles held between two horses is a covered chair, and on its door is a design—of a bird, its beak open, its wings outspread, rising out of a leafy tree.

Within a few breaths the horsemen and their cargo have passed by—impossible to see the person inside, the curtain was drawn.

Who were they carrying in such haste and secrecy to the Castle? And what is the meaning of the design on the door? I am sure I have seen it before.

Caterina is unlocking our front door when I remember.

I *have* seen that bird before. Saint Francis, I *have*!

I run upstairs and open my box.

The same bird—the very same—is on the face of my medallion.

VI

Before I have a chance to find my master and question him on this, there is a great pounding on the front door. If you live with Leonardo da Vinci, you get accustomed to people pounding on the door; there's always someone at it.

All right, I'm coming, I'm coming.

"Good day, Father Vicenzo."

Bad day. It is always a bad day when Father Vicenzo calls. And it's the third time this week. Father Vicenzo is the prior of the monastery of Santa Maria delle Grazie, where my master has been working on his biggest painting ever, the one I had the argument about in the market, the Last Supper. It shows Jesus and His Disciples at the moment when He announces that one of them will betray Him. I should say: It *will* show Jesus and His Disciples. It's not finished yet. In truth, it's barely been started. But when it *is* finished (if ever), it will cover a whole wall of the refectory, where the monks take their meals. And it's a big, big wall.

Perhaps it is not surprising, then, that Father Vicenzo has taken to visiting us so often. The longer my master keeps him waiting, the more excuses the prior must make to the Duke of Milan, and the more impatient the Duke becomes. We all have masters we must please, or suffer the consequences—even my master, who must serve the Duke before himself.

"Where is he?"

"At Santa Maria, father."

"He is *not*! That is why I am *here*, boy."

The prior is quite correct. He is not there. He is upstairs, asleep. Where he was when Caterina and I took ourselves to the market.

"I'll tell him you called, father."

I start to close the door, but a white, sandaled foot appears in the crack and prevents me. I notice that the toenails are neatly cut. You don't often see that in a priest; most priests have toenails like eagles' talons, but Father Vicenzo is not any old priest. He smells of rose water, too.

"You'll tell him I'm here," Father Vicenzo says. "Now." He pushes open the door and enters our little house.

"Come in, father, do," I say. "Please have a seat in the kitchen; it's warmer there. I'll go and see if he is in his room."

I leap up the stairs four at a time. The quicker I get this over with . . .

"Master?"

His door is open a crack. I tiptoe towards the bed where he is laid out, facing the wall, one arm dangling. He did not even undress himself last night. There are many papers with drawings and notes on the floor. I pick one up. Oh, so that's it. He has been working all night on one of his inventions, instead of the Last Supper. Why, it looks like some kind of—

"Giacomo?"

—Bird?

The paper falls from my hand, taking far too long to reach the floor. Fortunately, the Master is still rubbing his eyes when it lands.

"Time?"

"Past midday, Master. Father Vicenzo is here again."

"Then send him away again."

"I tried that, Master."

"And failed, I see."

How easily he forgets all the times I succeeded.

"He has been waiting a long time for the painting to be finished, Master."

A servant should not talk back, but I am no ordinary servant. I am Leonardo da Vinci's servant. If I did not say my piece, I would not be worthy of him. He gives me one of his looks. He has hundreds more.

"Your tongue is given too free a rein, boy. Must I remind you yet again?"

"Yes, Master. I mean, no, Master."

"Go down and show the peevish prior into my study. Did you fill my basin? It will take an ocean to refresh this face."

I run back down the stairs and into the kitchen. Caterina is showing Father Vicenzo her collection of crosses, all of them laid out on the table.

"And this one was blessed by Saint Barbara herself," she is saying, "and protects the wearer from being struck by lightning. . . ."

"Well?" he says, clearly relieved at seeing me.

"He's coming down, father. Please follow me."

The prior dabs at his face with a handkerchief. Lace, of course, and I thought monks swore a vow of poverty.

I knock at the study door, no answer; but when I push, it is open. In goes Father Vicenzo, and to his astonishment—he takes a step backwards, right onto my foot, *ouch!*—the Master is already sitting at his big table, holding a skull. How he got here so quickly is a mystery, but not a surprise; he is always somewhere you do not expect him to be.

This skull my master is holding is one of his prized objects. He says it is Donatello's, the famous sculptor who died many years ago, but I am not sure if I should believe him. The Master does not think much of sculptors.

He turns the skull towards the friar.

"Prince or pauper, priest or prostitute," my master says, "time erases all signs of our former standing on Earth. What survives, father? Tell me that!"

"The soul, Leonardo, the soul!"

"Art, father, *art*. Art is all we have to remind us that man has achieved something in this world, apart from his own ruin."

"Master Leonardo, I must—"

"Insist that you do not interfere, father."

"Eh?" says the bewildered prior.

"I simply cannot work with all these interruptions."

"The Master," I say, "means that he needs time to let his thoughts ripen, like grapes on the vine, until they are ready—"

"Be quiet, Giacomo, and go about your business."

That's what I get for trying to help. But when the Master orders me to leave the room, or suchlike, he does not really mean it. For one, he likes to hear what I have to say. For two, he likes it when I interrupt whoever is having a go at him, because that takes some of the wind out of their lungs. For three? Well, for three, I'll give you two and one. Adds up to the same.

"Come now, Master Leonardo," Father Vicenzo says, "you cannot argue that we have not given you time. It has been more than two years."

"What is two years to create a monument that will last for all eternity?"

"Do not talk to me of eternity, Master Leonardo. Our contract was for this world, not the next."

Father Vicenzo is sweating, though the weather is cool.

"You cannot put a time on creation," my master says.

"You can when we are paying you," comes the response.

My master is silent. He turns the skull round and round in his hand and points it once more at the prior. "You can have your money back, Father Vicenzo, every ducat. I will get it for you now."

The Master pretends to rise. It is a ruse, it must be, there's not a coin in the house. Though the Dominican friars are paying a monthly sum for my master's expenses, it is never enough. If my master cut back on his daily visits to the barber, that would help. But if I cut back on those, he would reply, who would cut back on my beard? He has an answer for everything.

"Master Leonardo," the prior says, "we do not want our money back—we want our painting! Now, when do you plan to finish the refectory wall?"

"Soon."

At this Father Vicenzo's face almost bursts into flames.

"Soon? *Soon?* Why, Milan's foremost artists were pleading with me for the chance to paint our wall! We could have had Felloni—"

"A felon! A felon!"

"Or Capponi—"

"A capon! A capon!"

The Master can be very comical, but his timing is off. This is the wrong person to be jesting with, and the wrong time.

"At any rate, Master Leonardo, it would be *finished.*"

"Yes," my master says, "and with it the name of the Order of Dominican Friars."

Father Vicenzo sighs and sits down on a small stool with a carved back, which straightway collapses beneath him. Now, where are we going to find the money to replace that?

"Are you well, father?" I say, helping him to his feet.

"Yes, yes, boy. Get me a proper chair. Must everything I put my trust in let me down?"

I find the prior a chair, and this time, thanks to its solid frame, it holds the sacklike weight. And when he is settled, my master says, in his loftiest of voices: "Am I not the greatest painter in the land?"

I knew the Master would not be tardy in using his best line. But this time it does not silence Father Vicenzo. On the contrary, the good prior gets up from the chair I went to such trouble to arrange for him and says: "That is why the Dominican friars hired you—so that other monastic orders would be green with envy. Right now, I am the one looking green. I commission you, I pay you, but you do not paint!"

Now it is my master's turn to rise. They stand facing each other. If looks were daggers, they would have pinned each other to the walls.

"You will get your painting, father."

"When?"

"When I am ready." He flicks some dust from his sleeve.

"The Pope is coming to Milan, Leonardo. It had better be ready by then."

"It will be, father, it will be," I say. "Will you stay for some wine?"

"There is a time to celebrate, boy. When the Last Supper is finished. And finished it will be, whether by Leonardo da Vinci or someone else."

And with that he moves to go. My master makes no effort to stop him.

But as Father Vicenzo prepares to pass through the front door, my master shouts out from his study: "No one but Leonardo da Vinci will ever finish the Last Supper!"

"We shall see about that," Father Vicenzo says. "Tell your

master that I am making a complaint against him to Duke Ludovico. This very day!"

I move in front of the friar. "Don't do that, father, my master does not deserve that."

"Get out of my way, boy, you and your master both."

He draws his robe around him and sweeps by me through the open door in a cloud of perfumed water and unwashed sweat.

This Father Vicenzo is planning to make our lives miserable, I think.

VII

What has my master been doing for the past two years? Not sitting on his hands, I can tell you. If the Duke knew how many sketchbooks had been filled up with studies for the Last Supper, he could not possibly complain that Leonardo da Vinci was shirking his duty. Not one book, not five, no—*nineteen* books, filled to the margins with drawings of the Disciples in every pose imaginable. But the Duke is not interested in sketches, he wants to see the finished painting. Everything else is just delay.

And the painting, there's no denying it, is well and truly delayed.

Work at Santa Maria delle Grazie began in the spring of 1495.

First, the wall had to be made ready. The plasterers Guido and Guilio came to Santa Maria on a cart pulled by a donkey with one ear. They unloaded a large wooden tub, two barrels, two buckets, and two trowels, and set up in the refectory. Using stiff brushes, they cleaned the wall, smoothed it down with blocks, and then began to prepare the plaster, which is a mixture of limestone, sand, and water. They wet the wall very thoroughly and with their trowels commenced applying the first layer of plaster. Before the coat was dry, they applied a second, and then a third. Finally, the last coat was worked over again and again with the trowels until the surface was smooth and polished. Then they told the Master they would see him when he was ready for them again, and off they went on their cart drawn by the one-eared donkey.

This part was completed in eighteen days.

Then Bernardo Maggio, Renzo's master—the one who is making him an apprentice next year—arrived on his own cart with three assistants and forty planks of wood, and began to construct the platform on which my master would stand to paint the higher parts of the wall. He built a solid frame with an upper platform and a lower platform, stretching all the way across the wall, with ladders at either end. On this the Master could then roam from one end of the painting to the other; when standing on the upper platform he could paint the top of the picture with his arm at shoulder height, and on the lower platform he could cover everything higher than his reach when standing on the ground. It was a beautiful piece of work, and the Master told Maggio so. It had taken eleven days.

Satisfied with the surface of the wall and the platform on which he would stand to paint it, the Master set to work planning the composition. With the use of a plumb line hung from the wall at various points along the upper edge of what was to be the painting, the Master marked straight lines from top to bottom. Then, with a set of large compasses and sticks of charcoal, he drew many intersecting arcs, until the wall was covered with half circles, lines, and crosses.

What was he doing? It was clear that the Master was dividing up the space for the composition of the painting, but it was only when he started to draw some rough outlines in charcoal on the surface of the wall that I saw what he was working towards.

In the very center of the painting was to be the head of Jesus. On either side of him would be six Disciples. And the more lines the Master drew, the more I began to understand: he was not merely going to paint Jesus and the Disciples sitting at a table—he was going to paint them sitting at a table in a room that would look as if it was joined on to the dining room! *Jesus, His Disciples, and the monks would be sitting and eating—together!—in one huge refectory.* Had another painter ever thought—ever dared to think—of something as novel as this?

It was midsummer, and the Master was ready to begin painting. Now, I imagined, when I heard the plasterers Guido and Guilio tell the Master to call for them when he was ready, that he was planning to paint a *fresco*. That is, every day the Master would select an area to which a fresh coat of plaster would be applied, and on this he would paint while the plaster was still wet, using colors mixed only with water, because when the plaster dries and hardens, it seals the paint and needs no addition.

But the Master never called again for Guido and Guilio.

That was a big surprise.

He was going to paint the wall *secco*—dry.

Most artists avoid painting on a dry wall. *Fresco* is acknowledged as the better way, being a method that actually improves with time, permitting the wall to retain the original colors, while resisting impurities and dampness in the air.

But my master had other ideas.

He was going to paint it dry, and he would therefore need to mix the paint with something, egg yolk or oil, to hold it on the wall.

He chose oil.

Since the wall was made ready for painting, I've accompanied the Master many times to the refectory, the wooden box Maggio made to hold his brushes, powders, and oils hanging from its leather strap on my shoulder. The streets are empty but for the beggars half asleep and the drunks half awake, and at this early hour there is a gray mist in the air.

And there I leave him standing before the wall, his hand already raised to begin painting. And, more often than not, I find him in exactly that position at the end of the day. Which is all very well, except that, more often than not, his arm has not moved since I last saw him. Or, if it has, it has painted a space no bigger than a nutshell.

Still, that is something. But then, *then*—Saint Peter, preserve us!—nothing. Days will pass and the Master is nowhere to be found within sight of the church. No sign of him anywhere, in truth, and he never tells me where he is going. Or he may indeed be at the refectory, but not painting, merely examining the wall. Hour upon hour. Staring at it.

What is going on in his head? Great thoughts, of course, stupendous visions, sublime constructions. (I hope so, anyway.) But on the wall? Nothing. *Nothing!* In the past two years my master has painted a bit of tablecloth, some of the ceiling above the Disciples, a few trees in the landscape showing through the window behind Jesus. In other words, very little. The rest of the wall is still empty except for the charcoal lines he drew in the beginning.

At the rate he is working, I calculate he will finish the Last Supper in, oh, about twenty-three years. But we will have been put out of Milan a long time before then.

And Michelangelo, or another one, will have been invited to finish what my master could not.

I do not understand why, after all this time, my master still hesitates. And the more time that passes, the less courage I have to ask. Why? Because I fear above all things that he might fail in this, his greatest endeavor.

VIII

But when I inform him of Father Vicenzo's threat, the Master just laughs.

"Ha!" he says. "Ha, ha!"

"Master, Father Vicenzo has the ear of the Duke."

"Let him have the whole head. I fear no priest. Now take this order to Messer Tombi."

But before I do, I remember to ask him if he knows the meaning of the bird on my medallion.

"What, Giacomo? Again? I have told you a hundred times that I do not know what it signifies. Why do you persist in asking?"

"Because this morning I saw the same design on the door of a covered chair being carried to the Castle."

He says nothing.

"Does it not seem astounding to you, Master, that I should possess a medallion bearing the same image?"

"Not at all. There are duplicating designs everywhere in

the world. That is Nature's art. Now, for the last time, take this order to Tombi."

"But, *Master* . . ."

Then I see the look in his eyes. There is a storm approaching, and I had best seek cover.

"Yes, Master."

He hands me the order for Bartolomeo Tombi, the apothecary, and tells me he will make his weekly visit to the public baths, it being Friday—the day reserved for men—and to have ready for him on his return two slices of the chestnut pie he has seen in the kitchen. Nobody told *me* about any chestnut pie.

So off I go to Messer Tombi's shop. I know the way, I go there almost every day. And this time I take my medallion with me. If the Master won't help me discover the meaning of the bird, maybe Messer Tombi will. He, if no one else, treats me as an equal.

And while I am walking, I am thinking. Why, when he knows so much about so many things, does my master not recognize the design?

But it's a long walk from our house to Tombi's, and I soon forget these unsettling thoughts as I pick my way through the streets that border the Cathedral.

A mother and her daughter walk towards me, and I feel the blood rush to my limbs when I see the young girl's face. Saint Catherine, she is a pretty creature! She gives me the swiftest glance as we pass: enough to show an interest, I think, but not enough to attract her mother's. After our paths have crossed, I turn back to have another look—and she is doing the very same thing! We stare at each other for a moment. Then she smiles at me! But her mother pulls her by the arm, and when she turns away her lovely face, I feel myself grow cold, as if the sun had hidden itself behind clouds. Where might I meet such a beauty? Renzo would know; he's got girls lining up to smile at him. But he'll say anything to please them, make up any story to impress, and I want to be myself, not someone I think a girl might fall for.

Now here I am at Tombi's shop.

An apothecary sells colors for painting as well as all kinds of herbs, spices, and drugs, for health and for sickness; and Messer Tombi is, according to my master, the most skilled of all the apothecaries in Milan (and this street near the New Gate on the northeast side is full of them). There is money to be made in this business, especially when the plague breaks out: that's the time everyone rushes to the apothecary to buy wormwood, juniper, and purple rue as protection. Nothing works against the plague, everyone knows that (especially the apothecaries), but herbs and prayers are all we have when the scourge descends on our city, and at least the apothecary makes the air—which is thicker than macaroni water during such times—smell sweeter.

Tombi's shop is a cave of wonders. The shelves are lined with jars full of wondrous substances—crystals, liquids, semiprecious stones—which throw off blue, green, and red reflections when the sun shines through the small window high up on the wall.

He is standing behind his counter as I enter, writing in

his ledger, garbed in his heavy black robe. It is not very clean, this robe, but I try to overlook that. Apothecaries are a strange breed, more alive to other worlds than our own. He looks up and curls his lip. That's a smile. At least, I think it is a smile. I do not like to think what else it might be.

"Ah, Giacomo, good day to you."

"And to you, Messer Tombi. A new order," I say.

I place it on the counter. Tombi opens the note and smoothes out the creases until the paper lies flat.

"Your master," he says, "is experimenting with every color in the rainbow."

And it's true. Today he wants *Vermilion, Ocher, Terre-verte, Azurite.*

I love the names of colors: so mysterious, so poetic, so majestic—like the names of ancient cities lost to time. There is magic in color, magic waiting to be conjured.

"But has he started painting the wall?" Tombi says.

"Dabs and daubs, here and there," I reply. "But not what you'd call *started*, if you know what I mean."

Tombi shakes his head and lets out a long sigh. "What is the delay, Giacomo? Why does he not make haste?"

"I wish I knew, sir. But he will not talk about it, and I dare not ask."

"The Duke will not permit your master this dallying for much longer," Tombi says. "I must speak with him myself, or we will both be put out of business: he by the Duke—and me by him."

"How is that, sir?"

"You know how much he owes me." Tombi sighs again, scratches his beard. "And I can't—"

"Oh, I do, sir, and one day you will get it all back, I promise, when the painting is done. But I have something to ask you . . ."

And, so saying, I take the medallion out of my purse and hold it up for the apothecary to see. Before I can say anything more, however, he has taken it from my hand.

"Where did you get this?"

His eyes are weak; he holds the medallion up close to his face to study it.

"I have had it since—"

"Do you not know the meaning of this design?"

"No, sir. That is why I—"

"Tell me how you came by this medallion," Tombi says, a bit sharply now.

"But I don't know, sir! I had it in my bag when the Master saved me. I lost my memory—I told you, Messer Tombi, remember? Because of the fever."

"You have here an object of great rarity," Tombi says. "And your master, he—"

"Does not know its origin. I have asked him. Several times."

Tombi turns the medallion round and round.

"It's a bird," I say. "A falcon, or an eagle—"

"Neither. It is a *phoenix*," Tombi replies. "And beneath it, see—"

"Leaves. A leafy tree—"

"No, boy—flames!"

And now I look at it again—yes, those are flames!

"See how it rises triumphantly from the fire, to be reborn. The phoenix can never be destroyed—by man or any other force. The phoenix in flames is the sign of the Brotherhood. The Brotherhood of Alchemists. You have in your possession a medallion belonging to an alchemist."

An *alchemist*?

My master calls alchemy a fantasy born of ignorance, practiced by people who suffer from the same deficiency. (He does not soften his words, my master.) But I have heard tell that true alchemists can turn base metals to gold, read men's minds just by looking into their eyes, and foretell the future by charting the course of the stars in the night sky. And some say that through their art they have unlocked the key to life itself—the secret of immortality.

But Tombi is speaking again: "There was a time, many years gone by, when alchemists were made welcome in the courts of kings. However, the Church, fearing their growing power, whispered treason into the ears of the great lords and turned them against the Brotherhood, whose members were forced into exile. The lucky ones, at least. Many others were whipped, tortured, burned, or beheaded. Those who are left now live and work in secrecy, fearing for their safety, waiting for their chance to rise again. But how did *you* come by this medallion?"

"Perhaps . . . perhaps it was given to me?"

"The medallion of the phoenix is proof of membership in

the Brotherhood. Why would someone *give* it to you, boy?"

"I don't know. But today I saw the very same design—the phoenix in flames—on the door of a chair being transported to the Castle."

"*What?* Is it true?"

"Yes, sir!"

For some moments he stares into the empty air. Then he says, as if to himself: "So the Duke has sent for an alchemist after all these years . . ." I wait for the apothecary to say more, but no further sounds issue forth—nothing save a faint rumbling, which I take to be the lingering effects of his breakfast.

"I must return to work, sir. My master will want me. May I have my medallion?"

Which he gives to me. I'm not letting that medallion out of my sight. Then the apothecary goes to his cabinet and opens various drawers, fills several small jars with colors, and hands them over. I place them in the sack over my shoulder. He no longer asks me for money. He knows I have none to give him.

As I walk home, every new thing I have learned brings forth more questions, until my head is full of tangled thoughts, like a net full of eels pulled from the Ticino River.

I have a medallion belonging to a member of the Brotherhood of Alchemists.

And now an alchemist has come to Milan.

He is the one who can explain everything to me.

I must make myself known to him as soon as possible.

IX

When I arrive home, the front door is open. Nothing unusual in that, Caterina is often next door, and she does not waste time with the lock when she has some important gossip to tell her friend Margareta.

But as I enter the house, something—some odd change in the air—causes me to hold my tongue, instead of loudly announcing my arrival as I am wont to do. This time I go in on tiptoe, like an inquisitive cat. And then . . . there are voices coming from upstairs. Low voices and the sounds of doors being opened and furniture moved. *Thieves!*

I reach under my jerkin and release my dagger from its sheath. At that moment the first intruder comes out of the Master's room and sees me below. My heart sets up a rapid twanging—he is clothed in black from head to foot. Not to tell you an untruth, he puts such a fear in me that the roots of my hair prickle my scalp like thorns.

"What . . . what is your business here?" I say, as loudly as

I can. It comes out as a sort of squeak, such as a tailless mouse might make.

No answer from him except the smooth hiss of his short rapier being drawn. It is a sword rarely seen in Milan, we prefer a longer blade. He slashes the air with it, two strokes, so cleanly I expect two slices to fall to the ground like slabs of cheese.

Now another one appears at the head of the stairs. They exchange a few whispered words. And then the pair of them fly at me from above, their cloaks rippling the air behind them.

I was frightened at first, the more because I did not know what I was facing; but now that I do, my blood unfreezes itself, and I prepare—to run. I may be a servant, but I'm not a complete dullard!

I turn like a top and throw myself through the front door—straight into the arms of the Master.

"What is this? Dancing again, instead of working?"

"M-M-Master! Behind me! Thieves!"

But he can already see them. He lifts me as easily as if my clothes contained nothing but air and places me to one side. The two villains are almost upon him, sword arms raised and preparing to strike, when, with one swift movement, he releases the tie on his cape—a bright red satin-lined, black velvet cape (God's oath, it must have cost ten florins)—and sends the ends swimming through the air onto the two swords lunging towards him. With a double twist of his wrist he turns the cape around and around, entwines the swords inside the folds (it all seems so easy, the way my master does it), and forces down the arms of the assailants, who, unwilling to release their weapons, are compelled to follow.

"Now hold your breath, boy!" the Master yells at me.

And he pulls a small vial from the pouch tied to the belt around his waist, releases the stopper with his thumb, and peppers the air with the contents, a bright yellow powder.

Thank the Saints that I followed his order!

There is a blinding flash, and a rolling cloud of smoke obscures the scene. Suddenly, everything is covered with a yellow fog. Our two assailants, having filled their lungs with the smoke, are coughing and spitting. The tip of a rapier cuts the air to the west of us.

The next thing I know, my master has me by the arm and is leading me away.

When we are clear of the yellow fog, he says: "Let them see us—I want them to follow!"

And when they do, we run down Spiders' Alley, so called because of all the washing lines that crisscross the narrow passage and give the impression of a web. Shirts, sheets, and hose hang dripping from above.

At the end of the alley the Master halts, tears a strip from a wet sheet above our heads, and ties it around my face, covering the lower half. Then he starts to do the same for himself.

The yellow fog is rolling towards us—hurry, Master, hurry! And just as he has finished tying his own piece of sheet, it envelops us until we can scarce see more than an arm's length ahead—but now, thanks to the wet cloths, we can breathe, at least.

"We'll meet them here, boy, where their swords will be more of a hindrance than a help."

What does he mean? I am too frightened to think. We are in a blind alley. We are unarmed. We can hear them running towards us. But the Master seems perfectly at ease!

One of them advances almost clear of the fog, cutting it blindly left and right with his sword, then once more is swallowed up by the cloud.

The Master points at the washing lines above our heads, which are falling as they are cut by the slashing swords—

"They have almost done our job for us," he says. Drawing another small vial from his pouch—this time containing a blue powder—he tells me to count to twenty, and then release it into the air.

And now he runs into the smoke.

"Master! Take care!"

I hear more shouts and must wipe my eyes continually to clear them.

What is happening in there?

Seventeen, eighteen, nineteen—*twenty.*

I pull off the stopper and release the contents into the air.

As soon as the blue powder touches the cloud, it begins to disperse. *Amazing!* And when the fog has lifted I can see the Master standing, arms crossed, above our two adversaries, who are lying on the ground, out cold and as much entangled in the wet laundry as if they had been bound hand and foot by it.

He removes the cloth from his face and signals for me to

do the same. There is a strong smell of bad eggs. "The blue compound, when inhaled in sufficient quantities, also numbs the limbs and renders a man incapable of action," he says, looking at me as if I would dispute the assertion.

But I can only nod my head in wonderment.

Then he bends down over one of them and lifts him up by his black doublet.

"Who are you?" he says. "Where are you from? What do you want with Leonardo da Vinci?"

The fellow's eyes slowly open. He twists his head, tries to raise an arm. The Master shakes him.

"Answer me!"

But the villain's head falls back, and once more he is senseless.

"Help me search them, Giacomo, before the Guard arrives. We must discover what they have taken from the house and on whose orders they were acting."

The Master lifts the fellow once more and searches through his pockets, the purse at his belt, the lining of his cloak. I take the other. Nothing. They have been stripped of all identity.

"If we had heard them speak," the Master says, "the accent might have led us to their place of origin. Now we may only guess at their masters."

"Venetians?"

"Perhaps. Wherever they hail from, these are no brigands, but paid agents."

Shouts from the end of the alley, the sounds of approaching men.

"Come, boy, we must leave this place before we are recognized. That will only lead to more questions."

At the end of the alley is a fence. Several struts are missing.

"Through there, Master, if we can make a bigger hole—"

The Master kicks at the wood and it soon gives. We pass through—I, rather more easily than he, whose shirt brushes against the grimy, greasy wall on the other side and sets him to complaining that it will be impossible to clean.

From there we take a roundabout route back to the house, avoiding the local folk running to the scene we have just left.

"How did you do it, Master?" I say. "How did you create the fog?"

He looks at me as if he did not hear.

"Then it does work, after all," is what he says.

"—And the blue powder? Master?"

"Oh, a simple combination of magnesium and—but here we are. Let us enter and inspect the damage," the Master says.

I pass into the house and call out: "Caterina?"

No answer.

While the Master goes upstairs to inspect his bedroom, I look in the kitchen.

Caterina!

She is laid out on the floor, a basket of laundry scattered around her.

"Master, come quickly! It's Caterina!"

I run to her and lift her head. Thank the Virgin, she is still breathing! And now she opens her eyes.

"Giaco . . ."

"Don't speak," I say.

She lets her head fall back into the crook of my arm. The Master enters the room at speed and joins me at her side.

"I did not . . . see them until it was too late," she says. "One of them struck me across the head with his fist. . . . I fell. Forgive me, Master. . . ."

"Lie quietly," the Master says. He inspects her head. "There is a bruise, nothing that would be serious in a younger person, but you must get to your bed, Caterina, and rest."

"I will take her there, Master," I say.

I make to lift her, but she pushes away my arm and stands up on her own.

"I'm not dead yet, boy," she says. "Save your lifting for my coffin."

If her tongue has recovered, I know that the rest of her will follow soon enough.

When she has lain down on her bed, I cover her to the chin with the blanket and say: "No more work for today."

"Then you must offer a prayer of forgiveness for me," she says. "To Saint Joseph. Tell him I do not waste my time willingly."

Then her eyes close and she sleeps. By my dagger, I hope I will meet the one responsible for this again. I will cut more holes in him than there are stars in the night sky.

Across the hallway, the Master is investigating the damage to his room. Everything has been overturned, and all the Master's clothes have been pulled out of their chests. Some of them are torn.

"Will you look at this doublet, Giacomo? Red velvet—and ruined! Where will I find the money to replace it?"

Where will you find the money to pay for it first, Master, as I am sure you still have not!

We descend the stairs and the Master tries the study door. Still locked.

"Thank the Saints that your arrival prevented those devils from gaining entry to my study."

"What were they looking for, Master?"

"Whatever it was, they did not find it. From now on, the front door must be kept bolted and barred at all times."

"Perhaps they were sent to steal your plans for the Last Supper—to delay the painting."

"The Last Supper is delayed well enough without outside assistance."

"And why is that, Master?" I couldn't help myself. I mean, all of Milan wants to know.

He frowns at me. Very well, I won't persist.

"Then will you tell the Duke, Master? He would surely provide us with an armed guard for the house."

"Neither the Duke nor anyone beneath him must discover what happened here. Can I trust you for once to keep your tongue under lock and key?"

"Yes, Master."

"Do not smirk, boy. I am more than serious. This matter must not reach the ears of anyone outside this room."

"Yes, Master. I mean, no."

"The Duke may not think so, but my inventions are worth money."

"What is to stop whoever dispatched these villains to do us harm, from sending more of them to do the same, Master?"

"They will find nothing of value here. I will ask Maggio to help us move certain of my materials to a safe place."

But what about *us*, Master? Where can *we* be moved to for our safety?

"Do not look so put upon, Giacomo. Our enemies are unlikely to try this again, thinking that we will be better defended in the future. So, you see, it matters little whether we are or not."

Little to *you*, Master, perhaps! But I do not have your fighting skills.

"Where did you learn how to disarm attackers, Master? You dealt with our foes like a man much versed in combat."

"I am keen to expand my knowledge in all matters of human understanding, Giacomo. You would be well advised to follow my example."

"I'll follow you well enough, Master. You only have to show me the way."

And his only reply is to nod and point upstairs to his room, where I must now set about restoring order.

X

Two days hence, Caterina is well recovered, by the grace of God, and is once more bustling about the house, although she has taken to asking me to look under her bed and inside the chests in case the thieves have come back and are lying in wait for her. But it looks as though the Master was right: since then, no one uninvited has come to our house—except one of Father Vicenzo's priests, to ask why the Master had not been seen at Santa Maria. But I got rid of him easily enough.

Yesterday, Maggio arrived with his cart, and he and the Master loaded it with several wooden boxes taken from the study. Because the Master did not ask for my assistance in the packing, I can only conclude that he did not want me to see what was in them.

Caterina tells me she'll be at the game tonight, and to look after my own supper. What game? Dice, of course. Milan's most popular pastime, after wine-drinking, lechery, feasting, fighting, and sleeping. Is it a sin for an old lady to roll the bones? Ask her confessor, Father Cristofano, who is often seen at the same game.

"I'll pray for your good luck," I say.

"Pray for my forgiveness, Giacomo, even though I do not think the Virgin would begrudge me an hour of idle time, if she is watching. And if you *are* watching me, Mary, mother of us all, and I know you are because you see everything, please guide my hand to throw some sixes so that I do not lose my savings, and please forgive me before I play, because I will play (that's for sure), and please forgive me after I play, because I will have played (and that's for certain)—I *must* play, I have to buy one of those holy crosses for sale by Father Benito, the ones the Pope himself has blessed. And I know, dearest Mother Mary, that in your heart you want me to win. Because if I don't, all the crosses will have been sold, and I believe it is a sin to say you are going to buy such a holy cross and then fail to buy it. . . ."

Caterina's collection of crosses would rival any cardinal's.

Then I hear that voice again. Which I've been ignoring.

"Giacomo, *how many more times* must I call for you?"

Caterina clasps her hands and closes her eyes in prayer. Wherever the Madonna is, she cannot but be moved by the old woman's entreaties.

I hasten to the study.

"Enter."

Should I go in with the broom, to make it look as if I've been working?

"I said: 'Enter'! What are you *doing* out there, boy?"

No, I'll leave it outside.

"Master?"

He is at his desk with the sloping top, scraping with his quill. Oh, he's writing backwards again, from right to left, a trick he sometimes uses to conceal his most secret thoughts. Impossible to read, I've tried it.

I stand at attention, waiting for him to look up. Meanwhile, I breathe in and out very quickly to give him the impression I have been working hard.

Now he sees me. But he doesn't seem to notice how *hard* I've been working. Ah, well.

"I have received a complaint about you."

Another servant, no doubt. They're a bitter lot, servants.

"Ugo Trocchi's footman claims that you stole money from his purse while he was in a tavern celebrating the Feast of Saint Michael."

Another servant! I knew it.

"Have you been drinking again?"

"Master, why listen to a footman's story? He has his brains in his feet."

"I am waiting for an explanation."

Explanation? Messer Trocchi's servant should be the one explaining himself, not me. The skull looks up at me with its curious grin. *You're in it again, boy!*

"Master, he spoke ill of you. I could not let it pass."

"Me? What have I to do with this? You are accused of stealing."

Master, why do you always take the word of my accusers?

When one of your students claimed that I had stolen his horse and ridden it to Novara, you believed him before me. But it was not I who took the beast, it was his brother, who confessed in the end.

"Why do you not answer, boy?"

Why should I? You never listen.

"Giacomo, how can I have trust in you when I receive such accusations? It is not the first time."

Master, how can you *not* trust me when every accusation has proved groundless?

"Answer me!"

His face betrays no feeling, but I can see his jaw working, a sure sign he is trying to control his anger. I have gone too far into this river now, and it is easier to wade to the other side than return whence I came.

"Master"—I take a deep breath—"this footman insulted you."

"What? What did he say?"

"That Felloni and Capponi were twice the painters you are, Master."

My master's face is now as stretched and white as dough before baking.

I wait for him to say something. Anything!

Nothing.

So I add: "Because they always finish what they start."

He knows what I mean. The Last Supper.

He snorts. "What they start is not worth finishing."

A dog barks. The Master and I stare at each other.

"Is that all, then, Master?"

"*Did* you steal the footman's purse, Giacomo?"

Can't he see that the real complaint is against him, not me?

"*Yes*, Master." If that's what you want to hear.

"Yes? You *did* steal it?"

Does it matter what I say? You always think the worst.

"I do not believe you," he says.

Yes, he doesn't believe me. *No*, he doesn't believe me.

After all this time, if he can't *see* my loyalty, can't he *feel* it?

Now I wish I *had* stolen it. Instead of defending the Master's name and then having to run like a hare to avoid a beating from the fat footman and his four friends. But why should I bother about his reputation, when he cares so little for it himself?

"You are an idle, insolent, ungrateful knave, and you do not deserve to live under my roof. Now go."

I must say something—I *have* to say something. I won't suffer any more of his insults. But, as they have done before, the words I need confound me and will not come out.

I turn and leave in haste, almost hurtling headlong into Caterina coming out of the kitchen, and to avoid explanations—I feel now as if I might shed tears of fury—I go directly to the front door, unbolt it, and run out into the open.

"Giacomo!" Caterina's voice follows me down the street. "Giacomo! Where are you going?"

Out. Away. Anywhere far from *him*.

I run towards the city walls, past the fine houses of the Visconti and Ricci families—so big we call them *palazzi*, palaces—with their four floors and flower-filled balconies and front doors fretted in bronze and silver, and straight on to the Vercellina Gate, where there is a long line of merchants waiting to bring their goods into the city for sale.

I slow down to a walk to watch all the activity.

It was a wise decision by our ancient city fathers to build seven gates in the city walls, to ease the flow of people and goods entering our city. Everyone who brings merchandise for sale here must pay a tax, and everything must first be inspected and valued at one of the gates.

Our city has more than 150,000 inhabitants now, bigger than Rome, Venice, or Florence, and we trade in everything on God's Earth. Fine leathers from Tunis in Africa. Ivory tusks, ostrich feathers, and turtles' eggs from the Barbary Coast. Pots and urns from Majorca. Maps from Barcelona. And Messer Boccanera, who sells animals from the lands far beyond our seas, has a monkey with white fur that can climb a tree in three bounds.

The line leaving the city is shorter, because there are no goods to tax, and soon enough I am crossing through the gate, which has a high watchtower built above it, manned day and night. Beyond that is the bridge over the wide moat that runs the full circle of our city, filled with the green water and plentiful wriggling eels of the Ticino River.

At last I have left the city walls behind and can breathe again.

Blessed Nature! How may I describe the beauty of our countryside to you?

To the north stands the great oak forest and, leading off towards the horizon, field after field in various hues of yellow and brown, the hedgerows dividing them up like squares on a chessboard, with elms and poplars standing here and there like scattered chessmen. The air is perfumed with the heavy scent of wild roses, ripe olives, lush blackberries—so rich it makes your head spin. If you look up, you might see in the sky, dipping and diving between the very currents of the air, a falcon with a fiery crest. The whole valley, the whole world, seems to welcome me as a friend—just the opposite of how I feel back home.

Autumn has carpeted the earth with red and gold, but even now the leaves are turning brown, the dull color of winter. I run directly to Santa Maria delle Grazie, which has a cloistered garden with a fountain at its center that is incomparable for soothing my distemper. The only sound is the water trickling from the head of the fountain, a fish's generous open mouth. Carved stone benches line the walls. It is so peaceful. I breathe deeply and try not to think about my master's accusations. But how can I not? He has been after me for imagined offenses ever since I have been his servant.

I close my eyes and listen to the silence.

All I want is to learn how to paint. But all *he* wants is to accuse me of villainy. We have a long journey ahead of us if we are to meet in the middle. If I was his son, and not his servant, would it be any different? Would he show me the skills he learned at the foot of his own teacher, Verrocchio, in Florence? Or would he still dismiss me when I asked? I must be *somebody's* son. If a rat or a dog has parents, where are mine? Always the same question, but asking it never brings an answer.

I take some paper and a stick of charcoal from my jerkin pocket and begin to sketch a rose. Drawing calms me and allows me to think clearly.

"What are you doing here, Giacomo?"

That voice.

"Father Vicenzo?"

He is standing behind me. The snake always sees you first.

"Where is your master, boy?"

"At home."

"Then why are you not there, too?"

The prior walks round in front of me. I get up quickly.

"Did you argue with him?" he says.

"No, father. I came here to rest."

"There is no rest for the ungodly. Confess to me your sins."

"What sins?"

"The sins of the flesh. One half of a young man is desire, and the rest of him is devoted to satisfying it. Have you ever had impure thoughts?"

"No, father!" And that is not a lie. The thoughts have me, not I the thoughts. They come without my bidding.

"If you have, you will burn in Hell's scorching fires, demons and devils striking at you unceasingly with their three-pronged forks!"

"And they never get a day off, father? Not even a Sunday?"

"Are you trying to make a fool of me?" he says.

Trying, Father Vicenzo? It costs me nothing in effort.

"Have you kissed a girl?"

"No, father." (Not what I'd call a real kiss, tongue and all.)

The friar is looking inside me, and his eyes are like fishhooks, hoping to catch on my every weakness.

"God in Heaven weeps for the sins you commit in Satan's name," he says. "Come to confession with me now and repent, or burn in everlasting Hell like a strip of roasting meat on a spit!"

He holds out his hand. What, he wants me to take his hand? Never ever.

"I go to the Church of San Giorgio for confession, father."

Well, I will one day; I promised Caterina.

He lowers his hand. I'm not going near that hand. Who knows where it has been? And where it wants to go.

"I have a proposition for you," he says, now toying with the rope around his waist. So does the Devil, for every man. "I am looking for a new servant."

"I have a master, thank you, father."

The friar smiles his sweetest smile. "I can give you instruction in many things, Giacomo."

"My master does that already," I say.

"Will he teach you . . . to paint?"

How does he—? Oh, he sees my drawing.

"I must return home, father. I am wanted."

"You are wanted *here*." Father Vicenzo reaches out and

holds my arm, just above the elbow. Now what? "If you come to the monastery as my servant, I will find an artist to teach you. I know Capponi and Felloni very well—they take a great interest in young boys. What say you to that, Giacomo?"

"Your offer is most courteous, father. I will think on it."

The answer is *no.*

"Do not, as your master does, let an excess of thinking delay the action."

Just before he releases my arm, I pull it away. Carefully.

"If he fails to finish the Last Supper, what will you do then?"

A cold wind is blowing the leaves across the stones, sending them skipping.

Father Vicenzo turns and walks into the shadows of the cloister.

I pull my jerkin around me and head for home.

XI

Evening. The candles are lit. Caterina is sorting through some linen in one of the chests and telling me the story of the three-legged dog that was eaten by a bear in the woods, but came back to the same place a year later as a ghost, to warn its master and save him from the same fate.

"Now, isn't that a story to warm your heart?" she says.

"True enough," I say, "but I'd rather you put another log on the fire to warm my feet."

Then the study door is opened, and the Master's head appears.

"Here, Giacomo, I wish to speak with you."

Caterina gives me a quick glance and scuttles off to the kitchen.

"Now, Master?"

He beckons me in and points to a chair. I sit.

"Why," he says, walking around to the other side of the table, "must you be so contrary?"

One of those questions I cannot answer without dropping myself farther down a deep hole I will be unable to climb out of unaided. And if I deny that I am contrary, he will only say that I am proving his point! Best to avoid the whole matter.

"I met Father Vicenzo in the garden at Santa Maria," I say.

"For what purpose, boy?"

"I did not choose the meeting, Master. But he offered me a position as his servant."

The Master says nothing.

"And he said that he would arrange for Capponi and Felloni to teach me how to paint."

"If you take instruction from them, Giacomo, you will learn nothing but bad habits."

"But if *you* would teach me, Master—"

"I will not. You are my servant, and so you will remain—"

"—while you are in my house." I know the line by heart.

I hear Margareta calling for her husband, Vanni, next door. The smell of beef roasting in a pot reaches my eager nose; how I long for a nice piece of beef, not that I'll ever get it while I am the Master's servant. In this house we may eat nothing that is not covered with leaves or pulled out of the ground by its roots.

"You are fortunate to be alive, Giacomo, remember that. Every day should be a blessing to you."

"Yes, Master."

"Now then. Your meddling friend, Father Vicenzo—"

"Not *my* friend, Master."

"He has made his complaint to the Duke. We are summoned to the Castle to explain the delay with the Last Supper."

"We, Master?"

"You will accompany me. You want to accompany me, don't you?"

I've *always* wanted to accompany you to the Castle, Master!

"I see you do. Well, we can't have you seen at the Castle dressed like a ragamuffin. I propose that we go to a tailor and have him make you a proper cloak for winter."

I jump up from the chair.

"Really, Master?"

I thought I was about to be thrashed and thrown out of the house—and here he is, offering to take me to the Castle in a new cloak. He can turn from anger to appeasement faster than the wind turns a weathercock from north to south.

"Which tailor, Master? We owe more than a few."

"We'll find a new one, then. A new tailor for a new cloak!"

And next day we set off to find this new tailor, who must not only be a master of his trade, but also willing to take the Master's credit.

Leonardo da Vinci always dresses richly when he goes out. Today he is wearing blue velvet hose with a red doublet and a black velvet cloak with a hood (lined with green silk, no less). The streets are thick with people about their business, but my master is easily seen. I've told him often enough to wear his hood up, but he won't listen.

"Hi ho, Master Leonardo, wait up! I need to talk to you about Dante!"

Dante is the Master's horse, and the voice is Fazio's, the owner of the stables where we keep him. The Master has not paid Fazio for Dante's upkeep. It's been due I don't know how long. Well, I do know. I'm the one who has to keep a record of our debts.

"The Devil take him!" my master says.

I *told* him to wear his hood up. Now Fazio is abreast of us.

"I can't talk now, Fazio. I am urgently required at the Castle."

"The Castle, is it this time, Master Leonardo? You are always looked for elsewhere, just when I have found you."

"Fazio, I cannot help the demands the Duke places on me. I shall visit you at the stables soon. How is Dante?"

"Very well, very well, considering what he costs me. What does Dante know, as long as he is fed and watered, eh?"

"Quite right, Fazio, let's keep the horse out of this, he is innocent."

"But what are you, Master?" Fazio says, walking in front of us.

My master halts.

"I? Why, Fazio, you know very well what I am! I am waiting for the Duke to pay me so I can pay you. And he is tardy, let me tell you, he owes me three thousand ducats."

"Three thousand du—!"

"*Now* do you understand? We are all at the mercy of the Duke!"

"Why, I—"

"Good-bye, Messer Fazio."

And Messer Fazio is left standing in the middle of the street. One cannot dispute that my master is a master at sidestepping his creditors.

The street in which most of the tailors' shops stand runs between the Church of San Giovanni, with its high-pointed spire, and that of San Nazaro, with its two iron bells. When they see the Master, several owners hail us from their shops—

"Special offer on sleeveless tunics—half off!"

"Cloaks, capes, *cioppi*—waist-length, knee-length, shin-length, ankle-length! We go to great lengths to serve you!"

"Hose! Beautifying hose! No thigh too fat, no shank too thin! Every defect hidden—bowlegs, flabby buttocks, weak calves! We turn short men into giants and fat men into athletes! Codpieces—small, medium, large, or lascivious!"

The Master dismisses them with a wave of his hand. Halfway down we halt outside a shop whose sign over the door announces MARTELLI, TAILOR, EST. 1479, and underneath: CLOTHES MAKE THE MAN, WE MAKE THE CLOTHES. The Master points to a roll of cloth on display on the table just inside the window and asks if that would not make a suitable cloak for me. It is a rich silver cloth. I am so surprised that all I can do is goggle. He has never made such an offer before, in all my seven years with him. Oh, I have been covered well enough, in dark jerkins and dull doublets, but this is decoration.

"Well?" he says.

"Master, I—"

"You don't like it?"

I *love* it.

Then he suggests that it might look good with a green velvet trim. A green velvet trim! Only the most fashionable young gallants wear such extravagance! I know we do not have the money for all this—we just failed to pay Messer Fazio, didn't we—but how can I refuse such a gift?

"No! I mean, yes!" I say. Yes, yes, *yes*!

"And we don't owe this one any money?"

"I don't think so, Master."

So in we go.

"I wish to buy a cloak for my servant."

"Ah, a cloak," Martelli says, coming to the front of his counter and rubbing his hands. "And you will be needing a jerkin, hose, cap, and—"

"How much do you want for this?" The Master is pointing to the silver cloth.

"My dear sir, it is a bargain—look, cloth of silver like this doesn't come cheap, it's made to order—a steal for a florin the half-braccio."

"What? A florin to cover half the length of my arm! *Too expensive!*"

"We can come to an agreement, sir, never fear! Lazzaro Martelli is not in business to make money, not a bit of it, but to please his patrons. Now, look at this material for a jerkin—"

"If you do not let me buy the cloak, and only the cloak, I will leave."

I'd better act quickly, or I'll lose my gift—and who knows when the Master will offer another one.

"Sir," I say to the tailor, "do you not recognize Leonardo da Vinci?"

"Master *Leonardo* . . . the *painter*? The honor is too great for me! Your name is like honey to my lips, sweetening the words of high regard I have always had for you!"

Martelli sweeps the floor with his bow. It's a miracle he doesn't crack his forehead on the stones. The Master, about to depart, halts. Oh, he loves extravagant flattery, does my master, he laps it up like a cat does milk.

"Boy!" bellows Martelli. And here a young lad appears from behind the curtain. "Take Master Leonardo's servant's measurements, while I retire for a moment."

For a cup of wine, no doubt.

And while I am holding up my arms for the boy to measure with the stick, I hear from behind the curtain: "—and some nice new gloves to go with it?"

The Master shakes his head, smiles at me, and lets fly with a great explosion of laughter. That's the first sign of mirth that I've seen from him in months.

Why, Master, if this fellow Martelli can bring a smile to your face, when nothing else seems to work, we should come here every day to buy me something new!

And the Master's laughter abruptly ceases, as if he has heard the very thoughts in my head and does not thank me for them.

We're going to the Castle.

At last!

XII

Monday morning. When I tell Caterina where we are going, she pleads with me—"Oh don't, Giacomo, don't go—not there! They say that the Duke throws men into the deepest dungeons just for daring to look at him!"

"I'll keep my eyes closed, I promise. Even if I fall into the moat."

"You imp, you'd better listen to me! Nobody escapes those dungeons, they are dug deeper than the graves of the plague dead. If you stand within a dog's bark of the Castle walls at midnight, you can hear the ghosts of the Duke's victims wailing!"

She continues to tell me tales while I eat my bread and honey: the amazing news she has just heard from her friend Angela, about the four merchants who were robbed on the road from Milan to Lodi—and suffered the same fate on their return from Lodi to Milan. *By the same robbers!* She gives a tremendous laugh followed by a loud burp, which sometimes happens when one of her stories is particularly amusing to her. Then she blushes like a schoolgirl and busies herself with some polishing.

My master proclaims that gossip is worse than wasted time, it is a disease that can only be cured by raising the intellect, but I disagree; without idle chatter there would be nothing to distract simple folk from their miseries. Work from dawn to dusk for a few coins and fall onto a hard bed half-dead from exhaustion? Is that a life? Most people cannot read or write, draw or paint, play music or chess. What do they have, then? I say an hour of gossip is kinder to a simple soul than any papal proclamation. Just look at Caterina's face as she talks, it is lit up like the Star of Bethlehem!

Then, at last, my master returns from wherever he was (not the Last Supper, and he's not happy I asked), and we set off for the Castle at a brisk pace. I am wearing my new cloak and prancing like a peacock. If I was on my own I might be more prudent with my swagger, but with the Master by my side I lack nothing in confidence. He walks down the street as if it was named after him, as one day I am sure it will be.

I am carrying various of my master's drawings for the Last Supper, secured between two wooden boards lined with silk and crossed with leather ties. It is a great honor to be allowed to carry the ripe fruits of the Master's mind to the Duke's table, and all the way to the Castle I am sweating under my doublet, fearful that the drawings will fall out of their casing and onto the streets, still glistening with the early morning rain.

"Be careful the boards do not come undone, Giacomo, or so will my plans."

Yes, Master. You trust me to carry your plans, but you will not hear me when I ask you for help with mine.

A hunchbacked man leading an old donkey carrying a great quantity of bricks on its back blocks the street while the obstinate creature refuses to move. The Master pulls me by the elbow in his haste to pass. He is, it seems, even more nervous than I am about our meeting with the Duke.

For some distance we follow the river called Nirone, a tributary of the Adda, which brings fresh water into the center of Milan. The Master comments that the water looks murky today, which reminds him that the Duke asked him to look at improving the Castle water supply and installing a heating system in the private apartments. Where the Master will find time for that is a question best left to the Duke's astrologers.

Then we join the Sforza Way, Milan's finest road, which crosses northwest to southeast from the Castle to the Roman Gate; halfway along it meets the Visconti Passage, which runs from the New Gate in the northeast to the Ticino Gate in the southwest. And there you have it: a big X dividing our city into four quarters. Four quarters equal two halves; two halves equal one whole—and *watch out, Giacomo, you're about to fall into one!*

The Duke should spend some of his gold on new paving stones, instead of wasting it on the more precious stones which only his mistress may have the benefit of.

But I must pay attention—the Master is lecturing me on my behavior inside the Castle, and what good is a lecture without an audience?

". . . don't speak unless I tell you to, don't wander off, don't play the fool, and don't look at the maidservants—or their mistresses. Yes?"

"I can't stop my eyes from seeing, Master."

"Then look at the floor. We are here on a serious matter."

The walk from our house to the Castle is one I have taken many times, curious to see what goes on within. You can always find a crowd of people at the main gates, hoping to catch a glimpse of the Duke. Some cheer when he rides by, but he pays no heed to that; others try to press petitions into his hand, but they are likely to lose whichever hand touches his person.

Milan Castle has the reputation of being impregnable. The walls are made of huge stone slabs that took thousands of laborers more than fifty years to put into position. At each of the two corners facing the city stand round turreted towers, higher even than the walls of which they form a part, each one capable of holding a hundred men ready for battle.

Inside the Castle are the grounds, barracks for the Duke's army, the Duke's own palace and apartments, and a highly fortified citadel deep within, known as the Rocchetta, built expressly to house the Duke's treasure in a room with walls a braccio thick, impenetrable by any cannon or mortar.

A deep moat surrounds the Castle, and the only way in is through the main entrance facing the city across a bridge. Visitors must pass through two sets of gates before they can enter the Castle, and the main gates themselves are vast doors carved from oak and fretted with black iron ribs and bosses. It would take a great army, maybe two, to storm this fortress with success.

There is a constant coming and going at the gates: carts loaded with food and materials, squadrons of foot soldiers, couriers on horseback. I have already tried—of course I have—to see inside, concealed among a group of laborers, but I was spotted—and warned that if I tried it again I would be thrown into the moat. With rocks around my neck.

We continue to walk towards the entrance in silence. Then my master says: "I made plans for a network of secret passages below ground, so that the Duke and his family could escape into the countryside, should the Castle fall to an enemy."

"Were they built, Master?"

"The Duke would not pay for the works. He says that the Castle can never be taken. That is called hubris, Giacomo, the belief that you are never wrong. Believing you are never wrong is an error that afflicts great men. I have learned that to be right you must first be wrong many times. Without making errors—and learning from them—a man cannot find the truth."

The Master is right. You learn more from your mistakes than from your successes. I must be learning a lot, then, with all the mistakes I make.

We cross over the bridge spanning the moat that circles the outer walls. The Castle has a score of white swans, graceful long-necked creatures with flecks of black in their wing feathers, which seem to float atop the still, green water without touching it, guided as if by invisible hands.

At the guardhouse, we are asked our business.

"Leonardo da Vinci and his servant to see the Duke."

We are told to wait. It is very dark in the passage. Then the inner gates are drawn open and our escort to the Duke appears. He is a fop, an *incredible* fop, tricked up in the latest fashions. His velvet doublet is intricately patterned with white and red roses, and draped over his left shoulder is a mantle in cloth of gold patterned with black oak leaves. Topping this display is an extravagantly plumed cap, much like one of those mythical birds that no longer exist on God's Earth. And low on his left hip he wears a rapier with a bejeweled hilt, which he'll surely never use, except in practice.

This, my friends, is how the rich live. At our expense.

He doffs his cap and bows deeply. He stays down. When I am beginning to think he might be stuck there, he raises himself up and replaces his cap with a flourish, as if he was describing a circle around his head. This they call etiquette.

"Master Leonardo, I am Count Pirzo de Brevi. The Duke extends his most benevolent greetings and bids you accompany me to him. Glory to invincible Milan and the name of Sforza!"

My master looks at me and I see the hint of a smile.

We pass through, led by the fop, and emerge into the inner court, a vast open field. The change from darkness to daylight forces me to close my eyes momentarily.

When I open them everything is in motion around me. A group of women in white aprons hurries from one building to another, carrying baskets overflowing with washing. Two old men in red robes pass before us conversing loudly in Latin, one shaking his finger, the other his head, their long gray beards swinging in the breeze. Geese are wandering about on the grass, squawking. The smell of horse droppings is mingled with the more inviting odor of roasting meat coming from the kitchens, and my ears are filled with hoarse shouts and the clangor of sword on sword as foot soldiers in the northwest corner test each other in anticipation of battle, knowing that when the time comes to raise their swords against the enemy, their blows must be made with the intention of maiming, not merely outmaneuvering, their opponents.

We walk across the field and reach the gates to the inner citadel, where Count Whatshisname pulls the bell rope, bows once more—and when I look round the doors are open and a new gentleman stands before us.

"I am Fausto dell'Aquila, Second Earl of—"

"Yes, yes, let us not keep the Duke waiting!" the Master says.

The gentleman (not as gorgeously attired as his predecessor, but still the mirror of fashion) says: "Then follow me, please."

We do: down long icy corridors through which the wind seems to follow us like an army of ghosts, and across musty halls with dull shields and limp banners hanging above the doorways. We pass nobody, see nobody, and hear nothing but our own footfalls.

"It is so cold in here," I say to the Master. No reply. "Why are you not wearing a cloak or furs?" I direct this to the gentleman, whose face has no color, though whether that is the result of the cold or his face powder, I cannot say.

The gentleman does not favor me with a glance.

"Then give your answer to me, if not to him," the Master says.

The gentleman sniffs. "The Duke has decreed that the Castle is not cold." The gentleman's lips are almost blue from this lack of cold. "And the Duke is right and correct in this as in all things."

We cross a courtyard and enter another building, guarded by two men-at-arms in the Sforza colors of silver and green, standing pikes crossed, which they open at a command from the Earl to allow us passage. This building has more sumptuous decorations than the last: some very beautiful tapestries line the walls, but many of them are also full of holes. Perhaps the Duke has decreed that there are no moths, either.

We mount staircases of varying length and incline, until I begin to feel like a climber on the snowy Alps. At last we stand outside two enormous doors set in a portal of carved, cream-colored marble, with cherubim playing around the edges.

This is it: on the other side of these doors is the man who holds the answer to my past, the alchemist. I feel inside my pocket for the medallion, which I now carry with me everywhere.

"Welcome to the Little Red Room," the gentleman says, and with a flourish of his cape he ushers us through the doors. "The Duke willingly attends you."

If this is the Little Red Room, the Big Red Room has to be as big as the dome of Milan Cathedral; there must be fourscore people in here, all dressed finely, all chattering incessantly. It is a bit warmer, too, thanks be to whoever is the patron saint of warm rooms.

I scan the crowd for someone who looks like an alchemist, but not being sure what an alchemist looks like, I fail in the task. Anyway, there is no one here dressed in anything embroidered with a phoenix in flames.

The gentleman leads us forward and the crowd withdraws. I hear mutterings and whisperings as we pass: "Leonardo, Leonardo," and "Our great painter," and "This is he who will not finish the Last Supper!"

Then one high, soft-voiced: "Look how pretty is the servant boy!" In spite of my master's warning not to look at any fine ladies, I turn to catch a glimpse of the beauty with the harmonious tones, only to be smiled at by a wrinkled old gentleman with beetroot-red lips. He blows me a kiss, and in my surprise I tread on the Master's heel. He gives me a good kick in the shin.

At length we have passed through the crowd, and *he* is standing before us, the object of our fealty and fear. The Duke. My master bows deeply. I follow. We rise. Now I know why he is called *Il Moro*, the Moor. His skin is as dark as saddle leather. Behind his back, men call him other names, too, like Devil's Hand and Viper's Tail, but whatever you want to call him, front or back, you don't want to anger him.

The Duke, let me be plain with you, has a reputation for making people disappear. His own nephew, who was made Duke of Milan before him, died suddenly in 1494. Very suddenly, some say, from poisoning; and, some say, *poisoned very suddenly*—by his Uncle Ludovico, no less, who then wasted no time in proclaiming himself the new Duke and winning over the people of Milan with the greatest celebrations ever seen. Weeks of feasting, jousting, horse races, and enough free wine to stop up the thoughts of any citizen inclined to complain. By the time the city had woken up from its merrymaking, it was all over. Ludovico Sforza was in control of the army, the churches, and the treasury. He was untouchable.

"Is this the man they call our country's greatest painter?" he says.

We wait. Nobody speaks. Not even my master. The Duke said it in a way that was not pleasing to the ear.

"Yes, this is Leonardo da Vinci," I say, when the silence has gone on too long, "our country's greatest painter."

And all I get from the Master in return is a look that would burn a hole in wood.

"And who is this?" the Duke says. His eyes seem to have no white in them. It is like staring into a lake at midnight.

"My lord, this is my servant, Giacomo."

"Giacomo, eh? He does not stint at speaking unbidden in the presence of Ludovico Sforza?"

"My lord," my master says, "he is young and rash."

"Rash, you call it?"

Someone comes forward and speaks into the Duke's ear.

"And be certain," the Duke says aloud, when the other has finished, "that there is prepared an abundant supply of lampreys for tonight. In garlic and lemon."

Those courtiers nearest us begin to cheer and applaud. The Duke raises his hand. They cease.

"And should I let it pass, this rashness," the Duke says, "as I would let pass a mad dog, fearing its bite? Or should I fell it now, while it is before me, before it can do further harm?"

"My lord . . ."

"Does his master let it pass, this rashness?"

He moves towards my master as if he might draw his sword on him; but, no, the Duke clasps him in an embrace. Then, just as quickly, he pulls away.

"Leonardo da Vinci!" he proclaims to the crowd. "The greatest painter in the land!"

And this time he means it, I think. The courtiers are not yet sure that he does, though, and, fearing censure, they remain silent. Then the Duke smiles; his teeth flash brilliant white; his tone brightens. "He is not in Naples, he is not in Florence, he is not in Rome—he is *here*, here in Milan, where my enemies cannot profit from his genius!"

Now there is unrestrained applause from the courtiers.

"My lord, I am your humble . . ."

But the smile has gone again, faster than a rat under a floorboard. The applause ceases almost as quickly. "And yet . . ." The Duke scratches the side of his nose, looks at his fingernails (polished and round), and shakes his head at Leonardo da Vinci. "And yet the Last Supper remains unfinished."

"My lord, I—"

"We have been waiting for it, Master. We have told the whole world that we have it, Master. And yet, Master, we are *still* waiting for it, we *still* do not have it, it is *still*"—the Duke sweeps his arm around the room—"not here."

No, I want to say, it is at Santa Maria delle Grazie.

From out of the circle that has formed around us, a very fine lady steps forward. She wears a jewel-encrusted dress in scarlet velvet cut square across her chest. Her necklace of ivory and jet is wound several times around her neck and hangs low in front, dividing her breasts, but doubling their attraction. The thinnest strip of gold encircles her forehead, and in the center is set a brilliant red garnet that catches the light now and then and dazzles the air. Her lips are painted the same color. Her auburn hair, parted in the middle and descending in two waves to her cheeks, is drawn back and tied behind in a net of sheer silk sewn with pearls. It hangs thickly down her back and swings like a bell rope when she moves.

Why do I go to such great lengths to describe her to you, when there is such serious business at hand? Because I have never seen such a living creature; her every movement is such that looking at her does not, as in other people, accustom the eye; rather, she becomes more fascinating, more impossible to look away from.

But this is no ordinary woman: this is Lucrezia Crivelli, the Duke's mistress. I recognize her from the portrait my master has been at work on for the Duke. She is lovelier even than his rendering of her, and it is a rare woman, having sat for my master, who can boast that.

"Master Leonardo," she says, "I wonder that you did not bring my finished portrait with you."

She looked at me, I swear she did. At *me*!

"I could not do that, my lady," my master says.

"Why, pray?"

"Because it is not finished."

"We beseech you to put aside your other works until it is."

"Then you must speak to the Duke, my lady."

"But I am speaking to *you*, Leonardo," she says, with an edge.

"If the Duke wishes me to neglect the Last Supper, then I may devote all my time to you. Otherwise, you must be disappointed."

"You would do well not to disappoint either of us, Master Leonardo," the Duke says.

Lucrezia puts a hand on the Duke's arm. The Duke takes it off. And then he says: "Now hear me, Leonardo! Father Vicenzo, the prior of Santa Maria delle Grazie, comes to me with a most serious complaint against you. It has been two years since you first raised your brush to the Last Supper, and he tells me that since then the brush has scarce touched the surface, in spite of the money I have paid you."

"If my lord would care to accompany me to Santa Maria, I would be—"

"Accompany you? Nay, Leonardo, you must find your way alone. This painting is yours before it is mine. Now then, to begin at the end: When will the Last Supper be finished?"

I am listening to every word, but I cannot take my eyes off Lucrezia: they are sewn to her front like the jewels on her dress.

"My lord," my master says, "to explain what art should be, and to examine why some works jump the hurdle of time and live forever, while others fall at the first fence, would be to—"

"Make me exceedingly weary. Speak to me not of the *how*, but the *when*."

"My lord, if you will look at my drawings—Giacomo!—you will see . . ."

I begin to untie the boards, but the Duke shakes his head. "No, Leonardo, no more drawings." So I tie them up again. "You promised me a *painting*—the finest painting ever made."

"And you will have it, my lord. But such excellence does not come without a price."

"You have been well paid, have you not?"

"The price, my lord, is time."

"In that case you have been *very* well paid. And now your credit has run out. State me your reason for the delay."

The Master does not reply at first. The courtiers are staring at us.

"Reason, my lord?"

I can smell cooking. Perhaps food is being served in the next room, and that is why the assembly looks so eager to see us go.

"Yes, Leonardo, *reason*; tell me the *reason*, before I lose mine."

My master hesitates—and in that brief moment I know he is thinking of a good excuse—then says: "I cannot find suitable models."

"Eh? Models? My dear Leonardo, you have the whole

court! Look around you at all my nobles, good and faithful men, every one. We have a thousand faces, Leonardo, would you have me lose mine by failing me?"

"I mean, Your Excellency, models for the faces of Judas and Jesus."

"Choose from among my courtiers, Leonardo, as I have just instructed you."

"But, my lord, how to choose the highest of men and the lowest? It cannot be done."

"Is that your problem? Is that it?"

"That is it, my lord, no more, no less."

The Duke claps his hands. "Then it is easily solved! You have my permission to use whomsoever you please."

"*Any*body, my lord?"

"My dear Leonardo, use your *servant* as a model for our Lord Jesus, if you have a mind to—just finish the thing, and finish it by Easter. The Pope will be visiting us, and I want to show him that Milan has the finest—and the largest—painting of Christ and His Disciples in all the land. Failure to finish it will result in my humiliation, and that will not be favorable for either of us. Do you hear me now?"

"Indeed, my lord, I could not fail to. And Judas?"

"Find *some*one, Master Leonardo. Take a beggar off the street, if you must. Paint it, Leonardo, paint it any way you like, but, above all, paint it quickly."

My master bows.

Then Lucrezia speaks. "You are our greatest asset, Master Leonardo. We wish to heap praise and rewards on your head, as soon as the Last Supper is finished—and that as soon as my portrait is done."

"My lady."

The Duke gives her a look, but does not speak. With a face like hers, Lucrezia can say what she wants.

"Our business settled, we may proceed to lunch," he says.

Thus the Duke brushes us off like dust from his sleeve. So much for the Last Supper, and so little for it.

The Duke looks at me as he passes. I bow. When in doubt, bow; it is safer.

"What is your name, boy?"

You were told that already, O forgetful ruler.

"Giacomo, if it please you, my lord."

"Please me? I cannot say. Does it please *you*?"

"Better than Donkey Ears or Monkey Face, my lord."

"Ha! A most insolent boy!"

"Giacomo!" my master says. "Giacomo, mind yourself!"

"This boy's effrontery reminds me of my Fool, but his face is better proportioned. My Fool's face looks like a badly stuffed cushion."

And a voice from within the crowd says: "Why does the Duke insult my face behind my back, when he knows full well it is on the front? But that is like everything around here—back to front."

The Duke's Fool pushes his way through the crowd—"'Scuse me." "Coming through." "That's a nice dress, did you make it yourself?" What a sight he is in his costume of red and yellow stripes and his hat a-jangle with bells. Why, he is no taller than a clipped hedge! I have always wanted to meet him, ever since I saw him in the Duke's procession to the Cathedral, running in and out of the crowd banging a drum.

"What errand brings you here, Fool?" the Duke says. "I did not send for you."

"And I didn't ask to come. But here I am."

Now the little man steps between the Master and the Duke.

"So this is the famous Leonardo," he says.

"This is he, Fool," the Duke says.

"The greatest painter in the land?"

"That is right."

"Who paints the Last Supper?"

"Yes."

"Never heard of him," says the Fool.

The Duke frowns.

"We must go, Giacomo," my master says. "The Duke's lunch grows cold."

"Leave the boy with me, Master Leonardo," says the Fool. "I will teach him how to wash the dishes."

"I already know that," I say.

"It will be a short lesson, then."

"Master, may I stay with the Fool?"

"No, boy," he says, "you are too much the fool already."

The Duke places his hand on my master's shoulder.

"Your genius is beyond our understanding, Master Leonardo, to be sure."

"Why, I thank you, my lord."

"As is your habit of disappearing at the very moment we have need of you. Keep me informed of your progress. Do not make me chase you so much, or one day I will be forced to chase you from Milan."

"My lord—"

"Do you see?"

"With the light of the summer sun."

"Not *summer*, Leonardo, *spring*! It must be finished by the *spring*."

The Duke makes a signal to the assembly and prepares to leave.

I give Lucrezia one last, longing look, but she has forgotten about me. The Duke takes her hand. She is escorted towards the door. The lords and ladies, courtiers and courtesans, handmaidens and hangers-on all follow in their wake.

The Fool, meanwhile, pretends to cry, then laugh, then cry, then laugh. He waves at me, shakes his fist at me, produces a horn from under his jerkin and blows on it, creating a noise fit to bring down a wall. Several courtiers cover their ears, wincing. My master pulls a face and looks at me as if I am to blame.

The Fool is the last one to leave. He gives one final blast on his trumpet and closes the doors behind him. Then there is silence. We walk to the doors and open them. No one about. Even the guards have gone off to eat, it seems.

"I want to show you something," the Master says, looking left and right. "Now, while we are alone and unattended."

XIII

He pulls me by the wrist up a flight of stairs and then down a corridor. We come to a door. He searches in the small leather pouch at his waist and pulls out a key. It opens the lock. We are inside a large room—a very large room, and cold—but it is too dark to see anything. The Master, however, has no hesitation in walking ahead of me, and soon he is pulling open two heavy curtains. Then he goes from window to window—four in all—repeating the action. And the vast room is filled to its farthest reaches with light.

The walls are hung with paintings in such quantity as I could never have imagined in the possession of one man. Every space, floor to ceiling, is taken up with panels large and small, square and round. And on the floor—more paintings stacked one in front of the other and sitting on easels dotted around the room. There is no order to the display. The Duke professes to be a lover of art, but this cold and gloomy room would seem to be a place he never visits.

"The Duke's private gallery," my master says. "I have a key copied from his own, unknown to him. There is a painting here that is as important to me as anything I have ever done. If I could not see it from time to time, I would not care to see anything."

My eyes rove the walls, trying to separate the lesser works from what I know will be a masterpiece. So many paintings! So many ugly, gaudy representations of pagan myths, of satyrs ravishing round-hipped, rosy-lipped women, many painted by Capponi and Felloni. I recognize these from my master's descriptions, although until now I have never seen them outside of my imagination. They are as far from matching his skill as an ass is from jumping a high fence.

Then my expression changes from disapproval to wonder.

"You have found her," he says.

"Oh yes, Master, she is—"

"She is Cecilia."

Cecilia Gallerani, the first mistress of Duke Ludovico, who lived with him at the Castle for nearly ten years, so my master told me, from the age of seventeen. I met her once, in 1491, just before she left Milan. She had come to tell my master that the Duke had grown weary of her and was going to send her away. The Duke was a fool. That must be why he keeps a Fool, to remind him.

In the painting her hair is quite blond, the same color as my own. That is not so common in Milan. Why, she could almost be my sister. But that is impossible—this was painted fifteen years ago.

"Master, you have captured her to perfection."

"It was the Duke who captured her; I tried to release her. In this portrait."

I look closely at it. She is even more beautiful than I remember—and I remember very well.

Her eyes, brown as ripe hazelnuts, hold a yearning that any man would die to be the object of, but she is not looking at the person facing the painting—that would be the Duke—but away, into the far distance. This, I think, is what the Master means when he says he has tried to release her—from the imprisonment of the Duke's ravenous gaze.

She has started to smile, but the Master has turned it into an expression of loss, as if all delight in her youth and beauty has vanished and been replaced with a rueful acknowledgment that what was hers by right has been taken by another.

Now I study the ermine she holds in her arms, her slim, elegant fingers lightly grazing its back. The creature's white fur and proud bearing serve to draw attention to Cecilia's white skin and noble character. It is the ermine, rather than Cecilia, whose head seems to be turning to face me as I look.

"What does it mean, Master?"

"I want you to tell me."

Let me think, then.

"The ermine is incorruptible," I say.

"Correct."

"As is Cecilia."

"You have it, boy."

Then it comes to me—this creature, hunted mercilessly for

its magnificent coat, is the bravest of animals. It prefers to die rather than be caught and humbled. My master wants me to conclude that Cecilia has a spirit like the ermine's, unbreakable, and that if a man—even such a man as the Duke—hunted her down, nothing could tame her.

I repeat this to the Master.

"Did I speak to you of this painting before?"

"No, Master."

If the Duke had known what Leonardo da Vinci signified by putting the ermine in Cecilia's arms, he would not have been very pleased—might, indeed, have fallen into a dreadful choler. But he had never thought about it. Why would he? To him it was an ermine, a mere animal, and he has worn enough of those around his shoulders not to have any regard for them other than as lifeless skins to warm him on a chill day.

"Let us go."

My master inhales deeply when we finally emerge from the corridors and mezzanines of the Duke's citadel. A trio of horsemen in armor, lances aloft, rides past us with a muffled thunder of hoofs on earth. We walk down the road leading to the main gates. My master, deep in thought, is silent.

Once outside the Castle walls, he halts abruptly, then says: "He sent Cecilia, the soul of purity, away from the Castle and replaced her with that—that *courtesan*! How much has changed during my time in Milan. When I arrived I was given gifts and lavished with praise. But, more importantly, I was left in peace to pursue my own interests. What I did was not questioned, and I performed my tasks for the Duke at my leisure. All that went when Cecilia did. The court is now no more than a circus of performing beasts seeking to please their master. He scolds me for not finishing the Last Supper, when any fool can see it is not ready to be finished. Does he expect me to do nothing about the insults he heaps on my head? Not if I am Leonardo da Vinci—no, I'll not take it! He'll see! He'll soon see!"

And with these inexplicable words, the Master turns in the direction of our house and sets off at such a pace that I must trot in order to keep up with him.

If Milan is not what it once was, then it must be true that neither is my master what he once was to the Duke. Perhaps it is time for us to consider one of those offers of work in Venice, Florence, or Bologna that the Master claims to have received. But I do not think he will ever leave Milan willingly—not while the Duke owes him so much money.

I hope not, anyway.

Not until I have met the alchemist and shown him my medallion.

But who knows when that will happen?

XIV

Evening, the next day. The dying sun is an orange discus hurled across the heavens by Zeus in a competition with Mars. The gods have battled enough. And so have I. Time for my dinner.

"Ah, boy, where have you been? I haven't seen you since the bell tolled midday," Caterina says.

I was with Renzo. We were on the scrubland to the northeast of the city, near the Lazaretto, which the Duke built to house victims of the plague outside the city walls, in order to prevent the spread of infection within Milan. The Lazaretto lies empty now, the city not having been infested for many years, thanks be to God. It is an excellent place for our practice, because no one comes near, fearing the ghosts of the plague dead.

Renzo throws a knife well and knows many moves employed in hand-to-hand fighting. He learned it all from an old soldier, Umberto of Lodi, who had retired from battle and was employed in Maggio's workshop to sweep up the sawdust and wood shavings. He had hurt his leg badly, fighting for the Duke in one of the wars, and could only walk sideways, in a kind of shuffle. For this he had earned the nickname "The Crab."

Today we were practicing the underarm throw, drawing the knife and letting it fly from below in one single action, releasing it at shoulder height. An especially effective move when fighting at close quarters, it has the advantage of surprise. Before your enemy has a chance to counter, the knife is buried to the hilt in his gut.

If the intruders return to our house, they will have more than the Master to contend with.

Caterina has prepared rice and fried pumpkin, pickled tomatoes and goat cheese. The Master is locked in his study, working, and Caterina takes him his food there.

While I am eating, I ask: "Caterina, what do you know about the Master and Cecilia Gallerani?"

"Why, what business is that of yours?" she says sharply.

"I saw her portrait at the Castle, that's all. Don't you think she looks very like me? Our hair is the same color, you know."

"I don't know anything about it," she says.

"Then what *do* you know?" I say.

"Nothing."

Nothing. It's not like Caterina to know nothing—she knows something about everything. I'll try another way: "Was the Master very close to her?"

"Oh yes. When the Duke sent her away he wept, I tell

you, and I have never seen the Master do that before or since. For days afterwards he kept to his room, eating nothing I set before him. The Master does not care for women, as a rule; but I tell you, Giacomo, he would have married our Cecilia, had such a thing been possible."

"And why wasn't it?"

"Marry Cecilia? Why, the Duke would never have given permission for a painter to be her husband. The thought of it! She was married off to a lord, a man with a great country estate where ostriches and peacocks roam the grounds. The Master—"

"Hush, Caterina! I hear his door opening."

And a moment later he appears in the kitchen. He is holding a brush and there is paint on his fingers.

"Come in here, boy."

We enter the study and over his shoulder I can see Lucrezia Crivelli! No, it is her portrait.

"Master, she is so real I almost bowed to her!"

How different her shadowy beauty is from the pure loveliness of her predecessor, Cecilia Gallerani. I could not, however, tell you who was the more beautiful, any more than I could choose between the differing glories of day and night.

Another painting is sitting on a second easel. It is already bound with cloth and rope. He does not want me to see it, then, but I will find a way.

"There." He applies the final dab of paint to her lip. "She is finished."

He stands away from the easel, and I stand back in wonder.

Whereas my master had shown in Cecilia's face shyness and pride entwined, a gaze that beckoned without surrendering, Lucrezia's eyes sparkle with scorn and seductiveness, challenging you to come closer, closer, if you dare. Her mouth, ripe with readiness, promises more than mere kisses. Cecilia was a child compared with Lucrezia. With his next mistress, the Duke traded innocence for experience.

But there is something new here.

"Master, on Lucrezia's face, a shading—"

"A new style I have been working on, Giacomo, a blending of colors at the corners of the mouth and eyes that adds depth and expressiveness to the face."

"It is truly miraculous, Master."

This is not flattery. Flattery is the result of intention. I said what I said without thinking. The painting is another great victory for Leonardo da Vinci; but however great his fame may be now, the future alone will record the true extent of it.

What I would give for him to teach me this new trick, along with all the other ones he has in his collection. If I show him how well I can copy the drawings from his sketchbooks . . . why, I'll run and get them now!

But, no, I *cannot* show him—not yet. I dare not! He will laugh at me. Tell me I am a servant and always will be. Oh, I know my work is still rough and unpolished. But I am improving. I feel it in my hand. And I can already draw a head or a hen or a hawk better than any of his students.

The Master sets down his brush in a clay pot.

"Tomorrow morning, I want you to take the painting of Lucrezia Crivelli to the Duke. That should keep her quiet for the moment."

"Yes, Master."

"I will wrap it and set it here, against the table." He points. "Hand it to the Duke himself. Can I trust you with this office?"

Need you ask, Master?

"Then we shall see whether the almighty Duke is satisfied with my work."

The Master has already left the house by the time I rise. I dress quickly and hurry to the kitchen. Caterina gives me a chunk of Parma cheese, hard and salty, my favorite, and a red pear. When I tell her where I am going, she says: "You went there once, boy. Do not tempt the Devil anew!"

"What have I to do with the Devil? I am delivering a painting for the Master. Do not trouble your head so, woman."

"That is how the Devil works, mark my words! And this time you might not escape so easily."

I smile. I nod. I eat my food. I have nothing to say to this; in truth, there is nothing she wants me to say. My job is to listen until she has exhausted herself. And when she has, I go to the Master's study—the door is open—and take up the painting bound with cloth and rope that he has placed against the table, where he said it would be. That other painting is still sitting on the easel. I could untie it now and take a look—but there is no time.

I set off for the Castle as fast as I can, clutching the important package to my side and keeping a watchful eye on every person I pass in the street. Perhaps this time I will have my chance to meet the alchemist. I walk all the more quickly.

A peasant leading a huge sow by a rope asks me the way to the market. I hope he will get a good price for her—his family must have had empty stomachs while he was feeding the beast to such a size.

Here I am once more at the Castle gates.

A head comes to the window. It's an ugly shaggy thing, this head.

"What do you want, boy?" the head says.

"I am Giacomo, servant to Leonardo da Vinci. I have a painting for the Duke. I must deliver it to him myself."

"Leave it there and shove off," comes the reply. "We're busy."

"You'll open the gate and let me in, or the Duke will hear of it," I say.

"You what?"

The guardhouse door is kicked open, and the brute and several of his fellows file out. Saint Francis, what have I done now?

One of them laughs and says: "Oh ho, we have a live one here, lads! He needs a lesson, and no mistake!"

The big brute moves towards me, his head turned slightly to one side, as if I am too insignificant to look at.

"Who are you, then, fool?" he says, now looking straight at me and standing to his full height. Saint Francis, are you listening to me? He is *huge*. "Whoever you are, when I've finished working on your face, even your mother will cross herself and swear she never saw it in her life."

"And when *you* came out of *your* mother," I say, "she must have given your face its first wash in quicklime."

That did it.

He roars at me and charges, in armor plate, too, and before I have time to move he has shouldered me a tremendous blow to the chest, knocking me down flat. Then he kneels on me and gives me a terrible whack on the side of my head with his gauntlet.

When I open my eyes once more, I am still lying in the dirt, looking up at the sky. I cannot move. One of my enemy's lead-heavy armored feet is planted on my chest. He starts pressing. He aims to crush the very life out of me!

And then—

"Aldo, look sharp. The Duke!"

I twist my head to see the Duke approaching on horseback with a small party of guests. A mere one hundred or so. They have been out hunting, to judge by all the dead game falling out of the saddlebags. He rides up to our group at the head of his party.

"What is going on here?"

"Lord," the guard says, "this knave—"

"Was delivering the painting—" I manage to say before the villain presses down again and squeezes all the breath from my chest.

"He threw a stone at the guardhouse and shouted, 'Death to the Duke!'"

"He did?" says the Duke. "Brazen boy!"

"Yes, my lord," the guard says, "and then—"

"But, don't I know you?" the Duke says, peering down at me.

"My lord, he—"

"Silence! And remove your foot from his chest!"

The guard obeys, and somehow I struggle onto my hands and knees, but I seem unable to raise myself farther.

"What are you doing down there, looking for worms?"

Some of the Duke's guests laugh at this. If *that's* the best he can do.

"Why, it is Master Leonardo's boy!" A female voice, soft as raised velvet.

"What? Look at me," says the Duke. "It *is* you! Jacopo . . ."

"Giacomo, my lord."

"What happened here, Giacomo?"

As I tell my brief, exhausting story, a woman dismounts from her horse and helps me rise to my feet. It is Lucrezia—Lucrezia Crivelli! When I am standing, with her support—she has an arm around my waist, the most gentle pressure—she beckons to a handmaiden for a cloth and, dipping it in the frosty dew on the grass, with strong fingers applying the lightest touch, cleanses my brow of the blood. A lock of soft, shining hair peeks out from under the hood of her cloak. She blows it away from her face. Her perfume floats on the air, something musky and sweet yet lemony and sharp, all mixed in with her sweat from the morning's hunt.

My nose reacts by igniting all my other senses until I am aflame with desire. I forget about the pain in my head and concentrate instead on the pleasure of having her near me. I am so entranced that I may have forgotten my own name.

Lucrezia's face is an inch from mine. She whispers: "You are a handsome lad, Giacomo, even with a nasty bruise."

"Well?" the Duke says to me. "What is it?"

"What is what, my lord?"

"It! That! There!"

"Oh, the painting you wanted from my master, sire. The Lady Lucrezia."

"Excellent, excellent. Leonardo is once again my champion of champions. Now, as for you—"

The armored guard drops to his knees on the ground with a noise like kitchen pots falling from a wall. He raises his hands in prayer. "My lord, I have been your faithful servant, have mer—"

"Take him away and lock him up in a cell so deep beneath my castle that only the rats may hear his prating," the Duke says, "and leave him there for a month. I will not suffer any man who does offense to my Lucrezia. Or her portrait."

The Duke's horse snorts and raises its front leg, stamping it back down on the hard earth as if strongly agreeing with its master's sentiments.

The Duke's captain waves to two Castle guards, who approach the still kneeling offender, swords drawn, and lead him away, his head turned back towards the Duke, pleading for clemency. We will not hear from him again. Nobody will, I fear.

A servant assists Lucrezia back into her saddle. The Duke and his entourage prepare to pass through the gates.

"Well, boy, are you coming?"

The Duke points at the painting, and one of the men-at-arms dismounts and gathers it up.

My other tormentors are standing in the shadows of the guardhouse, quaking. I just have time to give them a look that says they had better think twice before picking on the servant of Leonardo da Vinci ever again, and then the gates are opened and the Duke rides through.

I have to follow on foot? Yes, that is what I must do. My head is still ringing from the gatekeeper's blow, but I run behind them across the Castle grounds as far as the gates to the citadel. There the Duke and his party dismount, and he bids his guests farewell. Now the Duke is waving—at me—to accompany him and Lucrezia, and we enter his private apartments, attended by a small group of guardsmen and servants. When I follow too closely behind the Duke, I am held back. I should have known to wait.

Through a maze of corridors, through endless portals of limestone, of colored marble, of ornamented and inlaid woods, we at last arrive at the tall entrance to a room. When the heavy doors have been thrown open, I can see its walls are hung with tapestries of unicorns, horses, and bears. The Duke, Lucrezia, and several servants go inside. My master's painting is taken in and set down against a wall. I wait. Then I am told to enter. Now I see myself reflected in mirrors taller than I will ever be, enclosed in ornately carved and gilded frames. This room, unlike the others we passed through, is well heated: a fire large enough to warm a small village is blazing in the grate, and above it rises a chimney you could stand twenty men in, I swear it so.

And there—a very fine painting, round, of the Holy Family. Not by my master. Indeed, I do not recognize the hand.

The Duke sees me studying it.

"Ah, you have excellent taste, boy. This is one of my favorite works."

"Your favorites change with the weather," Lucrezia says.

I smile at her, my best smile, it almost touches my ears, which I hope she interprets as a great desire on my part to have her stand next to me once more and mop my brow.

"Your master has shown you many paintings, yes?" the Duke says. "Can you guess the author of this work?"

I look at it long and hard. No, it is a style new to me. The figures are almost like carvings, like sculptures, so bold and solid. I shake my head.

"A young man, not much older than you. Perhaps you have heard of—"

"Michelangelo!"

"You know his name!"

"There has been much talk of him," I say.

"There is always much talk of genius in Milan. I encourage it."

A long couch strewn with red and blue cushions looks soft enough to fall asleep on, which is what I fear I might do at any moment, my head is so dull and cloudy from the guardsman's blow.

The Duke flops down on an upholstered chair near the fire. Lucrezia settles full-length on the couch I was just looking at so longingly, making it doubly attractive. Two shag-haired dogs spring forth from somewhere and demand attention. The Duke fondles their ears and they nuzzle him in return. One tries to put its head between his legs and he kicks it away, which does not stop it from renewing its attentions; it must be used to the Duke's particular form of affection.

"Wine," the Duke announces to no one in particular.

Nobody has told me I can sit, and I have now learned to do nothing until I am instructed. I feel weaker than wet straw. Lucrezia is looking at me. The Duke is looking at her. I try to look away, though her face draws me like the sun.

Now the dogs have abandoned their master and are showing an interest in me. Get away, you brutes! They smell as if they have been rolling in dung. Or perhaps they always smell like this.

"They like you, boy," the Duke says, still looking at Lucrezia. "Fortunately for you." Then, for his further amusement, he watches the beasts nudge and poke me front and back, until finally, with an abrupt "Down, Agamemno! Down, Achilleo!" he dismisses them to their beds.

The wine appears on two silver trays, carried by two servants. It is poured. The Duke points at me, and I am given a goblet, surely made of purest gold.

A lute and its owner appear and music is struck up, but softly.

"Drink, boy."

I do so.

"Your master's painting," Lucrezia says, "does it become me?"

"No painter could ever hope to reproduce the beauty of Madonna Lucrezia," I say.

"Then I will not look at it," she replies.

"No painter save my master, Leonardo da Vinci."

"We shall be the judge of that," the Duke says. "Bring me the painting."

I put down the goblet. I bring the painting. I stand, holding the painting, still bound with its cloth and rope. The Duke is now sitting next to Lucrezia and whispering something to her.

"May I sit, sire? I feel so strange. . . ."

Before the Duke has answered, everything around me begins to melt—walls, ceilings, windows, chairs. My legs are giving way. I can see myself falling twelve times in a dozen mirrors. I just have a moment to set the painting against a table before the floor jumps at me, and I am kissing it.

When next I open my eyes, a man in a black cap and robes is standing above me. Some kind of doctor, by the look of him.

"The blood," he is saying, "has been corrupted by the blow to his head—see here, my lord Duke, and here."

"Oh," I hear Lucrezia say, although I cannot see her, "you must find some remedy for it now, Master Corso, you must save him!"

Master Corso pulls out a knife and glass cup from his bag.

"Yes, my lady, we must. To save him we must *bleed* him without further delay!"

"No knives, I beg of you! I am feeling much better!"

But when I try to rise, I cannot.

"Untie me the painting, you," the Duke is saying to someone.

Master Corso is floating above me with his knife. Now Lucrezia waves him away. She kneels beside me. She lifts my head from the floor and cradles it, brushing the hair from my brow. Her face is no more than a kiss away. I could raise my head a notch and graze those crimson lips with mine. But I won't. The Duke would have my lips sliced off for such impertinence.

Such bliss in her arms, such bliss.

I close my eyes.

"By the black claw of Lucifer!"

I open my eyes.

Now what?

A stream of oaths and curses flows from the Duke. Who has angered him so? Lucrezia ceases stroking my brow. She drops my head—*ouch!* The floor! I must try to rise, but—over there—the Fool! I want to signal to him to help me up. I have no strength. What? He is shaking his head and wagging his finger at me. What have I done wrong? Has the world gone mad? Now I see the Duke—he is holding a painting above me and pointing at it. Everything is fading, everything except—

No, take the picture away! It is ghastly, a horror—a woman's face, no, not a woman, you cannot call that thing a woman—it is staring, madly staring—red eyes and wide-open mouth, sharp teeth, oh, monstrous!—A nightmare that has found its way into day—a face filled with horror, hatred, and hurt—around the head writhes a hellish halo of serpents—a ghostly glowing green and yellow—so real I can hear their hissing!—

And now the Duke is shouting at me: "Did you not say your master had sent you with the portrait of Lucrezia Crivelli? Then why do you insult me with this abomination of a Medusa? Is this *your* doing, boy? Do you dare to mock *me*, Ludovico Sforza?"

Will he strike at me? Lucrezia has taken hold of his arm and is pleading with him: "My lord, no! Have mercy! He is just a boy!"

And then the curtain falls with a thump across my eyes, and everything turns to black: no more Duke, no more Lucrezia, no more doctors, attendants, dogs, musicians, or Fool. No more wondering, worrying, or waiting for my master to have faith in me, my parents to find me, or my life to reveal its meaning. The stage is empty. The actors have departed. What blessed relief.

No more me.

XV

When I have opened my eyes, rubbed them a few times, and touched my head (a bump as big as the dome on Santa Maria), I see that I am still in the Castle, still in the same room, and stretched out now on that couch I was admiring earlier. The Duke is standing ten paces from me, looking out of one of the high windows, hands clasped behind his back. Everybody else has departed, all save one man-at-arms stationed at the doors. It is early evening. The dying sunlight pushing through the window burnishes the Duke's dark skin and gives him the sheen of the bronze statue of Neptune in the fountain in Arengo Square. He is humming a tune, some ballad I once heard, called "Alas for Our Love, Her Love Is His, Not Mine."

The Duke, hearing me shift on the couch, turns as I am attempting to rise. "Stay where you are, boy. Hear me now. The Duke of Milan commands it!"

Well, in that case.

He comes towards me.

"Who bade you bring the face of the Medusa to me? Was it your master?"

"The fault is mine, lord, all mine." *Saint Stephen, my head is throbbing.*

The Duke finds a chair and draws it closer. He sits down. He looks uncomfortable. His doublet and hose are so tightly threaded, embroidered, and encrusted with jewels, it is a wonder he can breathe.

"Why is the fault yours?" he says.

"There were two paintings in my master's study. I must have taken the wrong one."

The Duke laughs.

"I do not think so. I think your master wanted you to bring the Medusa to me."

"No, my lord, never!"

The Duke stands up again. Clearly his doublet and hose are getting the better of him. He walks over to the vast fireplace, picks up a chunk of wood from the iron stand, and throws it on the blaze. You could cook a standing ox in that fireplace, you could.

"The q——on boy is wh——?"

"Forgive me, my lord"—I am shouting now—"I can't hear you over there. You're too far away."

The Duke brushes the dirt off his hands and comes back towards me.

"The question, boy, is why? What is the purpose of the Medusa?"

That's two questions.

"I do not know, my lord."

"This is not the first time your master has played a trick on us."

My master plays tricks? Yes, he played one on me, all right, when he switched those paintings.

The Duke tries to sit down again; then, thinking better of it, stands up.

"I value your master," he says. "We have grown accustomed to each other over the years. But no contract lasts forever. Now, I want that painting finished. I have told Pope Alexander it will be finished. And I *will* have it finished."

"Yes, my lord."

"By Easter."

"Yes, my lord!"

"Because His Holiness must see the Last Supper."

"Yes, my lord?"

"Must see it and must pledge his support to help defend Milan. Because this great painting must never fall into their hands."

"Whose hands, sire?"

"Why, the hands of the filthy French, of course. They have an army of fifty thousand knights and foot soldiers heading towards our borders!"

They do? Then *that* is why the alchemist has been summoned to Milan. To help the Duke against the French!

"Is it war, my lord?"

"It will be. We need the Pope. We need his blessing, we

need his money, and we need his army. Especially his army. I do not have sufficient forces to defend us against an invasion, and there may not be enough time to raise and train a new army ourselves."

"Will the Pope join with us against the French, my lord?"

"We hope so. But no alliance is certain until it is put to the test—and by then it may be too late. We need something else to ensure our safety, something so frightening it sends the French fops fleeing in fear! A new weapon—yes, that's what we need!"

"Then go to my master, sire. He has many designs for weapons."

"So he has often said. Even before he came to Milan, he wrote to me with promises of weapons never before seen. And that is just it—I have never seen any of them!"

The Duke should take a look inside the Master's sketchbooks . . .

A gigantic crossbow with a bow span of five braccia that will pierce walls of thickest stone with a bolt longer than a tree trunk.

A cannon with a mouth large enough to hurl a ball the size of a cathedral bell that explodes into thousands of pieces on impact.

A horse-drawn chariot armed with four scythes that rotate at ever-increasing speeds as the chariot is pulled towards the enemy.

The Master dreams up a new one almost every day!

The Duke paces up and down, clenching and unclenching his fists.

Now he is looking at me.

"Well, boy?"

"My lord?"

"Come now, Giacomo, I know there is more. Your master is working on something, is he not?"

"I-I don't know, my lord." But those thieves did not come to our house to admire the cleaning. "Whatever my master is working on, it is for the Duke of Milan."

"No, boy, I do believe that Leonardo is keeping his new creation a secret from me," he says. "But I am a man who knows more than his own subjects. If I did not, I would not be Duke."

"My lord, I am loyal to you, but I know nothing, therefore I can say nothing. Why not ask my master?"

"To ask him would be to quarrel with him, and I will suffer no further delay to the Last Supper. You will have to ask him for me, Giacomo, and bring me an answer, too, or by the hermit's beard I will take my revenge on you for insulting me with that monster of a woman, the Medusa. Do you hear?"

"But, my lord, I—"

He places a hand on my shoulder. This reminds me of my master, who often does the same thing; but then the Master always removes it soon after, as if he fears to leave it there too long. The Duke, however, continues to squeeze my shoulder, harder and harder. And *harder.* His eyes are as black as dead suns. His thumb bites into my sinew like a knife blade. Red-hot pinpricks of pain course up and down my arm. I try not to let him see how much it hurts, but soon I—

Then the doors are thrown open to reveal Lucrezia Crivelli

in a white silk dress. The Duke instantly releases his grip. She enters the room with measured tread. She has to—the train on her dress is so long it threatens to entangle itself around her ankles. Behind her, four—no, five—maidservants follow in her wake.

"One week, Giacomo," he whispers. "Bring me the answer in one week. And not a word to your master, or I, too, will hear of it."

Saint Francis, the look on his face. If I don't do his bidding he will kill me, and no mistake. My stomach clenches up—as if a gigantic snake is coiling itself in my belly. Oh, what do I do now—What?

"Are you tiring the boy, my lord?" Lucrezia says, drawing near. "He is not yet well."

"He is well enough."

A bell starts tolling. To judge by the fading light, it must be time for vespers. The Duke turns to Lucrezia.

"They are summoning me to prayer," he says.

"Then go, my lord," Lucrezia replies. "You know I have no use for it."

"Godless woman," the Duke says, smiling. He puts his arms around her waist. Her jeweled belt, worn low on her hips, presses further into her. Oh, to be that little belt. "It is your very disdain for prayer that I find so bewitching."

Lucrezia strokes the Duke's cheek.

And his wife, the Lady Beatrice, dead and buried no more than half a year. In childbirth, too, so it was put about. But with his mistress living openly in the Castle long before then, is it not more likely that the Duchess died of a broken heart?

Then he pulls away and says: "My lady, I must take my leave of you."

"Do not, sir, take from me anything I will not freely give. Come, we go together."

"Lucrezia." He takes her hand and kisses it.

Then she turns to me. "I want my painting, Giacomo. No more of your master's games. Bring it to me without further delay."

"Yes, my lady," I say.

"And—you can tell him that I am keeping the Medusa," the Duke says. "It shows great skill, even if its subject is repugnant to us."

Without further ado the Duke and Lucrezia make to leave.

When they are gone, a captain-at-arms enters the room and says roughly: "You, come with me. And leave that wine where it is!"

And before I know it I am once more outside the main Castle gates.

XVI

Whatever I dream

Whatever I dream of that night passes through my head like a bird through a roofless house, and the next thing I hear is—

"Giacomo! Wake up, lad!"

"Mmm?"

"Hurry up, you're late. He's waiting for you in the kitchen!"

"Caterina? Where am—?"

"Still in your bed, but you'd better be out of it soon enough, unless you want the Master to shake you out of it!"

"Oh, Caterina, I have slept too much!"

"You have drunk too much, that's the fault of it! Here, eat this crust. Now hurry!"

What *happened* last night?

Oh yes. Oh dear. Oh God.

I had stumbled towards home, but instead of going straight there I went to the Seven Knaves for a cup of wine. One became two, three, four. Well, I was all shaken up by the Duke and his threat. Shaken up? The business with the Medusa had petrified me. After the third cup I was about ready to make a run for it and leave Milan behind forever. But then I thought of the Master. I couldn't just leave him—not now, when he needs me here more than ever. But I have to find his invention and inform the Duke. Great Heaven, I have only a week to do it!

I make haste to dress, falling over twice in the attempt, and when at last I have managed to put on my shirt the right way round, I run to the kitchen. The Master is there and ready for work in the old hose and shirt that he uses for painting. He looks cheerful, well rested, and with a clear brow. I hate him for all of that.

"Now then," he says, "you are late. But I will say nothing about that."

"You just did, Master."

"Don't answer back, boy."

"Then I'll speak first." My blood is boiling now, and last night's drink only increases the heat. "You sent me innocently to the Duke with a horrifying portrait of the Medusa. At the Castle I was beaten almost senseless by a guard. And when the Duke saw the painting he was driven to a frenzy—"

"He was? Good."

"Good! *Goooood?* Master, I might have been killed for the offense!"

"The Duke will not harm Leonardo da Vinci's servant. Do you think I would have sent you if I thought he might?"

"You don't know everything that might happen, Master, although you may think you do."

"What do you mean by that, impertinent boy?"

"Nothing."

I have to sit down on the kitchen bench. My head is threatening to fall off my shoulders. Curse him, if he will not show some kindness after playing such a trick on me.

"Why did you send me to the Duke with the Medusa?" I say at last.

"Because I wished him to see it, boy."

"The whole court knows that by now—but *why*?"

He sits down on the opposite side of the kitchen table. "Why? I'll tell you *why*, boy: for everything that has gone from bad to worse in Milan. For the humiliating way he now treats me, when before he showed me some respect. And for sending away Cecilia, and replacing her with . . . the other one."

"Are those reasons enough to place me in peril?"

"I did not think it would be so, or I would not have sent you."

"The Duke is furious with us both."

"If the Duke is not furious with someone once a day, he considers the time ill spent. Never fear. I will deliver his Lucrezia, take back the Medusa, and all will be well."

"Master, the Duke is not planning to return the Medusa to you."

"No? So much the better. Let him look on her and contemplate his folly. Now then, the day is wasting. You seem well enough, in spite of last night's drinking. Get you to Messer Tombi with the order I have left on my table and meet me at Santa Maria with what you receive from him."

The Master sets to work on the food in front of him.

"And bring me some carrots, while you're at it," Caterina says, coming in too quickly. She was listening to everything outside the door.

Is that all he has to say to me? No apology? No sympathy? Not an ounce of feeling? Very well, then, I'll do the Duke's bidding, with no regrets and in good time, too.

"Master . . ."

"What *now*, boy?"

"That invention you were working on—"

"Which invention?"

"The one the thieves came to our house looking for."

"I told you, Giacomo, I do not know what they were looking for."

"Have you given it to Maggio for safekeeping?"

"There is nothing to keep safe."

"But you dispatched certain boxes to him."

"Old models, too many of them to keep here. Now, off you go."

"And remember my carrots, Giacomo, two pounds."

"You already told me, Caterina."

"Well then, so I did. And don't forget my carrots."

Two pounds of carrots, one pounding on the head, and six ounces of nothing for my pains. Is it because I am his servant that he treats me like a fool, or because I am me?

I enter his study and take the first paper I see on the table. Only when I am outside the house do I learn that I have made a mistake. It is not an order for Tombi, it is a letter—and the seal is broken. I open it, and instead of seeing the names of colors, I am reading a letter to my master . . . from Cecilia Gallerani.

Leonardo, dearest friend—

I write to tell you that I will come to Milan in early spring, while my husband is traveling in the south. It will bring me such joy to see you again after so many years; we have much to talk about. And I do want to see the progress of our Giacomo! He must be a young man by now, a fine young man, if he has had the benefit of my Leonardo's stewardship.

I have a request, dear Leonardo, and beseech you to fulfill it for me. I very much desire to take possession of my portrait. It is more than a painting—it is both a memory and a part of me that I must be reunited with. I am hopeful that you will persuade the Duke to part with it freely and without conditions. I need to have the painting near me, Leonardo, where I can see it every day. I cannot explain why, except to tell you that I find I can no longer live without it.

I will send word again of my arrival.

Cecilia Gallerani Bergamini

Cecilia is coming to Milan! She is coming to see me—and my master, too, of course. The thought of her arrival starts a strange pulse beating in my veins. I knew it would happen one day. I knew it! *A fine young man*, she writes. But more than that, she calls me "our" Giacomo. *Our* Giacomo? What does she mean by that—what?

I spin around and head back home.

"Did you read it?" the Master says, when I have explained my error.

What's the point in lying? "Yes, Master. Isn't it wonderful that Cecilia is coming—?"

"The Lady Cecilia to you, boy. She calls you 'a fine young man,' does she not? And fine young men do not read others' letters."

"Master, what does the Lady Cecilia mean by 'our' Giacomo?"

"Eh?"

"She calls me 'our Giacomo.' Why, Master?"

He hesitates. Presses his lips together. Picks up a pen and pretends to write.

"It's a figure of speech, boy. She takes an interest in you, is all."

"I see, Master."

I see that you're not telling me everything. But I will discover it, I surely will.

He hands me the order for Tombi and off I go again.

As soon as I have pulled open the heavy, iron-fretted door that permits entry to his shop, Tombi asks me whether I have found the alchemist I saw being borne to the Castle.

And I tell him that I have not, even though I have been there twice now on the Master's business. "But I have learned that there is a French army preparing to invade us, and that must be why the alchemist has been summoned to Milan."

"Yes, that may be it," Tombi says.

"What will the Duke require of this alchemist, do you think?" I ask.

"A great alchemist can do many things beyond the reach of ordinary men. He may see into the future—"

"Oh, Messer Tombi, I must find him and show him my medallion. I feel sure there is an important reason I possess it."

"You must take great care, Giacomo, should you meet this person. He will be a man of considerable power, and such men are apt to display it in unexpected ways."

I hand Tombi the Master's order.

"This is a long list," he says. "Are you confident that he will pay me as soon as the Last Supper is finished?"

"So he says, Messer Tombi. On completion of the painting he will receive five hundred ducats from the Dominicans."

"But how can I be sure he will pay *me* what he owes?"

And that is a question I cannot answer with any certainty.

"Because I have been thinking," Tombi says. "If you can assure me that I will be paid first, before all the others, then I will promise something to you in return."

"What do you mean, sir?"

"If you will bring me the money your master owes, as soon as he receives it, I will help you."

"How, Messer Tombi?"

"I will teach you my art: the art of colors."

"Colors? What—paints?"

He nods. "I will teach you the origin, composition, and use of colored pigments."

Is it possible? Will he really teach me about colors?

"I-I don't know how to thank you, Messer Tombi."

"Bring me my money, boy. That's all the thanks I need. Let's start today, shall we?"

He walks to the doorway leading to the interior of the house and pulls aside the heavy curtain. He beckons me to enter. I hesitate. Can I be sure the Master will give me the money he owes the apothecary?

"Are you coming, Giacomo?"

I'll get it somehow. This is my chance. It might be the only one.

Tombi waves me through into a room I have never seen before.

The heavy curtain falls back behind me and I am in another world.

A waxy yellow light glows dimly from a large glass egg almost the size of a wine cask, squatting on a metal stand, heated from below by a wick in a bowl of fat. Inside the egg are several chambers connected by glass tubes, and in these chambers colored liquids bubble and froth.

On the large table in the middle of the room there is a set of scales, various small silver dishes filled with powders and crystals, and measuring cups.

Very curious. But I quell my desire to question Messer Tombi further, because he has already started speaking: "The seven major colors correspond to the seven major planets in the cosmos: orange, indigo, red, blue, green, yellow, violet. We must distinguish between those pigments that occur naturally in nature—in rocks, plants, and earth—and those that we must make ourselves by combining and treating minerals, salts, and other elements."

My first lesson in paint has begun.

Some two or more hours later (I lost track of time, forgot all about Caterina's carrots) I emerge from the apothecary's shop in a state of great excitement. I have learned so much! For my first lesson, Tombi chose the color black. Together we made charcoal by cooking grape vine twigs in little bundles in a baking dish until they were burned, at which time we threw water on them and ground the remains.

Then Messer Tombi showed me how to "work up" a color. He brought out a square slab of veined rock that looked like marble but was red porphyry, thc best stone on which to grind colors, according to him. Taking a nut-sized portion of the black charcoal we had made from the vine twigs, he then gave me a smaller piece of porphyry and instructed me to grind the color against the slab with it. And when this was done, he told me to take some water from a nearby jar and mix it with the powder, and then to continue grinding for another half an hour.

"The longer you grind the color, the more its true self emerges," he said.

Finally, when my arm was aching from the to-and-fro, he bade me scrape the moist powder (for I was adding a small amount of water every now and then) and put it into a little jar, adding more water, until the jar was full; then I put the stopper in and lodged the jar among many others in a rack inside a cabinet.

The apothecary declared himself pleased with my work, because there were no lumps in the black, and he sent me on my way with the colors—*Malachite*, *Indigo*, *Ultramarine Blue*, among others—for my master. He laughed (a kind of soft growling, like a dreaming dog) when I said I did not want to go home again, but preferred to stay with him where I could learn more. He almost had to push me out of the shop.

"I will teach you all I know about colors," he said. "But your master will have to teach you how to paint with them."

"I will be waiting a long time for that lesson."

"Maybe your waiting will end sooner than you know, lad."

"Why, Messer Tombi, do you know something?"

"I know that you are a willing student," he says.

"Thank you," I say. "And when may I come for my next lesson?"

XVII

Today I must begin my search for the Master's invention in earnest.

There is no evidence of it in the house, and the study door has been locked ever since the thieves paid us a visit.

Where to look?

The place to start has to be Maggio's workshop, which sits in a street close to the main city hospital. He does a good trade in coffins. If you fall ill and are sent to the hospital, they say you won't leave unless it is in one of Bernardo's boxes.

I reach the workshop and throw open the two heavy doors with MAGGIO skillfully carved across them. Inside, a dozen carpenters are hard at it, sawing, hammering, and planing. All sorts of objects are being constructed: chairs, tables, cabinets, chests—three new houses are being built in Milan every day, and Maggio is as busy as he wants to be. But he always finds time to work for Leonardo da Vinci.

Even if most of the work is still unpaid. Oh, Renzo is a lucky fellow indeed to be offered an apprenticeship here.

I take in everything around me, but can see nothing out of the ordinary. Maggio is in a corner of the room, bent over a large table covered with drawings, talking to two of his men. A gray cat is asleep underneath, its tail twitching now and then.

Maggio looks up and sees me coming towards him.

"Giacomo? What is it? Does your master need something?"

"Oh no, sir, I was looking for Renzo."

He sends his men away and places a board over the drawings. And a heavy wooden mallet on top of that. There is something important under there.

"I haven't seen him all day," he says, "and I've been calling for him, too. Ever since I offered him an apprenticeship, he's forgotten his duties."

"He is very eager to start learning the trade, Messer Maggio."

"Perhaps that is it. No one wants to deal with the old when the new beckons, eh?"

Then one of his craftsmen asks him to inspect a cabinet.

"Wait here, lad, I have something you can take back to your master, if you will."

As soon as Maggio has crossed the workshop floor, I try to see the drawings he has hidden under the board. One of them is not well covered. I'll assume an air of innocence and give the corner a tug . . . just a bit more . . . aha! It's a drawing by the Master. . . .

But what in the name of the martyred Saints is it?

Long and curved like an archer's bow, filled with many thin struts, and pointed at the end—it looks like a wing, like a bat's wing! Amazing—

"Giacomo? What are you doing?"

I nudge the cat with my foot and it leaps up.

"Oh, Messer Maggio, this—your cat has taken a liking to my legs and wrapped itself around—"

"What? Bobo? What are you doing to the boy, infamous creature? Leave him alone!"

"No harm done, sir, a lovely cat, very bushy tail, you could clean a chimney with that tail, you could."

Then, with a mighty thrust of its solid furry legs, Bobo jumps up onto Maggio's table, knocking over the mallet and causing the wooden board to slip and slide its way off the table.

Maggio tries to catch the cat, and while I make a pretense of aiding him, I take a good look at the now exposed drawing.

Not one bat's wing, *two*.

And beneath them, attached to them, supporting them, and in turn supported by them, some kind of open box.

With a seat.

With a man sitting in it.

"Saint Francis, Messer Maggio, you and my master—"

I clamp my lips shut. Almost let that tongue out of its trap again.

Maggio has now gathered up the drawings and secured them once more under the board.

"I and your master *what*?" he says.

"Are the most excellent craftsmen in all Milan!"

"Indeed! Well, I thank you, Giacomo, but I prefer not to hear compliments. They are always followed by misfortune. Now, please take this piece of wood to your master and tell him it is fir tree and light enough, so I believe."

"It is light, indeed, sir. For what purpose?"

"Oh, a new panel for a painting."

I nod and smile. A panel for a painting. Ha! Too light for that. This wood is to be used for that bat's wing, or I'm a pickled egg.

When Maggio opens the doors to let me out, the wind seizes its moment to enter the workshop and whip up the wood shavings and sawdust into a whirl.

The doors are swiftly closed behind me.

Two wings, one man, and no more explanation necessary.

The Master and Maggio are building a flying machine.

"A *flying* machine!" I say out loud.

The words sound as impossible to my ears as the drawings seemed to my eyes. How can a man rise from the earth like a bird on wings, when he is scarce able to jump more than a chair's height off the ground? It would be necessary to create a source of power equal to that which lifts a bird, which is a creature that even of the largest kind weighs no more than a man's two legs, and whose wings are stronger than any man's two arms. The Master has been studying the flight of birds for many years. He has written hundreds of pages on the subject. This is what it was all leading to!

"Psst! Giacomo!"

From under a nearby portico, concealed in the shadows, a voice.

"Renzo?"

"Over here."

Together we walk away from Maggio's workshop.

"What are you doing? Your master is looking for you."

"Let him look. I've done enough work for today."

We pass by the Trivulzio family's *palazzo*, with its turrets and windows. Renzo points at it.

"Why should they live in such a house, Giacomo? Why them and not us?"

"They worked for it, I suppose."

"Did they? Many a rich man made his money outside the law. They're no better than us. Yet we are the servants. Why?"

"Well, *you'll* soon be a successful carpenter."

"Maybe I have something better in mind."

"What? What can be better than learning a skill you can use to make money and live an honest life?"

"Honest! Who in this world is truly honest, Giacomo?"

Sometimes I do not understand my friend. He has many good qualities. He can throw a knife straighter than a rook flies, catch a fish with no more than a hook and line, and never lets being a servant stop him from talking to girls. But the thoughts are often dark behind his clear brow, and watching him fight on the Feast of Saint Michael, it did not look as though he much cared whether he lived or died.

"Renzo, I beg of you. Don't do anything rash."

"No, nothing rash. Come now, let us eat something. Have you got any money?"

That's my friend. If he ever paid for a meal, they'd declare a new holiday.

We turn into the Street of Armorers, a hundred paces from the market.

"Well, well," Renzo says, "the gypsies are back again."

There is a large gypsy encampment on the heath that borders the city to the southwest, attached to the body of Milan like a strange limb. The Duke has banned them from entering the city, but they always manage to, somehow. They have to. How else will they live? They have no land of their own, no crops or other sustenance. They must survive by stealing.

As we watch, a young gypsy girl—scarcely more than a child—walks up to a rich man, smiling and blowing him kisses. He has stopped, what else, to stare. And now a group of five lively urchins, her companions, emerge from the shadows and surround the gentleman—one pointing, another shouting, a third waving his arms like a mad thing. The man does not know which way to turn, which way to look. And before he can decide what to do, nimble hands are threading through the folds of his cloak, sifting through his pockets, rapidly removing whatever gold coins and valuables he may have had on his person.

"Look at them go!" Renzo says, delightedly.

Faster than lightning can touch the ground, they have disappeared into the crowd.

The gentleman stands there, uncertain, bewildered, a bit fearful. Gradually, the spell cast on him lifts, and he soon discovers that the purse has been cut from his belt, the rings taken from his fingers, the gold chain removed from his neck. *Now* he understands.

"HELP! THIEF! I'VE BEEN ROBBED!"

You could have heard the cry in Cremona!

I turn to Renzo, who is full of mirth. This is excellent sport to him, to see the rich duped by the poor. He says it is forever the other way round. And he is not wrong.

When I have bought two roasted pigeons from a stall in the market, we walk to the Cathedral steps and sit down to eat. I pull the soft fragrant flesh from the bones and gobble it up, all the while worrying that my master might appear and scold me for eating meat. While we chew, there is a great coming and going in and out of the Cathedral doors by shaven-headed monks and black-robed priests. I'm reminded that the Pope is coming to Milan in less than half a year. God save us if the Master does not finish the painting in time.

Renzo has already finished and is licking his fingers. "I'd better get back to work," he says, standing up. "See you tomorrow for knife-throwing practice?"

"At the Lazaretto," I say. "Three bells, not before. My master's students are expected."

"Oh, that lot," Renzo says. "I hate the sons of the rich more than their fathers."

"They think no better of us," I say.

"Then bring me to the lesson," Renzo says, drawing his dagger, "and let them say what they think to my face."

He's serious, too. He'd take them all on before his dinner.

"You know I can't do that," I say. "Unless I want to find a new master."

Renzo shrugs, blows on his knife blade, wipes it on his sleeve, and sheathes it.

We shake hands and embrace. Before we part, I tell him: "Don't lose your chance with Maggio because of pride, Renzo."

He nods, but says nothing more.

I watch my friend walk away. Yes, we servants must better ourselves. But if the others won't, I will. I am resolved to. I have a great desire to run back home and take out my paper and charcoal and start drawing. There is a certain way the afternoon light falls on the mulberry tree in the garden that I have not yet captured successfully. And I must.

But my heart falls into my stomach when I think of what I still have to do. My master and Maggio are building a flying machine. And I have but a few days to find it and make my report to the Duke.

XVIII

From the street come loud echoes of laughing and cursing. The students. With a groan, I knock on the study door.

"They're here, Master."

"I'm finishing something. Look after them until I am ready, will you?"

"Yes, Master."

I hate being alone with the students.

"The Master will be with you soon," I say, opening the front door.

"Meanwhile," Tommaso says, entering, "we have to put up with *you*, Giacomo."

"No more than I you," I say.

"Watch your tongue, boy," Tommaso says, "or I'll have it pulled out by the root."

They stand around our front room whispering insults at me while I pull out the drawing materials from the chest. They each take a board, paper, and charcoal.

"The Master wishes you to draw this bowl of fruit," I say, placing it on a table under the window, where the light and shadow will make the scene most appealing. There is a bunch of grapes, two lemons, an apple, and a red pear.

"I'd rather eat it than draw it," says the pinch-faced Filippo, who curls his hair and wears it to his shoulders like a girl.

"It will certainly look better in your stomach than it ever could in your drawing," Tommaso says.

They all chortle at that, even Filippo, after some hesitation.

The students take their seats around the table and pretend to draw. But before long they turn their attention back to me.

"Don't just stand there with that ugly look on your face!" says Simone, a particularly unpleasant fellow with bulging eyes (from a noble family of eye-bulgers).

"He always has an ugly look on his face," Filippo says. "He was born with it!"

"He must get it from his parents. Whoever *they* are," says Marcantonio.

"Yes, who are they, Giacomo? You never tell us. Peasants? Gypsies? Or wild dogs?"

My head feels like an eggshell which their words are cracking open.

"In my opinion," Tommaso says, "Giacomo has no parents. I think he was found under a bush!"

"I do have parents!" I cry out. "I do—"

Now the Master appears from behind his door.

We all turn to statues.

"What is going on in here?"

No answer.

"Is this an art class or a cattle auction?"

Someone laughs.

"Draw in silence, or do not draw at all. Gentlemen, if you cannot show some restraint, I will have to cancel the lesson and send you off to the friar for moral instruction."

"If you do that, Master," says Tommaso, "you will corrupt us utterly."

The whole group bursts into laughter. Even the Master smiles now, may his eyes fail for it. "Settle down, gentlemen. Please!" he says. "Why is nobody drawing?"

"Because your servant has not brought the wine," Tommaso replies. "God's blood, Master Leonardo, if I had a servant as lacking in attentiveness as your Giacomo, I'd whip him morning, noon, and night."

"Master, please—"

"Giacomo," he says, "go to the kitchen and bring the wine."

"And don't spill any this time, emptyhead!"

I depart the room to hissing and whistling.

In the kitchen, Caterina is chopping, chopping, chopping—great Heaven, she has cut her finger! "Look what you've done!" I cry.

"The Devil is passing through our house," she says.

I take a rag and wrap it around her finger to stop the bleeding. She sits down, forlorn. "Here, drink this," I say, and offer her a cup of the wine I am pouring for the students. She shakes her head.

"My mind was wandering," she says, "and then my knife did. I'm getting old, lad; my limbs no longer obey me." And, in truth, there is no spirit in her face today.

Now I must sit down, too. I am shaking with rage.

"The students say I do not have any parents. But I do, Caterina, I know I do!"

I feel a terrible pain welling up inside, along with the old questions. Where are my parents? Who are they? Why have they never come looking for me?

"Who am I, Caterina? Who?"

I sit down beside her and bury my face in my hands. "Now, now," she says. "Don't fret so. Of course you have parents, boy. And perhaps they—" Then we hear him calling for me. "Well, you'd better wipe your face and go," Caterina says.

"I have to know. I have to find out who they are."

She shakes her head. "Don't ask me, Giacomo, I'm just an old woman."

"But the Master received a letter from Cecilia Gallerani in which she called me 'our Giacomo.' What does that mean, Caterina? '*Our* Giacomo'? You told me the Master would have married her, had it been allowed. But you don't need to marry to have a child. What if they—"

"That's enough, boy. Don't fill your head with such thoughts; they are pure foolishness and will only bring you more misery. Now hurry back to the Master."

When I return with the wine, the students are seated at the large table with their drawing boards aloft, and the Master is walking up and down, inspecting their work.

"I have always said that it is better to draw in company than alone, because the presence of others will inspire you to greater efforts. But, gentlemen, to judge from your work, the lack of accomplishment in one has spread to you all."

Silence.

"Have none of you received any benefit from my classes?"

"Oh, indeed yes, Master," Tommaso says. "For an hour each week we have not had to listen to our fathers telling us that we drink too much, eat too much, and gamble too much. All of which is true," he adds, "but the more the old folk scold, the less we obey them."

The Master looks lost. Then he says: "If you can learn nothing from me, I must inform your parents that I will no longer teach you."

"We'll go and study with Michelangelo, then."

The air in the room freezes on the instant.

My master coughs. "What?"

Silence.

The Master closes his eyes. He takes a deep breath and says, in a voice as mild as May: "Will whoever spoke last please repeat what he said. I promise not to be angry. I merely wish to know what the gentleman means by it."

Somebody sneezes.

"I only want to hear about Mich-Michelangelo," the Master says. "Come, surely you can share with me what you know."

The students continue to look at their feet.

Then Tommaso looks up and says: "Michelangelo is coming to Milan."

My master takes a deep breath.

"Ah. Indeed."

"Yes, Master," Marcantonio says, eagerly joining in. "Have you not heard? It is all the talk at the moment."

"I do not listen to gossip, gentlemen, and neither should you. Michelangelo will never leave his home in Florence."

"He is in *Rome*, Master, just at the moment," Marcantonio says. Insolent dog. "But he is looking to move, and my father has heard Duke Ludovico say that he will be made very welcome in Milan, should he choose to come."

The Master lets out a long breath. "I see," he says. "Well then, let us, while we wait for the great Michelangelo to arrive, proceed with our lesson."

My master has recovered. Well done, Master! But it has taken all his strength; he looks like he has run a league.

Someone yawns.

"Giacomo," my master says, "would you be so good as to serve the wine."

"Yes, Master."

"And hurry," someone says under his breath, "or by the time you finish, we'll all be asleep."

I do hurry. I do not want to miss the lesson. The Master begins his lecture: "Painting is based on perspective, which is nothing less than a thorough knowledge of the function of the eye. And what is the eye, gentlemen?"

The window of the soul.

"The window of the soul. Wasn't *anyone* listening last week?"

As I serve Tommaso, he leans towards me and whispers: "I have to show you something, Giacomo. Meet me after class."

"No."

"Giacomo! Stop talking and do your duties, or out you go."

"Yes, Master."

"See the trouble you get into by refusing me, Giacomo?" Tommaso says. He smiles, revealing even, white teeth. His hair is black as a raven's wing. He ruffles mine.

"Don't *touch* me."

I pull away with a sudden movement, sending the jug of wine leaping from my tray. It lands on the floor with a crack and a swiftly spreading pool of red.

"Now look what you've done, boy!" Tommaso says.

"What is going on here?" The Master has drawn near without my noticing. "What foolishness is this, Giacomo?"

"Master, it was my fault," Tommaso says, hanging his head. "I apologize. I asked Giacomo if there was something in my eye, but it seems to have gone now."

He looks up and winks at me. I do not want to be his fellow conspirator, but I must stay silent or suffer for it.

"Giacomo, go to the kitchen. Now, boy! The rest of you—back to your drawings."

Then, just as the class begins to settle down, there is a knocking at the front door. Four men and horses outside: three in armor, one in black robes. I have never seen them at the house before. A fifth horse, perfectly white except for a black ring around the left eye, stands nearby, without a rider.

"What is it?" I say.

The one in robes replies: "We have come for Master Leonardo."

"Your business with him?"

"Is none of yours. Summon him."

The look on his face cautions me. I turn back inside.

"Master? Visitors."

"Yes, tell them I am coming, and to wait."

Which I do. But they are not happy about it. What a fine creature the white horse is. I reach out to stroke its mane.

"Leave her alone, boy," one of the men says.

"Gentlemen," the Master is saying to the students, "I am wanted. Finish your drawings and leave them with Giacomo. I will look at them later."

"Master, where are you going?" I say, as he prepares to leave. "I don't want to be . . ."

. . . left alone with the students.

"I will return by nightfall, Giacomo. You are in charge here until then."

"We'll be sure to finish up our drawings, Master," Filippo says.

"Oh yes," Tommaso adds, "we'll finish things, all right."

As soon as the door has closed, they rise from their seats and come towards me. I should run now, I surely should. But I cannot do that, I have been left in charge. "You heard the Master," I say, trembling now. I can't help it. "Finish your drawings and leave."

"Giacomo, come over here. I said I had something to show you," Tommaso says. I hear Simone's high-pitched squeal of laughter. "You've never seen anything like it, I promise you."

"Keep away from me."

Marcantonio comes at me and I lash out with my fist, catching him a glancing blow on the chin. "You little turd!" he cries.

Then Filippo draws his sword.

"No, none of that," Tommaso says, "use your fists."

Filippo gives him an angry look, but sheathes it once more. Now they have formed a semicircle around me, forcing me into a corner.

Before I can land more than a punch, I am thrown to the floor. Drawing boards are sent flying and papers are scattered everywhere. The Master's easel falls over with a crash. They are all on me now, pressing me down. I manage to kick at Simone, hitting him in the chest—but now my legs are held fast. Tommaso is standing over me.

"Hold him, lads, I want to see how much pain the gypsy boy can take before he cries."

Then someone enters the room—what, Caterina? Before anyone can stop her, she brings down a heavy iron pan on Tommaso's head! A dreadful thud. He falls to the floor.

"Get off my lad," she says. "All of you."

They let go of me, though whether that is because of her order or the shock of seeing Tommaso laid out, I cannot say. I get up. My enemies stand back. Tommaso lies there, unaided. Caterina is still holding the pan in front of her, like an ax. Her hands are shaking.

"Do you know whom you have struck, old woman? That is Tommaso Bentivoglio, son of Milan's Chief Magistrate!"

"Then let his father be the judge of his actions here today. The lesson is over."

I look down and am relieved to see Tommaso move. He groans. Simone and Marcantonio hold him under the arms and lift him up. They cannot support him. He falls to the floor again. Simone lets out a giggle. Marcantonio slaps his head. "Shut it, Simone."

Again they raise Tommaso, and this time he stays up. They back away towards the front door, Tommaso sagging between them.

"We'll get you for this, Giacomo," Simone says.

"You won't get anybody," Caterina says, "or you'll feel my pan against *your* head. Come back to study as gentlemen, or do not come at all. It's all the same to me."

"You expect us to return after this outrage, woman?" Filippo says. "If we do, it will be with an armed guard to take you away." Then he turns to me. "Keep an eye out for us, gypsy boy. It may be the last thing you see."

The door closes behind them, and we are alone—and alive, thanks be to the Virgin. And Caterina.

"Don't say anything, boy. I'm an old woman, near the end of my stay here on Earth. If they'd knifed me I would have thanked them for hastening my journey."

"Caterina, you saved me—"

"The good Lord did, when he told me what to do and gave me the strength to do it. Now, let us clear up this room before the Master returns, or we'll have some real . . . some real . . . explaining to . . ."

She stumbles—*Caterina*! I go to her and she grips my arm; we make our way to the kitchen, where she sits down on her favorite chair by the kitchen fire. I'll put another log on, though the Master will scold me for doing so. He does not like us to use more than four logs in one day, even when the air outside is cold enough to freeze blackberries to their stems.

How did this old woman wield such a heavy pan?

She pulls the blanket up over her knees and closes her eyes.

Then I hear the bells of nearby San Ambrogio. One . . . two . . . *three*. I agreed to meet Renzo for knife practice at three! I should stay and watch over my Caterina. But she is sleeping. There is nothing more I can do for her now.

XIX

I set off at a run for the Eastern Gate.

In our street, children are playing kick with a ball made from stitched cloths. From an alleyway, the metalworker's hammer strikes his anvil with a repeated *Ching! Ching! Ching!* There are no more leaves on the tree whose branches hang over our garden wall. Winter is here.

As I turn a corner, a man pulling a full cart, head down and struggling with it on the uneven stones, bumps into me, and we both fall. A hundred apples are released into the air and bounce off in all directions. The accident attracts several ragged children, who seize handfuls of the fruit and then dissolve into the shadows.

"Fool!" the apple seller shouts at me. "My apples! Someone save my apples!"

"I am sorry!" I help him up. He shakes me off.

"This is a street, boy. I have a business to attend to. Stay in bed if you want to daydream."

And away I go, while he shouts oaths at my back.

The Eastern Gate is just ahead and there is only a short line of people waiting to leave the city—hurry, hurry, Renzo is waiting for me!

I pass through and now I am on the road to Monza, which leads away into the hills. Monza has always lived in the shadow of our city; they call it "Milan's little sister." And, like all little sisters, it seeks to mimic its elder. It even has a cathedral, but it is no more than a shed compared to ours.

I leave the road and cross the open grassland towards the Lazaretto. There is the oak we use as a target. No Renzo. The sky has turned a dull gray, and the clouds sit uncomfortably on the horizon, as if waiting for something to happen.

Perhaps he too was delayed. More likely he came here and left when he did not see me. He doesn't like to wait for anyone, my friend. Even me.

I'll throw a few knives, warm up my arm.

One: overhead, raising the elbow high, forearm snap.

Not bad. I go to the tree and pull out the knife from the thick bark.

Two: from the left, holding the blade by the tip, flicking the wrist.

Hmm. Too much twist. The knife hit the trunk and bounced off.

Three: underarm, bringing the hand up with a snap.

Hurrah! Direct hit! One day soon I will be as capable as Renzo.

But I don't feel like practicing on my own. What happened with the students has greatly upset me. I am tired of their insults. I must find my parents. And my master must help me too, he owes me that, or—I will leave him.

But what is this? A horse has appeared from behind the west wall of the Lazaretto. A fine white horse. And no rider. That's strange. I saw a white horse not an hour ago. Then it turns its head . . . *it has a black ring around the left eye.* It's the same horse that was brought to the house—the one that I was told to keep my hands off!

I approach with a soft tread.

"Gently, girl, gently, I won't hurt you. What are you doing out here all alone? Don't shy away, now, I'm your friend."

Every time I draw near enough to touch her, she trots away. But if she is here, where are her masters? And why the Lazaretto? Who ever comes here except Renzo and me? This is where the plague sufferer is sent to live out his final days or hours, his boils swelling and bursting, his hair falling out in handfuls, sweating hot tears of blood from his skin. Only a madman would think of entering such a place willingly.

Only a madman like me. Something is going on here. I mean to find out what.

There is no chain on the gates, but they are firmly locked. From the inside?

I'll try the ragged old bell rope. One tug—and it falls off! Surely there have been no visitors here for many years, and the white horse is merely an odd coincidence.

But I have heard the Master say that coincidence is the visible result of invisible intention, as if God wanted to draw our attention to something, but was waiting for us to do the work.

And here's one shutter broken on its hinges. I could pull it . . . open . . . and . . .

I'm in. A small dusty room, the plaster falling from the walls. The frame of a bed, the wood old and rotten. A chair lying on its side. How many unfortunates have died here? I'll open the door of the room slowly, quietly, someone might hear. (Who? There's been no one here for years.)

But as I leave the room, there is a soft sigh, as of a woman's breath. I turn around sharply, my heart quickening, in time to see a gray shadow pass into the wall and disappear from sight. Great Heaven, what was that? I wait for another sign, all of my senses straining, hardly daring to breathe. But there is nothing more.

I walk down a dark, drab corridor, through another door, and out into a central courtyard, open to the sky.

And in the middle of it . . .

A gigantic bird.

The same design as I saw in the drawings at Maggio's workshop.

But fifty times the size.

Its wings are very like a bat's in shape and form, curved in the center and pointed at the tip. The ribs are still uncovered wood, so finely crafted that you might think Nature herself had created a new race of wooden birds.

Underneath the wings is a kind of open box with a seat, pedals, and a lever. Beneath that, in a smaller box, a jumble of coils and springs of sundry sizes, some tightly wound, some loose in their casing.

And two wheels sitting under the machine, for ease of transport.

It is incredible. It is impossible. It is inexplicable.

And it is here, right before my eyes.

My master has built his flying machine.

And then, from behind me, I hear: "I told you he'd find us, Master Leonardo."

I turn to see my master and Messer Maggio walking towards me.

"So you did, Maggio. But can you tell me why the boy followed me, when he knows not to?"

"Master, I did not follow you! I was here to meet my friend and I saw the white horse—"

"I do not have the time to argue with you, Giacomo. You have seen what you came to see. Now get you home. You should not be here!"

"But, Master, now that I am, will you not show me how you made such a miraculous machine?"

The Master's face softens. Explanations are his special pleasure.

"By approaching the task as a man of science, not superstition," he says. "To make it simple for you: A bird is a mechanism for flight. Flight is governed by mathematical laws. Man made those laws. Therefore man can make a mechanism for flight. Which is what I have done. With Maggio's invaluable help, of course."

"And the bat, Master? Why did you choose the bat as your model?"

"Because its wings are suitable for our needs, being covered with light, smooth, strong skin. It requires less power than feathered wings to produce flight. We have built the machine using those same principles of lightness and strength."

"But how can a man work the wings rapidly enough to raise his own weight above the earth?"

"He can't." The Master points to the wooden box beneath the pilot's seat. "Unless, that is, someone has invented a way to multiply his natural capacity many times, through a system of linked, weighted springs, which, when operated by the pilot, will cause the wings to beat as if propelled by twenty men, lifting him clear of the earth and into the sky—higher than trees, roofs, steeples, spires, and clouds—for as far as his strength and endurance may take him!"

Thoroughly fantastical.

"And how are the springs to be made to work, Master?"

"Why, by the pilot pressing down on these pedals—here and here, down and down, as if he were pressing grapes. And with his hands, using this lever to steer the craft left and right (note the rudder on the tail for that very purpose)."

"Remarkable, Master!"

"Yes, I do believe it is." He turns his back to me. "Maggio, I trust the thick fustian cloth will be suitable for the body of the craft. For the wings, we will cover them with the treated silk, which is light and strong, not dissimilar in texture to the skin that covers a bat's wings. What say you?"

"What *can* I say, Master Leonardo? Every moment I am asking myself if this is not all a dream."

"My dear Maggio, this will be a dream come true, if we can conclude what we have so successfully commenced," the Master says.

"Night is drawing in," Maggio says. "I will tidy up inside before we leave."

"Thank you, Maggio, that will be most welcome," my master says.

And we watch him walk away.

When he is out of hearing, the Master takes my arm and pulls me towards him: "Now, boy, I want the truth. Without further delay. The truth!"

"The truth?" I can feel my lips quivering.

"Why were you following me, Giacomo?"

"Master—on my word, I wasn't!"

"You came here by chance?"

He looks at me with stony eyes, and in them I see the old mistrust. But mistrust cannot make a traitor out of me. I will tell the Master what the Duke has ordered me to do, even if I perish for it. Truth be told, I would rather forfeit my life than betray my master. I will tell him everything.

"Yes, Master, I swear it was chance that brought me here. But there is more. It is a long story."

"Shorten it."

"The Duke is desperate for a weapon to use against the French army, which even now is approaching our borders. Somehow he knows that you are working on an amazing new invention. He has commanded me to spy on you and report back to him."

"You will tell him nothing of what you have seen," the Master says.

"Yes, Master. I mean, no. But he has threatened to take his revenge on me if I fail him."

"Not if he wants me to finish the Last Supper. He tried to frighten you, is all."

He succeeded.

The sky grows dark. We must leave soon or be cloaked in blackness.

"Master," I say, "who were the men who came to the house today?"

The Master ignores the question.

"You can tell me, Master, surely you can."

He shakes his head. "Must you always know everything?" he says. I nod. He sighs. "They wish to buy the flying machine."

"What, Master? You are double-dealing the Duke?!"

"Lower your voice, boy. It is the Duke who has been double-dealing me! Why is Michelangelo invited here to Milan, if not to usurp my position? Why should I not look elsewhere to secure my future, if the Duke will not secure it for me?"

"Then who are they, Master?"

"You do not need to know. But I can tell you this: My new patrons are very generous, unlike the Duke—why, even today they gave me the white horse, freely and without conditions, they were so pleased with what they saw. The flying machine, after twenty years of thinking and planning, is almost ready to fly. But it will not fly for the Duke!"

Oh, Master, you have not betrayed Milan and offered it to the French, have you? I pray you have not. They are our enemies. There is no reward great enough to sanction the act of treachery.

"What about the two intruders who broke into our house, Master? Were *they* working for the Duke, do you think?"

The Master shakes his head.

"I still do not know," he says. "And it troubles me."

"And the Last Supper . . ."

"What about it, boy?"

"Master, the Pope is coming—"

"Giacomo, I am more than aware of the Pope's intentions. How could I not be, when you remind me at every turn?"

There is a strange stillness in the darkening air. No birds fly over this house of death.

"I do not want you emptying your mouth to anybody about this," the Master says to me. "Not to the Duke, not to your friends. You will say *nothing*. Is that understood?"

I nod my head.

"Swear it."

"Yes, Master."

"Say it, boy."

"I do swear not to tell anyone what I have seen."

"This invention is my—our—chance to leave Milan," he says.

"And when the Duke comes looking for me, Master? In a few days he expects an answer."

"Let me worry about the Duke."

You won't worry alone. Then another thought comes to me—

"Who will pilot it, Master, when it is finished? You will need someone brave of heart and strong in the leg to fly it for you, someone like—"

"Enough, boy. It is too early to consider who should have that honor."

Now Maggio has joined us once more.

"I am not too tall, Master, and will fit snugly in the seat—"

"Enough, Giacomo. The hour is late. Maggio, what say

you we cover our great bird against the night air and return to Milan?"

"You read my mind, Master Leonardo."

What was that noise? It sounded like a tile falling off the roof.

"Do you hear something, Master?"

"The wind in the trees, boy."

"Or an unhappy spirit returned to its place of death," Maggio says.

"Maggio, I took you for a man of reason. There are no ghosts in the Lazaretto."

Neither are there any trees, Master.

Maggio and the Master begin to gather up the waxed cloth that lies in a stiff pile to one side of the flying machine.

Then the Master says: "We have enough work here for you, too, Giacomo, if you care to help."

But—"Master! There's something up there!"

I point to the roof. I thought that I saw something. Someone.

He does not even glance upwards.

"Giacomo, I am not falling for your tricks. Take a corner of the cloth and help us cover the machine."

Now clouds as fleecy as spinning wool pass before the moon; and when they have drifted across the sky there is nothing—no one—to be seen.

"Now that you know what we are up to," the Master says, on our journey home, "you can return here tomorrow. We have need of another pair of hands."

XX

I wake to the sound

I wake to the sound of Caterina calling for me. A rock could not sleep through such a summons, I swear.

Outside my window, the sun is up, but it is sickly; it can scarce crawl out of its bed to give us light. The leafless branches of the trees show like black lines against the silvery sky.

"The Master's been and gone," she says, when I have stumbled into the kitchen. "And he left without his breakfast. He'll be sorry he did."

"Gone without me? He promised that I could help him work on—Caterina, I'll be back later to do my chores!"

I run out of the house and across town to the Eastern Gate. The air is cold, which persuades me to run all the more swiftly. At the Lazaretto I bang on the doors and call for the Master. No answer. Then I must again climb through that window with the broken shutter.

In the central courtyard all is quiet. No Master. No Maggio.

And no flying machine.

Gone. Gone? *Gone!*

Somebody has stolen the flying machine!

And, to judge by their absence, somebody has stolen my master and Maggio, too.

The day passes more slowly than a cart with a broken wheel.

He has still not returned by the time Caterina and I go to our beds.

Sleep is impossible. Every noise jerks me awake. A dog barking. A shutter slamming. An argument in the street between two drunks, which turns into a fight. Plenty of that when you live near The Dangling Bat, a notorious tavern. Nonetheless, this house is better than some we've had. Father Vicenzo chose it for its closeness to Santa Maria delle Grazie. Perhaps he thought that it would help the Master finish the painting more quickly; if so, as you alrcady know, he was sadly mistaken.

"The Master never returned last night," Caterina announces, the next day. "What will we do?"

"Oh, he wouldn't abandon us, Caterina."

"How can you be sure?" she says.

Wherever he has gone, he has left us unprepared. Sometimes he drops a few coins in the clay pot in the kitchen. I take a look. I run my hand around the inside. Nothing. Nothing but air.

"There's a dice game tonight," Caterina says. "The astrologer Massimo told me I will have good luck."

"You'll have good luck if he does not take all your money," I say.

I sit down before the fire. Five more logs to go, five more logs to freezing.

"We've still got the shopkeepers," I say. "They won't refuse us if they know the Master is away and we are left penniless."

She shakes her head. "I think they've had enough of Leonardo da Vinci," she says. "It's the dice, or starve we must."

"No, Caterina. We must save what we have, not lose it."

"Then what?"

"If I managed to survive on the streets, I am sure I can think of a way for us to survive in a house."

Fine words. My mouth is full of them. But they won't fill our stomachs.

The day passes. I stare out of our front window, and when that fails to bring forth the Master, I leave the house and walk up and down our street, expecting at every moment to see him turn the corner. No sign of him by midday.

I'll wait some more.

The last thing I want to do is visit the shopkeepers and plead with them to let us eat for free, when we already owe them so much. Caterina is right—they have all had enough of Leonardo da Vinci and his excuses. My welcome at the market has recently become as frosty as the weather.

We busy ourselves with our chores: washing, polishing, sweeping. Today is laundry day, and in the afternoon I help carry our dirty linen to the canal, where Caterina will spend the next hour gossiping and laughing with other old women. (Sometimes they even do the washing.) If I ask her kindly,

Caterina will also darn the holes in my shirts. I have only two shirts, and they are both full of darned holes. Yes, those holes are a nuisance.

I leave her there with her friends and walk back to the house.

Almost as soon as I have returned, there is a hammering at our door.

I'll go and—but, wait! Supposing this is an armed guard from the Duke, come to take me away for not bringing him news of the Master's invention? A week has now gone by and who knows what, if anything, the Master said to the Duke in my defense?

More hammering. That door wants to deafen me, I swear.

I open it, and before me stands a short, bald, aged gentleman with a sparse beard, dressed in white hose and a tunic of burgundy velvet. And shoes with high heels. Even so, he does not reach the top of my head.

Not an armed guard from the Duke, I think.

"Am I to be kept waiting until Christmas? Where is the famous Leonardo da Vinci?"

"Will you come in, sir?" I say. Perhaps this is a new patron for my master, someone who'll hand over money for the promise of a painting.

"I've come this far," he says. "I expect another few paces won't kill me."

But as he crosses the threshold, he stumbles. I catch him before he lands on his head.

"Damn these new shoes!" I restore him to an upright position. "Double-damn them! Who are you? Where's my son?"

His *son*? I take another, closer look at him. This birdlike creature with the bony knees and eggshell head is the father of the great Leonardo? Not possible! Not *possible*!

He lets me peer at him a while longer, my mouth half open, and then he says: "What, have you swallowed your tongue, boy? I asked you—"

"I am Giacomo, sir, and your son, if he be your son, indeed—is not here."

"Typical! I come all this way to Milan—ten days by horse, I'll never sit down again in comfort—and he is nowhere to be found. You two, stay out there and wait." This last order directed at two servants standing outside our door, shivering.

I escort him (unsteady in his high heels) to the fire and he sits down on one of our chairs, holding his hands out to the flames to warm them.

"He writes to his brothers, pleading for money," the old man says, "but not a word to me. Wouldn't ask his father for a florin, too proud for that. What a fool he is! Thus I decided to come to Milan. We have not seen each other these many years, you know. And as soon as I arrive, he's gone! If that is not my son Leonardo, I don't know who is. How long have *you* been in the house, then?" he says.

"I have been your son's servant for seven years."

"Seven years, eh? You were just a little boy, then, when you came here?"

"I was, sir. The Master rescued me from certain death."

"He never told me about you. I wonder why. No, I don't. He never tells me anything." The old man runs his finger across the table and inspects it for dust.

"Damn these shoes, they pinch like the Devil's tongs." He gets up again. "I won't stay. Tell your master—tell my *son*—that if he wants my money, to come and see me at the Inn of Forty Steps. I'll wait three days for him. No more."

"If you leave the money with me, sir, I give you my word that he will get it."

"Leave the money with you! Ha ha! What kind of fool do you think I am?"

The worst kind.

"I don't like that look, boy. You remind me of him. Stubborn as a farm gate, he is. His letter said he was desperate. If that is truly so, then let him come to me for help. No one else will give him any. He has no friends. Let him come and beg for the money he hates me for."

Now I am too hot to stop myself—"What has he done to you, that you wish to humble him so?"

This won't help the Master. I should have kept my mouth shut. Too late. Again.

"What? A servant asking questions outside of the kitchen? I won't answer an insolent ragamuffin boy!"

He looks at me through eyes that betray no emotion except, perhaps, indifference; they just sit in their sockets, as wet and gray and unfeeling as oysters in their shells. Then he says: "But here's a question for you, young man, from an old man who has seen his fill of war, plague, and rebellion: Why do you think you're his servant? Eh? The answer may unsettle you, if you discover it."

"What do you mean by that, sir?"

"Did he tell you that before he left Florence he barely avoided an appearance before the magistrate?"

What?

"No, of course he didn't, why would he? It's nothing to be proud of. An anonymous complaint—in writing—was made against him. In '76. When he was twenty-four."

Why has this news set my heart to jumping inside its box?

"Nothing was proved. That's in his defense. But that some-one should have accused him, that is quite enough!"

"But what—what was the complaint?"

"Indecency."

". . . Indecency?"

"With another man."

"Another . . ."

"Do you understand what that means, boy?"

"I . . . don't know."

"No, you don't, do you. Not yet. But you might," he says, looking me up and down, "and maybe sooner than you expect. Now open the front door."

What does this mean? *What does this mean?*

His two servants are still outside, shivering in the cold.

I close the door on them all.

In the kitchen, a few coals glow orange and red in the hearth, but the room is growing cold. I'll put another log on the fire. Caterina will be home soon, and she needs to be kept warm; her blood is thin.

Why *has* the Master kept me here as his servant all these years?

And then I remember the Master's sketchbook, the one with the drawings of the youth, Fioravante, who looks like me. That was dated 1476, too, the year of the accusation! And underneath the drawing my master had written *my most beloved friend.*

The same year he draws his friend, he is accused of indecency.

What really happened between this Fioravante and my master?

And then a horrible thought inches its way up my spine like a black and poisonous spider—

Oh no, dear God, *no.*

He brought me to his house because I reminded him of that youth.

And he has been waiting, waiting, until I reach a certain age—

No, I will not believe it. I must not. Such thoughts will make me mad. The Master has always been good to me. There is no proof of anything sinister.

Yet.

XXI

By the next day the Master has still not returned, and whatever uneasiness his old father has awoken in me is overtaken by other concerns, far more pressing.

How do we live without money or food?

"I went to see Bagliotti, the baker," Caterina says, coming in through the kitchen door. "He would not give me any more bread without being paid. But I did not come home empty-handed. I saw he was throwing out an old loaf and asked him for it."

It's there on the table. Covered in greenish mold.

"Poisoning ourselves won't help," I say to her. "I'll go and see the moneylenders."

"Giacomo, you know the Master hates moneylenders."

"Because he can't run away from them, like the shopkeepers. They'd send hired men over here and burn the house down."

"The moneylenders won't give you a hello," she says. "You're just a lad."

"We'll see about that," I say.

I have something they might be interested in.

I go to my box and take out the ring. It's a thick, heavy circle, and the jewel in its center, though dull, has depth. It might be worth something, after all. I am loath to part with it, but we must eat, and I have nothing else of value, except my medallion. And I would *never* offer that for a loan.

I don my cloak and forthwith set off. There is frost underfoot, which gives a pleasing crunch and soothes my drumming heart. Oh, I'd be in a delightful mood on this fine winter morning, if only the Master was here and we had a full pot of money and the Duke had forgiven me for my failings and the students did not hate me and, and—and all was well with the Last Supper.

I follow the back streets until I come to the Sforza Way, turn right, and continue past the Broletto and then the Cathedral (where a procession of brown-robed priests—Franciscans, probably—is just ascending the steps), finally arriving at the Exchange, which sits in a tree-lined square called Duke's Court. This is where the moneylenders conduct their business.

The Exchange is a many-windowed building three floors high. Two thick marble columns flank the front doors. On the first floor are the grain dealers, on the second the silk and cloth dealers—I need the third. I enter and run up the wide marble staircase, open the shining bronze doors—and find myself in the midst of such shouting and waving of hands that I begin to wonder if I took a wrong turn and have entered a madhouse.

There must be a hundred tables in here, stacked high

with silver, gold, and copper coins, some with five or more moneylenders working behind them. The wooden rings on the abacuses fly back and forth, filling the room with a constant whirring sound as the lenders make their calculations. Many customers are wandering between the tables, bargaining for the best rate of interest on loans. Now, where—

"Over here, young man, over here! That's it, I'm the one you're looking for, you'll get the best deal from me, you ask anyone, Valentino's the name, been here in the Exchange thirty years. Now then, sit on this chair, what can I do for you?"

Do I have a choice? He looks determined enough to grapple me by the legs and pull me down if I try to escape.

"I need to borrow some money, sir."

"That's why we're here, lad: you on that side of the table, me on this. How much?"

I think ten florins would be enough for our food, wood, and candles until the end of the month. When I name this figure, he says: "And what have you got for security?"

I must be looking at him like a fool, because he adds: "I can't lend you money unless you give me something to hold until you can pay me back with the interest, see? Otherwise, how would I know whether you were going to pay me back at all? You could run off to Venice with my money—it's happened to me before."

"I do have this."

And from my leather pouch I pull out the ring and hold it up for Valentino to inspect.

He takes it from the air faster than a rook snatches a flying beetle.

"Well, well, well," he says. "You do have security, after all. A nice little round fat jeweled piece of security. Now then."

From the drawer in the table he produces a thick, smooth circle of glass which he holds up to his eye, and through this he inspects the ring, turning it left and right. It is a big ring, after all—much bigger than it looked in my small room—and it is attracting some attention from Valentino's neighbors.

"Good God!" he exclaims, so loudly that I jump up from my seat.

"Wha-what is it, sir?" I say.

Valentino is holding up the ring and waving it back and forth as if it was the prize for winning the annual Christmas horse race.

"Do you know what this is?" he cries.

I won't bother to say no. I'll just think it.

"This ring has the Duke's mark engraved on the inside. This ring belongs to the Duke of Milan!"

Now I can't help myself. "The Duke of Milan?" I cry. Oh, not the Duke again, not him—please!

And now the room, which before was filled with chatter and cry, empties itself of all sound. A silence like the inside of a coffin.

Valentino is still holding up the ring—

"Look at this, all of you!" he shouts. "The Duke's ring! This boy has a ring belonging to the Duke!"

"But, I didn't—"

"He's a thief!" Valentino screams. "A thief!"

And on every side, accusing faces and fingers are pointing towards me.

"Thief!"

"Take him, someone!"

"The Duke's ring! An outrage!"

It's clear that I will not be given a chance to explain myself. How do you, after all, explain being in possession of the Duke's ring? I should stay and try to prove my innocence—but they are not concerned with my innocence, I see. They want my blood!

Valentino is still waving the ring in the air.

"It's mine!" I say to Valentino.

And before he can shield himself, I pluck the ring from between his thumb and finger—

And run straight for the window.

"Stop him! He has the Duke's ring!"

As you may remember my telling you, I had ascended to the third floor of the Exchange. Thus, you would not be remiss in thinking that I have lost some of the stuffing in my head, preparing to jump out of the window—undoubtedly I'll break my neck when I land headfirst on the stones.

But, look you, I am gambling on the branch of the tree just outside the window being strong enough not to crack and break when I throw myself on it.

It's a risk. But if I am caught now, there is no one to look after Caterina, and who knows when the Master will return. Or if he ever will.

A greasy-cheeked lender rises sluggishly from his table and throws out his arms to take hold of me as I pass. I duck under them. I don't stop running.

The shouts and cries behind me lend fuel to my legs and I do not hesitate as I draw near to my only chance of escape—

"The young fool is going to jump out of the window!"

Hardly are those words in the air when I, too, join them and plunge through the opening in the wall.

Thanks be to Saint Peter—the branch is just outside the window, and I can easily catch it with both arms—*got it*! It's bending, it might break, it will break—Mother Mary, save me! Should I let go and take my chance with the fall? No, I'll hang on, I'll hang on—

The branch holds! It holds my weight!

From the open window, oaths and curses follow my exit, but words cannot harm me now. I drag myself along the branch to the trunk and then, using the creases in the bark as a ladder, clamber down to the ground.

I hold up the ring—let them all see it one last time!

Then I bow low, as any gentleman would, and race across Duke's Court and down an alleyway to safety. They can call the Guard, but the Guard is slow. My legs, when I am fearful, can almost fly.

Down one street, up another; across a square, a garden, over a crumbling wall; through one arch, two, and I am in the marketplace behind the Cathedral. I hide at the rear of a stall selling clothes, peering out from between a row of dusty shirts and shriveled hose. No one about. I lost them, I think.

Work has already begun on the Christmas market. Soon traders will come from all over Lombardy to sell their wares: bracelets, purses, necklaces, needle cases, ribbons, rings, gloves, mirrors, candlesticks, holy relics, mulled wines, pies, lemons, and quinces. The sounds of hammering and the merry calls of the carpenters mingle with the smell of newly sawn wood.

I must hide myself and rest. My legs are shaking, and I am covered with sweat. Where? The Cathedral.

So in I go, there to find a quiet corner until I can recover.

The few worshippers at this time of day have only come in to escape the cold, to judge from the noises. Instead of hushed prayer, there is a constant recitation of coughs and sighs. And the Cathedral, being almost empty, is like a huge cavern, magnifying every sound. I might as well be in Milan Hospital.

I pull my jerkin tight around me and settle into the shadows.

The Duke's ring? I stole a ring from the Duke? But *how*?

I must tell the Master about this ring, as soon as—but can I do that? If he knows I have the ring, he will surely force me to surrender it to the Duke. And the last thing I want is to see *him* again.

No, no, I must keep this ring to myself. When I leave Milan—*if* I leave Milan—I will be able to sell it for a good price in another city, where the Duke's mark will not be recognized.

But now I must return home. Caterina will wonder where I am. And I have yet to find a way to feed us.

When I give Caterina my report on everything that has happened to me today, she listens in silence, sometimes shaking her head, sometimes nodding. Often doing the one when you would expect the other.

"What do we have left to eat?" I ask, when I have finished my sorry story.

"Dust and mice droppings, boy. And the mouse, if you can catch it."

"I couldn't eat the mouse, Caterina, it's lived here longer than we have."

"You won't be saying that if there's a famine. Why, I remember one winter, what, thirty years ago now, it must be, we were so hungry we were boiling the—"

"Nothing? Nothing at all in the house?"

"Just a corner of cheese. And Bagliotti's bread."

Well, I said I wouldn't touch it, but I will. We scrape off the mold and share it out between us.

And then Caterina finds an apple that had rolled under the cupboard. We eat it with great ceremony, slicing it carefully down the middle and separating the halves: one for Caterina, one for me. But two halves do not fill the hole.

XXII

The next day, early, I open the door to—

"Messer Maggio! You're back, thanks be to God! And my master?"

"At the Castle. Somehow, that night you discovered us at the Lazaretto, the Duke did, too. I'm afraid that your master blames you for it."

"Me? But I never told the Duke anything!" Maggio gives me a questioning look. "Tell me what happened, sir. I must know!"

"We rose at dawn the day after your visit and were unlocking the Lazaretto," Maggio says, "when a squad of horsemen rode up and, despite your master's protests, escorted us directly to the Duke. He accused Leonardo of conspiring with the French. Your master accused the Duke of conspiring with Michelangelo. The Duke desired to know why Leonardo had not told him about his new invention. Your master asked why he should, when the Duke never pays him what he owes. Back and forth it went. 'You have failed me!' the Duke cries. 'No more I you than you me!' your master shouts back. 'I will send you away from Milan!' says the Duke. 'I will willingly go!' says Leonardo."

"Messer Maggio, I forget myself—please come into the kitchen and have some water."

And there, having drained three cups, Maggio continues. "I thought it was all over for us. The Duke rose from his seat and looked ready to send us to the chopping block. Instead, he breaks into laughter. He laughs! And then the Master starts laughing! And then the both of them are holding each other in an embrace, the best of friends once more!"

I can scarce believe it.

"Oh, it's true, lad, I was there. Great men, you cannot reckon with them."

"So—"

"So the flying machine is now installed at the Castle, inside the Rocchetta, the safest, most heavily fortified part. No spy will get in, and Leonardo will not be able to get out!"

"Then you will remain at the Castle, you and the Master?"

"That is right, boy. Until we finish the work and ready the flying machine for use against the French."

"And why didn't my master come to me with this news? We have been waiting so long to hear from him."

"The Duke will not let him out of the Castle, fearing, perhaps, that Leonardo might take the opportunity to depart Milan without warning. Now I, too, must return in good time. I was given but an hour to see you." He hands me a crumpled note. "And to pass you this message from your master."

"Thank you, Messer Maggio. You cannot imagine how Caterina and I have worried."

"Your master is safe, so long as we finish the work."

"Messer Maggio, we have no money. Could you—"

"I have only these coins on me, but, look, you can have them."

"I thank you, sir. I know my master owes you money. I do not wish to enlarge the debt."

"Your master has promised to pay me everything he owes, as soon as we finish the flying machine and the Duke has paid him."

Oh, then I fear you will *never* receive what is due to you, Messer Maggio.

When Maggio has left, I find Caterina, and together we eagerly open the message.

But all it says is that I must look after the house while he is at the Castle, tell no one where he is, and await his return, about which he has no further information to give. Not one friendly word. It would seem that what Maggio told me is true: the Master really does hold me responsible for revealing his secret.

And now what to do about the Duke? I failed to report back to him—and he found the Master's invention himself, without my help. Does that mean that he will soon come looking for me to exact his revenge?

It seems that I am caught between the Master and his

master—and I will suffer some kind of agony from either or both of them. But now I must hasten to Messer Tombi; it's time for my next lesson, and I don't want to miss it. Today he will teach me everything about the color that runs through all of us, the color red.

XXIII

The weeks have passed. It's Christmas Eve.

On every corner groups of strolling musicians play the lute and recorder, raising our spirits with the songs of the season. The air is sharp and clean; and the stench of rubbish, so strong in summer, no longer assails the nose with every step. Wreaths of holly and branches of fir hang from the doors of Milan's better houses. How can one not rejoice? Let the streets come alive with voices singing joyful songs! Tomorrow is the birthday of our Lord.

That much we can be sure of. Whether the Master will ever return is not so certain. There has been no more news from him.

We have finished the last of the cabbage soup Caterina cooked up with the money Maggio gave us, and tomorrow, while we go hungry, the good folk of Milan will be exchanging gifts and gathering around the kitchen table to feast on roast boar in pepper sauce, goose in red mustard, spicy meat sausages, fresh white figs, soft, sweet-smelling marzipan, pine nuts in melted sugar, and—*stop now, Giacomo, stop before you drown in your own spittle!*

Feeling lonely, I decided to take a stroll through the market. They're lighting the lanterns for the midnight celebrations. The air is spun thick with seasonal spices—cinnamon, cloves, ginger, nutmeg, cardamom, and myrrh. Although the crowd presses on every side, nobody curses or spits; it is Christmas, after all, when we set aside our complaints and embrace one another in brotherly friendship. So the story goes.

But it pains me to see all the food on display and to have no money to buy any of it, when other folk are laden down with their packages.

I leave the market and find a stone bench in a small square behind the Cathedral. It is cold. I wrap my cloak all the more tightly around me. What if the Master has left us for good?

And then the Cathedral bells let loose their music on my head with a joyful tolling—I nearly forgot my duty! I promised to accompany Caterina to midnight Mass. She never misses it.

I run home past bands of monks, their hands in prayer, families out walking with lighted candles, vendors selling hot chestnuts. The tavern doors are open, and the friendly hubbub from within spills out onto the streets. There'll be no fighting, not tonight, not on the eve of our Lord's birthday.

"Caterina! Let me in! It's Giacomo!"

The door opens, and she says: "Can't you hear the bells? I thought you'd forgotten."

"Me, Caterina?—never! But you look too tired to leave the house. Let us stay here in front of the fire and keep warm."

"Not a chance, boy! And you promised, remember, and to break a promise is to put a coin in the Devil's purse."

But the old woman is not well enough to walk out tonight, and she knows it. She opens the front door and takes a look. It is starting to snow.

"Maybe you are right, after all. I don't feel so steady. Will you read to me from the Scriptures, then?"

I smile and nod. I love to read to Caterina.

We mount the stairs, and soon she is tucked up in bed.

"Now then," I say, "what will it be—one of the old stories, or the oldest story of them all, how God created the world?"

"Thank you, Giacomo," she says, "for staying with me."

"I will never leave," I say. "Even if my parents come looking for me."

And she says, almost in a whisper: "Maybe they know where you are already."

"Caterina, what do you mean?"

She turns to the wall and falls asleep as quickly as a weary child. I will learn nothing more tonight.

So I go to my own room, undress, and jump into my cold bed.

Does the old woman know something about my parents? Sometimes I think she does. But perhaps it is just out of kindness that she raises my hopes from time to time.

Tomorrow is Christmas Day, 1497.

And I am hungry. Very, very hungry. For food, for answers, for a new life.

We awake to the glorious sound of the Cathedral bells.

Later that morning I am making the fire in the kitchen, when there is a knock on the door—and Margareta is standing outside holding a big platter, which she sets down on the kitchen table. She pulls off the cover and reveals a half side of roast beef, still steaming from the spit!

"Our master has too much to eat," Margareta says, "enough for ten, and there's only him and his wife. He asked if any of our neighbors—"

"Margareta, you are an angel!"

"Well," she says, "it is the time of year for them."

I hug and embrace her—and as soon as I have led Caterina to the table (where she then leads me in a proper prayer of thanks), we fill our skins with food that could not have tasted better had it come directly from the Duke's kitchen.

The rest of the day passes peacefully. I do some drawing, read to Caterina from the Bible, and we retire to our beds. But I cannot sleep. Jumbled thoughts fill my head and turn over and over like mill wheels on a racing river.

And then it comes to me.

The answer I have been looking for, which, like my own nose, has been right in front of my eyes, but unseen all this time—

A way to pay our debts, fill our stomachs, and settle the matter of who will be the models for the Disciples!

I sit up straight.

Let me think, now. I have sometimes suggested to the Master that the merchants we owe money to would be glad to cancel our debts in return for a painting. But he has always dismissed me with a wave of his hand.

"What?" he has said. "A Virgin Mary for a pound of Peroni's cheese? A Baby Jesus for two pairs of Martino's hose and a doublet? A Holy Family for Fazio's horse and saddle? Never! I would rather be sent to debtors' prison!"

Now, I know he does not mean *that*—my master hates the damp.

"But instead of painting a picture for each of them," I say to the wall (standing in for my master), "why not put them all in one painting?"

He'll look at me as if I am mad, and *then* I'll say to him: "That's right, Master, *use the merchants as the models for Jesus' Disciples in the Last Supper*—and they'll cancel all our debts, down to the last ducat!"

That'll get his attention.

He'll think for a moment, and then he'll say: "Giacomo, you are ingenious!"

Better than that, Master. This is the best idea of the century.

And there are only two more years until the new one.

XXIV

Early the next day

Early the next day I venture forth to Benedetti, the paper merchant, to try my plan for the Last Supper. He's the one I can speak with most comfortably. And if it pleases him, I think it might please the others.

When I arrive at his shop the shutters are drawn. Of course, it's Saint Stephen's Day. He will be at home next door.

I pull the bell rope. No answer. Again, then.

"Yes, yes, I hear you!" A woman's voice from within. "Will one of you idle girls stop making mouths in the mirror and answer the door? Can't you see my hands are full?"

A long pause, then the door swings open. One of Benedetti's daughters stands before me.

"Hello," I say. She starts giggling. In a moment she is joined at the door by her sisters. Soon they are all holding hands and giggling.

"Hello, girls," I say.

"Who's at the door?" Benedetti's gruff voice could strip the wax from the insides of your ears.

The girls are still giggling. Two of them are bent double with it.

"It's Giacomo, Messer Benedetti, from Master Leonardo," I say, over their heads.

"Hello . . . GIACOMO!" they shout in unison. More giggling.

"Giacomo? What brings you here on Saint Stephen's Day? Come in, my boy," Benedetti says, holding out his hand. It is warm and dry. A good sign. He is at his ease. "What can I do for you?"

"I would like to speak with you privately, sir."

"Of course. But permit me first to introduce my daughters to you: Chiara, Clara, Clarissa, Corinna, and Emilia, our youngest; we ran out of *C*s. Every one of them a gem!"

"Father, really!" Clara (or is it Corinna?) says.

"I am honored to meet you all," I say, bowing so low I can count the whorls in the planed wood floor. And when I rise at last, I am delighted to be wearing my new cloak, it makes an elegant flourish.

Benedetti claps his hands and rubs them together.

"You are jolly, sir."

"Indeed I am, Giacomo, indeed I am. Christmas is my favorite time of year, and one of my girls—that one, Clarissa, give us a curtsy, my dear—just a week ago received an offer of marriage. Now she's been snapped up, I have high hopes of handing over the lot of them within the next year!"

"Father!"

"Don't talk like that, father, or we'll never leave you!"

"Yes, yes," Benedetti says, "now off you go and help your mother. Emilia, wait for me outside. I have a task for you."

The giggling girls sweep off in a cloud of perfumed velvet and lace. Benedetti ushers me into his study.

"Emilia comes to me this week and asks to work. Doesn't want to sit around the house, wants to learn my trade! Have you heard the like?" Benedetti says.

"No, sir, but I like what I hear."

"And her face won't break any mirrors, eh? Make someone a fine wife."

"Is she not too young to wed, sir?"

"They're never too young to wed. The sooner we get these girls off the streets—where every man looks at their bosoms as if 'Touch Me' were written on them—and into the arms of honest husbands, the sooner I will be able to sleep peacefully again."

It is so pleasant to be inside a warm house with a happy family that I almost forget why I came here. Oh, yes—

"Sir, to the point. My master owes you money."

"Money! Ah, money. It always comes back to that."

"Yes, sir." I hope this is not the beginning of a lecture.

"Yet money has only one purpose, Giacomo: to buy things. That, in itself, does not bring happiness."

It is a lecture.

Messer Benedetti sighs, peers out of the window. He places one hand on his heart, looks up at the sky, and recites:

"I wish that I could be a bird,
I'd fly from tree to tree,
But I'm a man and have no wings,
No man is ever free."

He takes his hand from his heart and looks at me. "What do you think, lad?" he says.

"Did you write that, sir?"

He smiles. "When I was just a young man."

Age has not improved it!

"Ah, if I had spent my years writing, instead of becoming the biggest paper supplier in Lombardy . . ." He stops to adjust a small statue of Cupid on his mantel. "I would probably be living in a hut, instead of in this fine house. Now, Giacomo, what was it again?"

The artistic yearning has passed by for a second time and probably took no longer than the first, for who would choose an uncertain future over a chinking bank account? Only a true artist. Or a fool.

"Money, sir. We owe you."

"That is correct and has been for some time now. But we both know this. Do you have it with you?"

"No, sir, but—"

"Giacomo, we are friends. I hope so, at least. Your master owes me hundreds. I've stopped counting. I know very well he thinks that because I am a simple merchant—"

"Never, sir! He has never called you simple!"

"—A simple merchant, he can play games with me. And,

Giacomo, what is worse, I let him, because he is a great painter, and I am in awe of him. But enough is enough. If he wants to purchase more paper, let him not send you to plead with me, no, let him come here himself and do it."

"But, Messer Benedetti, I am not here about the Master's paper."

"No, you are here about more credit! The mother-in-law wants me to hire someone to knock him down in the street," Benedetti says. "She'd probably do it herself, if I paid her."

The door opens and a tall, handsome woman appears in a blue dress, cut low on the shoulder, her chest bulging against the material. Her necklace is a string of pearls, shining as if freshly plucked from the seabed. Benedetti's money has been put to its best possible use; at least so far as his wife is concerned.

"I heard voices," she says, smiling.

"Elizabetta, my wife," Benedetti says. "Giacomo, the servant—"

"Of course—Giacomo. My husband speaks of you often."

I offer a small bow at this, though I am not sure why. Perhaps because it is the end of Act I.

"Well then, Giacomo, why *are* you here?" Benedetti says.

At last! Act II. Time for my speech.

"Sir . . ."

"Yes?"

"You are a successful merchant—and your success, I think, comes from your quickness to seize on a good deal."

"That's part of it, of course. Then there's attention to detail and—"

"Here's a good deal, sir. The best you will ever be offered. How would you like to be—" and the first word that comes to mind is "—*immortal*?"

"Now you're mocking me, Giacomo, you're worse than your—"

"I mean it, sir."

"What are you getting at, eh?"

"Cancel all the Master's debts—everything, the lot, down to the last soldo—and he will paint you into the Last Supper."

"Come again?" He looks at his wife, but she is looking at me, her eyes large. "How's he going to paint me into the Last Supper?"

"Your face, Messer Benedetti, your face. The Master will use your face as the model for one of the Disciples. Think of it! You could be John, or James, Peter, or Bartholomew! You could be a figure in the largest and most celebrated painting of Christ and His Disciples in all the land. Think of the fame, the glory! The whole world lining up outside the doors of Santa Maria delle Grazie—to see you!"

By degrees, Benedetti's face begins to shine. And soon he is gleaming.

"Benedetti, the paper merchant?" he says. "In the Last Supper?"

"Yes, sir, you, sir, there. Sir."

"Oh husband," Elizabetta Benedetti says, taking his arm. "Imagine what that would do for our daughters' prospects in marriage! And think how jealous the Vergiliano-Tassos would be!"

"One more thing," I say. Oh, why not, I've come this far. "As well as canceling our debts, we will require a small payment."

"Eh? Payment? Now I see you are more horse dealer than servant! What kind of payment?"

"Ten ducats."

It was the first figure that came into my head.

"Ten ducats?! Why, that's five reams of parchment, that is!"

"Not so much to pay, sir, to become famous throughout Lombardy."

"Giacomo, would you sit down? Wife, call the servant for some wine for the boy. Let's you and I have a little conference outside."

Almost as soon as the door is closed behind them a servant enters, an old fellow with a stoop. As he wobbles his way towards me, I get up and take the glass of wine before he drops it, thanking him for his trouble.

Well, this is the life. Wine at eleven. A fine chair to sit on, not like the ones in the Master's house that sag as soon as you place your rear on them. And being treated with respect instead of contempt. I could take some more of this life, I could.

Then the door opens again and a pretty head appears, sees me, and is followed by an equally pretty form: Emilia. She glances back to see that no one is about and then comes in, closing the door behind her.

"Is it true you serve the great Leonardo?" she says.

"I have that honor."

"Then could you—would you arrange for me to meet him? More than anything, I want to learn how to paint."

"You do? That's what I—"

But now the door is opening again, and the Benedettis are entering.

"Emilia?" Elizabetta Benedetti says. "What are you doing in here?"

"I wanted to ask Giacomo about Master Leonardo—"

"You ask too many questions of too many people about too many things," her mother says.

Too many questions? I like this Emilia more with every passing moment.

As soon as his daughter has left the room, Benedetti says: "We've talked it over, my wife and I, and I agree—*we* agree—to your proposal, Giacomo. Your master will use my face in the Last Supper—not Judas, mind, not Judas!—and I will cancel all his debts and pay the sum of ten ducats."

"Agreed! Let us shake on it."

We do. Several times.

By the Virgin, what have I done? Some good, I hope, for the Master. But for Caterina and me, I do not need to hope: I know. Tonight we eat.

"When will we see it?" his wife says.

"As soon as it is painted."

"And when will that be?" Benedetti says, rubbing his hands together.

"When it is done."

Benedetti and his wife smile delightedly at each other. The Vergiliano-Tassos will have to admit they are beaten.

"Giacomo, I tell you truly, my wife and I are thrilled. What other merchant in Milan will have his face in a painting by Leonardo da Vinci, our greatest painter?"

To that I will give no answer. There are twelve Disciples. One place taken by Benedetti leaves me another eleven to fill. And we owe money to a multitude of merchants. My friend Benedetti will have plenty of company at the Last Supper.

And now he escorts me to the front door, his arm around my shoulders.

"A fine young man, yes you are, don't argue, a fine young man. I'll prepare the document annulling your master's debts and have it sent over to you. Which Disciple will I be, Giacomo? May I choose?"

"I'll have to ask the Master."

"Oh, don't put him to any bother, wherever he can fit me in."

Benedetti knows very well that arguing with the Master is a profitless exercise.

As I pass through the door, I turn and say: "I'd like the ten ducats now, if you please, sir."

He looks at his wife. She nods. Benedetti fishes inside the purse hanging from his belt and brings out the coins. ". . . Seven, eight, nine, ten. There now. We are settled. When do I come for the sitting, eh, Giacomo?"

"Just as soon as my master is ready for you."

Whenever that will be.

"I do have one more request," I say.

"Anything, my boy, anything."

"May I take some paper for drawing?"

"What—are you an artist, too? Come to the shop tomorrow. By all means you will have your paper, as much as you can carry."

As I walk down the street something tells me to look back—and both Benedettis are waving at me as if I was their long-lost son! I would have no objection to them as parents, none at all, except that the last thing I would want to be is Emilia's *brother.*

And now, as soon as the Master returns, I'll tell him how successful my plan has been with Benedetti, and he will surely agree to let me make this offer to the other shopkeepers.

XXV

The New Year is knocking on Milan's gates, and in a few hours it will enter. Will it be any better than the last? Only God knows, and He isn't telling.

At midnight the cannon will be fired from the Castle and the annual display of fireworks will begin, the so-called Battle between the Giants and the Gods. It's a gift to the people from the Duke, and it lasts an hour or so; for the rest of the year he will not give, he will take.

Once more my friends and I are met at the Seven Knaves.

Renzo will not yet say if he has accepted Messer Maggio's offer to make him an apprentice. By Saint Francis, I do not understand why he delays. You never know what Renzo is thinking. Sometimes I wonder if he does any thinking at all.

Jacopo is watching over his customers with a falcon's ready eye; he awaits the next disaster, knowing it will come, but not what form it will take. Just now an old lady, drunk as a young maid on her first night out, slipped and fell into the fire, and precious water had to be wasted putting her out. Much madness will take place tonight. It is New Year's Eve, and strange spirits are let loose.

Caterina is spending the evening next door with Margareta, whose master—Messer Montevecchio, the trader—is having a final celebration before he leaves for Spain on business. There will be music for dancing and plenty of food, and even if Margareta will be serving instead of sitting, and Caterina will be in the kitchen helping to wash the platters, they will make merry together. I am glad that she will have company this evening; old folk feel the passing of time more keenly on this night than any other and should not be alone.

But here in the Seven Knaves the riotous revelry that fills the tavern top to bottom scarcely touches my sides. I am as sober as a tree stump. I have good reason. This morning a message came from Messer Tombi: *Tonight at midnight. The shop.*

Nothing more. No welcome, no farewell. A command, plain and simple. Which I am meant to obey. And the manner is so unlike the friendly apothecary's that I wonder if he wrote it, or if his hand was guided by another.

Who would want to lead me into such a trap? The Duke? The one who sent those thieves to our house? But why send me to the apothecary?

Such speculation is useless. I must go; I have to. Something is going to happen tonight, something important. I can feel it.

"What's wrong with you?" Renzo says. "Not joining in the singing? I've never been able to stop you before. God's breath, how I've tried!"

"I have heavy thoughts," I say.

"Drink some more, then, and lock the door on them. It's New Year's Eve, Giacomo!"

I raise my cup and we toast each other, but I set it down again untouched.

Claudio, by character cautious and shy, is more the opposite tonight. His round face is shining from the heat and drink, and he laughs as if he has just now discovered how.

"Giacomo, my dearest friend, did I tell you how much I love you?"

"Only a dozen times."

He claps his arm around my shoulder.

"My master has invited me to join his family for the fireworks tonight. And his daughter Alessandra is the loveliest maid in all Milan. Perhaps I will be seated near her!"

"Then this is your big chance, Claudio."

"But I fear I will make a fool of myself."

"You will if you go on drinking. Stop now, is my advice to you."

Then Antonio starts telling us about this monk, Teofilio, who has a prayer that can cure bad breath, and how he, Antonio, has bought it from him for a bottle of pear brandy (which he stole, anyway), and how he is going to print a hundred copies of the cure and sell them from door to door. While he drones on about his new scheme, my mind drifts away to thoughts of my master, and what might be happening at the Castle. Have they finished building the flying machine? And will the Master let me be the one to pilot it?

"Come on, Giacomo, drink up, you're lagging behind," Antonio says.

I raise my cup once more—"My Lady's Cheeks!"—one in a list of ten pledges that begin with the lady's hair, then progress south by eyes, lips, neck, and so forth, as far as the lady's secret parts, at which point some overzealous drinkers halt and linger for the rest of the night.

The serving girl sets down a fresh jug of wine. Renzo gives her a look. It's almost worth staying just to see what will happen next—but the hour of midnight is almost come.

"Friends, a joyful New Year to you all! I must leave now, I am expected."

We shake hands and embrace. And out the door I go into the shivering night air.

I cling to the shadows, head down, and when I turn into the Street of Apothecaries, the shops are all dark—all except Tombi's, where I can see a greenish glow flickering behind the shutters.

"Messer Tombi, open up! It's Giacomo."

Tombi peers through the peephole and, satisfied that my voice does not deceive him, opens the door.

"Come in, boy, be quick about it."

He beckons me through the curtain into the workroom. There is no candle lit, but a glass jar is giving off a strange light. He sees me staring at it.

"The tails of glowworms, boy, caught at dawn. Cheaper than candle wax, and they last longer. The waste pit outside the city walls is an excellent place to find them. I go there every day."

That may explain the persistent strong smell on Tombi's clothes.

The creatures are wriggling and writhing behind their glass wall. Is it agony or ecstasy that possesses them?

"Why did you send for me with such urgency, Messer Tombi?"

He says nothing at first. Then, from deep inside his robe, he draws out a silver disk. But it looks like the medallion—

"*You*, Messer Tombi? An *alchemist*?"

"A true member of the Brotherhood," Tombi says. "Indeed, the last alchemist left in Milan. When the Duke began his purge of my brethren, I disguised myself in a beard and old robes and became the apothecary. I waited. And waited. I have been waiting these many years. Then you came to me that day and told me—"

"—about my medallion and that I had seen someone arriving at the Castle!"

"That man is Ottavio Assanti, Grand Alchemist, and Second Brother of the Brotherhood."

"Second—?"

"Second in rank to the First Brother."

I take a deep breath. "Will you help me to meet this Assanti?"

"Better than that. When I told him about you, he came here himself."

Tombi holds out his hand by way of introduction, and as he does so, from out of the shadows appears a tall figure, hooded.

He stands before me, fully half a man taller.

I can see nothing of his face, hidden as it is by the cowl.

Then he places one of his hands inside the folds of his robe and pulls out a medallion. He holds it in the palm of his hand for me to inspect.

"The medallion of the Brotherhood," he says, in a voice that defies argument. "I have been told that you possess the same."

"I do, sir. I have had it since I was a child."

I take it from my purse and hold it out to him.

Assanti comes towards me and pulls off the hood that obscures his face. He has a shaved head and short gray beard. His nose is long and bent slightly to the left. His eyes are blue. It is a face that commands respect.

"But you have forfeited your memory, so I am told. What would you give to have it restored to you?"

"Anything, sir. Everything!"

"With my art," Assanti says, "I can probe the inmost corners of your mind. Together we will discover what lies behind the veil of forgetfulness and return to you the past that is rightfully yours."

Straightway, the blood rushes from my head and I feel faint with excitement.

"You could do that, Master? You could?"

Assanti smiles. "It merely requires time. Which, at the moment, I do not have. The Duke does not let me wander very far before he sends his men to look for me. He needs me at his side, and he does not trust himself when I am not."

"I would give anything to know more, Master."

"And so you shall. There is much for you to learn."

"Thank you, Master, *thank* you! I will do everything—"

"Not everything, boy, one thing. But now I must return to the Castle, or I will be missed. Listen to what Tombi has to say."

Assanti moves through the curtain and without another word departs Tombi's shop, his cloak billowing behind him.

"Messer Tombi, is it possible? Can Master Assanti restore my memory to me?"

"He is capable of many things."

"Then tell me what I must do."

"The Second Brother wants you to perform a small service for him."

"Anything I can do is little enough to receive the answers I seek."

"The Pope is coming to Milan."

"Nobody knows that better than me, Messer Tombi!"

"Master Assanti wishes to meet with His Holiness."

"Why does he need me for that?"

"The Duke will never permit it. He needs the Pope's help against the French; and the Church, as I told you, is not a friend to alchemists. The Duke will want to keep Master Assanti as far from the Pope as possible."

"But why does the Church hate alchemy so much?" I ask.

"It considers our work sacrilegious, but most of all it fears that one day we will discover the secret of immortality, which would render the Church's own teachings worthless. If man could become immortal while he yet lived, who would care for the Christian faith, which says you must die first?"

Now, that *is* sacrilege!

"The Church, however, has the advantage," Tombi continues. "The First Brother fears that alchemy will one day vanish completely unless we make our peace. Master Assanti has been given the task of winning the Pope's confidence and proving to His Holiness that henceforth alchemists will work together with the Church to bring about a better life for all mankind."

"What must be done, Messer Tombi, and when?"

"Master Assanti understands that Pope Alexander has requested to see the Last Supper. You will gain access to the refectory at Santa Maria delle Grazie and help the Second Brother to obtain an audience with His Holiness. After this fruitful meeting our two faiths will be drawn together in one happy union. Giacomo, with your help we will change the course of history!"

It sounds worthy.

"I'll do it, sir. Tell Master Assanti he has my agreement."

"Now, you must speak nothing of this to anyone. Least of all to your master, who might well deny you this chance, much as he has denied you the chance to learn painting."

The apothecary speaks truly. Why does my master seek to hinder my progress in the world?

I bid farewell to Tombi and hasten home to a New Year, 1498, and, God willing—and not so far distant from now—a new life. The celebrations are still going on in the streets, and my heart rises up with the thought that I will one day soon have something to celebrate as well.

In three months the Pope will come to Milan. Now, more than ever, I must make sure that the Master finishes the Last Supper in time. If it is not done, the Pope will never visit Santa Maria delle Grazie, and I will never learn the truth about myself.

This New Year promises to be the first truly happy one of my life.

Before I fall to sleep I take out my drawing board and paper and draw the Second Brother, Ottavio Assanti. His proud head, his keen eyes, his imperial nose.

I work at it for an hour or more.

In the candlelight I see that I have made a passable likeness of the alchemist. It's not quite done, but I am too drowsy now to draw any more. For safekeeping, I'll put it inside the cover of one of the Master's sketchbooks lying here by the bed and finish it tomorrow.

XXVI

The next morning I am too tired to rise early, and without the Master here I have no one to complain at me if I don't. It is New Year's Day, after all. Even the dogs are sleeping it off.

Caterina brings me some soup at midday, and I am soon dreaming once more.

When I awake it is late afternoon.

I hear talking in the kitchen.

My master has returned!

I jump up and pull on my clothes. I'm about to go in, when I hear his voice: "Has he been stealing?"

"I do not know where he found the money, but he did," Caterina is saying. "That is how we ate while you were away. The shopkeepers refused to give us anything more until they were paid."

"What! No more credit? I'll speak to them, they won't deny me."

"You left us with no money," she says.

"Nonsense, woman! It was in the pot, where I always leave it."

I step into the kitchen.

"There was nothing in the pot, Master."

"Well, you haven't starved to death, anyone can see that."

"If I had not been given money by Benedetti, air is all we would have had to eat, Master."

"Benedetti? He loaned you money?"

"Gave, Master. Freely." And why he gave it is a subject I will have to address with you very soon.

"If he can give you money, he certainly does not need mine, then. No more payments to Benedetti! Now, boy, I have much to tell you, but even more to ask you."

Here it comes.

"Who told the Duke that I was working at the Lazaretto?"

"Don't look at me like that, Master! Do you—can you—believe that I would knowingly betray you?"

"But the very day after you found me, the Duke's horsemen appeared at the Lazaretto! How do you explain that?"

"I told you I saw someone on the roof that night. And you didn't believe me."

"I believe you now," he says. "And you must have been followed. That was careless of you, Giacomo, very careless. But what is done cannot be undone. Let us say no more about it."

No more about whether *you* might have been the one followed, rather than me.

He leaves the kitchen and goes to the study. I arrive soon after.

"Master, may I enter?"

He is seated before the fire.

"Hmm? What is it now?"

"Your father was here, Master."

His head snaps up, his eyes wide.

"What? My father—Piero da Vinci—came to Milan?"

"Yes, Master. He saw the letter you sent to your brothers. He had money for you."

"I will never take money from my father. Unfortunately, neither will my brothers lend me any."

"Why is that, Master?"

"Because they do not consider me a proper member of the family."

"But—why, Master?"

He pokes the fire with the iron and stares into the flames. Then, after long moments have passed, he turns to me.

"Did he say anything else to you, Giacomo?"

"What do you mean, Master?"

"Did you talk?"

Should I tell him what the old man told me? No. Better I keep that to myself.

"Only hello and good-bye," I say.

"That is more than he has said to me since the day I left Florence. And more than I would want to say to him."

"Anyway, Master, it is too late for your father's money. He has left Milan."

"And good riddance to him."

He turns to the fire and warms his hands.

"Water, please, Caterina. I know you are outside the door listening."

And I can hear her shuffle off to fetch the jug.

"Master, there is food ready for you, but please serve yourself," she says, entering with the cups. "I do not feel so well. I'll go to my bed."

He continues to sit in front of the fire, staring at the flames.

"Come, Master," I say, "let us see what Caterina has left for us."

We go to the kitchen and sit down to cat the bean soup that she has prepared, along with half a loaf of millet bread. Now I must tell him my plan for the Last Supper.

"Master, we must act soon," I say. "We owe so much money to the merchants, and Father Vicenzo, well, nothing would please him more than to throw us out of the house. He has already stopped payment for your expenses—"

"He has?"

"Yes, Master."

"Why didn't you tell me?"

"I just did. Even now the Duke may be welcoming Michelangelo, and who knows what will happen to us after that. Our task is to finish the Last Supper as soon as possible, if we do not want someone else finishing it for us. And we need to eat, too."

"You have a great talent for re-stating the obvious, Giacomo. We have a tree full of worries, and all you can do is shake the branches. Instead of endlessly repeating the problems, give me a solution."

Very well, then, I will.

So I tell him what I agreed with Benedetti: that in return for canceling our debts, his face would appear on the shoulders of one of the Disciples. (I do not mention the ten ducats, which I gave to Caterina for food—he would surely demand them.)

"And once I have proposed a similar arrangement to the other merchants—our debts are paid, the painting is finished, the Duke is satisfied, Michelangelo is sent away, and your position will be secure. There, Master, you asked for solutions. How does this one sit?"

"Whose idea was this, Giacomo?" he says sweetly. "Yours or Benedetti's?"

"Why, mine, Master, of course."

He's going to shower me with thanks and praise!

No, his expression is changing, the smile has gone, the eyebrows are lowering, and now he is shouting loud enough to make Donatello's skull cover its ears, if it still had ears. Or hands to cover them.

"I will never, ever compromise my art to pay off a few merchants. You have done many foolish things in the past, Giacomo, and I have managed to forgive you for them. But you go too far! *Nobody* tells Leonardo da Vinci how to paint, what to paint, or why to paint. I, and only I, Giacomo—hear me for the first and last time!—make those choices."

"Master—"

"Learn the business of art, boy, before you meddle in another artist's business. That time is many, many years hence."

Never has Pride, newly attired in the soft robes of Self-respect, been obliged to undress so quickly. I press my lips together to restrain the profanities seeking to escape. He is like a man who prefers to stand in the rain on his own rather than ask for shelter from another.

And the way he is looking at me now, he is about to rain a tempest down on my head. I'd do best to leave the room without delay. His father was right about one thing: Leonardo da Vinci is a very stubborn man!

But I cannot leave without saying something, anything—to show my respect, of which he now thinks I have none.

"Master?"

"Yes?"

"Happy New Year."

He looks straight through me and gives a slight shake of his head.

"Is it?" he replies. And turns away.

There go my painting lessons, perhaps forever.

XXVII

For the first time ever since I came to live with the Master, Caterina is not already awake and bustling about in the kitchen when I rise the next morning. She complained of feeling unwell the night before, true, but illness has never prevented her from being first in the kitchen to light the fire. It was a matter of pride for her to rise before us.

That she is still in her bed frightens me.

I run upstairs to her room. She is sleeping peacefully. Poor thing, she has exhausted herself. Maybe rest is all she needs. When I think how she hit Tommaso over the head with her pan, I have to laugh. But then I remind myself that one day he and his cronies will creep up behind me and—

"Giacomo, where are you? There is no breakfast!"

I run back downstairs and into the kitchen. The Master is waiting.

"Where is Caterina? Never mind. Forget breakfast. You are coming to Santa Maria with me, boy. Now. I grow vexed with your constant complaints about the Last Supper. You have been hinting that I am unable to finish it. No, do not deny it. Put on your cloak and off we go."

The Master and I walk out together into the air. The water trough is sealed with a layer of ice. A rough gray sky covers the earth like a beggar's blanket.

He takes long strides and urges me to walk more quickly. We pass through the Vercellina Gate and head towards Santa Maria, our breath clouding the air before us. A cart lies in the ditch, one of its wheels off. The driver is nowhere to be seen.

Soon we come to the refectory. The Master searches through his leather bag.

"The key! I do not have the key."

"It's in your hand, Master."

He looks at it as if for the first time.

"So it is."

I take the key from him, put it in the lock, and turn. A part of me, if not all of me, wishes I had the wrong key and that we would never again enter this room to stand before the Last Supper.

The doors open slowly, grinding their hinges. There is a scampering in the darkness. I feel a strange comfort, knowing that the mice have not deserted the refectory. Perhaps they have faith that the painting will be finished, even if the rest of the world does not.

The Master takes two candles from his bag and lights them. He walks straight to the Last Supper, mounts the ladder to the upper platform, and holds the candles aloft while he inspects the surface.

From left to right he paces, then from right to left. He descends to the lower platform and makes a further inspection.

Still he says nothing, but shakes his head.

Then he steps down to the floor, stands back a few paces, and takes in the whole surface. Now he turns to look at me.

"Why do you think I have been hesitating to finish the painting, boy?"

"Because you could not decide which faces to use as models for Jesus and Judas?"

"Come, Giacomo, you know better than that. There is another reason, far more important."

I know. That's why I've been worrying.

"What is the meaning of that look? Do you think I deliberately waste my time? That I do not paint the Last Supper because I cannot master it?"

"No, but—"

"No painting has ever defeated me, or ever will."

"Yes, Master. I mean, no."

"Come here, boy. Look! Look closely at the surface of the wall. Well?"

"Master, I see nothing."

There's nothing to see, nothing having been painted on it!

"Touch it, boy, touch it."

"It's—it's—?"

"It is. Damp. Not much, just a little, but enough. For the past two years I have waited for the plaster to dry itself out. I have tried applying all manner of coatings to the surface: beeswax, boiled oil, varnish, resins. Nothing has worked. I have even tried prayer. And now I am trying a chalk-and-limestone mixture. The problem is not so much this side of the wall—the other is where the dampness comes from."

"But—what do we do, Master?"

"Do? We should abandon this place and paint the Last Supper in another refectory in another church! I suggested as much to the Duke—and he bellowed all Hell at me. His late wife, the Lady Beatrice, is buried in Santa Maria. No other church will do. When I told him that the dampness renders the surface unsuitable for paint, he told me not to bother him with petty grievances and to remedy the matter."

"So now you must finish it on a damp wall?"

"Given more time, I can find a solution—I know I can. But he won't give it to me! Easter, it has to be done by Easter, in time for the arrival of Pope Alexander. He will compel me to finish a painting that should not be finished—and doom what was to be my eternal monument to an early death!"

"Oh, Master . . ."

He lightly touches the surface with his finger and inspects the residue.

"And that is why you decided to paint the wall *secco*—in oil? Because you thought it might hold better on the wall?"

He nods.

"I could not use *fresco*, because that relies absolutely on the plaster drying. The problem would be visible right from the beginning. With oil, at least, we have some time before—"

At that moment there is a pounding on the refectory doors, followed by voices: "Is he in there?" and "Come out, Master Leonardo!"

"If that is Father Vicenzo," my master says, "tell him that the Duke has promised to hang him up by the ears if he interferes with me again."

"Yes, Master."

I go to open the doors. Some ten persons are standing there—shopkeepers, the ones we owe money to. I close the doors behind me.

"Right," says Fazio, "where is he?"

"Not here," I say, without thinking. I know the routine. "Gone to Rome."

"Not without you, he hasn't," says Rossi, the greengrocer. "He'd lose his way."

"We know he's here," Bagliotti, the baker, says. "We've been watching him."

From behind the doors I hear my master shout: "Let them in, Giacomo, let them in. If I can yet finish the Last Supper with all these interruptions, they will account me a greater artist than ever before."

The group of claimants enters. The Master is still staring at the wall.

Fazio speaks. "We're here for our money. Or rather, we're here for your money. We've waited long enough."

Now the Master turns and says: "Did you want to be paid yesterday?"

"Of course we did," Rossi says.

"But you weren't," my master replies. "So please do not tell me that today is any different."

"Is that all you have to say?" Fazio asks.

"It is all I am going to say." My master crosses his arms. "Now, gentlemen, if you please. I have work to do, by order of the Duke."

"We all have work to do, Master!" Peroni says.

"You call what you do *work*, Peroni?"

"Master Leonardo, you have eaten my cheese—"

"Once was enough."

(A while ago my master had a bad attack of stomach cramps after eating some of Peroni's gorgonzola, our famous local cheese, which is left to age naturally in caves, where the mold gives it its blue veins. It happened that some bats took up residence in the same caves. The cheese was tainted. Since eating it, my master's mood has been the same.)

"Blame the bats for that cheese, not me!" Peroni says in a high voice. "I would have been pleased to give you your money back—if you had paid me in the first place."

"What about my health?" the Master says. "How do you plan to give that back to me?"

"Master," Bagliotti says, approaching him, "we did not come here to insult or be insulted. We came here for our money. And if we don't get it within the next seven days, we will have to take the matter to the Court of Justice."

"Do as you must. You will never receive my business again."

There is general laughter at this response.

"We don't want your business again, Master," shouts a voice from the back. "We just want your money!"

"I don't have any. Good day, gentlemen."

"Don't expect any of the other shopkeepers to deal with you in the future, either," Peroni says. "The whole market is behind us. If you don't pay, you don't eat, Master Leonardo. Insult your way out of that!"

The Master is, in fact, silent. I look at him. We could solve this problem *now* if he would agree to use their faces in the Last Supper.

"Master, please . . ."

He shakes his head at me.

"There is a way we can avoid all the unpleasantness of the courts," Rossi says. He has several long stray hairs on his lumpy chin. Could he not see them in the mirror? Surely his wife could, even if he chose to ignore them. She must love him very much, to leave them hanging there like that.

"Yes," my master replies. "Desist from making the complaint."

"No, Master," Bagliotti says, "the complaint *will* be made. Unless . . . well, we understand from the paper merchant, Benedetti, that he has come to a private agreement with you concerning the payment of your debt to him."

My master turns to me. Is he going to shout again? I'll avoid his gaze and look out of the window, as if I have just seen someone I know fly past.

"What agreement?" he says.

"Why, Master Leonardo, you agreed to paint Benedetti's face in the Last Supper," Fazio says.

"You are wrong," comes the reply, and in a rising voice. "I never made any such agreement, my servant did, and without my approval. Talk to him, if you like, but as I do not plan to honor this arrangement, you may find your discussion a bigger waste of time than your visit here today."

The Master turns back to the Last Supper.

"So whose faces will you use, if not ours, Master Leonardo?" Fazio says, the persistent fellow, I have to admire him. "Are we not grand enough for you? Is it only the rich and important who appear in your paintings? Yet the Disciples were simple men, Master, whose hands bore the marks of a lifetime's labor, as do ours."

He makes no reply, even though Fazio's speech deserves one.

"Gentlemen," I say, "let us leave the Master to his work." Nobody moves. "Please."

I take Fazio by the arm and guide him away before the Master becomes incensed, and I can tell from the way he is standing, hands on hips, that he soon will be.

When I have herded them like reluctant sheep out into the cold air, I say: "You all know the Master will pay, in time. Even now the Duke owes him thousands of ducats."

"Always the Duke, isn't it!" Peroni chirps. "The Duke is not responsible for eating Leonardo da Vinci's cheese, is he?"

"No, but—"

"Then why should he be responsible for his bill?"

Can't argue with that.

"Nor is your master courteous," Rossi says, "not that we

expect much of that from an artist. But he should be asking for our forbearance."

"Then offer it to him anyway, gentlemen, and he will be all the more in your debt."

"The last thing we want is more of Leonardo's debt!"

There is some laughter at this. And if there is still laughter, there is still hope.

"Will he paint Benedetti, or no?" Bagliotti says.

"I made the arrangement without the Master's consent. I did not anticipate an objection." But I should have.

"The last thing we want, Giacomo," Fazio says, "is to take the matter to court. Even Peroni, whom your master insults so freely, is against it."

What Peroni wants more than anything, I think, is an apology for my master's mockery. And, like most things that one badly wants, he is unlikely to get it.

"But it is Father Vicenzo who brings us here," Bagliotti continues. "He has been whispering in our ears that the Dominicans have stopped paying your master and are about to throw him out of that house you live in. We have been very patient, but this news has doubled our worries. Now we are thinking that Leonardo da Vinci might be tempted to leave Milan in the middle of the night—and us with our unpaid bills. He would not be the first artist to do so."

So Father Vicenzo was behind this visitation.

"Gentlemen, I thank you for your honesty. I will speak to the Master again. Please give me some time to find a remedy."

"One week, Giacomo," says Fazio. "One week and no more."

The merchants shake hands with me and then set off for their various places of work. I feel sympathy for their predicament; but to help them, however, I must first help the Master.

If only he will let me.

I open the refectory doors again. There he is, still staring at the Last Supper as if it will tell him what to do. Then he mounts the ladder to the top of the platform and once more begins his pacing from left to right and right to left.

"Are you still there, boy?"

"Yes, Master."

"Then you shouldn't be. Caterina is not well. You will have to attend to her chores until she is."

I am just closing the doors behind me, when he says: "And keep those infernal tradesmen away from me, Giacomo. I will not endure their complaints and demands!"

"You won't have to for much longer, Master," I shout back. "If we don't pay them within a week, they will take the matter to court."

He makes no reply to that, but I know he heard me.

As I am leaving the refectory, Father Vicenzo is coming out of the church. I duck behind a statue of the young David, a clumsy piece of work that Father Vicenzo particularly admires. I wish that I, like the true David, had a slingshot; I'd put a nice round pebble in it and make a deep hole in the prior's ugly head.

XXVIII

Tuesday

Last night the Master did not return from Santa Maria, or wherever he went. I ate what was left of the potato pie Caterina made two days ago.

This morning, Rodolfo, one of Maggio's assistants, still wearing his carpenter's apron, knocks at our door with a message: My master has returned to the Castle to help Maggio with further adjustments to the spring-and-coil mechanism of the flying machine, which will not release cleanly. He will stay there until the problem is remedied.

"I've been working on the flying machine for weeks now, and every time I stand back and take a good look I shake my head," Rodolfo says. "And then Bernardo Maggio asks me why I am still shaking my head, have I contracted the palsy? No, I say, I'm well, thank you, Master. And he laughs at me! I feel sure that if one of the holy fathers saw our craft, they would condemn it. But we are doing it for the Duke, aren't we, so we are safe."

It's the Duke we may not be safe from, Rodolfo.

No, it's the Duke *I* may not be safe from. He has not sent one of his men to murder me—yet—but I am sure that he has not forgotten how I failed him.

Wednesday

Caterina is well enough to rise. She has spent much of the day sleeping in her favorite chair by the kitchen fire, her thick red blanket wrapped around her legs. I am seated at the table, drawing with charcoal, trying to copy the way the light cast by the flames falls on her face. It is the hardest thing in the world to draw light and shade, but it is also the most important. An artist who cannot draw the difference between day and night may as well spend his time in a barrel.

Whether the Master is working or not, I am. I spend two hours every day copying from his sketchbooks. A little more each week adds up to a lot more every month.

In the afternoon I go to Tombi for another lesson in colors. This is my ninth.

Thursday

I have been experimenting with a pen made from a goose quill. The Master buys these feathers by the dozen, cuts and shapes the ends with a very sharp knife, making the points broad or fine, according to his needs. I have borrowed one of his old ones to practice with. The quill is very responsive to the force of the hand. Every stroke must be clean; the slightest pressure can change a line from thin to fat. For more shadow, you make more lines—but not too many. How much paper I have already used up, trying to obtain the right effect! We have almost run out again.

Tomorrow I will visit Benedetti. Perhaps Emilia will be there. Please let her be there!

Friday

The baker Bagliotti came to our house and asked if any word had been received from the Master concerning payment. I had to tell him that no word has been received from the Master on *any* subject, because he is at the Castle. Very well, Bagliotti says. So be it, he says. If that's the way it is, he says. And strides off.

In the afternoon, I head for Benedetti's shop. I have a surprise for Emilia. On the way I buy myself a big chunk of Maiden's Promise, which is a sweet made from cinnamon, nutmeg, ginger, and aniseed, all hidden inside a powdered sugar coating. If you ever had doubts before, a bite into this will reassure you that Heaven really does exist. I am so eager to see Emilia, I eat the whole thing!

And here I am, the wooden sign above the shop swinging a bit in the wind.

BENEDETTI † PAPER MERCHANT
"NEVER OUT OF STOCK"

The door is open and inside there is paper, paper, paper everywhere! White, green, gray, yellow, light blue. Parchments, all types. Boards, bindings, blocks, and bookmaking materials.

The shop has clean white walls, and the large front windows let in plenty of light. Oh, it is a marvelous sight! The shelves are stacked high with clean, fresh, fragrant, inviting paper!

Benedetti is standing in the center of the room. The shop is shaking with buyers. Government officials in black and white robes, their medallions of office proudly displayed on their chests. Poets (I suspect, by their inky fingers) scratching their beards. Clerics. Bankers. Everyone is bantering and bartering with Benedetti, who stands firm like the captain of a galleon, directing his assistants hither and thither to satisfy his customers.

And there is Emilia in a green dress, her dark brown hair tucked under a cloth cap, running to and fro with stacks of paper, as keen and able as any of her father's men. By Saint Barbara, she is beautiful!

Benedetti sees me enter.

"Giacomo, my boy, welcome, welcome. Emilia, look who's here!"

But Emilia is too occupied to notice me.

"Need some paper? I thought so. Emilia will see to you in a moment."

And when she has finished with her customer, she turns to me and smiles. It is a lovely smile—an invitation to dance, do somersaults, sing French *chansons*, and generally fall over myself like a bad tumbler.

I'll just smile back. That's easier. But my lips are quivering, which makes it harder.

"Good day, Giacomo," she says. "I've been wondering when you would come by—excuse me a moment. Father, Messer

Fidero wants five hundred sheets of the plain middle weight. Oh, we are so busy here today. And the Duke wants a thousand sheets printed, too."

"Oh? What is the announcement?"

"It's war, Giacomo. Haven't you heard? War against France."

So it's official. Any Frenchman living in the city will be ordered to leave. No more French wines on the tables of the rich.

"My father tells me you are an artist, too," she says.

"Still a student," I reply.

"How much paper would you like?"

"I'll take whatever you can spare, Emilia."

And I promise to pay for every page, if my master will not paint your father.

"Here's a hundred sheets. It's not our best—"

"But, Emilia, it's too fine for me. Give me some of—"

"Nonsense. Take it, Giacomo, with my father's blessing."

He'll soon be cursing me when he finds out what has happened with the Last Supper. Now he is calling for her from across the room.

"I must go. Please come and see us again," she says.

"Before I do, this is for you."

And I hand her the drawing I have been laboring over for days.

"What, Giacomo? Oh . . . it's me!"

Thanks be to Saint Catherine, the patron saint of artists—Emilia recognizes herself!

And now she is blushing. That is a good sign, I think.

Caterina says blushing invites the interest of the Devil. Let him come!

She is still looking at it, a big, beautiful smile on her face.

"Oh, it's very, very good. Father, look! Giacomo has drawn me!"

"I'll go now," I say. But only to come back again.

And she smiles at me some more, before running over to her father with the drawing.

And I run all the way home, a smile on *my* face.

Saturday

Two more days until . . . oh Master, where are you?

And then, just as swiftly as he disappeared, he returns.

He tells me he has finished his work on the flying machine and left Maggio and his assistants to complete the gluing and underpinning.

Then I remind him about the shopkeepers.

"Master," I say, "they are going to take us to the Court of Justice on Monday. But if you would agree to use them as models for the Disciples—"

"Giacomo," he says, "please. I am worn out."

He leans over the mantel above the fire and rests his head on his forearm. I watch him while the fire burns down to a soft glow.

"Master, what is wrong?"

"Wrong? Everything." He takes his purse from his belt and holds it open for me. Empty. "After all the years of labor, I have nothing but debts and no means to repay them."

He throws his purse into the fire!

"No house. No land. No reward. Curse the Duke, I say! What does he know of art? What does he care for the agony of creation? The endless time necessary to contemplate and prepare the work and, once begun, the innumerable daily labors—labors that would make Hercules himself hang his head in defeat!—before the result can be achieved. Why, Giacomo, only a fool would call himself artist; it is a life filled with hesitation before the work, uncertainty during it, and regret afterwards."

"Master, your art has made you famous and will be your future monument. Is that not reward enough?"

"I have no time to think of the future, when the present demands all my attention." He yawns and stretches. "I must rise early on the morrow and go to Santa Maria."

He turns away, and I follow him out of the kitchen. He plucks a book from the shelf, lights a candle from the fire, and prepares to ascend the stairs to his bed. When he is halfway up I call to him: "Master? Have you thought any more about my painting lessons?"

I bite my tongue. You *fool*, Giacomo. Now is not the time—look how tired he is.

He stops as if to reply, but continues to slowly mount the stairs, until both he and his candle have melted into the shadows.

Later, I poke my head inside Caterina's door. She is asleep, her breathing quiet and steady. I hold up the candle to her face; her skin is so thin I can see the blood flowing beneath it. So many broken veins on her cheeks. So many years of labor. And for what? What has been her reward for a life of faithful servitude?

Sunday

As still and sad a Sunday as I have ever experienced. The Master leaves the house early and does not return until very late.

I go for a walk along the canal.

Some winter days hang like ghosts over the streets, turning familiar paths into foreign places.

Perhaps I'll call at Benedetti's house and see if Emilia is at home.

No. I can't do that. Not until I find the courage to tell him that the agreement we made has been forbidden by my master. And I'll owe him the ten ducats I took. And the money for the paper. When Emilia finds out how foolish and rash I have been, how I have humiliated her father, she will never look at me again.

Anyway, tomorrow the bailiffs will come for us, just as soon as the shopkeepers have made their complaint and the Court of Justice has sworn out the warrant for the Master's arrest. I won't be seeing anyone for a long, long time.

Monday

The Master summons me to his study. I have been praying to the Virgin for a miracle. And I get one.

"You win, Giacomo."

"I do?"

"I cannot risk an appearance in court. If I end up in jail, I can hardly finish the Last Supper, and I will not have it finished by Mich-Michel—"

"Michelangelo?"

"Yes. Him."

"Master, do you mean—?"

"You may advise those impatient shopkeepers that I agree to paint them in return for canceling my debts. Yes, Giacomo. I will use them as my models for the Disciples."

Without thinking, I do a little jump and clap my hands together.

"You will, Master?"

"The more I think on it, the more I think of it. Why *not* paint the faces of our industrious Milanese? They have as much right to be on the wall of the refectory as any of the Duke's noblemen. He wants me to decide for myself? Very well then, I will. I am resolved, Giacomo; I will use your merchants and paint the refectory wall, whether it is damp or not. We have delayed long enough. Now let us set to work!"

My feelings precisely, Master—let us set to work!

We have Benedetti's agreement, and I am sure, after what they said to me outside the refectory, that I will obtain the approval of Rossi, Bagliotti, Peroni, and Fazio. That would be five, with seven to go to make up the twelve. I relate this to the Master.

"Eleven. The face of Judas is already settled."

I dare not ask who he has chosen for that infamous role; whoever it is will not be content when he discovers it.

"And our Lord?"

"That I have not decided. If the Duke is so keen for me to finish the painting quickly, perhaps, as he once said in jest, I should use *your* face as the model for Jesus."

I cross my fingers. Oh yes, Master, choose me, choose me!

He smiles. How that fills my heart with warmth. If he would only do it once a day, I would not need a new winter shirt.

"You would use my face, Master? Really?"

Or do my ears play tricks on me, as they have done before when something I badly wanted to hear turned out to be a lie?

"We shall consider it, boy. But, for now, bring me your tradesmen and shopkeepers—bring me the whole of merchant Milan, if you must—but tell them there is to be no discussion of who sits where at the table. I am the artist and will make the artistic decisions. Are we understood?"

"Yes, Master!"

"Then don't stand there gaping at me! Go your ways!"

After all my wishing, worrying, and waiting, he changes his mind just like that.

So I set off to find Fazio, Bagliotti, Rossi, and Peroni.

I know I have done the right thing when the four merchants greet me and my news most enthusiastically later that same day. Not only will they clear our debts, they will each pay me ten ducats (forty ducats in my purse, God's truth!)—and they are more than eager to tell their friends of their good fortune. That will make it easier for me to approach the other merchants and fill the remaining places.

That night, after I have given the Master the money (he took it without a great show of thanks, which was disappointing), I sit down and count up some of the other merchants I might approach to exchange our debts for a place in the Last

Supper. There are plenty to choose from. I've just now made a list of the most promising, along with their trades, and the goods we have not paid for.

Bernardo Maggio. Carpenter. Master's bed, chests, platform for Last Supper.
Lorenzo Delitto. Goldsmith. Master's gold cross and chain.
Vittorio Veroli. Shoemaker. Master's shoes and boots (various).
Gregorio Rinnucci. Saddler. Master's saddle with silver stirrups.
Cesare Cabrera. Swordsmith. Master's rapier with decorated hilt.
Girolamo Martino. Tailor. Master's black cloak, two jerkins, five undershirts.
Paolo Vecchio. Tailor. Master's other cloak (red), doublet, hose (four pairs?).
Pierfrancesco Festa. Bookseller. Master's books: too many to list on one page!

But what about Tombi?

The Master owes him as much as any of these merchants.

And I owe him much more. Not only has he been teaching me about paint, he introduced me to Ottavio Assanti, who will soon restore my memory.

But how *can* I offer Tombi a place in the Last Supper? I have to keep him away from the Master, who would surely pluck from him the whole truth about my pact with Assanti.

XXIX

I arrange for the sittings and the Master chooses Fazio to begin. They meet at the refectory, and the Master is not late, nor does he leave until he has made many sketches of the subject.

Fazio returns the next day, and the next, and the next, until the Master has made a full-sized drawing of his face. Then he makes small holes in the outline and features of the face on the paper; when that is done he takes the drawing, pins it to the wall (not so difficult, because of the dampness), and, using a small bag filled with soot, taps it against the paper (artists call this pouncing, which makes you think of a cat jumping on a rat).

After he has covered the drawing several times, he unpins it, and—behold! The soot has penetrated the little holes and left an outline of Fazio's face on the wall, exactly as the Master drew it!

(When he sees this, Fazio stands up, astonished. The Master thanks him and tells him not to sit down again, it is time for him to leave.)

Then the Master takes his paintbrushes, oil, and colors and begins to fill in the outline. Before another few days, we have Fazio's face, wrinkles and all, up there on the wall.

And then the Master asks me to summon Rossi.

The days pass, and I see little more of him than the front door opening and closing. He seems to have put aside all hesitation and doubt. I do not want to take the credit for this (not all of it, anyway), but I cannot help thinking that some of his newfound purpose may have been caused by the thought that the more he paints, the quicker he rids himself of his debts. In the meantime, the money I have given him from the shopkeepers serves to pay for our food and firewood.

And then, one afternoon, with the Master hard at work on Bagliotti's face, and me in attendance watching from the shadows (a blanket around my shoulders—it is so cold in here, I don't know why the Master's fingers don't freeze), the refectory doors swing open. Vanni, the husband of Caterina's friend Margareta, appears with his dog, Poppo, a scratch-haired old fleabag whose excess of girth attests to a lifetime of overindulgence by his owners.

"Giacomo! Master Leonardo! It's Caterina!"

No. Please, *no.*

"My wife says come quickly, come quickly!"

We do not need to be told twice. The Master sets down his brushes, throws on his cloak, and we both make for the door. The four of us hasten back to the Master's house.

Margareta is kneeling by Caterina's bedside as we enter the

room. It is hot and smells of something bad. Her skin is the pale yellow of wax; her eyes are closed.

"Giacomo, fetch me some water in a jug, and a cloth. Bring the green box from the shelf in my study. Here, take the key."

"Master," says Margareta, "will our Caterina die?"

When I return, they are waiting for me outside Caterina's room.

"She wanted to speak to you, Giacomo," Margareta says. "You were the one she asked for. May the Lord have mercy on her soul! Poor Caterina!" And with this, her tears start to fall. Vanni comforts her, and while he does so, Poppo takes the opportunity to lie down on the floor for a sleep. I go to the Master.

"Wet the cloth and wipe her brow, Giacomo," he says.

He opens the green box, pulls out a vial of powder, and pours the contents into a cup, adding water from the jug. The result is a dark brown mixture that does not give the appearance, or the odor, of being pleasurable to drink. I draw the damp cloth across her brow and cheeks. The Master holds up her head with his left hand and gently presses the rim of the cup to her lips. She sips. Swallows. Her eyes open. She coughs, twice. Her hand reaches out.

"Giacomo?" she says.

I come closer.

"Giacomo," she breathes into my ear, "Giacomo, listen . . ."

The Master rises from the bed. "Caterina, this is not the time to tax yourself with talk. You must rest."

"I'll be resting soon enough, Master."

The Master hesitates a moment, as if he is about to say something more, then leaves the room.

"Is the door closed?" Caterina asks. "Now, while I have the strength, I will answer you all those questions that I have been avoiding until now. But God has shown me that I must tell you all, everything—"

"Everything?"

"About our master. And me." She puts her hand on mine. "And you."

Her voice is so low that I can hear my heart beating above it, *thud, thud, thud.* I hold her hand more tightly. She takes a deep breath, and the light in her eyes grows stronger.

"It was fifteen years ago. I had been your master's housekeeper but a few months, when one night he knocks on the door of my room and pleads with me to accompany him to a house on the Arengo Square. To help deliver a baby, he says. Would I refuse such a request? Water . . ."

I put the cup to her lips. She sips.

"Inside was a young girl—fifteen or sixteen, at most. I saw she was in terrible pain, sweating and moaning, but radiant as Saint Catherine in her agony. The Master went to the bed. He took the girl's hand."

"Please, Caterina—please go on," I say.

"I did not have much to do at first, except heat and fetch the water—the Master did not leave the girl's side, and it was he who mopped her brow and spoke words of encouragement. The girl's spasms came and went for hours."

I try to breathe slowly, but my thoughts are flying around inside my head like the birds trapped in the Cathedral vaulting, of which there are many. I put my hands over my eyes to calm myself. What if . . . ?

"Suddenly it began. The girl cried out: 'Oh, Leonardo, I shall die, I shall die!' I began pressing on her down there to help the baby find its way out. And then the Master said: 'Have courage, dearest Cecilia!'"

"Did you say *Cecilia*?"

"Aye, I did. Now don't—"

"Caterina, describe this Cecilia to me."

And so she does. Before she has said five words, I know that her Cecilia is the same one in my master's portrait: Cecilia Gallerani. *My* Cecilia.

"Are you still listening, boy?"

Listening? I could not listen harder had I ten heads and the ears to go with them.

"After the infant was born, she lay there, poor thing, quite exhausted, but as lovely as any angel at rest."

"And this was the year you came to the Master's house?"

"Yes. 1482."

The year of my birth, so my master has told me. And he would know! *He would know!* This is what I have been looking for all my life. The truth about my parents.

"But you must not think—"

"I need not *think*, Caterina—I *know*. I am that child."

She holds up her hand as if to halt me.

"No, Giacomo, wait—"

"Look at me, Caterina! I am not an orphan, a thief, a servant. I am *someone*—I am the son of Leonardo da Vinci!"

This is why he has kept me in his house all these years. And why he could never tell me—because of the Duke, who became Cecilia's lover soon after I was born! To tell me would have put her—all three of us—in peril.

I am going to confront my master. *I am your son. I am the son of Leonardo da Vinci and Cecilia Gallerani.* The thought of standing before him and telling him what I know fills me with so much hope and fear I think I will split in two and fly to the opposite ends of the earth.

"Giacomo, I promised the Master never to speak of this matter to anyone, and I have broken that promise." She looks at me most pitifully. "I do not know whether you are the son of Cecilia and the Master, but, if you are, you should be told. God forgive me for speaking what I can no longer keep to myself. The Master is a great man, and he has his reasons, but the truth belongs to those who need to know it, not those who try to hide it."

"I promise that I will use what you have told me honorably, Caterina."

"Now I must seek my master," she says.

"He is nearby, Caterina. I'll go—"

"No, Giacomo, my *master*. The One . . ."

She closes her eyes. She no longer has the strength to resist the pull of the Earth; and soon her soul will be as light as air, rising on wings to its destination.

For long minutes I sit by her side, watching her slow breathing. Sometimes her lips move; she is praying.

Outside, a cart is being pulled across the stones, its wheels scraping and squeaking, the driver cursing the ass for its slowness.

I cannot tell you what goes through my head at this time. All I can do now is hold her hand, although it no longer seems to belong to her.

And then she sighs, and I suddenly understand that I will never see her again—"You will not die! I will not let you! What will I do if you go?" I cry.

And she replies, in a voice more like an echo, as if she has already left me: "You will find your way, Giacomo, as we all must do: alone."

The strain departs from her face and she looks at peace.

She sleeps.

"Caterina?"

Her breathing has stopped.

"*Caterina?* Master! She is going! Help, Master, save her!"

The Master flings open the door. He bends over the old woman and listens to her heart.

"Don't let her die, Master," I say. "Please, please don't let her die."

"Nothing to be done," he says. "She is gone, Giacomo."

Then he pulls up the sheet and covers her face.

I cover my face, too, with my hands.

"Death is one puzzle even I cannot solve." He looks at me as if he would say something more, then turns away.

Oh God. Oh God. Oh God. Why did you have to take her?

Soon Father Cristofano, the priest from the Church of San Giorgio, arrives, but too late—too late to take her confession. Caterina is dead. She, of all people most deserving, has died without being absolved of her sins. But what sins can the Lord hold against her? Surely Saint Peter will open the Gates of Heaven without question and give her entry to the place she has been looking forward to all her life.

May God have mercy on her soul.

I go to my room and lie down on the bed. In spite of my grief, which threatens to overwhelm me, I cannot weep. I am too angry to weep. Instead, my body seeks solace in sleep.

When I awake it is night.

I find the Master in the kitchen. He is eating something with great vigor, but the thought of food makes my stomach turn inside out.

"An old woman," he says, "and not as foolish as some."

He goes on eating. Is that all he has to say?

"She was our friend, Master. Should we not show her some grief?"

"I leave the outward show of grief to those who wish to impress others with it. Caterina was my servant. She will receive a decent burial, if I can find the money. That is how I will show my respect for her, and that is enough. She is gone, boy. Be happy that she is free of her cares at last."

The Master's words are like a freezing wind that leaves you

gasping for breath. Is that how he feels? Then perhaps he has no feeling left; perhaps it has all gone into his art, for others to feel what he cannot.

The doctor, Grimaldi, comes from two streets away. For five soldi he gives us a paper certifying her death.

The Master has called for Bernardo Maggio to make the coffin. I show him into Caterina's room. She is wrapped now in her white sheet.

Maggio produces his stick and begins measuring her.

"Oh, this is sad," he says, "too sad. She often said to me that one day I would make a chair for her, one with a high back, such as a fine lady might sit on. And now she has a coffin instead."

We both look at poor Caterina, dressed for her final journey. Maggio continues with the measuring. He gives me quick glances, as if he wants to say something, but cannot decide when to do it.

So I decide for him. "Messer Maggio, whatever it is you want to talk about, please do not let Caterina's death hinder you. We are friends, and friends may speak, whatever the time."

"Well, I thank you, lad. This is not the right moment for such a conversation, but I confess the matter has been on my mind too much of late."

"Yes?"

Maggio returns the measuring stick to his bag of tools.

"Why hasn't your master offered me a place at Christ's table? Benedetti is in, I hear. Fazio, Rossi, Peroni, and Bagliotti are in. Why not I, his faithful carpenter?"

So that's the difficulty! Easily solved, then.

"Will you agree to the same arrangement I made with them?" I say.

"You know I will, Giacomo, or I would not have asked!"

"You'll cancel his debts and pay us the ten ducats?"

"I'll clear everything he owes me before I started work on the flying machine—but, for all my work on that, and the materials, I think it only fair that I be paid an additional fee."

"Agreed," I say. We shake hands on it. Neither he nor my master will ever see any money for the flying machine, given that the Duke suspects my master was planning to sell it outside of Milan.

"Oh, but this is a great day for me and for all of Milan's carpenters," Maggio says. "We are looked down on by the other guilds, don't ask me why, when Jesus himself was one."

I tell him that a carpenter has as much right as any other fellow to sit with our Lord. After all, without a carpenter there would have been no table for the Last Supper.

"Why, I never thought of it like that," Maggio says, with a laugh.

"May I have the ten ducats now?" I ask.

"I'll have to bring you them later; I came out in a rush," he says.

"And deduct the money you gave me while the Master was away," I say. "It saved our skins."

"God's blood, Giacomo, am I really going to be in the Last Supper?"

"You'll be there until the paint falls off the wall, Messer Maggio."

Which may not be a time too distant, if the dampness spreads unchecked.

"I'll be back with Caterina's coffin, and your money, as soon as I can," he says.

Maggio shakes my hand again, picks up his bag, begins whistling a tune, and leaves.

The day passes.

I sit in Caterina's room and try to pray, but my thoughts drift here and there like leaves blown by a random wind. What should I do? Should I tell the Master what I now know—what Caterina told me, the secret of my birth? I rise. I sit down again. I cannot speak to him. I do not yet have the courage. I will have to wait until I do.

Word of Caterina's death travels down our local streets faster than the fire in the bakery behind the Church of San Lorenzo a year ago, which almost took the church with it. People soon begin to knock on our door to pay their respects. Caterina has many friends that I have never seen before, and only a few of them have the bitten fingernails and darting eyes of hardened dicers.

Eventually, the last mourner leaves and the knocking on the door ceases.

I replace those candles around Caterina's coffin that have gone out and sit down in a chair next to her. Now I feel a great tiredness. I rest my forehead against the smooth wood of the coffin.

Giacomo?

Yes? Is that you, Caterina?

I like it here.

You do? Oh, that makes me so happy!

I don't have to cook a thing, it's all done for me. Tonight we had pheasant baked in raspberry juice. And they gave me warm milk and honey laced with spices before bed. Every Tuesday there's a dice game, and I'm allowed to win as much as I want. Oh, and I've seen my husband, Giorgio, and he's well. Better than one could hope for, seeing he's been dead all this time. But age means nothing up here. He said to me, he said he thought I was never going to get here, he'd been waiting so long. I told him that he shouldn't have left me so quickly, then, and we both laughed. Oh, Giacomo, don't fear death; it's just the beginning. Just the beginning, Giacomo, not the end, not the—

XXX

"Giacomo! Giacomo!"

"Uh? Master? What—what time is it?"

"After sunup. What, have you been sitting here all night? The funeral has been set for midday."

"Where were you, Master?" My head feels as if it has been stuffed with straw.

"The Last Supper. I worked like someone possessed. As if God had given me a new arm. Do you have the rest of those heads ready for me to paint?"

"I'll bring you one today." The good Maggio.

"I have paid out fifty soldi for the funeral arrangements," he says. "Father Cristofano and the curate will be here at eleven. Be ready for them. I am going to sleep for an hour or so."

"Yes, Master."

"Wake me when they arrive."

"Yes, Master."

"Do not forget."

Yes, Master, yes, yes, yes.

The floor is dirty. When Caterina sees it, she will surely—but she won't. She won't see any of my hasty cleaning ever again. Oh, Caterina, I promise to scrub the house top to bottom, so that when you look down on me from Heaven, you are not ashamed of my work.

I throw open the window shutters and the front door to let in the fresh air. I bring out a pail of water and wash down the steps. And then I fetch the long-handled broom and sweep the street all the way to the juniper tree.

On my return to the house, a group of some dozen local merchants and tradesmen (most of them on that list I made) are standing at the door. And at the front is Messer Benedetti, his hand raised.

"Ah, Giacomo, there you are. I was just about to knock."

"You can save yourself the exercise," I say. "If your friends have come for money, they must go away disappointed. Today we bury our Caterina."

"No, Giacomo, you've got it wrong. These fine gentlemen are not here for your master's money; on the contrary, they're here to cancel your master's debts. If you can promise them seats at our Lord's table in the Last Supper, that is." He moves closer to me. "Bagliotti and his friends have been boasting about it all over town. You didn't tell me that others were being offered a place!"

"I didn't say they weren't."

"Yes, well, it rather takes the shine off for me. Nonetheless—"

Nonetheless, I do not think you will complain too loudly and risk losing your own seat at the table.

"Caterina's funeral is set for midday. We do not have time to conclude the matter now. Let us meet tonight—at the Seven Knaves."

"Very good," Benedetti says. He shakes my hand and leads the merchants away.

Two hours later, the Master awakes, in time for us to welcome Father Cristofano, his curate, a priest, and four coffin bearers.

We make our procession to the Church of San Giorgio, and there we bury Caterina. Then the Master returns to the Last Supper and I to home.

The rest of the day I spend in my room.

I lie on my bed and think about what has happened and what will.

Caterina is gone forever. She has given me my life at the same time as she has taken from me her own. And now that I know the truth, I must find the right time to face the Master and tell him what I know. But when? If he never trusted me before with the knowledge that I am his son—thinking that because I cannot control my tongue, I would one day let slip to someone that he and Cecilia are my parents—why would he change his decision now?

He might even try to convince me that Caterina did not tell the truth!

But I cannot keep this to myself, I will not. I have waited too many years to discover the truth. But I must hear it from his own mouth. I will confront him, whatever the consequences.

When? Of course, when Cecilia comes to visit us. That's the perfect time—with both of them here together, they will have to confess. If the Master tries to deny me, Cecilia will prevent him. He must have been preparing to tell me, anyway. He cannot complain if I have discovered the truth sooner than he anticipated—he knows I am a fast learner!

But now that I have uncovered my past, I no longer need Assanti's help to restore my memory. I will have to tell Tombi as much.

The bells are ringing for late Mass as I hurry towards the Seven Knaves. The streets are strangely silent tonight, as if everyone has been commanded to stay indoors as a sign of respect for my friend's death.

But the quieter the streets, the more I feel that someone is following me and means to do some mischief. Perhaps Tommaso and his devil-friends are watching me even now, patiently waiting for the moment to strike. And the Duke? Perhaps my master really did settle the matter, and I have nothing to fear. He said he would, after all. And now that he has the flying machine, perhaps the Duke has put me out of his mind. But the Master's dealings with the Duke are never certain. My instincts tell me that I am not yet safe.

At last! I am here. I thrust open the rusted hinges of

Jacopo's citadel, and the scene greets me with its customary warm embrace. I feel better on the instant.

I am studying a group of shoeless friars in thick black robes grouped around the fire and raising cups to one another's health in a strange language, when Jacopo's wife, Marta, pats me on the back.

"Nice burial, was it, Giacomo? Poor Caterina, we were sorry to see her go, but we've all got to go sometime, as my husband says when he is closing up the tavern and kicking out the drunks! Speaking of my lord and master, he has settled your company in the back room." She laughs and returns to her business, lifting foaming cups and brimming goblets, the Venus of the tavern, the goddess of the grape.

Through the old curtain and into the back room, to be greeted by cheers and shouts. I'll soon settle them down.

"Gentlemen, please!" I say. "Today was the funeral of my master's faithful housekeeper, Caterina. Show some respect, I implore you." And that's the first time I've ever had the pleasure of telling others to pay the respect that I'm usually accused of not paying myself.

But I got their attention. They're all looking at me now. Then Gregorio Rinnucci, the saddler, raises his finger and points at me: "Respect, the young fellow says! Respect! Your master owes *me* respect—and fifty ducats!—for the fine saddle of leather with silver stirrups. Lovely work, if I say so myself. Now, I want in on this Last Supper!"

"Stand in line, then," says Lorenzo Delitto, the goldsmith, elbowing his way forward. "Giacomo, you know me—"

"He knows me better than you, Delitto," Rinnucci says, giving him a shove.

I hardly know either of them, except to run when they come for money.

"Pah! I was serving Master Leonardo when you were still an apprentice," Delitto says.

"And I'll still be serving him when you're lying three braccia under the earth!" Rinnucci retorts.

"Well, who gets to be in the Last Supper?" And that's Paolo Vecchio, the tailor.

"Gentlemen! Gentlemen!" I raise my voice above the hubbub. "We must decide this matter in a seemly manner. Please be seated."

The merchants do so, pushing and shoving for the best places on the two long benches.

"That's right," Benedetti says. "Behave yourselves, or Giacomo will cancel the auction."

"Auction?" someone says. "Nobody said it was to be an auction!"

And the uproar commences once more.

"Gentlemen! If you cannot restrain yourselves, I am leaving!"

Oh, that shut them up. This is more fun than sweeping the yard! Nobody except Caterina ever listened to me before, and even she with only one ear—now I have Milan hanging on my words like silken bell ropes.

So I begin, and what comes out is a surprise, even to me.

"Messer Benedetti," I say, "the Master sends you his greetings and bids me tell you that your seat at the Last Supper is no longer assured."

His brow furrows; time to sow the seed.

"We have been offered more by others who wish to take your place."

The colors in Benedetti's face run into one another. The result is a kind of green.

"What," he starts to say, "is . . . *this*?" It ends as a shout.

The other merchants look at Benedetti. Then they bend towards me, all ears.

"It is simple, sir. There are certain persons who most earnestly desire to be seated at Christ's table, and they are prepared to bid higher for the honor."

"*Who* is prepared to bid higher?"

"I cannot tell you that, Messer Benedetti. The question is whether you are willing to ensure your place by offering a sum that is agreeable to the Master."

I want to laugh out loud! Never have I had such a feeling of power. Indeed, I've never had any feeling of power at all, until now.

"This is madness, Giacomo!" Benedetti says. "It's not what we agreed."

"I'll pay!" says Girolamo Martino, another tailor the Master owes. "I'll cancel Leonardo's debts and give him a new cloak with fox trimming! What else would he like?"

"He'd like twenty ducats in addition," I say. Ten more than the last lot paid. And why not.

To which Martino replies forthwith: "Very good! His debts

are gone, he'll have twenty ducats, and I'll make him a new cloak—all for a place at our Lord's table!"

"Your master has owed me for two years past," says Rinnucci, the saddler, his voice rising to make itself heard, "but I forgive the debt. He can have his twenty ducats as well, and I'll throw in a new saddle, free of charge. What say you, Giacomo?"

Then they all rise from their seats and begin speaking at once; it sounds like the Monday cattle auction outside the New Gate.

"Gentlemen, you do me wrong, when I am so honest with you," I say. "You mock my master with your miserliness!"

Really, I have to clench my teeth to stop the laughter.

They stare at me, mouths agape. But not for long. Another one stands up—I don't know his name—and says: "Leonardo's debts to me are canceled, if he will grant me a place at the table. And I will give him three pairs of—"

"—Shoes and a pair of soft leather boots for you, Giacomo," Veroli, the shoemaker, finishes the sentence. Now, that is a proposition worth considering. New boots, without having to foot the bill!

Delitto is back again: "I'll make your master an ivory medallion inlaid with gold, with his name on it in Latin: *Leonardus Pinctor Magnificus.* A gift, and freely given. Who can match that?"

"I can, for one!" The bookseller Pierfrancesco Festa is pressing a book bound in soft red leather into my hands. "I have the only copy in Lombardy of Pliny's *Natural History*!

Yes, that's right, its value is greater than gold, the Duke was after me for it—but your master can have it, if he will paint me seated near Christ in the Last Supper. And he need not pay me for the books he still owes: the two by Pulci, the *Epistles* of Filelfo, and the others. I can't remember all the names in this madhouse!"

"Gentlemen," I say, "I thank you, but we have only five places left—"

"Five? We heard six!"

"Here, Giacomo, listen here! Come and live with me on my country estate near Pavia! Fish in my private river on weekends! Just get me a place at this supper, wherever it is, I cannot bear to miss a good meal! I am Gherardi, the banker. Call me Ercole, my dearest friend!"

"Sir," I say, "do you know the name Leonardo?"

"Leonardo . . . Leonardo . . . I know a Leonardo Zanetti, he makes wine barrels. Is that the one?"

"Off with you, sir, you are in the wrong tavern!" I say.

"Gentlemen! Gentlemen!" Benedetti is still trying to keep order. And failing.

Delitto and Rinnucci are pushing and shoving each other, Veroli punches Vecchio's shoulder, and Vecchio tries to kick him in the shins—and misses. There is much hurling of angry threats and bitter curses.

Then some fellow—I thought he was asleep, his head on the table—sits up and says: "Shir, from your young lipsh come the wordsh of a gentlemans, and I am a gentlemans, sho I will respond to them." He stands up and sways over the table. "What shlay you—what shay you to four hunnerd, four hundred ducatsh and my daughter for a place at the Lush Sipper? Thus shpeaks Count Girolamo di Berto . . . da Campo . . . Fregoso!"

My first thought is: How did you get in here, you old sponge? My second is: Four hundred ducats? Saint Matthew! And his daughter, too? Well, I'd have to take a look at her first. But, no, that won't be necessary. We do not want or need a gentleman at the Last Supper; indeed, I insist we have no gentleman, highborn or self-proclaimed, especially one the length of whose name will leave no room at the table for anyone else.

"Sir," I say, "we thank you for your generosity. But the bidding is between friends. I cannot accept your offer."

"Do not inshult me, shir," Count Girolamo says, reaching for his weapon. He makes two full turns, like a dog chasing its tail, before he gets a hold of it.

My hand goes to my dagger.

But Jacopo's short, strong arm holds mine in place.

"Have a care, Giacomo." Then, turning to the gentleman, Jacopo says: "Sir, the boy means no offense. And he is right. This is a private meeting. Not knowing who invited you or why, we must ask you to leave."

"Well, shir," the Count says, trying to pull his sword from its scabbard, "if I mush leave, I'll take every one of you devilsh with me!"

While the gentleman is once more struggling with his weapon, Jacopo turns, picks up a cask as if it was a paperweight, and drops it squarely on his head. The Count collapses into his cloak and falls to the sawdust floor with no more sound than a stuffed pillow.

"I'll lug his lordship to the neighboring tavern, The Falling Star," Jacopo says, "and when he wakes up, he'll more than likely have forgotten what happened or why. Continue with your business, gentlemen. More wine in here, Marta!"

While the others are being served, I confer with Benedetti, whose face has not yet regained its former aspect. Drawing closer to his ear, I whisper: "I am using you as bait to raise the price of admission to the other tradesmen. You have been a friend to Leonardo da Vinci, sir, and I am a man of my word." A man of my word! I like the sound of that, yes I do. "Your seat in the Last Supper is secure."

Benedetti's face straightway finds its original, happier composition.

"I knew you were a clever lad," he says, "but this is the height of cunning! Brave boy! Your master will be proud of you, I warrant."

I had hopes that he might feel that way, yes.

Let the bargaining begin.

Between cups of wine and chunks of spit-roasted mutton, long into the night, with Messer Benedetti acting as my help, and with a strong word from him to whoever uses one on me, I make an end to the question of who should be seated in the Last Supper.

And this is what has been decided: the remaining five places will be taken up by Pierfrancesco Festa, who has already given me the valuable copy of Pliny's *Natural*

History to take to the Master; Cesare Cabrera, the swordsmith, who has offered a silver dagger with a pearl handle for his place; Lorenzo Delitto, the goldsmith, who has promised to start work on the gold-and-ivory medallion as soon as he returns to his shop; Vittorio Veroli—new shoes for the Master, new boots for me, and free repairs for as long as we are in Milan; and Girolamo Martino, the tailor, who promises a new cloak trimmed with fur for my master, and a new jerkin and three shirts for me.

What is more, they each agree to cancel all debts incurred by the Master and to pay nineteen ducats in coin. (And they are overjoyed, too, because I asked for twenty and let them beat me down!)

And I'm taking the money now. We need it, after all.

While those tradesmen who have been fortunate enough to gain their places in the Last Supper congratulate one another, I commiserate with the other members of our auction who would not bid, or bid enough. I am thankful there is no ill feeling. We all shake hands, and Jacopo shows them out.

"Messer Benedetti, my thanks—and Leonardo da Vinci's. You have not yet been to sit for him, and he is waiting for you. Do not be tardy, sir, or your place may be taken—"

"What? Let's have no more of that, Giacomo, please! I'll be there tomorrow, first thing!"

Benedetti wraps his arm around my shoulders and asks if he can bring his wife as well. Without a doubt, Benedetti, without a doubt.

"And Emilia, too," I say. "If she can be spared from the shop."

"Business first, Giacomo," Benedetti says, smiling, "but I dare say I can let her out for an hour. She showed me your drawing. Now, my boy, why didn't you tell me you were such a fine artist?"

"Because I am not, Messer Benedetti. Not yet."

Dawn is breaking when I emerge from the tavern; the darker sky is rent apart with gashes of pink and rose. I feel newly born into the world, and my hopes are high. I have not drunk a cup all night—what need have I of drink, when my success in this venture gives me more pleasure than any wine? I have cleared all our outstanding debts and, in addition, can hand over ninety-five ducats to my master. (Not forgetting that rare copy of Pliny's *Natural History*.)

Look what I have accomplished, Master—and think how much more I will be capable of when you recognize me as your true son.

XXXI

“Master?”

“Master?”

No answer. I run upstairs. His door is open. He lies on his back, his arm across his chest, breathing heavily.

Wake up, Master, wake up, I have excellent news to tell you!

In the kitchen I start up the fire. Nearly out of wood again. So many things to think about now that Caterina is gone. I put the money from the shopkeepers in the clay pot, and then I take two buckets and go down the street to the well. The air is cold, but it is refreshing.

The buckets full, I start for home. Some water goes into the pot over the fire for heating. The rest into our drinking barrel. I take the broom and begin the housework. To my astonishment, I need neither rest nor sleep. My night’s work has given me strength, not taken it away.

An hour later, he appears in his robe.

“Anything to eat?” he says.

Now he expects me to cook for him, too?

“Wait here, Master, a moment.”

I run to my room and bring back Festa's book.

"Master—this is for you, from Pierfrancesco Festa. Look! It is a book you have long coveted, is it not? And listen to this: I have made the contract with the other merchants. Our debts are erased, and in addition you will have a new dagger from Cabrera, shoes from Veroli, an ivory-and-gold medallion from Delitto—"

"What? What is all this, boy? You are making no sense."

"Don't you understand, Master? In return for painting their faces in the Last Supper, the merchants have agreed to cancel our debts. And I got more out of them, too—they were so eager to be in the painting that they offered us gifts and money. I have ninety-five ducats for you!"

"You do? I don't believe it!"

"Well, look in the pot."

He hesitates—probably thinking I will play the same trick on him he once played on me, claiming there is money inside when there isn't.

He goes to the shelf and picks up the pot. Yes, Master, it's heavy, isn't it!

Then he pours out the coins onto the table.

Ninety-five ducats, the Duke's head on every one of them. More money than we've ever had in the house, I swear.

"They paid this money to you of their own free will?" he says.

Does he think I robbed them all at knifepoint?

"Well, well," he says, when I do not answer. "I see I must thank you, then."

Not if it's too much trouble.

"I'll take the money to my study and lock it in the coffer for safety."

We go together, and when he has done that, he says: "Thank you, Giacomo, you may go now."

I bring him ninety-five ducats and I get no more thanks than for one.

"Master, when would you like me to bring these merchants to Santa Maria delle Grazie to sit for you?"

"Mmm?"

He has this habit of drifting away like an unmoored boat at the very moment he should be anchored firmly before the coming storm.

"Master!"

"You are worse than a wife, Giacomo. I can never remove you from my ear. What is it now?"

"The merchants, Master, when may I bring them to the refectory?"

"Did I not already say? Bid them come to me one by one. Now go."

"Yes, Master."

"And you may bring the first four to see what I have done. They are finished."

"What? Fazio and—?"

"Yes, yes, Rossi, Bagliotti, and the other one."

"Peroni."

"Peroni. The one who tried to murder me. Yes, him."

"Oh, Master, that cheese was not his fault, you know."

He says nothing. He goes back to his drawings. And just as I am passing through the door, he says: "I have received another letter from Cecilia, boy. She is coming to Milan at the end of next month."

Cecilia! She will soon be here. My waiting is almost over.

"Did you ask the Duke whether you could have her painting?" I say.

"He will never agree to that. She will have to live without it."

But that was what she said she could *not* do.

And then, because he does not seem to care that it is Cecilia's dearest wish, I say: "We could take it ourselves in secret from the Duke's gallery, Master. You have the key. He would never miss it, after all. It sits in the dark among a hundred other paintings."

"That is exactly the kind of foolish suggestion that will get us both thrown into one of the Castle dungeons, boy. And we have already come too close to that of late. Let me not hear such talk again."

"Yes, Master."

Then he says he is going to the Last Supper, and to be ready to take an order to Tombi.

"Give me some money, please," I say.

"Money? I have no money."

"Master, I just gave you ninety-five ducats!"

He writes out the order and reluctantly, very reluctantly, unlocks the coffer, puts his hand inside, and pulls out a ducat for the colors he needs. I am never asking for credit from any of our friends again, I vow. If the Master won't give me the coins, he can go himself.

"And don't forget the change," he says, as I am leaving.

Outside, the sky is a delicate pale yellow that makes me think of dried saffron, Caterina's favorite herb. She told me once that it did wonders for the lungs, chest, and liver. And I said to her: "What about the elbows, feet, and ears?" She cuffed me round the head for that one. Oh, I will miss her slaps as much as her hugs.

I hand Tombi the order (*Cinabrese*, *Giallorino*, and *Lac*) and relate Caterina's story from start to finish.

"How can you be so certain that you are Leonardo da Vinci's son?" Tombi asks.

"The date of my birth, for one. My master said that I was eight years old when he found me, which means I was born in 1482—the same year as the child. Also my blond hair, which is very like Cecilia's. And a letter from her to my master, in which she called me 'our Giacomo.' Are they not proofs enough?"

"Perhaps. But you are failing to answer one important question, boy."

"Which is?"

"Why your master has never told you that he is your father." Tombi waves his finger at me. "There's the hole in your story," he says. "And it's big enough to lose all your other evidence in!"

I smile. I already know the answer to that one. I tell Tombi that if my master's secret had been discovered, all three of us would more than likely have been murdered by the Duke for betraying and humiliating him.

Tombi nods his head once. I think he believes it, too.

"Remember one thing, Giacomo," he says. "The truth is never given out in one piece to the seeker, like a slice of pie to a hungry man; it must be assembled from many parts."

"Sometimes, Messer Tombi, the truth is standing right next to you."

"And what about your contract with the Second Brother, Master Assanti?"

"Well, I have found my past now, so I do not need him to find it for me."

Tombi looks at me. He says nothing.

"Did you hear me, Messer Tombi? I don't need his help now."

"You made an agreement with us, Giacomo."

"I have not forgotten."

"But it appears that you have, because you no longer wish to honor it."

"Perhaps this is all for the best, my discovering the truth without the alchemist's help. I have not been at peace with the thought that I was deceiving my master."

Tombi nods slowly.

"May I have the colors now, sir? I must meet my master at the Last Supper."

"Be careful, Giacomo, that the devil lurking in every man's soul does not take possession of yours."

"Messer Tombi, I have seen enough of devils to know how to fend them off."

"It is the Devil's talent that he makes everyone think that, boy."

"Please tell Master Assanti that I offer my apologies. No doubt a man with his powers will find another way to meet the Pope."

Tombi says nothing, and I leave.

Later that evening, the Master calls me to the study.

"Tomorrow," he says, "I want you to take the portrait of Lucrezia to the Castle. The Duke is calling for it."

That's the last place I want to go. It would be like putting my head, covered in honey, into a bear's mouth. And asking it to bite down hard.

"Master, I cannot return to the Castle."

"Why not? You have nothing to fear from the Duke."

"So you say. But I have failed him once already and never explained myself. He will surely want to do me some ill."

"I already told you I would take care of the matter. The Duke will not lay a hand on you. Do you want to be of help to me or not?"

"You *know* I do, Master."

"Then take the portrait of Lucrezia to the Castle tomorrow. Now off with you. I have work to do."

"Master?"

"Yes, what is it?"

"Have you yet decided who will be the face of Jesus?"

"I will decide that when it is time."

"It would be a great honor—"

"Yes, it would. Now leave me, please."

"Don't be late for supper, Master. I'm making a pie."

"So you *can* cook, can you?"

"Be in good time tonight, Master, and you will find out."

So it's back to the Castle. At least I can be sure of one thing this time: I will not be carrying the Medusa, which I know is sitting in the Duke's gallery, slowly gathering dust.

XXXII

Early the next day the Master gives me the portrait of Lucrezia, bound in silk cloth and tied with leather bands, and I set off for the Castle once again.

Within a hundred paces I am sweating, but I cannot be sure whether that is because I fear losing the painting to some thief, or because I fear another meeting with the Duke. Whatever the reason, I clutch the painting to my side and hurry on, my eyes searching the crowd for villainous faces.

At every street corner there is one of Benedetti's printed sheets announcing the coming war with France, and a crowd of people fighting with one another to get a closer look at the contents.

And soon I am at the Castle entrance.

"What's your business, lad?" the gatekeeper asks. A new man, and a friendlier one than the last, thanks be to Saint Francis.

This time the gates are opened almost as soon as the

words are out of my mouth. The Duke must be panting for his painting!

A man-at-arms escorts me across the Castle grounds, and once again I mount staircases and stride down hallways, until I find myself in the immense room with mirrors and tapestries.

The Duke and Lucrezia are already seated and talking softly to each other. Today she is wearing a dress of forest green, threaded with gold. Her hair is twined with tiny glittering pearls. The smell of her perfume settles over me like a soft mist, turning my legs to jelly.

I stand at attention and wait for them to acknowledge me. After some time, the Duke looks up and says: "Why did he not bring it himself?"

"My lord, the Master is hard at work on the Last Supper."

"He is? We hear nothing of it."

"The Master will send for you and the Lady Lucrezia, my lord. Very soon."

"Good. And tell him that I will require a demonstration of his flying machine."

"I believe the flying machine awaits your pleasure, sire."

"Now show me the painting."

I undo the ties, the silk cloth slips off, and Lucrezia sees her face looking back at her.

She raises a hand to her cheek (not a good sign, oh dear), then rises from her seat and comes towards the painting.

She stops in front of it. I hold it up, the better for her to see. It is not a large painting, just a wood panel, unframed, an arm's length in height and three-quarters that in width.

She turns to the Duke.

"I do not like it. Your painter has made me look like a German."

"But, Lucrezia, Leonardo has bestowed on you every quality a woman could ask for: grace, elegance—"

"He has given me a parrot's beak for lips! And why am I looking upwards, as if I were watching the clouds? I told your painter that I wanted to look directly ahead, so that my eyes would be always meeting yours, Ludovico. He has disobeyed me—worse, by disobeying me, he has disobeyed you!"

"Come now, Lucrezia, your face is tempting enough to make a priest break all his vows and run to—"

"And he has painted shadows on my neck—it makes me look as if I have three chins!"

"Nonsense, Lu—"

"It is an entirely new method, Lady Lucrezia, invented by my master," I say, "a blending of color and shadow that makes the subject's flesh look as natural as in life."

"I do not want to look *natural*—I want to look *perfect*!"

She turns away and walks back to the Duke.

"I will not look at it. Take it away. I will not look at it ever again. *Never!*"

The Duke takes her hand.

"Lucrezia, my precious, my angel—"

"I told you I wanted Capponi and Felloni. You gave me Leonardo. He has never liked me. I told you he would try to humiliate me. And now he has. If I ever see this painting again, my lord, do not think of coming to my bed."

She rises and walks out of the room without another glance at him or me.

The doors close behind her.

The Duke looks as if he has just had his stomach removed. But he soon recovers his senses and turns to me, saying: "Ha ha! This is what I love about her—her passion. When you are older, boy, you will see how sweetly a fiery temper lends itself to lovemaking. Desire and anger are the most potent of mixtures, and when they meet, they burn with a force no comfortable love can match. I will go to her room now and console her."

"What about the painting, my lord?"

"Take it back to—no, go with my captain to the gallery and lodge it there. And, while you are there, now I think on it, find the Medusa and return it to your master. We have tried to look at it; we cannot. There is something more than evil in that face. It stares at us as if we have committed some crime! Take the Medusa, boy, take it far from the Castle, and leave the portrait of Lucrezia in its place."

I wrap the painting in its cloth once more.

"Now then, I must go to my love before she cools."

The Duke signals to the guards standing by the doors, which are instantly held open for his departure.

"One thing more, my lord," I say. "Now that my master is well advanced in painting the Last Supper, will you honor us by dismissing Michelangelo from the Castle?"

The Duke laughs. "He was never here, boy. I put it about to hasten your master's progress. Leonardo is not the only one who can play tricks, you know!"

"Thank you, my lord."

"And," the Duke says, "do not think I have forgotten that you never made your report to me concerning Leonardo's invention."

"Sire, I—"

"Never mind. I obtained it from another source. You are forgiven. Now that the flying machine is mine."

At the door the Duke speaks to the captain and then disappears from sight. I take the portrait of Lucrezia and follow this fellow until I once more arrive at the entrance to the Duke's gallery. The captain looks to his ring of keys and, after several attempts to find the right one, succeeds in opening the lock.

"In you go, boy, and be quick about the Duke's business."

"Are you not coming with me, Captain?"

I can feel a bead of sweat work its way down between my shoulder blades.

"Do I look like someone who would enter the Duke's gallery? I have no business with art, nor it with me. All paintings are an affront to God's eyes, and if He will not look at them, neither will I. So, in you go, lad, leave whatever it is you're leaving and take whatever it is you're taking, as the Duke commanded. I'll be waiting."

And I won't be delaying.

Once more I enter the tomblike room. This time I know how to find the curtains, and I only trip once before I succeed in opening them.

First, unwrap the Lucrezia and set it down somewhere.

On that easel. Now to find the portrait of Cecilia. When the Master and I were here before, it was on the wall opposite the windows, near the center. But it no longer seems to be there.

I cast my eyes up and down, right and left.

"Have you finished in there, boy? They're ringing the bell for me."

Where in the name of Saint Peter is it?

But what's that empty space halfway up the wall, a square without dust?

Of course! The nail has come out of the wall and Cecilia has fallen on top of a stack of paintings. Ah, there she is, face down. You should never be facing the earth, dearest Cecilia—your beauty was meant to bedazzle the heavens!

Now to wrap it up in the cloth, tie the bands, and hope that nobody wants to inspect it before I leave the Castle.

And nobody does, thank God.

I walk down the Sforza Way with the portrait of Cecilia Gallerani tight under my arm. *I have rescued Cecilia!* The Duke can keep his Medusa, like it or not (I hid it behind a stack of other panels), and Cecilia will have her youthful likeness returned to her.

I have done for her what my master's painting skills could not—set her free, at last.

I'll hide the panel under my bed. It won't leave my room. Cecilia is coming soon! Cecilia, my own dear mother!

The next day, the Master says to me: "Was the Duke pleased with my Lucrezia?"

"Oh yes, Master, most gratified." *She* wasn't, but I'll let that rest.

"I dare say the lady had some complaints, eh?"

"Why, Master—"

"I wanted her to see herself as I see her: a vain, sensual, proud temptress."

"Nonetheless, Master, for all Lucrezia's faults, you did not neglect to show her beauty."

"Giacomo, what is the difference between a beautiful woman and an ugly one?"

And before I can answer, the Master says: "It is not the way she looks, but the way she is seen. I painted them both as they are in life. But, to me, Cecilia is an angel from Heaven, and Lucrezia was sent here from the other place."

You haven't had your brow mopped by her, Master, or you'd soon change your mind about that.

XXXIII

What time is it?

What time is it? Still dark. Morning has advanced no nearer than night has retreated.

I had a dream. Nothing strange in that, but it was a strange dream, as many are. Even as I try to recapture it, it eludes me—away it flies, away, on soft wings, lighter even than a thought. All that remains is the feeling that something was about to happen, something was—some*body* was—

Somebody *is*—in my room!

"Who's there?"

I sit up—where's my dagger? Where? Have the two intruders returned to the house to put an end to me? Where is the Master?

A solid black shape, no more than an arm's length from my bed. Growing bigger, blacker, blooming, spreading, unfurling, a blackness enveloping me—

"Master? Master, no!"

"Your Master is not here."

"Wh-who are you?"

"Have you forgotten me so soon?"

Is it him—the alchemist, Master Assanti? I can see nothing through the dense blackness.

"Do not be afeared."

Yes, it is!

"But, how did you enter—?"

"Tombi tells me you wish to cancel our contract."

His voice fills my head. How near is he? Near enough to strike? The air grows heavy around me and it takes all my strength to remain upright.

"Well, boy? Does he speak truly?"

"Master, I did not—"

"Do you feel the air around you pressing down? I could crush you like chalk between my fingers, if I so wished. Turn you to a powder and mix you into a potion to cure forgetfulness. You made an agreement with me, boy. Nobody dismisses Ottavio Assanti."

I can hardly breathe. He's taking away the air—he's going to suffocate me! Saint Catherine, have mercy!

"Master—" I gasp.

"You *will* help me to my audience with Pope Alexander."

"Yes."

"And willingly."

"Yes, Master."

"And you will be rewarded for your part. I will teach you a secret that only I can give you, and only you will ever receive."

"Yes, Master."

"It will be something given only once in a lifetime," he says. "Do you understand?"

"Yes, Master."

The air seems less dense, easier to breathe. Whatever spell he cast on me is lifting.

"Now tell me when the Pope will visit the Last Supper," he says.

"Before he leads the Easter Mass on Holy Sunday at the Cathedral. We are still to learn the day and time."

"When you know, you will straightway inform Tombi. Say nothing to your master—*nothing*, do you hear—or you will never learn from me what I have to teach you."

"Yes, sir."

"You are a servant, Giacomo, but what you will become is something only I am aware of. And it is more, much more than you may imagine."

"Will I become a great artist?"

No answer.

The room grows lighter. The black turns to gray.

The alchemist is gone.

I lie back down on the bed, trembling.

Can I trust this alchemist? I have no choice. Tombi warned me that a man as powerful as Assanti might act unpredictably. I have seen proof of that now. But he has promised to tell me a secret, something that only I may know. Yes, Assanti means to do me some good if I please him, I am sure of it. I must carry out my part.

If only I could tell the Master. But that is not possible. Assanti would certainly discover it.

What can I do but follow the course I have already set and pray to God that all will be well.

XXXIV

The great work is

The great work is slowly taking shape.

And the Master, though he might delay and delay when he is not ready to begin, when he is, he will not move from his task for hours or days, his hand moving over the painting like a bird in flight, only the light around him changing, while he remains constant.

When I come at midday with bread and cheese, he holds the brush in one hand and feeds himself with the other. In the afternoon I bring him a drink of water. He takes a sip and sends me away. When it is time for his evening meal, he tells me to leave it on the kitchen table. He often returns after I have gone to bed. And some nights he does not come home at all, taking his rest on the platform in front of the Last Supper.

The landscape of trees and meadows and sky seen through the windows behind our Lord is finished. The ceiling above Jesus and the Disciples is also done (the Master has chosen to paint it in the guise of wood panels). The table and cloth on which sit the bread, plates, dishes, and glasses—all are close to completion. There is still much to be done on the walls to the right and left of the table, and, of course, on the Disciples themselves.

In between working on the background and the table, the Master has been painting the faces of the five merchants who were successful in bidding for their places in the Last Supper. But will it be done before the Pope arrives? Though the Master works without cease, we have no more than seven weeks left.

Truth be told, I do not think he can finish it in time. Even if he had two new arms, each one holding two brushes.

Then, one morning, at Santa Maria delle Grazie, he says to me: "I will not finish it in time."

There he goes, reading my mind again.

He wipes his brow with a cloth, leaving a small streak of paint behind.

"Master, your forehead has a blue—"

"Giacomo, do not interrupt me, please. I was about to ask you if you would do something for me."

"With pleasure, Master."

"Something useful."

Very comical, Master.

"Help me to finish the Last Supper."

"Master!"

"Sit down, boy. Do not wave your arms like that, and do not speak until I have finished telling you what I want."

"Yes, Master."

"I just told you not to speak!"

"Yes, Master. I mean, no."

"You are to do exactly as I say."

I nod. I wave my arms a bit more.

"Tell me you have understood."

"Why yes, Master. But you told me not to—"

"Enough! Now listen: I want two things. The first is to cover with my special varnish that part of the wall I have painted each day. Can you do that?"

"Why yes, Master, of course."

"And the other way you can help me, after I have instructed you, is to mix my oil with the colors, in readiness for me to paint."

"Master, will you really—?"

"And may God help both of us if you do not repay my trust."

"You need ask no help from God, Master. I will do the job myself."

"What do you know about colors?" he asks.

What do I know about colors!!

And I explain how Messer Tombi has been teaching me these past months and how I know all about where colors come from, what they are made of, how to grind them, mix them with water, and prepare them for use.

"All this time Tombi has been teaching you?"

"Yes, Master."

"And he never told me."

"Perhaps he thought you might be angry with him."

"Why would I be?"

"Because *you* do not want to teach me."

"That is something else entirely."

"Why won't you teach me, Master?"

He tilts his head. "Eh?"

"Is it because you hate the thought that I might become more than a mere servant?"

"You *are* more than a mere servant. You are Leonardo da Vinci's servant. That makes you much more than a servant to me, Giacomo. You know that."

Do I, Master? How much more than a servant—as much as a son?

"Now then," he says, "will you help me or no?"

"You know I will, Master. And you will see how quick I am about it."

"But you are not to paint on the Last Supper. Not a smear. Is that understood, Giacomo?"

I nod again.

"Do you think that anyone may become an artist, merely because he has the intention? Do you?"

"No, Master."

"Every man has a dream. Dreaming is man's balm and comfort, his recompense for an unendurable life. But, for most men, a dream is all they will ever have. They are not prepared for the years of hard work and perseverance required of them."

"Yes, Master."

"Very well. You will start tomorrow. Now please bring me the next merchant."

✦ ✦ ✦

With every step home, my humor improves. Tomorrow I will help the Master. And the next day, well, the next day the Master might turn around and help me!

I am walking down the Sforza Way, when from behind I hear three rapid blasts on a horn—and I turn to see the Duke's heralds, a dozen of them in capes of black and gold, running down the road in lockstep, at full speed.

They halt near the Fountain of Graces, and a crowd gathers.

When a hundred or more folk are milling around, there is a lengthy fanfare on the horn, and one of the heralds is lifted up above the crowd. Then he proclaims in a mighty voice: "By Order of the Duke of Milan, harken this! War against France! The Duke calls on all men older than fifteen years to enlist in his army, for the glory of Milan. The French enemy is at our borders. The Duke has decreed that they will advance no farther! All honorable men be present this Sunday at the Eastern Gate, from midday. Free uniform and two meals a day. Join the Duke's army now, for the defense of our great city! By Order of His Excellency, Duke Ludovico, High Guardian of Milan, Most Benevolent Protector of Lombardy!"

Another three blasts on the horn and off they run to broadcast the message at their next stop.

Voluntary recruitment, is it now? And how long before volunteers become conscripts, and every man with more than one leg is forced to sign up? The Duke's army has been shredded by all the petty wars with his neighbors; he will need every one of us, if we are to offer the French some real opposition. All the more reason why the Master and I must leave Milan—I'm not going to war for the Duke, to lose a hand or an arm in the fray! How would I hold a paintbrush then?

The next day, just after sunup, the Master and I walk together to the Last Supper.

He watches over me as I varnish the wall with the brush. The varnish is as thick as pitch and as hard to spread. I make each stroke with care, again and again, until the surface is smooth and free of bubbles and holes. My wrist aches badly and my fingers are already blistering.

"You'll have to work faster, boy, or I might as well do it myself," he says.

"Yes, Master."

I expected him to find fault at first. And I *will* go faster, too, just as soon as my hand stops shaking.

The morning passes. My shaking stops. I work faster. The Master looks better disposed towards me. He inspects my work and nods. At midday we open the basket and eat the bread, cheese, and fruit I packed.

When he has finished eating, the Master drains the water from his leather gourd, wipes his mouth, and goes to his bag. From it he pulls out a drawing, turns it the right way round, and hands it to me. He says: "Do you know who drew this?"

It's the drawing of Master Assanti. I forgot to remove it from inside his sketchbook, where I put it that night! All that time spent worrying when I would show him my work, and he found it for himself.

"I did, Master."

"I know you did. Who else could have left a drawing tucked inside one of my sketchbooks? Indeed, who else could have been taking my sketchbooks from my shelves and copying my drawings? I know what you have been doing, boy. For some time now."

He knows everything. Why has he said nothing before?

"It's not a bad drawing."

"It isn't?" I say.

"No, it isn't. Why have you never shown me any of your drawings?"

Oh, Master, it's hard to explain. You see, I never felt worthy of you and my work was not good enough and I was worried you would laugh and then I knew you did not want to teach me and I am only a servant and—

"I don't know, Master."

"Who is the owner of the face?"

Oh, let me not have to explain Master Assanti.

"Master, it's just some fell—"

"It is Ottavio Assanti. I could never forget that nose and those eyes. Or the sound of his voice. It is impossible to stop up his prattling."

"You *know* him, Master?"

"Oh, yes. I know him of old."

"But, how—?"

He gives me a long look. Presses his lips together. Furrows his brow. And sighs. (Signs I know well: he is about to tell me something astonishing.)

"I studied alchemy for five years. In Florence, a long time ago."

Whaaaaaat?

"That medallion you keep in your box is mine. It was given to me . . . by Ottavio Assanti of the Brotherhood."

Now, this is too amazing, even for my ears. They'll fall off the sides of my head with this news, I swear.

"No, Master! You told me that alchemy—"

"Was neither art nor science, but their unholy offspring," he says.

"A fantasy born of ignorance, practiced by people who suffer from the same deficiency."

"I commend you on your memory, boy."

"But, Master—"

"And I would not, could not have made those assertions had I not seen for myself that alchemy is a wasteful pursuit, of little use to mankind, but of much greater use to rogues who seek to gull the gullible. Gullible people like the Duke."

"Why did you spend five years studying it, then, Master?"

"I wanted to learn what alchemy could and could not do. And it is capable of the latter far more than the former. In other words, it has little merit. But how would I have known that if I had not delved into it most thoroughly?"

"But why did you give the medallion to *me*, Master?"

"A good question, Giacomo, and worthy of answer. But I do not have one. All I can say is that I did not yet wish to dispose of it, but neither did I want it near me. So I gave it to you. A gift, if you like."

"Master, you do not know how much time I have wasted on fruitless speculation concerning that medallion—how I came to have it, and what I was or might have been to its former owner. Could you not have told me?"

"I just did. Now I want to know where you saw Assanti, what he was doing, and why you drew him. In fact, everything."

I have to think quickly. I can't tell him about Tombi, about my contract, about what I must do at the Last Supper.

So I cook up a story involving the Duke, my trip to the Castle, the Medusa, and my medallion. And how I met the alchemist, briefly. And at the end of it, my master says: "But why did the Duke never tell me that Assanti was working for him?"

"Assanti's presence here is a closely guarded secret, isn't it, Master? What with all the French spies in the city. The Duke swore me to silence."

The Master nods, slowly.

"Very well," he says. "For now, let us continue with the Last Supper. The afternoon is under way and I do not wish to waste the light."

And we continue with our work. But although I give the wall my every attention, I cannot help wondering if the Master is satisfied with the story I told him about the alchemist.

Side by side we work on the Last Supper. Every day I mix the oil with the colors he plans to use that day, and then he paints. And when he has finished painting, I varnish the part of the wall he has painted. And so it goes on. By Saint Peter, it looks as if we are going to do it in time!

Then, a month before Easter, he tells me that he will finish the painting alone, and that I am no longer needed.

This upsets me greatly, but instead of getting into an argument, I thank him for the chance to work by his side. I tell him that I have learned a lot. But I also tell him that I still have a lot to learn. I think he understands my meaning.

XXXV

Two weeks have passed. They caught some French spies trying to pass through the Roman Gate. There was an announcement. And now there's going to be a burning.

It's evening. Claudio, Antonio, and I are met at the Seven Knaves.

We have seen nothing of Renzo since New Year's Eve. The story is going round that he has run off with a girl, one Patrizia Bandino, who works at the market with her mother, selling fish. But I begin to suspect that he has been knifed by some villain; he has always been quick to anger, and I have had to pull him away from a brawl more than once.

Antonio has been watching me strangely.

"What is it?" I ask him.

"Nothing," he says.

"Nothing?"

"Are you going to join up?" he says.

"The Duke's army? No, I'm not."

"Don't you want to fight against the French?" he says. "I'm going to the Eastern Gate tomorrow."

"I want to be an artist, Antonio, not a soldier."

"Artist? Pah! You're a coward, Giacomo, that's the truth of it."

"You may think that war is a fine thing from afar, but I doubt you will be so pleased with it if you come home without an arm or a leg."

Or not at all.

"I do not fear dying," he says. "It is an honor to die for the Duke of Milan."

"Perhaps, but I doubt the Duke would do the same for you."

"That's treason, talk like that."

"Only if someone overhears us," I say. "We can speak plainly to each other, can't we?"

He says nothing and looks away. If what we witnessed last Saint Michael's Day is any guide, Antonio will more likely run behind a tree at the sound of the first cannon.

"And you, Claudio?" he says. "What about you?"

"Me? Why, I—"

"Another coward!" Antonio says. "A pair of weaklings."

"Antonio," I say, "think hard before you do this. There's no going back."

"There's no going back anyway. I've been ordered to leave my master's house."

"Why?"

"It doesn't matter. But I cannot stay there. It's the army or the street."

He probably stole something and tried to sell it, if I know Antonio. So much for honor and glory.

"Are you so keen to hurry to your death in battle," I ask, "that you won't stop a while longer with your friends and talk it through?"

"I'm done with talking," Antonio says. "I have but one more word for you: Farewell."

Antonio gets up to leave and pushes his way through the crowd.

"Are we cowards?" Claudio says. "For not wanting to fight?"

"I don't care what he calls me," I say. "An artist fights another kind of battle."

But Antonio's taunt is not so easily forgotten. Or forgiven. We stare into our cups.

"What happened on New Year's Eve?" I say, hoping for happy news.

"Oh, that. I drank too much. I don't think they will invite me again."

"Ah, I'm sorry for you."

"I was a fool to hope for more," Claudio says. "In future I'll stick to servants for friends and marry a laundry girl. Come with me to the burning, Giacomo, eh? You are my best friend, you know."

I have no wish to go to a burning, but I'll keep Claudio company as far as the main square, then turn back for home.

We make our way towards the Cathedral, and the closer we come to it, the slower our progress. I have not seen a crowd like this since last year's midsummer carnival, when the big attraction was twenty whores whipped naked through the streets. Their crime? They were Venetians, and they took away trade from the local girls.

The mood is festive; the crowd is merry. Are we really about to see a burning, or the celebrations marking a new saint? No, it's a burning, all right, and what a burning it will be. Three enormous bonfires, still unlit, are piled to the sky—they must be taller than the trees they were cut from.

The mob is pressed up against these stacks of firewood, and everyone, young and old, is shouting and hollering. At the pinnacle of each of the three bonfires, high, high above the ground, is a human form tied and bound to a stake. One with his head hanging down, another twisting from side to side, the third—Saint Francis, it's a woman!

Now the priests are making the sign of the Cross. Now the burning torches are thrust into the branches.

The fires spark and catch, and in a few moments there is a *whoosh!* as the flames ignite the dry wood.

A huge cheer goes up from the crowd. I have lost sight of Claudio. The crowd pushes against me, eager for the kill. As the fires take hold, silence falls over the multitude. For a time, all that can be heard is the crackling and snapping of the wood. The flames circle, hesitate, and then, sensing no resistance, attack the inner branches. Within a minute, all is blazing orange, yellow, and red.

The fire has licked the feet of one fellow, and he screams. This brings renewed cheers and whoops from the crowd. The tethered figures are swiftly enveloped by the flames. Soon they will be as blackened and charred as pigs on the spit.

I have to leave this accursed scene now, as quickly as possible—I can take no more of this brutality. At last, after what feels like an hour of pushing and a gallon of sweat, I have made my way through the mass of onlookers, whose faces, lit up by the flames and twisted into strange shapes by their shouting, no longer seem human at all, but like lost souls in Purgatory.

I sit down in a doorway. Sundry groups of Milanese pass by: wives, mothers, sons, fathers, rich and poor—they are in such a fine mood, laughing and smiling as if the world was a sanctuary of goodness and love, instead of a damnable hell pit. When the wind turns in my direction, the smell of roasting meat—*burning human flesh*—penetrates my lungs before I can stop up my nose. It is horrible, horrible. The noise from the square rises and falls with the wind.

I raise myself at last and turn in the direction of home. There is a strange tremor in the air, it is heavy and bloated, as if a storm was about to break. The moon, milky and clouded, hangs over the rooftops like a blind man's eye, seeing nothing of the madness going on below.

I wander I know not where and find myself in a small garden square. In the middle stands a tree, beneath it a stone bench. I sit down, trembling with passion and exhaustion. I do not recognize this place. How did I come here?

"Gia . . . co . . . *mo*!"

"Giacomooooooooh!"

"Who's there?" It can't be—

"You're ours now, gypsy boy!"

They've found me. My heart doubles its pace. Oh God, what should I—I'll run, I can still—but in which direction? Their voices seem to come from everywhere—

"We've been waiting for you, Giac-Giac-Giacomo!"

The fight against the apprentices was just practice. This is war.

Now four figures separate themselves from the gloom: Tommaso, Marcantonio, and their cronies, Simone of the bulging eyes and Filippo, the pinch-face.

"Good evening, Giacomo," Tommaso says. "Taking the air?"

"Giac, Giac, Giacomo!"

"Shut up, Filippo."

I reach for my dagger.

By all the Saints, it's not there! I forgot to wear it today!

I stand up, my back to the tree, and wait for my enemies to draw closer.

I will not go wherever I am sent, be it Heaven's bright halls or Hell's burning fires, without a fight.

"What is it you want?" I say.

"Only what you owe," Marcantonio says. "Your life."

"I owe my life to God alone," I say.

"Your death is what God will get," Tommaso says. "A suitable gift from a peasant who will never have anything else of value."

The cold night air rakes a claw across my cheek, but I am sweating, either from fear or eagerness to start the fight, although I suspect the former.

"Kneel, Giacomo," Simone says. "Kneel and take your punishment."

"Never."

"If you don't do it willingly," Tommaso says, "you'll do it anyway."

"I prefer to die."

Filippo says: "Oh, you'll die, all right. But not until we say so."

At a nod from Tommaso, they rush me. I land a solid blow under Filippo's jaw with the flat of my hand. He falls away. Simone, the half-wit, starts laughing at that; I use the moment to kick him between the legs. He gasps and doubles over. Tommaso has crept behind me and now catches hold of my arms, but he has come too close and I butt him with the back of my head, grazing his chin—

He lets out a roar of dismay.

"You urchin!" He wraps a forearm around my neck and pulls tight. "I'll make you hurt for that."

Though I can scarce breathe, these words fill me with alarm and set me to work swinging and kicking with all my might. Little use in that, however; with Tommaso on my back they have soon pulled me down to the ground. My arms and legs are held apart like a staked animal.

I cannot move.

The wine they have already consumed comes off them in hot, foul-smelling gusts. Marcantonio's face floats above me; he wrenches back my head until I think my neck will break. I twist and spit in his eye. Got him! He slams my head to the ground.

"Tommaso, I want him dead—*now*," he says, wiping his face.

"Somebody—help! Help!" The only response is the sound of a window being shuttered. "Summon the Nightwatch!"

My fear is gaining mastery over me, my legs and arms have lost all their strength. I twist and turn, but they have too many hands. A heavy knee comes down like the blacksmith's hammer on my back.

"Someone! Some—"

A kick to my side and my ribs twang like lute strings, knocking the breath out. There is no more struggle left in me. I am done. I lie still.

"Pull him up, boys, and let's see him beg for his life," Tommaso says.

Filippo and Simone take hold under my arms and haul me onto my knees.

Dear God, forgive me for my sins and for all my—

"Leave him be, you sacks of toad venom!"

Eh? I raise my head. Instead of letting me die, God has sent me a vision of my friend Renzo. I blink once, twice. He's coming towards me. It *is* him! My friend is here to save me!

Tommaso's cronies are so taken aback that they drop my arms and freeze. Meanwhile, I get to my feet and, clutching my sides, stagger towards Renzo.

Tommaso recovers first. "Draw your rapiers, gentlemen," he says, "and let us skewer these pieces of rough meat!"

"No weapons," Renzo says. "Fight hand to hand, like men, if you are men, which I am not yet inclined to believe, when you can set four onto one and call it sport."

"Well, well—we'll sheathe," Tommaso says. "Simone, give me a hand breaking the head of this villainous clown. Marcantonio, you and Filippo stifle Giacomo until I am ready for him."

Renzo curses and spits. "Remember Saint Michael's Day, Giacomo," he says, "and show them that servants are made of stronger stuff than they know!"

Tommaso shouts: "Come, gentlemen, for the Duke and our family honor, let us send the peasants crawling back to their sties!"

We meet them in the middle of the square, man on man, and they are more than us, but we are many in spirit.

Marcantonio roars at me and charges, but I know him now for a rash opponent and quickly move aside, giving his thigh a furious kick as I do. He cries out and falls. Filippo, who already received a jaw blow from me, is more wary. He picks up a stone and moves in a circle, waiting to strike.

But a more thrilling fight is taking place a few paces hence.

Tommaso is as well-proportioned as a thoroughbred horse. Renzo is tall and skinny, a human ferret. When they have at each other, Tommaso has the sinew and the straight back, but Renzo has the quick and unerring strike of the rat killer. After exchanging several glancing blows, they set to grappling. Tommaso tries to twist Renzo's head off his shoulders, Renzo answers that with an elbow in Tommaso's gut—he staggers—Renzo turns, and without further hesitation calmly jabs his thumbs into Tommaso's eyes—sending him backwards, screaming.

Simone waits neither to help Tommaso nor to see what tortures Renzo may have in store for him; he turns and runs like a proper gentleman, which is to say, like any fearful peasant.

Renzo laughs. And that makes me smile. I haven't smiled for hours, and it feels exceedingly good. My friend is back!

As soon as Marcantonio and Filippo see what has happened to Tommaso, they too retreat like whipped dogs and, each taking a separate point of the compass, disappear into the shadows.

Tommaso, meanwhile, is on his knees, still cupping his eyes.

"I'll have you both murdered!" he shouts into the air.

Renzo laughs. "No, you won't," he says. And he kicks Tommaso in the behind, toppling him to the ground, where he remains.

"Leave my friend in peace," Renzo says, leaning over him, "or I will leave you in pieces, so help me God."

There is no sound from Tommaso, who has always loved the sound of his own voice. He is either too scared or too hurt to respond.

And then we hear—

"Hold right there, you two! The Nightwatch commands it, in the name of the Duke!"

Someone did summon them, after all. Milan is full of surprises. But they're too late to help me. As the old saying goes: The Nightwatch is never at hand when you need it, and always ready to lay a hand on you when you don't.

They've brought the hounds with them, too, by the frenzied baying and barking I can hear on the other side of the square.

Renzo lifts his legs and I follow his example. We run into the darkness.

If they catch us, there won't be any excuse we can make to save our hides. All we can hope for is that Tommaso keeps his mouth shut. I think he will. He'll say he was set upon by two robbers, rather than risk having his throat slit later by my friend.

Now Renzo is pulling my arm—*Which way? Over there, then, down that alley*—another twenty paces, and—a high wall. No way out!

They are almost on our backs—we can hear shouts, barks, wild oaths—

I'll try this doorway. *Come on, open up, curse you!*

We put our shoulders to the door and it cracks open just as the Nightwatch enters the alley. We leap in.

Blackness.

Voices outside.

"Did they go down this one?"

"I didn't see. Tonio, go and look."

"Yes, chief."

Footsteps passing by. A dog panting.

"Do you smell 'em, boy? Get 'em, Duke! Tear their legs off!"

Angels of grace defend us, they are on the other side of the door! The dog is barking and scraping at it with his paw—

"What's that, eh, boy? Are they in there?"

"Have you got them, Tonio?"

"Hold on, chief! Ach, you stupid animal, leave that alone! He's only gone and found an old bone! Come off that, you brute!"

The dog lets out a whine. A kick in the ribs, must be. I know what that feels like now.

"Then get yourself and that idiot dog back here and let's finish our rounds."

"What about the lad with the bloody eyes?"

"Taken home to his father. Who knows if—"

I miss the rest; they are too far away.

We listen until the night silence has once more been restored.

Only then do we open the door.

When we are safely away, I take my friend's hand and say: "Thank you, Renzo. If I have ever said a bad word against you—and I fear I have, God forgive me—I take them all back twice on my own head. You saved my life tonight."

"It was an honor to be of service, my lord," Renzo says, bowing low with a flourish.

"Can you jest so soon after a fight almost to the death?" I say.

"Why not? Life is a comedy, Giacomo. We should all laugh before we die."

"What does that mean?"

"It means that in doing you harm I did you good."

"What? What *harm* were you doing me? I owe you my life!"

He looks away. "It was not by chance that our paths crossed tonight."

"It wasn't? Then you'd better tell me the truth," I say.

And when he turns to face me again, I see—guilt. But for what, and why?

"The truth, then," he says. "Though I wish it were a lie."

The night air seems warmer now, but the sweat drying on my back wraps a chill around my whole body. My ribs are aching, and I can barely move my right arm. But I must listen. As we walk home, he tells me the story.

"I was in a tavern, couple of months ago. The Upside

Down, you know it? I'd drunk too much. This girl comes up to me and we talk. Now I often get girls coming up to me, as you know, so I thought nothing of it. God's blood, Giacomo, she was a witch or something; she had spells I could not resist. By the next day I was hopelessly in love. And I'm the one the girls fall in love with, not the other way round. We saw each other every day. She made promises to me. Lured me in until I said I'd do anything for her. And then, when she knew she had me, she told me that she worked for the Duke. And that he wanted to offer me employment. Giacomo, I was so in love—"

"You've been recruited to work for the Duke?"

"I have. I'm one of his men now. I'm a spy."

"A spy? Great Heaven, Renzo, that's a step up from servant!"

We stop at the Goldoni Fountain and Renzo scoops up some water to drink.

"And my first order was to spy on you, may God forgive me."

"Me?"

"Yes, you. Because you are the servant of Leonardo da Vinci."

"No, Renzo, no! You wouldn't! I won't believe it!"

"That's how I saved you from those cowards tonight. Because I was on your tail. I've been watching you for weeks."

"But—me, Renzo? My master? Why?"

"To find out what it was your master had invented. And whether he planned to sell it to the French."

"So it was you I saw on the roof of the Lazaretto."

He nods. "Instead of meeting you for knife practice, I

followed you. And you found what the Duke was looking for."

"You told the Duke—"

"Yes."

"How *could* you, Renzo?"

"How could I *not*? It was the Duke's command. Who can refuse him?"

"And you've been following me all this time?"

"Oh, Giacomo, you cannot know how confusing these past months have been for me. Whenever I thought of telling you—and I wanted to, every day—the girl seemed to sense it and twisted me around until I forgot everything except her. She told me she loved me. I could not resist her. I still can't. I would die for her—even now, if she asked me. By God, I would kill myself if she told me to!"

"And she was more important than our friendship," I say.

"Try to understand. Please, Giacomo."

"But you were *spying* on me—and my master."

"I had to, don't you see?"

"No, Renzo, in God's name, I don't."

"Well, don't forget I saved your life tonight."

"I won't. But you might have been the cause of my death, too, if my master *had* been working for the French."

Renzo just nods and hangs his head.

We walk together some more.

"And the girl?" I say.

"Gone. I was work to her, nothing more. The Duke has sent her elsewhere."

We walk the rest of the way to Bernardo Maggio's house in silence, and with every step I feel my resentment melting away. He is still my friend, whatever has happened.

"Tomorrow I leave Milan," he says. "I will make my way behind the French lines, to report back to the Duke's spymaster on their position and movements. My life is no longer my own, Giacomo. I swore an oath until death."

"Renzo—"

"Yes?"

"I may never see you again."

"Forgive me, then," he says, "in case you don't."

"I have already. We were once the best of friends."

"You will always be my friend, Giacomo. Don't forget me."

"Nor you me," I say. "Milan will not be the same without you."

"Oh, it will," he says. "I am the one who will not be the same."

It is true. Renzo's life is changed forever. Not in the way I was expecting, but in the way that it was destined.

And what is *my* destiny? Is it art—or something else? Ottavio Assanti holds the answer to that, I think.

We embrace quickly, and Renzo turns away.

When the door is closed behind him, I head for home.

Our house is quiet. The Master has not returned.

And now I am tired. So very tired.

What a night.

I surrender myself to what remains of it and fall into a deep sleep.

XXXVI

"Giacomo! Giacomo? Where are you, boy? I've been calling forever!"

The Master!—and—yes, where am I? Still in bed. The sun is pressing soft fingers through my small window. *Saint Michael, how my ribs ache.*

"Coming, Master, coming!"

I run out of my room, trip over the broom I forgot to put away, and hop on one leg along the corridor until I regain my balance—right in front of the Master coming out of the kitchen.

"What games are you playing now, boy?"

"Um, nothing, Master."

He is looking very—*very*—pleased with himself. A new commission, perhaps? A medal from the Duke? He's got a smile wide enough to drive an ox and cart through.

He takes me by the shoulders, shakes me a bit.

"I've got something to tell you!"

"M-master?"

"I worked all night, you know!"

"You d-d-did?"

He releases me.

"Now what day is it?" he says.

"Mid-March. The fourteenth."

"March the fourteenth, in the year of our Lord, one thousand, four hundred, and ninety-eight! What an auspicious day, what a glorious month—what a year! The Last Supper is finished! I am done!"

"Oh, Master, is it true? Really? This is the best news! When can I see it?"

"Soon, boy, soon. My trial is at an end. And I am free. Now it is up to God and the weather."

". . . God and the weather?"

"They will be jointly responsible for keeping the wall dry enough to hold the paint until we are safely out of Milan."

"Is the Last Supper in that much danger, Master?"

"It will not stain for a few years—five, maybe ten. But by the middle of the next century, boy, it will be a bigger miracle than Jesus' resurrection if the faces in my painting still look like faces, let alone the faces of Benedetti, Fazio, and, and . . . and I am hungry, Giacomo, what do we have?"

I go to the kitchen to find food for the great Leonardo da Vinci. Margareta, that good and kind woman, left us a pie early this morning. Still warm, too. And on the table there is cheese and bread, tomatoes, apples, and pears.

He has settled in his study.

I take the pie and some fruit to him, and he is soon hard at it. I watch him eating. After a while, he looks up.

"You know, Giacomo, I had my doubts about finishing it."

We all did, Master.

"My doubts about whether it *should* have been finished, I mean, given that it is not going to remain in the best condition for very long." He sighs. "But we'll let those who come after us worry themselves about that, eh? We have enough to think on. Oh, and—"

He puts down his knife and smiles.

"—Have you seen Father Vicenzo recently?"

"Not for weeks, Master."

"I have. Been seeing quite a lot of him. Every day, in fact. You know why that is?"

Not until you tell me, Master.

"Because—ha! Because I have used his face as the model for Judas!"

The Master slaps the table and bursts into laughter.

I have to smile, too. It's a fate worse than anything I could have dreamed up for him. Apart from being eaten alive by wild boars. And that might still happen, if I pray hard enough.

And now I must ask, though I fear the answer—"Tell me, Master, whose likeness did you use for Jesus?"

Did he take the Duke's suggestion? He could not be blamed for it afterwards, having been given permission, even if it was given in jest. And it would be a way of thanking me for my efforts, without actually having to thank me, which I know only too well is difficult for the Master.

"Ah, yes, the face of Jesus."

Is it me, Master? Is it?

He stops to cut up an apple and raises a piece to his mouth. Puts it back on the plate. Then he says: "For the face of Jesus I chose someone—someone whose true closeness to me must never be revealed."

Whose true closeness . . . must never be revealed? It's *me*—it *has* to be me! Of course! I am the Master's son—and it must remain a secret, or the Duke will have our heads!

"I understand, Master." Oh, I understand, at last.

"I am glad you do," he says.

I need say nothing more.

"We will go together to the Last Supper, as soon as I have made a few small improvements."

"Soon, Master?"

"Very soon."

The Master, having finished his food, retires to his bedchamber for sleep.

The news has stirred my thoughts into a whirlpool, and I go from room to room, picking up a vase here, putting down a book there. I clean candlesticks and door frames and kitchen pots and *I'm the face of Jesus—the face of Jesus!* I'll clean everything in the house—the hearth, the stairs, the ceilings, the roof—and when I've finished those, I'll reach up and polish the very sky! The Master has given my face to our Lord Jesus! This is as good as a confession from him—Leonardo da Vinci is truly my father!

It cannot be much longer before he tells me himself. Perhaps when we visit the Last Supper together.

For some time this thought lifts my spirits so much that I brush and scrape and sweep and scrub with the arms of ten men, but gradually the dull ache in my ribs and head compels me to sit down on the chair near the kitchen fire.

The next thing I know there is a voice in my ear. I open my eyes. How long have I been asleep? Margareta is peering at me through the window.

"Oh, I—what time is it?"

"Late afternoon, with dusk following on its heels."

The Master—I must wake him.

"Thanks for the pie, Margareta. We ate every bit."

"Oh, I'm glad. The only good pie is the one that's been eaten. That's how you know it was good. The least I can do, now that the shopkeepers treat me like a real lady—all smiles and kindnesses—when I tell them I have come from Leonardo da Vinci. Why, only this morning Bagliotti gave me two extra loaves for free. They're all waiting with great anticipation for the public opening of the refectory. The whole of Milan will see them on that wall your master painted. Peroni says it is the best advertisement for his shop he could ever have. He's thinking of buying a farm and making his own cheese."

Far away from bats, I hope.

"Thanks for all your help since Caterina died, Margareta."

"If your master would do me a little painting of the Virgin, even a drawing, that would be all the reward I'd want."

"I'll be sure to ask him."

But I won't hold my breath for an answer. Unless I want a purple face.

"Your food, candles, and other supplies are where Caterina, bless her, used to store them." She stops, quickly wipes her eyes with her apron. "Poor Caterina. Now I have the washing to do."

As soon as Margareta has gone, I run up the stairs to wake the Master. Then, before I can accomplish this, I have to run down again, because there is a loud knocking at the front door. There has been so much loud knocking at our door, for so long, I wonder it has any more knocking left in it. Still, it must be answered, unless it can be taught to answer itself.

"Where is he?"

"Good day, Father Vicenzo."

"Did *you* tell him to do it, Giacomo? Was it you?"

"Whatever do you mean, father?"

"I offered to help you!"

"Father Vicenzo—"

"To give you my protection! And now this! I am Judas, and my face is to be mocked for all eternity!"

"Father, I had nothing to do with—"

"You lie, villainous boy! It was your idea. I will swear an oath on it."

"No, father," I say.

My master, in his sleeping gown, is at the top of the stairs.

"I find," he says, "that whenever you approach our door, Father Vicenzo, sleep flees this house faster than a friar from a poor vintage."

"Master Leonardo! You are not dressed!"

My master descends the stairs and stands before the prior of Santa Maria delle Grazie. He takes several deep breaths, as if the air coming through the window had arrived fresh from Lake Como, instead of stinking of the rags they are burning in the next street.

"I have finished the Last Supper," he says.

As if the words have to be pulled out of him with tongs, the prior says: "I know you have, Master Leonardo."

The Master smiles. Smirks, really. After suffering three years of the prior's torments, it is hard for him not to show his glee, now that the task is done. "And I think you will agree that it is the finest painting in the land," he says.

Father Vicenzo blanches.

"You did not think I could do it, Father Vicenzo. You had no faith. I was always told that you priests were made of the stuff. Nonetheless, the Last Supper is done and finished, reverend father."

The prior's hands are trembling, and he is pulling at his robe.

"Why did you use my likeness for the traitor Judas?" he says.

"*Your* likeness, father?"

"Don't juggle with me, Leonardo! He has the same eyes, the same nose—he is closer to me than my own skin!"

"Do you have a beard?"

"No—"

"But *he* does, Father Vicenzo."

"You gave him a beard to deceive me—"

"Father Vicenzo, you are deceiving yourself."

"Then who was your model?"

"A villain, a knave of knaves, whose name protects him from the noose, but who deserves to hang as much as any murderer, for trying to murder a work of art by forcing it to be born before it was ready, and for putting poison in the ears of his betters concerning matters of which he has no understanding." My master pauses. "But not you, father."

Father Vicenzo raises his finger and waves it at my master. He has never done that before. It is a great insult to do that. The Master's hands are strong enough to snap off Father Vicenzo's finger at the knuckle, but he does not move. Nor does he need to. He has already beaten the prior without having to touch him.

"You think *you* have suffered?" the priest says. "You have made me so ill with your delays and stubbornness that I have not slept a full night these three years past, nor eaten a meal without it giving me the cramps. I gave you employment, Leonardo!"

"My employment with the Dominican Friars is now terminated. The Last Supper is finished. It will attract novices to your order and pilgrims to your church. The Pope, when he visits Milan, will praise it to the skies—and you, too, no doubt, for your part in commissioning it. Be content now and let others argue over the merits of my painting. We have argued enough."

"But my *face*—"

"Your face is not my affair. What I have painted is. Let be, father."

"You think you have bested me, Leonardo. You and your servant both. Nonetheless, I will have the last word. You must leave this house, now that your contract with the Order of Dominican Friars is fulfilled. We reclaim this house for our use."

"When you have paid me the balance of what you owe, father."

"We owe you nothing, painter."

"Oh, but you do. My expenses for the past three months have not been paid, nor has the sum agreed on for finishing the work."

"Then you will receive it in good time."

"And in good time I will vacate your house."

The prior does not say more. He straightens himself, turns, looks at me through narrowed eyes—I half expect darts to come flying from them—and then marches to the front door.

"Good day, father," says my master.

The only response is the sound of the door being slammed shut behind Father Vicenzo, the prior of Santa Maria delle Grazie.

"What is today, Giacomo?"

"Friday, Master. A very good day."

"Because I have finished the Last Supper."

"And because we have surely seen the last of Father Vicenzo," I say.

"I think not. He will be on the wall of the refectory every time we return there."

It's hard not to smile at that thought. Then the Master says: "Now, if it is Friday, I will visit the baths. I think I have earned some reward for my efforts, eh?"

Yes, Master, you surely have.

"And, Giacomo," he continues, "you have been a great help to me, boy."

Why, thank you, Master. Perhaps you do have a heart, after all.

"I wish to show my gratitude to you for everything you have done."

I think I can hear it beating too, by Saint Peter's keys!

"Well, how may I reward you?" he says.

"You know, Master. You know! I want—"

"—You to pilot the flying machine at the demonstration for the Duke."

Wha—?

"Pilot the flying machine, Master?"

"And then we shall see."

"We shall . . . ?"

"Tomorrow you will accompany me to the Castle for training."

"Yes, Master."

Yes, yes, a hundred times yes!

And then, after I have proved myself on the flying machine—and then . . .

XXXVII

The next day the Master commences my flying lessons: how to guide the lever and thereby control the rudder on the tail to direct the path of the machine in flight; how to press on the foot pedals in such a way—left, right, left, left, right, right, left (the correct order being of the utmost importance)—so as to contract and release the spring coils, which will cause the wings to rise and fall like a bird's and carry me into the air.

"Of course, Giacomo," he said to me after a few days' practice, "this is our first flying machine. I am confident that it will rise from the ground, but I cannot tell how far it may travel or for how long. That will depend on your vitality and mental application. If you reach a certain height and then lose the rhythm of the foot pedals, or misdirect the machine's tail rudder, you will come down to earth rapidly and without warning. You will probably kill yourself, true, but, more importantly, you will cause the ruin of my years of work, which would greatly dismay me."

I was bent over the foot pedals, adjusting the straps, when he said this. Did he really care more about his infernal creation than me? Then he could pilot it himself!

But when I looked up he was smiling, and behind him Bernardo Maggio was trying to hold in his laughter.

"By God, boy, your face!" the Master said. "For a lad with such a comic turn of mind, you are easier to anger than a wet cat!"

"Master, I—"

"Have no fear, boy. You will not fall from the sky like a piece of rock from a cliff. Even if you stopped pedaling for a half hour, the stored up momentum of the spring-coil mechanism would keep you aloft until you reached safe ground to land."

On the Sunday of the week following, the Master invites me—at last!—to accompany him to Santa Maria delle Grazie to see the finished work. It's a warm day and the larks are singing as we pass through the Vercellina Gate.

Drawing closer to the church, we notice several Dominican friars cleaning the walls with scrubbing brushes. They wave at the Master as he passes.

"When will we see it, Master Leonardo?"

"Is it a good likeness of our Lord and His Disciples?"

And the Master answers: "I have given you Jesus as you would wish Him to be, my friends: brave, compassionate, and suffering—a man much like us, only much better."

"God save you, Master Leonardo!"

The Master takes out the key and fits it in the lock. Then he turns back to the monks and says: "Wherever you sit in the refectory, you will find the eyes of Jesus looking down on you in His goodness and infinite wisdom."

"Thrice blessings on you, Master!"

"We at Santa Maria are honored above all our Dominican brethren!"

"At last we'll have somewhere to eat!"

The Master opens the doors.

"Yes," he says to me, "and the monks will also see that what the Lord gives, the Lord takes away."

And the Master fixes me with a look. What does he mean? I must study the finished painting to answer the riddle.

The afternoon light shines in through the western windows.

The room has a warmth I have never felt before.

It must be the majesty of the painting.

I run towards the wall—I cannot wait any longer to see Jesus' face.

But—but that is not me! That is not my face!

"Master, Jesus—Jesus looks like me, but it is not me. . . . His nose is less. . . . His eyes are more. . . . That is not my face! Master, you promised me I would be the face of Jesus!"

The Master is directly behind me when I turn.

"Did I? I do not think so," he says.

"You made me believe—you said that you chose someone whose true closeness to you must never be revealed. That was me, wasn't it? Who else could it be?"

"Foolish, prideful boy. Are you the only one I have ever been close to?"

"I don't know, Master."

"No, you do not. There is much you do not know."

"But I do know that face. It is not me, but I have seen it before. In your sketchbooks."

"It is the face of my childhood friend, Fioravante di Domenico."

My master is staring at Jesus with such sadness in his eyes. This Fioravante meant more to him than I will ever know. Saint Francis, what a fool I am, always thinking of myself—

"I am sorry, Master. I am sorry for speaking out so hastily. You honored your friend, and you should be honored for that. When he sees—"

"My friend will never see this painting, Giacomo. He is dead a dozen years. Thrown from a horse. This painting is to keep his memory alive in our world. Nobody but you and I will know the truth about the face of Jesus."

But why could the Master's true closeness to Fioravante never be revealed?

And then I remember that word spoken by old Piero da Vinci. *Indecency.*

Oh God. The accusation against my master was on account of this Fioravante.

"Why do you stare at me like that, boy?"

"Master, I—your friend Fioravante, was he the one—?"

"The one? What do you mean, Giacomo? Speak up!"

"Your father, Master—I did not want to repeat what he said, but—"

"My father is an evil old man who resents my fame. Do not listen—"

"He told me that you were accused of indecency."

The Master's face turns a shocking red. It is true, then. His father was not lying. Does this mean that the old man was also telling the truth when he said that one day I would find out—

He is coming towards me!

"Master? Master? What are you doing?"

I move to one side but he takes me by the wrist—his father warned me, too late now—*oh God, why didn't I listen to him?* My master was only waiting for me to reach the same age as his Fioravante and then he—

"You little fool, will you *listen* to me?"

"No, Master—! Not that! Don't touch me—please, no!"

"What is the *matter* with you, boy? I only want to tell you the truth!"

"Master?"

"Stand still and listen. What my father told you is true: I *was* accused of indecency with another man. But I swear to you, on God's oath, that the accusation was a lie. A lie told for a vile reason, as all the worst lies are."

He looks up at Jesus, then turns to me and says: "Fioravante and I grew up together. He was my childhood friend. He gave me the affection that my father always denied me. We were closer than any brothers. But our friendship did not please his father."

"Why, Master?"

"Because . . ."

"Yes, Master?"

"Because I am a bastard, born out of wedlock."

Whaaaat?

"My father, I see, did not tell you *that*. Yes, Giacomo, Piero da Vinci is my father, but he never married my mother, who was a simple peasant girl."

My master takes a deep breath. I have never seen him like this—ever. He is shaking with the effort of controlling his emotions.

"Master? Are you—?"

"Yes, boy, let me continue. Fioravante was from an important family, the di Domenicos, close allies of the Medicis, the rulers of Florence. It was *his* father who composed that anonymous letter accusing me of indecency. He did it in order to have an excuse with which to part me from his son. And his son had no choice but to obey. Because of that letter I was never allowed to see my friend again. Because of that letter I became an outcast. My life in Florence from that time on was almost unendurable. But I did not have the courage to leave the city, until the invitation came from the Duke of Milan. Then I took my chance. I found a new life in Milan and have not regretted it."

The Master's head is bowed; he has brought a hand to his face. It is the first time I have ever seen him—but, no, he takes away the hand and his eyes are dry. Yet I feel that he has been weeping inwardly for his companion.

We stand in silence and stare at the face of Fioravante, the Master's beloved friend.

Outside, in the cloistered garden behind the refectory, I can hear birds and, in the distance, monks are singing the praises of our Lord. Their voices have such purity and truth that I feel ashamed of myself, though I do not know why, except that I should not have doubted my master. He has always been good to me. How could I have thought that he meant to do me harm?

"Thank you for trusting me with this confidence, Master."

And yet I have never felt more miserable.

He nods. I hope we can both forget my outburst.

Now the Master is pointing at Jesus.

"As we were entering the room, I told you that the monks would discover the truth of the words from the Bible: 'What the Lord gives, the Lord takes away.' Now, Giacomo, look at the Last Supper and explain to me what I meant."

What the Lord gives, the Lord takes away? How am I supposed to know what he means by that? He has crossed his arms. He is waiting for me.

What the Lord gives, the Lord takes away.

Think, Giacomo. Look at Jesus.

What a piteous expression he has given our Lord. What unutterable sadness. He always knew He would be betrayed. But He did nothing to change His fate. Why? Why did Jesus not try to escape? We cannot deny it—He allowed Himself to be betrayed. He *wanted* to be betrayed! To die, for us. To die, so that we might live.

What the Lord gives . . . *Jesus' hands, His blessed hands—*

"I see it, Master! I see what you mean! The Lord gives, and the Lord takes away!"

"Well, Giacomo, stop hopping up and down and tell me!"

"Jesus' arms are stretched out towards us. He is looking down, drawing our attention to His hands."

"Correct, boy. Continue."

"Our Lord's left hand is shown with the palm facing upwards. He is offering something to us—the bread on the table. The bread is the Lord's flesh. What the Lord gives—"

"Yes, Giacomo, yes, what the Lord gives—"

"—the Lord takes away! You have painted Jesus' right hand with the palm down, fingers outspread, about to take the wine, His holy blood. His left hand gives, His right hand takes. What the Lord gives, the Lord takes away. We live, but we must die. That must be it! Am I right, Master? Am I right?"

"There is no right and wrong, boy. There is only interpretation. Your interpretation of Jesus' gestures does you credit, however."

"Thank you, Master."

And now I think I understand why the Master painted Jesus like this: to remind himself that despite all the gifts he had been given by God, and despite all his past and future successes, the life of Leonardo da Vinci would one day be taken away.

"I am proud of you, Giacomo. You have been watching me, and you have learned much. I was right to think that one day you would show yourself capable of deeper thought."

"Master, I do not know what to say."

"Say nothing, then. You will be surprised how good it sounds. Even more so to others. There is yet something in the painting you have not seen. Study the Last Supper some more. Here is the key; lock up after you."

"Yes, Master."

I watch him leave the refectory. I have missed something—something important.

My master has given his figure of Jesus such quiet strength, such astonishing presence! It seems as if the Disciples are being pulled towards Him and pushed away at the same time. Look at how they are in motion as they argue, complain, deny, and plead! There is Judas, reeling backwards as if what he hears is a surprise, when all the time he knows he is the culprit! Has guilt ever been painted so truly? Oh, Father Vicenzo, now I feel pity for you, when I never did before.

See, my master has painted Judas's left hand reaching out at the same moment as Jesus' right hand—they are almost touching.

And now I grasp even more of the Master's intention.

The highest and the lowest are *opposites*—and yet they cannot exist without each other. Judas needs the comfort of touching the hand of the one he will betray. Our Lord Jesus needs to forgive the betrayer even as He condemns him. *They need each other.*

That is what the Master wanted me to see. Everything must have its opposite. Life and death, good and evil, happiness and sadness. One cannot exist without the other. It is the truth of all existence.

Now, let me study the figures.

To the right of Jesus are our three old friends—

Peroni, in the role of Thomas the Doubter, pointing up to Heaven disbelievingly (here, I fancy, poor Peroni is alluding to the bats in that cave of the tainted gorgonzola).

Fazio is James the Greater, arms outstretched in dismay (the same gesture he used to make when the Master told him he had no money).

And Rossi plays the role of Philip, who is leaning forward to hear what Jesus has to say, just as Rossi does in real life (he's a bit hard of hearing, you know).

On their right are the Disciples Matthew, Thaddeus, and, at the end, Simon.

The Master has given the role of Matthew, the tax collector who gave up his wealth and position to follow Jesus, to the goldsmith Delitto. Ingenious, Master, giving a man who works with gold the role of a taxman!

To his right is the gray-haired bookseller, Festa, in the role of Thaddeus, who was known for keeping his own counsel (just like an unopened book, I think, whose covers conceal the knowledge within).

And at the end of the table is Simon, the Disciple known as the Zealot, played by Veroli, the shoemaker. But why him? Let me think. Simon is known to have walked a thousand miles or more to preach the Gospel—he'd need many pairs of shoes to do that!

Now, at the other end of the table, to the farthest left of Jesus, is Bagliotti, the baker, playing Bartholomew, the Disciple who was called "without guile." And surely there is no more honest a man in Milan than our good Bagliotti.

On his right is James the Lesser, who has been given the face of Maggio, our carpenter—and rightly so, because James's symbol is the saw (I saw through you, Master!).

To the right of James is my good friend Benedetti, of course, as Andrew, who was Jesus' first Disciple (just as Benedetti was the first to get a seat in this painting). And next to him is the armorer, Cabrera, in the role of Peter, the fisherman—but, why? *Think*, Giacomo! Yes, yes—a suit of armor has pieces that overlap to protect the wearer, just like a fish's scales!

In front of Peter is Father Vicenzo—Judas—and behind him, sitting next to Jesus, is John. Why, he looks a bit like—

That's *me*—that's my face!!

The Master *did* give me a place in the Last Supper, after all—he has given my face to John, the favorite of Jesus.

Why didn't I notice this before? How could I not have seen—? Because I was not *looking* properly. That was what my master was trying to tell me—I was so sure that he had given my face to Jesus that I did not think to look at who was seated *right next to Him*! Oh, Master, thank you—thank you for giving me this great honor. I will do everything in my power to prove myself worthy of it.

But—what will become of Martino? He also paid for a place in the Last Supper. In order to paint me in, the Master has been obliged to leave him out.

I continue to study the great work. This is my last chance to be alone with it before the rest of Milan comes to stare.

There is the wooden stool on which the Master was wont to sit and contemplate his work. And the old sheet he used to cover the floor against drips and spills is now a rainbow of colors. The brushes are still in the cleaning pot, the colors snug in their jars, and there the clamshells my master uses to hold the paint-and-oil mixture before applying it to the wall with the brush. Red shells, blue shells, green shells, yellow shells.

Is it possible that from these simple materials the Master has created the greatest painting in the world? Yes, it is. The artist is the link between man and God, sent to this Earth to show us the infinite possibilities of life. God grant me the courage and devotion to become a true artist, like my master, and I will endure any sacrifice for it.

I sit on the Master's stool and continue to study the painting.

Another hour passes. The room grows colder. But I do not want to leave yet.

Folded up in the corner is a blanket. I wrap it around my shoulders. The light is fading.

I will stay until I can no longer see the outlines of the figures on the wall.

XXXVIII

As I hurry home, the

As I hurry home, the moon is masked by shifting layers of black and gray. A few moments later a streak of lightning rends the sky, followed by a giant's groan, as if the lightning had pierced his thigh. Then comes a bellow of furious thunder.

The rain begins to fall as I enter our street. Three small children are standing under the downpour and laughing, even as they are soaked.

I leap for the front door—it is barred and bolted.

"Master! Open up, Master, it's me!" I pound on the wood with my fists.

Even if he is disposed to hear me, the storm must drown out my voice. I run down the alley and peer through the half-open shutters in the kitchen window. There he is, sitting at the kitchen table, and next to him is a woman with golden hair. Her head is bowed. The Master is holding her hands, talking to her. She raises her head. It is—it is Cecilia Gallerani.

"Master!" I shout through the window. "Master!" He looks up. Does he see me? "Master!"

He rises, opens the shutters. Now Cecilia sees me. She smiles. She remembers me. Of course she does. She called me "our Giacomo." *I am her son.* The Master points to the front door. He could as easily have opened the kitchen door for me. I run back down the alley and am there before him.

"Master, I-I—"

"You are out of breath and indisposed, Giacomo. Please go to your room and clean yourself, then come into the kitchen. I have someone here who wants to see you."

"I know, Master. She's come at last. It's Cecilia—our Cecilia!"

"Do not be presumptuous, boy. She is Lady Cecilia to you."

I pass Cecilia Gallerani's maidservant, who has been waiting in our front room. A pretty thing, too. Before I can smile at her, I notice another servant standing in the shadows: a male, a big brute, who stares at me as if he would take a club to my head if I so much as twitch at him. So I twitch in the other direction.

I go to my room and change my shirt and hose. My jerkin is sodden. I hang it on a nail. Then I take out the portrait of Cecilia from under my bed and carry it to the kitchen, leaving it outside, standing against the wall.

When I enter, the fire is unlit. My master should have thought of his guest. I go towards the pile of logs, then turn to Cecilia. I do not know what to do next. I bow. I take her small white hand and place my lips to it.

"Giacomo!" my master says. "Remember your place!"

"Master—"

"Leonardo, do not be so hard on the boy. Do you remember me, Giacomo?"

"My lady, you are never far from my thoughts."

"There, Leonardo. Such a gentleman has every right to kiss my hand. Now, let me look at you." She holds both my hands. Scans me up and down. "You have grown into a handsome youth, Giacomo. And look, Leonardo, his hair is exactly the same color as mine—blond, as blond as the wheat fields in summer. But yours is curlier, Giacomo."

"And you, my lady, are lovelier—you outshine the painting my master made, the pride of the Duke's collection."

"Ah, I was young then, Giacomo. Have I not grown old? Does my face not show signs of age?"

"My lady, your face can only improve with age."

"Leonardo, Giacomo has become a poet since I last saw him. A very pretty poet."

My master ignores this speech and addresses me thus: "Madonna Cecilia has come to Milan to see the Last Supper."

"Yes, Master. Have you seen it yet, my lady? Is it not the most wonderful painting in the world?"

"It is, Giacomo. Your master has so greatly surpassed himself that I doubt he will ever catch up again. It is a painting that will be honored for all time."

My master tries to smile. We are all silent for a moment.

"I am so pleased to be sitting here with you both," Cecilia says.

The shutters fly open and the rain, still fierce, forces its way inside. I leap to the window, knocking over a chair in my zeal, and secure them once more.

"Giacomo, the fire," my master says.

"Yes, Master."

"Now, Leonardo," she says, when the fire has caught, "tell me how you managed to persuade the Duke to give you my portrait. You did obtain it for me, did you not?"

"My lady—" he begins.

"We had to use some guile, Lady Cecilia, which we hope you will forgive us for."

"Giacomo?" my master says.

"Master, I only wanted to tell Cecilia—"

"*Lady* Cecilia, boy—"

"*Lady* Cecilia, *sir*—that we had to obtain the painting with a measure of craft. In short, my lady, it was not given to us willingly."

"How wonderful, you deceived the Duke! Tell me how you did that, my brave boy."

I glance at my master. He is glowering at me, but holding his tongue, it seems, until he fully comprehends my intention.

"My lady, I have something here for you."

I run out of the kitchen at the same time as my master shouts "Giacomo!" at me, but whether he is correcting me for leaving Cecilia so hastily, or trying to stop me from doing what he suspects I have already done, is no matter. It is done. I can't be stopped.

In two breaths I am back in the kitchen with Cecilia's

portrait, which I place on the kitchen table, holding it up for her and the Master to see. Cecilia stands up; she is trembling. She looks at me, then at my master, then says, "Leonardo! My champion! I knew you would not disappoint me! My portrait—oh, if only you knew how much this means to me! Thank you! Thank you!"

"Giacomo, what have you *done*?"

Cecilia is taken aback by his sudden change of tone. "What is it, Leonardo? What is wrong?"

"He has *stolen* your painting from the Duke's gallery."

"Master, Cecilia, I did take the painting without the Duke's permission, it is true, but he will never notice its absence. He no longer cares what is in his gallery and what is not!" I turn to my master. "You saw the disorder in that room, paintings everywhere, one on top of the other. I thought that he would not miss the portrait of the Lady Cecilia—and, look, Master, look how overjoyed our lady is to have it back!"

"Giacomo, you have done a terrible thing! You must take it back forthwith and explain yourself!"

"But, Master, I cannot—the Duke!"

"Leonardo," Cecilia puts a hand on his arm, "this is not theft, is it? No, it is kindness, to return to me what is rightfully mine—my youth. Do not send him back with the painting, it is too dangerous."

"But, Cecilia, if the Duke discovers his loss, we will all suffer for it!"

"I, for one, am ready to take my chance," she says. "I know

Duke Ludovico's habits well. I lived with him for nearly ten years, remember. Once he has ownership of something, he soon loses interest in it. I would wager that he has barely looked at my portrait since you painted it for him. And now he has a new mistress, does he not? Why would he go looking for the old one?"

"If we permit Giacomo this liberty, Cecilia, what more will he be capable of, thinking that he will not have to pay for his actions?"

"But, Leonardo, he did it for me—to show us that he was courageous and faithful."

"I will not support a thief in this house!" he says.

"My Leonardo, you are too harsh on the boy."

"I am accustomed to it, Lady Cecilia," I say. The fire is just beginning to blaze. "By always denying me my accomplishments, he seeks to bury the truth about me."

Cecilia looks at my master. His face grows hot; and it is not the fire that is responsible, I vow, but his guilt.

"The truth about you?" the Master says. "What *truth*?"

I poke the fire with the irons. The flames leap up. This is it. The time has come. I am ready to say what I must. I turn around to face them.

"Come now, Master, we both—we all—know who I really am!"

My master rises as if I had thrown a burning log and told him to catch it.

"What are you saying, Giacomo?"

"I know what happened that night in 1482 when Madonna Cecilia gave birth."

"Leonardo!" exclaims Cecilia. She puts a hand to her mouth. Her eyes are round with amazement. My lady, forgive me for causing you some pain—I cannot stop now!

"You know *nothing*, boy," my master says, his face blazing.

"Nothing? I know *you* were there, Master. You were by the Madonna Cecilia's side while she bore her child. Nothing? I know *everything*! Caterina told me all on her deathbed. She was there—you made her take a vow of silence afterwards, to safeguard your secret. But she told me, she had to, because the truth must out."

"Giacomo, that night had nothing to do with you," my master says.

"Nothing to do with me? How can that be, Master, *when I was that child*?"

Leonardo da Vinci and Cecilia Gallerani stare at me, slack-jawed. I have them—I have them at last! Before they can deny me further, I say: "I was born in 1482. I have blond hair. I am no more a servant than you are. I am your son and the son of Cecilia Gallerani. I was never an abandoned orphan, was I! I grew up in secret with Leonardo da Vinci—and on that terrible day, when the fever took away my memory, I lost my way home and was forced to live on the street, fending for myself until I was reunited with my true father when I fell from the Cathedral roof."

"Giacomo—!" Cecilia says.

"I forgive you Master, Cecilia. I understand why you could not tell me. It would have been too dangerous for all of us if the Duke had discovered who I really was. Oh, you cannot know how much joy it gives me to be able to let it all out at last!"

"You little fool!" the Master bellows. "What madness have you succumbed to now?"

I hear my master's voice, but as if in a dream I have at last awoken from.

He looks at Cecilia, shakes his head. "Say something to the boy, Cecilia!"

And she does. "Oh, Giacomo!" she says. "We are not—we are not your parents."

"Don't lie to me, my lady, please," I say, forgetting my place. "Not now, I beg of you. My whole life has been a lie."

"Dear Giacomo." She takes my hands. "The child I bore in 1482, my poor boy, was not you."

"I will not believe it."

"You must," says my master. "She speaks the truth."

"But, what about—my hair?"

"It is beautiful hair, Giacomo, the hair of a young Apollo," Cecilia says. She strokes my head once. "Sadly, it does not signify that you are my son."

"Master, you were there at the child's birth!"

"Cecilia had no one else," he says.

"And you are not the father?" I say to him.

He shakes his head no. Now I am lost.

"What does this mean, Master?"

He sighs and sits down. Looks at Cecilia. She nods.

"I will tell you my story, Giacomo," she says. "It is not one I would have wished to repeat, it hurts me to do so, but you need to hear all. So shall you know the truth of the matter." She pauses. The Master fills her cup from the water jug.

"I was a little older than you are now. The Duke saw me one day when I was out riding and sent a message to my father, praising my beauty and grace. He desired me for his mistress. Do you understand, Giacomo? My father, who could not or would not refuse the Duke, decided to make the best of it—for himself, if not for me. He sold me to Duke Ludovico for two hundred acres of rich farmland and one thousand gold ducats. That was my price, the price my father extracted from the Duke before handing me over to him."

No! How could her own father do such a thing?

Cecilia coughs. For a moment her eyes fill, as if she would begin weeping, but she quickly recovers.

"I had a secret, however. I was already in love with a young man. He had told me that he loved me, and we had lain together. I was carrying his child. I had not yet summoned the courage to tell my father, but now I had to. He was more than enraged with me, of course, but still more fearful of the Duke's wrath, should I not be delivered as promised. He managed to put off the Duke, without revealing the true reason, thinking to delay my going until after I had given birth. But the Duke was impatient; if he was to be kept waiting, he wanted a portrait of me while he did. That is how I met Leonardo, who became my true friend. It was he who stood by me, when my parents would not."

"What about the young man you loved?"

"The father?" Cecilia says. She rubs the table, as if there

was a mark on it. "He would not have come to my side if I had been dying."

"And the infant?"

"Taken after the birth to the nuns at the Convent of Santa Beatrice in Pavia."

She hangs her head but, like a true lady, raises it again, even though the effort has cost her much. Then she says: "I went to the Castle some months after the birth and became the Duke's mistress. I was there for nearly ten years. Then he grew tired of me and I was sent away to be married to one of his nobles."

She gives a small, sad smile. "My place at court has been taken by a new and younger woman. Lucrezia Crivelli. I believe you know her."

She smoothes a crease from her dress.

"That is my story."

I cannot look at her. I cannot bear to hear more. My heart will crack, I swear.

"Are you listening to Lady Cecilia?" my master asks.

What does he think I am doing—playing the fiddle?

"That is why I was present at the birth," my master continues. "Not because I was the father, but because she had no one else. Do you hear me, boy? I was there to help her, nothing more. I was the only one she could trust."

"Your master saved me, Giacomo. Without his kindness, I would surely have taken my life and been sent to Hell for it."

I look at my master. His face is a mask he will not remove. What is he really feeling inside?

"What became of this child?" I say.

"He died after seven months. I never knew my little boy."

Her tears will come now, I am thinking, her eyes must spill. But no, she holds them back. Neither she nor my master will surrender to their sorrow. And neither will I.

I want to go to her, to hold her. I look at my master. I make the smallest movement. His eyes warn me away.

Long moments pass. The wind howls, and the rain rushes at the shutters in waves.

"They will be waiting for me. I must go." She sniffs, gives her head a little flick, and she is ready. "Perhaps now you understand why having this portrait means so much to me. It reminds me of who I was, and of who I truly am. Your master, Giacomo, saw in me what no man could take away. To have this portrait will be a great comfort. Thank you, dear boy, for what you have done, even if it was done without your master's consent."

When she has gone, the Master invites me to sit down.

"Since tonight we are being so honest with each other, I have a confession to make to you."

"Master?"

"The ring, the one with the red jewel you keep in your box."

"Yes, Master?"

"You did not steal it."

"I didn't—?"

"The ring was a gift to me from the Duke," he says. "He

took it off his own finger one day, when he was in a very cheerful mood, and placed it on mine. It has value, Giacomo. If ever something should happen to me, you can take it to the moneylenders and sell it, or procure a loan. It is yours."

No, Master, I can never take it to the moneylenders. Not in Milan, anyway. They won't let me run off with the Duke's ring a second time!

"And the cross?"

"Ah, it was not I who gave you that—"

"Caterina!"

"Who else?" he says.

From her precious collection of crosses. Blessed by the Pope, among others.

The medallion came from my master. The ring from the Duke. The cross from Caterina. Gifts, every one.

But, then—

"You told me those things were in my ragbag, Master. Now I know they were not. What *was* in the bag?"

"Nothing much, my boy. A half-eaten apple, some old crusts of bread, a smooth, black pebble, probably plucked from the riverbed."

Outside, the rain has ceased at last. Just the steady *drip, drip* from the roof to the paving stones.

For some time we continue to look at each other.

"You told me I was a thief."

"I did, I did. Try to understand. When I brought you to my house you were such an unruly child—I had to find a way to control you. By suggesting you were a thief—"

"You did more than *suggest* it, Master! You *proclaimed* it."

"Yes, yes, but listen a moment: I had to stop you from running away. In Milan, youth is merely a coin passed from hand to hand until it loses its luster and all value is spent. A lovely face only hastens the decline. You would have been corrupted and lived a life of pain and anguish. And, I suspect, died an early death. I wanted to save you from such a fate, Giacomo. I had to keep you here, and to do that I had to scare you. Do you understand?"

"Yes, Master." Sort of.

"Then why was I being chased that day, Master?"

"You were seen at the same time as another small boy, who was the true thief. He was later caught."

"What happened to him, Master?"

"That . . . I do not know."

I am not a thief. I was *never* a thief. Not even of Cecilia's portrait. After all, the Duke had no right to take Cecilia's youth from her. All I did was return it to its true owner.

But I am still no closer to finding the truth about myself.

Who are my parents? Why was I abandoned? For how long did I live alone on the streets?

He is turning to go. His candle flickers in the doorway.

"Master?"

"Yes, Giacomo?"

"Thank you for painting my face in the Last Supper."

"You are most welcome, boy."

"And I am sorry—sorry for thinking that—"

"No more need be said on that matter. You are safe with me, Giacomo. You always have been, and you always will be."

"What do we say to Martino, who paid for his place and will now be disappointed? My jerkin is ruined by the rain, and he promised me a new one for a seat in the Last Supper."

"Don't fret about Martino. I'll go to his house tomorrow and offer to paint a portrait of him and his wife. He'll be more than content with that."

I've no doubt he will, Master. Let's see how he feels when a year has gone by and you have not yet begun it!

The Master rises and moves to the door.

"Giacomo, I—"

"Yes, Master?"

"I wish you good night."

"Do you really know nothing of my past, Master? Nothing at all?"

"No more than you, boy. You have my word."

And then he is gone. I watch the fire slowly die away, and then I too make my way to bed.

XXXIX

Spring has come at last to Milan. Today, Margareta showed me the new pear trees in the garden next door, and how the buds hang heavy like drops of glass.

The refectory of Santa Maria delle Grazie has been opened to the people of Milan for the two weeks before Holy Friday, and soon after the announcement was made in the main square a line of eager visitors formed outside the refectory doors from early morning until late in the evening, on some days stretching all the way back to the Vercellina Gate. It makes me proud to see such a multitude waiting patiently to see my master's greatest work. However, I have not told any of my servant friends that my face is in it. They would never believe me, even if I showed them.

The Master—after paying a visit to the refectory on the day it was opened, and satisfying himself that Father Vicenzo was not allowing anyone to touch the wall, and telling Father Vicenzo that if anyone did, the Duke would hear about it directly, and reminding Father Vicenzo that he still owed my master a good deal of money—has not since returned to Santa Maria delle Grazie.

It is as if, now that the work has been done, he has no more interest in it. If I had painted such a thing, I would go there every day, rain or shine. But my master is not like that, he does not need to congratulate himself for a work whose deficiencies he is already privately cursing, even if he is the only one who can see them.

Meanwhile, inside the refectory, the friars are fully occupied with the crowd. You may stand in front of the Last Supper for only a short span, but many onlookers are so affected by the scene before them that they become like statues and have to be prodded until they shift, while others weep openly, point, and shake their heads in disbelief. But they too, if they will not move when entreated, are pushed or pulled until they do.

"We must prepare for the Pope's visit," the Master tells me. "He is arriving with his retinue on the Monday before Holy Friday and will stay at the Duke's apartments in the Castle. He has requested to see the Last Supper by candlelight on the Thursday evening, in private."

"Why then, Master? Surely daylight would be better."

"What could be better than to view it at the same time he supposes the Last Supper actually took place?"

So Assanti knew all along that the Pope was planning to see it alone. He must have someone high up in the Vatican, a secret friend of the Brotherhood, who reports back to him.

And now I must pass on this news to Tombi. But until the

Duke has paid the Master, I would prefer not to see him in person and have to explain that I still do not have his money. So later that day I put a note under his door, giving him the time for Pope Alexander's visit to the Last Supper, and advising him that I will meet Assanti by the fountain in the garden at Santa Maria one half hour before.

Everything is coming together. The Brotherhood and the Church will soon be reconciled. The start of a new era for mankind! And I will have played my part in it.

I wonder what reward Master Assanti has in mind for me. Perhaps he will teach me how to turn lead into gold, which is one of the legendary alchemical skills. The Master would never again have to worry about paying the merchants!

The Pope and his attendants arrive on the Monday, but there are no cheering crowds to greet him; the only sign of His Holiness's presence is the Vatican flag, red with a white cross and four white keys, flying high over the Castle gates alongside the Sforza colors.

The lack of pomp and ceremony attending the Pope's arrival in Milan bespeaks the grave matter that occupies the minds of our Duke and His Holiness. An invasion by the French is a threat to be taken most seriously, the more so because this is not the first time they have been at our borders. They crossed them once before, in 1494—at the invitation of our very own Duke Ludovico, who was pleased to help them pursue their claim on the Kingdom of Naples, if it meant the overthrow of King Alfonso, his detested enemy. The French accomplished that, but they had also decided to attack Rome on the way and would only leave when Pope Alexander paid them thousands of gold ducats from the Vatican treasury.

Our Duke was then afraid that the French would turn against Milan, so he made a new alliance with the Pope against them, and together they fought the French at Fornuovo in July of 1495. There was no outright winner, but the French king, Charles VIII, his army spent and war-wearied, went home.

And now Charles is dead, and Louis XII is the new French king.

And now Louis is threatening Milan, which he claims is his by right, because of a marriage long ago between one of his ancestors and a Visconti (the family that once ruled Milan).

"But is the Pope our ally or not?" I asked the Master.

"Nobody is very sure," the Master said to me. "However, it is rumored that he has sent one of his sons to France to find a wife. And that does not bode well for us."

Everything—the fate of Lombardy, Milan, and Duke Ludovico—now depends on whether my master's painting of the Last Supper can so dazzle the eyes of His Holiness that he renews his alliance with Milan and pledges his support to save the painting from the enemy.

XL

On the Wednesday before Easter the refectory was again closed to the people of Milan, and all day Thursday the Dominican brothers have been at work sweeping and washing the inside and outside of Santa Maria delle Grazie in preparation for Pope Alexander's visit.

And now it is night. The sky is a deep, dark velvet blue, and the wind is sending the clouds across it at a gallop. The movement in the heavens seems to foretell the great events that will occur here below. Inside the refectory, bunches of fresh flowers sit on the floor below the Last Supper, giving off a heady fragrance. And four large tapers on gold stands have been placed nearby, throwing a hazy light upwards and across the painting.

Even the Master seems pleased with the effect, walking to and fro before the wall and inspecting the work from every angle.

"It is a sight worthy of a pope, Master."

"Hmm? . . . Well, let us hope so, and then he might invite

us to Rome. He is a liberal spender, our Pope, unlike Duke Ludovico. We could do worse than get a summons to the Holy City to paint a few ceilings."

"We'd better leave, Master, the Pope will be arriving soon."

"What's the matter, boy? You look perturbed."

"Me, Master? Why, no, well—I'm just a bit on edge because I so much want the Pope to admire your painting."

"No need to trouble yourself on that account, Giacomo. I give you my word he will esteem it highly. Come, then, let us depart. I do not wish to meet the Pope before he sees the thing and be obliged to explain myself. It is always those who have no understanding of art, I find, who are most insistent that the artist listen to their opinion on it. Come, now."

Outside, a large group of Dominican friars has gathered to greet the Pope on his arrival. After we have managed to elbow our way through them, I bid good night to the Master.

"Where are you off to, boy?" he says.

"Oh, just for a walk, Master, before it gets too dark."

"No tavern visits, I trust."

"Oh no, Master, you know me!"

"Only too well," he says.

I notice that the Master is wearing his sword, which is rare for him. He says a sword gets in the way of his thinking.

As soon as he has disappeared into the darkness, I turn back to Santa Maria and, avoiding the monks gathering outside the entrance to the refectory, enter the main body of the church, walk down the nave, and leave through a side door into the cloistered garden for my meeting with Assanti.

I set myself down on the lip of the fountain, which gurgles soothingly behind my back.

Should I have told my master what I am up to? I think I should have. But Tombi is my friend, I can trust him. And Assanti needs my help. All will be well, surely. And yet, I begin to wonder if—

"Giacomo."

I peer into the shadows. My heart skips three beats and twists itself into a knot. The alchemist is here.

"Come under the walkway, where we will not be seen."

I leave the fountain and cross the garden.

"It is a fine night," he says, when I am standing before him.

"It is, sir."

"A night that will change all the days that come after."

I clasp my hands together. They are cold. Freezing.

"Are you ready to learn what I am here to teach you?" he says.

"If you are ready to tell me, sir."

"I am. Now lead me in."

We walk along the cloister until I see the door that gives entry to the passage leading to the refectory. An owl hoots in the distance. I look up, as if expecting to see it on the church roof. It's a rare thing to hear an owl in the city. But tonight is a rare night.

I turn the handle of the door, gently, gently. The passage is damp and dark. Too dark to see anything. We begin our walk. Master Assanti is so close behind me that I can smell his breath in the air. Spices. His sandaled feet give off soft slaps against the polished stone floor. Then my hand touches wood. The door to the refectory. I find the latch and open it.

Inside, the tapers are burning with a silvery-gold light.

Assanti follows me in. "A fine painting," he says, looking up.

"The finest," I say.

Although the platform on which the Master stood to paint has been dismantled, Maggio has not yet been here to remove the planks, which stand upright against the far wall. I have already decided that these are what we will use.

"Crouch behind those planks, Master Assanti, sir, and I will drape this painting sheet over them. Thus you will be concealed until you wish to be made known. The Pope will be here soon, let us not delay."

But the alchemist seems in no haste to move.

"Did your master tell you he once studied alchemy?"

"Yes, he did. But he—"

"Considered it beneath him. The work of lesser minds than his own. Tonight I will show him how artful an alchemist can be. Tonight I—"

"Master, please hide yourself, the Pope—"

"Leonardo could have been the greatest of all alchemists. Together, he and I would have discovered the secret of immortality. Instead, he abandoned me. It was a terrible thing to do. I trusted him, Giacomo. And I envied him his mind."

The Pope will be entering at any moment—he must be near, I can hear horses—

"Do you like—do you love—your master?" he says.

"Yes, sir, I do. And I would do anything for him."

"Do not waste your feeling on Leonardo. He does not feel."

I don't like the way he said that. What is he up to? Does he *want* to be discovered before he can meet the Pope? And now he is looking at me strangely. Something is wrong, here—something—

"Giacomo, are you ready to learn what I promised to teach you?"

"Yes, sir, but after—"

"There is no after for you, my boy, except the hereafter."

Oh God, I was right about this alchemist. I should never—

"The secret that I have come to tell you is this: Tonight you must die, so that the Brotherhood may live."

"What—?" A terrible urge to vomit overwhelms me. I clutch at my stomach. "I don't—"

"Hush, boy, I will tell you all, but quickly now. You will die. You must. And Pope Alexander must follow you."

And from his black robe he withdraws a short sword, the like of which I think I—why, it is the same type of sword that the intruders were wearing, the ones who broke into my master's house! Then the Duke had no hand in it, after all.

But what is Assanti saying now? The Master was right, he is a terrible prattler—but a very dangerous one. He's rehearsing the story he will tell later, it seems—

"You see, my lord Duke, I had been praying at Santa Maria, and then I went for a walk in the garden. I heard shouts in the refectory and ran to help, but too late to stop Leonardo's servant from murdering Pope Alexander. I drew my sword and killed the wicked youth, but not before he confessed and laid the blame on his master, Leonardo da Vinci, who ordered him to do it."

He looks at me triumphantly. Perhaps he now expects me to applaud. I must think quickly. *My dagger—*

"And then, when the Duke trusts me as never before, I will poison him most painfully and take control of the city. And for the trifling sum of one hundred thousand gold ducats, I will surrender the keys of Milan to the French!"

—I have slipped it out of its hiding place while he has been talking.

The underarm throw is quickest from this position.

I flick it as hard as I can at the alchemist, and—

Impossible! *I missed!* The knife has embedded itself in a wooden post behind his right shoulder.

"Foolish boy, you—"

"—Are finished, Assanti. So says Leonardo da Vinci."

The Master! Coming through the door that leads to the cloister. But how?

"Leonardo! Leonardo, the traitor to alchemy, the man I—"

"You talk too much, Assanti. One of two reasons I left the Brotherhood. The other being that there was nothing more to learn. Stand back, Giacomo."

The Master draws his sword and advances on the alchemist.

"Primitive, Leonardo. A true member of the Brotherhood can do better than that."

Assanti reaches inside his robe and pulls out a small leather ball. He throws it with great force to the ground in front of the Master, and as it hits the stone—*pflatt!*—it breaks apart and green dust billows into the air.

The Master walks right into it, his sword arm raised to strike at the alchemist.

And starts coughing. And drops his sword. And falls to his knees. And clutches his throat.

Master!!

He gasps! He cannot breathe! Without another thought I take a deep breath and hold it in. Assanti has produced a black hood, which he has drawn over his head—it must be some kind of protection! His voice, strangely distorted from beneath the covering, proclaims: "So I am no match for you, eh, Leonardo? Breathe deeply, the deeper the better! It's poison of the deadliest kind! You once declared that alchemy was neither art nor science. Oh, Leonardo, how wrong you were—it is both art *and* science! You believe only what you can see with your own eyes and prove with your own deductions. But there is another world, Leonardo, closed to your eyes, the eyes of the unbeliever. The world of alchemy!"

The Master is crouched on the floor, gasping.

While the alchemist has been giving his speech, I have worked my way behind him and now I am pulling—out—my—dagger—*come on, curse you!*—from the wood in which it was embedded. I have only a few more seconds of breath left—

"Now I will have to kill *you*, painter. I had hoped the Duke would be the one to do that, and slowly, too, but your arrival has changed things. My story now requires that you and your servant both are dispatched by my sword, in order to save His Holiness, who dies soon after you. Good-bye, Leonardo, good—*aaaargh*!!!!"

I threw my dagger once more, and this time it landed in his thigh. Not the best place—that would have been in the center of his black heart—but good enough.

He turns his attention from the Master, takes hold of the dagger's hilt, and pulls it slowly, sickeningly, from his leg—

"You will drown in your own blood for this!" he bellows.

And he raises his rapier and comes at me as well as he can with a ruined leg—

And then the main doors of the refectory are opened and Pope Alexander enters with two cardinals.

The Pope says: "What?"

And everyone halts where they are.

The thick green smoke is straightway swept out through the doors. Gasping, I take in a lungful of fresh night air.

One of the cardinals shouts: "Your Eminence, withdraw forthwith!" and tries to pull him back through the doors.

Assanti looks left and right, undecided who to kill first. Then he turns from me to the Pope and raises his sword.

But two armed attendants run into the refectory and stand in front of the Pope as a shield, while the cardinals pull him, stumbling, out of the room.

Assanti roars like a trapped beast. His black hood is shaking with the pent-up fury inside. And then he turns back to me and says: "Boy, you have done more damage than you know. But time means nothing to me. I have *eternity* to play with. Fear me, boy. I will come to you again, as I did once before. And next time will be my final visit. And your final day on Earth."

Once again he reaches inside his robe and pulls out another leather ball, which he hurls to the ground—*paff!!!*

There is a blinding flash. Suddenly, everything is covered with a yellow fog, and the air is filled with a strong smell of old eggs. (Isn't this?—It is!—exactly what happened when the Master emptied his glass vial over the heads of the thieves who broke into our house!) Once more I take a deep breath before the fog envelops me, and then I run to the Master, grasp him beneath the arms, and pull him towards the doors.

It is the hardest task I have ever undertaken. For a start, the Master is heavier than he looks, but he is also senseless from the dust he inhaled. It is like dragging ten full sacks of grain.

Slowly we make our way through the yellow fog, although I cannot see if we are moving in the right direction. Then a fresh pair of strong arms, this time belonging to one of the Pope's guards, helps me to lift the Master and remove him from the refectory. Oh, let the vile dust not have poisoned him!

The doors are shut behind us.

"Open the doors again!" I shout. "Let the smoke out—it might harm the painting!"

The Master lies on his side, but his chest heaves—he is alive, thanks be to God! And then his eyes open, they are streaming; he spits, he coughs, and he retches on the ground.

"Water!" I cry. "Bring water!" And one of the friars scurries off to do so.

I help the Master to his feet.

"Enough, boy. I can stand, thank you."

I let go. He doesn't like to be touched. He rubs his eyes.

"Didn't Assanti say that it was poisonous, that powder?"

"Yes, Master, he did."

"Well, I'm still alive, aren't I?" (*Cough! Cough!*) "So much for the claims of alchemy. By Heaven, the Last Supper!"

He runs back into the refectory, with me following a pace behind.

Inside, the yellow smoke has almost dispersed. Assanti has made good his escape—through the cloister door, to judge by the drops of blood leading to it.

The Master, however, does not concern himself with following the trail of the alchemist. He is looking up at the Last Supper, holding one of the large tapers close to the surface.

"No damage—at least, no damage visible. You did well to open the doors, boy. The smoke did not have time to settle."

"Master, Assanti threw a second ball—it gave off a yellow fog, just like the one you—"

He turns around.

"Yes, boy," he says, "it is the same substance: a rock found near volcanoes that Assanti and I discovered together when we were in the Brotherhood."

So alchemy does have its uses.

He turns back to the painting.

Saint Francis, I was almost responsible for the death of the

Pope! What a fool I have been. And now I will pay dearly for my failing. My dreams of becoming an artist are over. When this story comes out, I will surely hang for my part in it.

"Master, I-I have done a terrible thing."

"Hmm," is all he says.

"Going behind your back to meet Assanti. I wish I had told you everything before."

"So do I. Then I could have warned you about him. He is a schemer, always has been. And you are an innocent—don't interrupt me, boy!—who thinks he already understands the ways of the world. Let me tell you, Giacomo, you have much to learn about the wiles of man! I did not know what Assanti had planned, other than treachery of some kind. I thought it might happen tonight, and your uneasiness confirmed my fears. That is why I wore my sword."

"You saved my life again, Master."

"And this time you returned the favor."

He continues to look at me.

"What was your arrangement with Assanti, boy? For giving him admittance to the Pope?"

"He said he would tell me a secret. I hoped it would be a secret power, a spell or a potion, but it was my death he planned to reveal to me. I was greedy, Master, and I was nearly undone by it, but my motives for helping him were not entirely selfish. I was told that he planned to unite alchemy with Christianity and make a better world for all men."

"Ah, that is Assanti, all right, cunning as a twice-escaped ferret. He knew how best to lure you in."

"And he has no secret powers?"

"None that I know of. Unless you count the ability to talk for an hour without drawing breath!"

And the Master laughs. I want to join him, but I do not. After what happened in my room I cannot doubt that the alchemist possesses powers far beyond a normal man's.

"What will become of me now, Master? I will have to confess to my part, however innocent, in this plot to kill the Pope."

"Let me worry about that, boy," he says.

The next morning, Holy Friday, the Master is summoned to the Castle to offer his explanation for the dire occurrences of the previous night.

When he returns, it is to say that he told the Duke a story in which I played no part, and that at the end the Duke thanked him for saving the Pope's life—and Milan's future alliance with the Church. But if the Pope *had* been killed at Santa Maria, the Church would surely have turned against Milan and made an alliance with the French—and I would have been responsible for that calamity, as well!

My master has earned high praise for his part in foiling the plot and saving the life of the Pope (being no longer in the story, I had to forgo my share of the glory). His Holiness, meanwhile, has been confined to his bed to recover from the unspeakable events. He will return to the refectory to view the Last Supper as soon as the doctors permit it.

The Duke has issued a new proclamation against all

alchemists, vowing to wipe the land clean of them forever. Even now, bands of armed guards are preparing to scour the city and bring any suspects to the Castle for interrogation.

In the evening, I hasten to Tombi's shop to warn him of the impending danger. I do not yet know how great a part he played in Assanti's plot, but my heart tells me that he was no more aware of the alchemist's true mission than I was.

I knock on his door again and again before the peephole is uncovered and Tombi's eye appears at the opening.

I hear the door being unbolted and unbarred, and I hasten inside.

"You must leave Milan, Messer Tombi. Tonight!"

"Wha-what has happened, Giacomo? Did Assanti's audience with the Pope go badly?"

He knows nothing, after all. He is innocent.

I start to explain what happened at the Last Supper the night before. While I relate the order of events—me, Assanti, my master, the fight, the Pope, the guards, the smoke, the Master's near death, Assanti's narrow escape—my tale is interrupted repeatedly by Tombi's exclamations—

"No!"

"I do not—"

"I will not believe it!"

"Not Master Assanti, no!"

"Never!"

"Alchemists are not murderers!"

—So that it takes me twice the time it should to give him all the news, and that is twice as much as I wanted, because time is something Tombi no longer has. Not in Milan, anyway.

By the end of my story, the good apothecary, or alchemist rather, has sunk into a chair, his head in his hands. "No!" he says, one last time. It is more of a whisper, this last one. "I am ruined. All is done!"

"We must pack up your belongings and have you out of here by dawn, Messer Tombi. The Duke's men will be searching the city, and they are sure to visit the Street of Apothecaries first."

"But why, Giacomo? Why are you helping me after what has happened? You, your master—you were both almost killed!"

"Because I believe you for a good man, Messer Tombi. I know you were not aware of Assanti's true intentions."

"He convinced me I was helping the alchemists to make peace with the Church, not start a war with them. What a fool I was! And now—"

"And now I will help you pack," I say.

"God bless you, Giacomo, for giving me this chance, which I do not deserve."

"Messer Tombi, you have been a valued friend to me, a good and true friend, one of the very few in my life."

He thanks me again and again—his eyes are shining, poor fellow, he is almost in tears.

"I will take myself across the mountains as far as Germany, by foot if need be. I have a friend in Heidelberg, a doctor, who will hide me until I can contact the Brotherhood and obtain their assistance."

"And for the lessons you gave me," I say, "I promised that my master would pay you as soon as the Duke—"

"Never mind that, Giacomo, it is too late to worry about my debts."

"The Duke has still not paid us, sir. But I have brought you something . . ."

The ten ducats that Maggio gave me for his place in the Last Supper, the only money I did not hand over to the Master.

Without further delay I give them to him.

"Why, Giacomo—"

"I am sorry I cannot pay you more of what we owe. But I will. One day."

We shake hands and I turn to leave. Then he takes my arm and says: "Farewell, Giacomo. We shall find each other again, I hope."

XLI

On the Sunday we are up in good time to make our way to the Castle to join Maggio and the flying machine. The Master takes long strides and lectures me continually on the working of the wings and pedals (which he has already been lecturing me on for weeks, now). He is very nervous and speaks in short bursts, calling the machine "the great bird," as is his wont.

"Be mindful of the wind's whirls and eddies—that they do not overturn the great bird—respond to the pressure of the air raising you up from below or pushing down from above—by subtle manipulation of the lever, left and right—it must be handled with great care—especially when the craft has risen more than ten braccia from the ground."

"Yes, Master. I understand."

"All it requires is the smallest movement of the lever, and the wind's current will do the rest for you."

"Master, I have not forgotten."

While the Master continues the recitation of his list of

reminders and instructions, my mind drifts as if on its own wings to the Street of Apothecaries. I pray Tombi has made his escape. The Duke's men will not have been slow about their duties.

But here we are at the Castle gates.

We are admitted without delay and walk out into the vast, dazzling green square inside. In the middle, right in the middle, is the flying machine, fully assembled and ready to launch. It has been moved from the Rocchetta in readiness for its voyage. Maggio's two assistants are underneath the body of the craft, screwing and hammering at something. Maggio is adjusting the rudder at the back.

And suddenly I think: *I am going to fly this thing—today!*

The sun has come out and the wind is favorable; I am glad I will not have to worry about the weather, when there is so much else to worry about. Everything looks set fair for the flight.

The Master tugs my sleeve.

The Duke's Castle Guard, some five hundred men, perhaps, have filed out of the barracks and are lined up side by side the length of the walls. In front of them, at intervals of perhaps ten paces, are a hundred or more knights on horseback, riders and chargers both in full ceremonial armor and bearing the Sforza crest on banners and pennants. But most unexpected of all is the viewing stand, covered with a golden canopy, which has been erected for those invited to witness the flight. Even now, these important personages are filing out of the Duke's apartments to take their places, radiant in purples and pinks, greens and golds, with attendants and servants following. By the laughter and loud voices, I judge there has been drinking and feasting at the Duke's expense.

"Master, was this not to be a secret demonstration for the Duke?"

"He has turned it into a spectacle for the rich to goggle at and invited all of Lombardy, the fool."

But perhaps the Duke is not such a fool after all. In order to keep the support of his allies, Lombardy's greatest families, against the French, he must convince them that Milan has something truly extraordinary, a weapon that will cause the enemy much consternation. If the French have cannons on wheels, the Duke must have something better—and what can better a flying machine? Once the word goes abroad that he has such a remarkable invention, perhaps the French will call off the attack!

"Well, Maggio, are we ready?"

"Not long now, Master Leonardo."

"Very good. Please examine the foot pedals one more time before Giacomo enters the box."

"I will," Maggio says. "Quite the crowd, eh?"

"Indeed it is, though I wish it were not." Then the Master turns back to me. "Now remember, Giacomo, the sequence of the pedals: left, right, left, left, right, right, left—"

"Master, you have told me this a hundred times!"

"Then one more repetition will seal the others in your head. And take rests on the wind currents whenever you can, without losing your forward impetus, which will be maintained by short stamps on the pedals. You must treat our machine like a musical instrument, playing according to the tempo, and at all times sensitive to the most harmonious combination of pedals and lever."

"Yes, Master." Musical instrument? He really has lost me.

The Duke has emerged and is coming towards us, a group of counselors and servants in attendance.

"Ah, Leonardo, you're here at last, thank goodness! After what happened at Santa Maria, I have been afraid of another mishap."

"My lord, there will be no mishap here today."

"For weeks I have been telling my friends of your wonderful machine, and my hopes that it will so affright the French that they run home cowering, hands over heads—ha! ha!—but now I see it in the open, I can only say that it looks less . . . less *menacing* than I remember."

Before the Master can respond, I say: "My lord, it will look menacing enough to the French when it is dropping iron balls on their heads."

"Silence before the Duke!" someone thunders.

The Duke waves him down as if he were swatting a fly, and the fellow shrinks back into the assembly.

"My lords, you have not met Master Leonardo's faithful servant," the Duke says. "Leonardo never goes anywhere without Giacomo to defend his name and uphold his reputation."

Well, somebody has to do it.

"I am also the pilot of the flying machine, my lord."

"Are you, now! Your master has high expectations of you—even as high as the clouds! Ha ha!"

The assembly smiles and titters at this uninventive jest.

"Now then, Master Leonardo, show us how it works."

"As a bird works, my lord, by the flapping of its wings," my master responds. "When the pilot places his feet on the pedals and pulls on this lever here (activating the springs there and there), the wings will beat and thence raise the structure off the earth."

"They will?" The Duke looks dubious.

"They will." The Master looks masterful.

"There, gentlemen," says the Duke. "I told you that Leonardo had more up his sleeve than paintbrushes! How fortunate we are to have him on our side!"

"My lord," one of the counselors says, his bald head reflecting flashes of the sun as he walks to the fore, "this machine is more suited to Mount Olympus than Milan, the airy invention of an artist with his head in the clouds, who imagines he can transport the rest of himself there with it!"

"It *will* fly," my master says. "I vouchsafe it."

"He may have his *head* in the clouds," another lord says, "but I vow his *feet* will never leave the earth!"

They're mocking my master! Look at him blush. I must say something—

"My lord Duke, there is only one way to test my master's invention. Let me fly it for you now!"

"Giacomo, you speak well. We cannot talk it down before we have given it a chance to rise. Leonardo, do you take up the challenge?"

"My lord, I am ready. Let your counselors bear witness to the invincible mind of Leonardo da Vinci, who can take the wings of a bird and give them to a man, who was never given them by God! Giacomo?"

I bow to the Duke and prepare to enter the wooden box. What will it feel like, to float above the Castle turrets? To look down on the Duke and his lords, instead of being looked down on? I will soon find out.

"Giacomo . . ." My master takes my arm as I am entering the box. "Before you go, I want to thank you. For your courage, for your loyalty, for your faith in me and the Last Supper—and for saving both of us from Assanti. After Easter, God willing, we shall commence your painting lessons. So be diligent with the controls and come back safe!"

He is still holding my arm. I place my hand over his.

"Oh, Master, do you—do you really mean it?"

"I never say anything I do not mean, boy. Not intentionally, at least. And meaning without intention can hardly be called the result of considered thinking."

He's lost me again.

"Now, lad, the Duke is ready and waiting."

He gently removes my hand and places it on the box in which I will sit.

"In you go, then," he says.

"Thank you, Master." I won't waste time with more speech, but in my mind I am endlessly repeating *thank you, thank you, thank you.*

He will teach me to paint—HE WILL TEACH ME!!

I already feel light-headed, and the craft is not yet off the ground.

Maggio is giving the signal that all is ready.

Rodolfo approaches and says: "Don't pull too hard on the lever. It's been known to seize up, and if that happens you'll go into a dive. I'll be praying for you!"

He shakes my hand and retires. At this moment one of the Duke's trumpeters sounds the ready. The Duke stands and waves at me. I wave back. Then he sits. The crowd of nobility in the viewing stand follows his example.

Well, my friends, here we are.

After many years of deliberations and delays, one of my master's inventions has finally been built to full size and will now be tested.

I cast a last look at my master. He stands ten paces from the flying machine, his arms crossed. He smiles at me, and in that smile I see something I have never seen before: pride. And something else, too . . .

My heart tightens, and I feel joyful and sad, both at once.

If only Caterina was here to see me!

But now I must clear my mind and concentrate.

I begin to press down on the pedals. Now, what was that sequence again? How could I forget! Left, right, left, left, right, right, left . . .

Thanks to the ingenious system of interlocking springs that my master has designed, one thrust of my leg on the pedal produces the same power as twenty. Therefore, each time I press down once with my right and left legs, I achieve a motion forty times greater than a man is capable of producing, without using up any more of my strength than I would if I was raising my legs up and down to walk.

Left, right, left, left, right, right, left . . .

The momentum is building. The springs are contracting and releasing in concert.

Saint Francis, the wings have begun to move! One beat, two beats—and now they are developing a rhythm—one and two, and one and two—it's working, by Heaven! My master's calculations were correct, every one of them. And what is so amazing is that with every thrust of my foot, yet without exerting more pressure, the wings beat faster and faster.

Now I must draw the lever back slowly, slowly, to adjust the angle of the wings to allow for the craft to lift—

"Master! It works!"

He has uncrossed his arms and raised two fists to the sky in jubilation (I've never seen him *jubilant* before). He's urging the great bird upwards—

Now to release the lever a notch to permit the machine to find its balance—

It's rising! It is rising from the ground!

Cheers have broken out from the soldiers lining the walls! They're shouting "Long live the Duke!" and "Leonardo—our hero!" and "Death to the French dogs!"

And now the Duke and his assembly have raised themselves from their seats and—and they're applauding! The nobles and counts and earls and ladies and all the rest of them are *applauding*—and *cheering*, as well!

Now I have found a steady rhythm—left, right, left, left, right, right, left—the wings are beating smoothly, and the machine has lifted more than one braccio from the earth . . .

. . . Two braccia! . . .

. . . *Four*, and still it rises!

Now I understand what the Master meant—it *is* rather like playing a musical instrument! As I ascend above the heads of the crowd, I decide that—yes!—I'm going to fly the Master's creation over the Castle walls and down the Ticino River! I want all of Lombardy to see the great bird and bear witness to my master's genius!

Now that I am more than twice the height of a man above the earth, I will try to direct the nose of the craft towards the western walls. The great bird is responding with such ease that I should be able to clear them in a short time.

Many of the Duke's nobles have left their seats and begun making their way towards me. All those rich robes, the plumed hats, and velvet cloaks—trying to get a better look at *me*, Giacomo, the servant! Many of the Duke's foot soldiers have also abandoned their posts and come running.

But where is the Master? And Maggio? They have been swallowed up by the crowd now assembled below—all cheering and waving hats and swords.

Master, where are you?

And then I see him, standing quietly in the center of the throng.

He is still looking up at me and smiling.

And finally I understand—

He was always there by my side, even when I doubted it.

He was watching over me from the very first day.

And when he scolded me, sometimes too harshly, it was because he worried.

He is not my father. But he has been everything a son could want in one.

Suddenly, the machine lurches and begins shaking—Saint Francis, the thing is trembling like a branch in a storm! I can scarce hold the lever—the right wing is tilting down—oh no, I think we're falling—but keep pedaling, Giacomo, keep her in the air—don't let her down yet or you will let down the Master!

Then from the crowd comes a voice like a hammer striking the anvil: "Bring that creation of the Devil back to earth at once!"

Everyone's head turns to see whence the order was issued—over there? No, from the other side of the square.

I'm still treading up and down, up and down on the pedals, and the machine is somehow staying aloft, but it is no longer rising, and the shuddering of the wings is almost uncontrollable—

Now the Master is waving at me—but he's waving me back to earth!

Someone is standing beside him, someone in robes of white that shimmer in the sunlight like distant waterfalls. Is it Pope Alexander? By Heaven, it is! Behind him are five gentlemen in scarlet robes with glittering gold trim. His cardinals.

The crowd below has dispersed—the cheering has ceased.

"Bring her down, Giacomo—now!" the Master shouts up at me, hands cupped around his mouth.

All right, Master, if that's what you want. It was coming down anyway, if you want to know, whatever I chose to do with it.

So I reverse the order of the pedals—left, right, right, left, left, right, left—and attempt to bring her down as gently as I can, though the spring mechanism is making a frightful scraping and squeaking noise as I do. I fear the Master still has some work ahead of him before the flying machine is ready to be used in military action.

The Duke is hurrying over to where my master and the Pope are speaking to each other. Something has gone badly wrong, if the Duke can be made to run in haste across his own castle grounds.

My legs are bursting with the effort—the craft felt so light in the air, but the nearer it comes to the ground, the heavier it seems. But I do not cease pedaling until the machine lands safely back on the grass with a solid bump.

And then the right wing makes a terrible cracking sound and falls off.

I undo the belt that secured me to the seat. Rodolfo is there to help me out of the box. I am trembling violently.

There is no more cheering, no more applauding. The whole Castle has gone silent. And as I jump down to the ground, I hear: "Blasphemy!"

Spoken, nay, shouted, by the Pope. It seems he is well recovered from the attempt on his life three nights ago.

To which my master replies, hands on hips: "Nonsense!"

I remain underneath the left wing of the flying machine,

unsure whether to advance. The Duke has now joined the Pope and my master.

"Your Holiness," the Duke says, bending to touch his lips to the Pope's heavy gold ring, in the center of which, like some ruby toad, squats the largest red stone I have ever seen.

"Your Holiness," Duke Ludovico says once more, receiving no reply, "how have we offended?"

"I am almost murdered in one of your churches, Ludovico, and now I bear witness to one of the Devil's instruments in your very own castle!"

"This is no winged demon, Your Eminence," my master says, "it is a machine for flying. And I built it."

"*You* built it?" the Pope says.

"Yes, I did."

He's forgotten Maggio's part in the construction. Perhaps that is a good thing, given the Pope's visibly increasing wrath.

"No, no, the Devil built this. It is the Devil's work! I have an infallible instinct for the mark of his black hand."

"Your Excellency, this is no devil, this is the great Leonardo da Vinci, painter and inventor to the Court of Milan," the Duke says. "He saved your life in the refectory of Santa Maria delle Grazie."

"That was you, was it?" the Pope says.

The Master does not reply.

"So you believe that man has the power to fly like a bird?"

"Believe? There is no need to believe," the Master says. "We have all seen it with our own eyes."

"That is heresy, Master Leonardo. A man cannot fly, or it would be written in the Holy Scriptures."

"Nonetheless, Your Eminence, a man *did* fly. You witnessed it yourself!"

The Master looks around him, but the Duke and everyone else are looking at the grass.

"You are not listening, my dear fellow," the Pope says. *"A man cannot fly."*

The Duke and my master exchange glances.

"Am I being clear enough for you?" the Pope says. "Man was not meant to fly. It is heresy to suggest he can. It is blasphemy to attempt to prove he can. And it is treason to contradict the word of the Pope, who says he cannot. And there's an end to it. God did not give a man wings."

Everybody looks at my master.

"Neither did God give man fins," he says, "yet he crosses the oceans."

The air around us seems to grow colder on the instant. Pope Alexander's accompanying cardinals turn to him to see what will happen next. The Pope raises his hand.

"Master Leonardo, I see that the Duke of Milan permits you certain license here, and for his sake, as we are newly reunited, our policies and intentions mutually agreeable, I will not at this time have you censured for your liberal tongue."

"Your Holiness, I meant no offense."

"What you *mean*, Leonardo, is for me alone to decide. I traveled here to Milan, at great personal discomfort, let me add, for two reasons: to discuss the threat of the French with

Duke Ludovico, and to view the Last Supper for myself. I have now accomplished both of those aims. What happened here just now *did not happen*, and there is an end to it."

Silence. Nobody moves. The Pope is staring at my master, almost daring him to argue further.

But my master is not a fool. He changes the subject instead.

"Did Your Excellency find my painting worthy?" he says.

"I would take issue with the meaning of the gestures you have given to the Disciples. You have interpreted the Gospel in a way that is disputatious and vexing to me."

The Pope turns and prepares to depart.

Is that it? Is that all His Excellency, Pope Alexander VI, has to say about my master's work? No—the Pope turns back.

"Let me add that I have never yet seen the equal of this painting, and I heartily wish that it were on the wall of one of our Vatican chapels, instead of here in Milan. The face of Christ is a triumph, and I do not use that word lightly. It has inspired me for today's sermon at the Cathedral. The theme is resurrection, Leonardo. The resurrection of our Lord and the resurrection of the Church's union with Milan. But remember this, Master Painter-Inventor: Only God has free passage in the heavens, and only His angels have wings."

And without waiting for a response, the Pope and his cardinals direct themselves towards the Duke's apartments.

With the Pope gone, the Duke now looks very pleased with himself.

"Did you hear that, my lords? The Pope wishes he had our

painting in the Vatican! But he never will, unless God gives him the power to move walls!"

Or my master follows him to Rome.

"Well, Leonardo," the Duke says, "it seems that the flying machine will not fly again."

"My lord, you are not going to let the Pope—!"

"Peace, Leonardo. Let be. His Holiness is pleased with the Last Supper. Milan will have a firm ally in Rome, God willing, and in good time, too. If the flying machine must remain on the ground, that is a small price to pay for our larger safety. The Pope has an army of fifty thousand. We will need every man."

"I am your obedient servant, my lord Duke."

The look on my master's face bespeaks another answer entirely, something containing a few choice insults.

"Now, now, my worthy painter, do not despair. The French are not so near that we cannot continue with our other work. I want you to start the portrait of the late Duchess, my Lady Beatrice, on the wall opposite the Last Supper."

The Master says nothing. He looks too tired to speak.

"What say you to four hundred ducats?" says the Duke.

"Four hundred, my lord? Well . . ."

That woke him up! Money always does.

"Five hundred? Done, then!" the Duke says. "You start work on it after Easter."

"Yes, my lord, willingly."

"That's what I like to hear—we are friends again, are we not?"

"We were never not, my lord, and, I hope, we will still be always."

And the Duke looks as bewildered by the Master's words as the Master wanted him to be. With a quick shake of the head, as if to clear his mind of the confusion, the Duke says: "Then I release you to your work and me to mine. Come, counselors, we have much to decide concerning our joint response to the new French king."

And while the Duke strides off, trailing his advisors and attendants behind him like great Neptune his fronds of seaweed, the knights on horseback dismount and lead away their steeds, the Duke's armed men march in formation to their barracks, and the nobles and courtiers disperse to resume their pleasantries and pastimes.

Soon the Master, Maggio, his two men, and I are the only ones left on the grassy plain. We, and our faithful flying machine. The odor of roasting meat coming from the Castle kitchens makes the Master wrinkle his nose with distaste, and my mouth fill up with water. I haven't eaten yet. I hope Margareta has left something out for us.

"Shall I commence taking apart the flying machine, Master Leonardo?" Maggio asks.

Judging by the broken wing, it will not need much assistance.

"Leave it where it is, Maggio, for the moment. I am too tired to think right now. But if we are not allowed to fly it, I can see no reason to have anything more to do with it."

"But, Master, will we not build another one, faster, more powerful?" I say.

"That decision no longer rests with us," he replies.

He thanks Maggio for all his work, and Maggio thanks

the Master for the honor of working with him. And then they embrace each other. Perhaps, between Maggio and me, we have taught Leonardo da Vinci, who has always worked alone, that he can share his work with others, without sacrificing his reputation.

I shake hands with Rodolfo and the other one whose name I cannot recall or have never known. Maggio goes off to find his cart. The Master and I make our way across the Castle grounds.

At the gates there is no farewell ceremony, no gift from the Duke, not even a courtier with a plumed hat to wave us out.

We walk home in silence. The Sforza Way is deserted. Everyone has gone to the Cathedral to hear Pope Alexander speak. But neither the Master nor I have any desire for that, I think. We have heard the Pope speak enough.

I want to say something to the Master, to thank him for the honor of flying his machine, and to reassure him that one day I will fly it again, or the like of it, only better. But I cannot find the words.

The Last Supper is finished, but it has already begun to decay.

And the flying machine will remain on the ground.

Now I ask you, after all the work, has anything been accomplished?

XLII

It is a warm day in early May. More than a month has gone by.

I am walking to Santa Maria, carrying the bag with the Master's tools. I will take the measurements for the wall opposite the Last Supper, in preparation for the painting of Lady Beatrice that the Duke wants him to start forthwith—and is making a great noise about, too, because he has not. But neither has my master been paid the five hundred ducats that were promised.

Father Vicenzo still has not managed to rid himself of the Master and me, even though he pleaded with the Duke to send us—or him!—elsewhere to work. The new painting in the refectory means that we will keep our old house for a time yet—perhaps for a long time, knowing the Master—and Father Vicenzo will be obliged to suffer us in silence. Indeed, he has not said a word to me since he came to our house and complained about the face of Judas. Long may this state continue!

And the Master will begin my painting lessons tomorrow. So he has said, anyway. He promised to start them the day after Easter, but there was too much to do. Well, after all, I understand. The Master is not like other men. He simply has more in his head than the rest of us, and what he has takes up so much more of his time.

I wish Caterina was still here. I miss her. And her voice, which I heard so strongly in my head after she died, has not returned. But I know she will always be with me, close to me, somehow. She would have had much to say about everything that has happened recently. Her tongue would have unhinged itself telling her friends and neighbors all about the Pope and the Last Supper and the flying machine and everything!

The earth underfoot is dry, a pleasant buzzing and droning of small insects fills my ears, and the fields are changing color as the crops grow and ripen. There is a faint smell of lavender in the air. They say it will be a good year for olives and lemons.

A red fox is running between the hedgerows, a dash of brightness in the brush; and skimming the treetops to the east is a golden eagle, as easeful on the currents of the air as the Master's flying machine will, I fear, never be. But I have no doubt that one day man will float above the clouds as easily as he now runs beneath them; the Master and I will be long gone by then, although we will always have the honor of knowing that we were the first to raise a man above the earth.

Our flying machine did not remain in the Castle grounds for very long. The Master requested permission to have it moved back to the Lazaretto, where he might rebuild the right wing and make adjustments and improvements, and to keep it there until such time as the Pope comes to his senses and decrees that a man with wings does not contravene the Gospel. But it was too late. The Pope had already demanded that it be transported to Rome for examination by the Holy Inquisition, which had taken a great interest in it. The last thing anyone wants is the interest of the Holy Inquisition. They do not love art or invention. Indeed, they do not love anything. They live to hate and to destroy whatever they think is a threat to the Church.

It is even possible that the Master will be summoned to Rome to explain himself. You do not want to have to explain yourself to the Holy Inquisition; if you fail to do so successfully, you might find yourself in their torture chamber. And even if you succeed, there is a good chance of ending up in the same place.

But, thanks be to God and His holy Saints, we have thus far heard nothing. Let us hope it stays that way. No doubt the Pope has more on his mind than Leonardo da Vinci, which, sadly, is probably the reason we have not been invited to Rome, in spite of His Holiness's admiration for the Last Supper.

The French are still, it is rumored, somewhere beyond our borders, waiting to attack. But the city of Milan goes about its business as if they weren't. We only fear the unknown. Now that we know they are out there, we prefer not to think about them. If we have to fight, we will. Is the Pope our faithful ally? That is a question yet to be settled. My master says that His Holiness did renew his pact with the Duke, after seeing the Last Supper. But rumor has it that the Pope's son, Cesare, the one who was sent to France to look for a wife, has married a niece of King Louis.

The Duke, meanwhile, has been strangely silent of late.

Cecilia has written to us from her country estate. My master read me the letter. The painting hangs in her bedchamber, where she can look at it every night before sleep. And, as I suspected, the Duke has not missed it, among so many others.

Tombi made his escape from Milan. And just in time. When I returned to the Street of Apothecaries three days later, everything was in ruins. Doors had been broken down, awnings torn away, and everywhere there was broken glass, colored powders, and shattered crystals. The Duke's men had entered the street without warning and forced their way into the shops, chasing out the apothecaries while they searched. But whatever it was they were looking for (and it is unlikely they knew), they did not find it. The whole event was staged purely to give vent to the Duke's fury. When a great man has been duped, he will always take it out on those lower down.

I hope Tombi will send word soon. It would make me happy to hear that he is safe. And Assanti? My master says that he will not be back, if he values his skin. But a man like Assanti does not forget the injuries done to him, nor those responsible for them. I sleep with my dagger under the pillow.

One of these days I am going to invite Emilia to the Last Supper for a private viewing. Yes, I think I will. I know rather a lot about it, after all. And perhaps, after the Master has started giving me my lessons, he will not object if she joins us. I think she might like that. I know I would.

I intend to have finished my first painting by Saint Michael's Day. It will be a poor effort—how could it not be?—but it will be a start. Every artist has to start somewhere. The important thing, once started, is to keep going until you come to the end.

My friends, we are almost there now.

After a long struggle, I have finally won the Master's respect. That means the world to me.

I still have not discovered the identity of my parents, but that can wait, because I have learned something just as important: who *I* am.

I am Giacomo, and I am going to be an artist.

The past can stay where it is. The future is what matters now.

The future with my master, Leonardo da Vinci.

What will happen to us? That's a story for another time.

But now it's time I began measuring this wall!

The doors are opening; I can hear someone entering the refectory.

Ah, it is my master.

I'd better look busy.

"What, Giacomo, have you not finished that simple task yet?"

"Soon, Master, soon."

He makes me smile, my master. No matter how much I change, he'll never change the way he speaks to me.

And, truth be told, I do not think I ever want him to.

The Fate of the Last Supper

Soon after the Last Supper was completed, it began to deteriorate.

In the 1540s a contemporary observer called it "half ruined"; in 1568 the artist and writer Giorgio Vasari called it "nothing but a blurred stain." Twenty years after that, Paolo Lomazzo, in his treatise on painting, wrote: "Today the painting is in a state of total ruin."

Since then it has been restored several times; the most recent attempt was completed in 1999, but what now remains of Leonardo da Vinci's masterpiece is little more than a shadow of his original work.

CHRISTOPHER GREY

is from London, England. He has worked as a waiter, a hotel manager, a hospital porter, a jeans salesman, a rock musician, and a tour operator. This is his first book. Originally inspired by a visit to the *Last Supper* in 1992, it was not until he came into possession of an old, faded copy of *Leonardo's Notebooks* that the story began to take shape. The rest is—almost—history.

"Once upon a Time"

is timely once again as fresh, quirky heroines breathe life into classic and much-loved characters.

Renowned heroines master newfound destinies, uncovering a unique and original **"happily ever after. . . ."**